JULY

In the Name of the King

D0754838

By the same author

Honour and the Sword

In the Name of the King

A. L. BERRIDGE

PENGUIN BOOKS

PENGUIN BOOKS

Published by the Penguin Group
Penguin Books Ltd, 80 Strand, London WC2R ORL, England
Penguin Group (USA) Inc., 375 Hudson Street, New York, New York 10014, USA
Penguin Group (Canada), 90 Eglinton Avenue East, Suite 700, Toronto, Ontario, Canada M4P 2Y3
(a division of Pearson Penguin Canada Inc.)
Penguin Ireland, 25 St Stephen's Green, Dublin 2, Ireland (a division of Penguin Books Ltd)
Penguin Group (Australia), 250 Camberwell Road, Camberwell, Victoria 3124, Australia
(a division of Pearson Australia Group Pty Ltd)
Penguin Books India Pvt Ltd, 11 Community Centre,
Panchsheel Park, New Delhi – 110 017, India
Penguin Group (NZ), 67 Apollo Drive, Rosedale, Auckland 0632, New Zealand
(a division of Pearson New Zealand Ltd)
Penguin Books (South Africa) (Pty) Ltd, 24 Sturdee Avenue,
Rosebank, Johannesburg 2196, South Africa

Penguin Books Ltd, Registered Offices: 80 Strand, London WC2R ORL, England

www.penguin.com

First published 2011
1

Copyright © A. L. Berridge, 2011
All rights reserved

The moral right of the author has been asserted

Set in 11/13pt Dante MT Std
Typeset by Jouve (UK), Milton Keynes
Printed in England by Clays Ltd, St Ives plc

Except in the United States of America, this book is sold subject
to the condition that it shall not, by way of trade or otherwise, be lent,
re-sold, hired out, or otherwise circulated without the publisher's
prior consent in any form of binding or cover other than that in
which it is published and without a similar condition including this
condition being imposed on the subsequent purchaser

ISBN: 978-0-141-04374-6

www.greenpenguin.co.uk

MIX
Paper from
responsible sources
FSC™ C018179

Penguin Books is committed to a sustainable
future for our business, our readers and our
planet. This book is made from paper certified
by the Forest Stewardship Council.

Acknowledgements

In the Name of the King is a work of fiction, but many of the people and events depicted are real. André de Roland's journey takes him through one of the most turbulent periods of French history, and would never have been possible without the map and compass provided by so many experts in the field.

I am particularly grateful for the inspiration of Robin Briggs of All Souls, Oxford, who first alerted me to the ambiguities surrounding the fate of the Comte de Soissons, and also to Dr Jonathan Spangler of Manchester Metropolitan University for his invaluable assistance in uncovering the mysteries of the Battle of La Marfée. I would also like to thank the many historians of the H-France community who have generously guided me in my research, especially Professor Melissa Wittmeier of Northwestern University in Illinois for her help deciphering some obscure passages in the *Mercure François*, and Professor Orest Ranum for advice on mid-seventeenth-century Paris. Theirs is the credit for any historical insights offered by this novel; any mistakes, I'm afraid, are my own.

I have also profited enormously from the advice of experts in the use of historical weaponry, in particular Kevin Lees and Ian Shields for practical help with the musket, and Cris de Veau of the Tattershall School of Defence for his advice on swords and swordsmanship.

I'd also like to thank my agent Victoria Hobbs and editor Alex Clarke for their faith and editorial help, Stephen Guise for his sensitive and meticulous editing of the manuscript, and my long-suffering husband Paul Crichton for his patience. Last but not least, I must express sincere gratitude for the encouragement and support of my colleagues in the Thirty Years War unit 'Hortus Bellicus'. To them and the thousands of men and women just like them, who freely give their time to make history come alive for those who now rarely encounter it in schools, this novel is very respectfully dedicated.

Editor's Note

It is with this present collection of the Abbé Fleuriot's documents that the story of André de Roland really begins.

The papers published under the title *Honour and the Sword* related those circumstances that shaped him as a national hero: the murder of his parents during the Spanish Occupation of Picardy, his upbringing among his former subjects, and his final victory in restoring the villages of the Saillie to French rule. Yet the man who survived these events is also a hybrid. Educated from birth to uphold a strict code of honour, he has since imbued not only the gentle humanity of his illegitimate half-brother, former stable boy Jacques Gilbert, but also the libertarian creed of soldier and former tanner Stefan Ravel. These qualities proved admirable in the defence of his home village of Dax, but now he is to encounter a France rigidly divided by caste and convention and already torn by civil conflict within the greater context of the Thirty Years War. How he fared there, this history will tell.

But it is not I who will tell it. I present the reader only with my translations of the Abbé Fleuriot's papers, comprising in this case a handful of letters, the diary of the girl André loved, and a series of remarkably frank interviews conducted by the Abbé himself. As before, the translation preserves the informality of the verbal accounts by substituting modern idioms for those of seventeenth-century Picardy, but I have taken fewer liberties with both the written sources and the remarkably controlled and occasionally stilted expression of the tavern girl Bernadette. Hers is one of the voices new to us, while others are familiar, but the reader must use his own judgement to determine which are the most reliable.

Edward Morton, MA, LittD, Cantab
Cambridge, March 2011

Maps

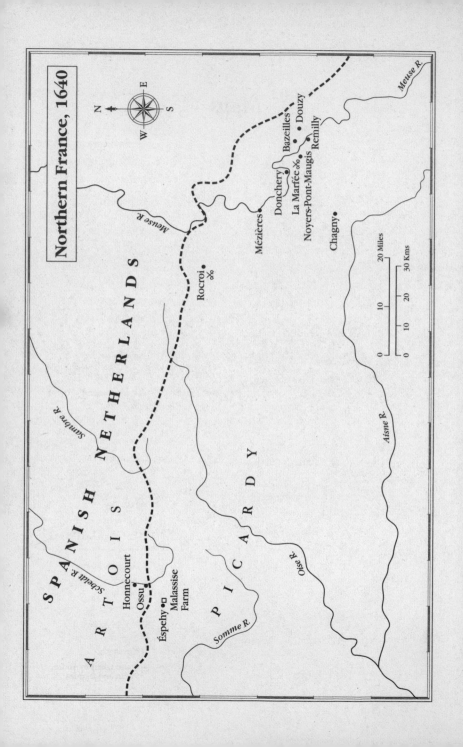

Northern France, 1640

SPANISH NETHERLANDS

ARTOIS

PICARDY

Sambre R.

Scheldt R.

Meuse R.

Meuse R.

Aisne R.

Oise R.

Somme R.

Homecourt
Ossu
Éspehy
Malassise Farm

Rocroi

Mézières

Donchery
Bazeilles
La Marfée
Douzy
Noyers-Pont-Maugis
Rémilly
Chagny

N E
W S

0   10   20 Miles
0   10   20   30 Kms

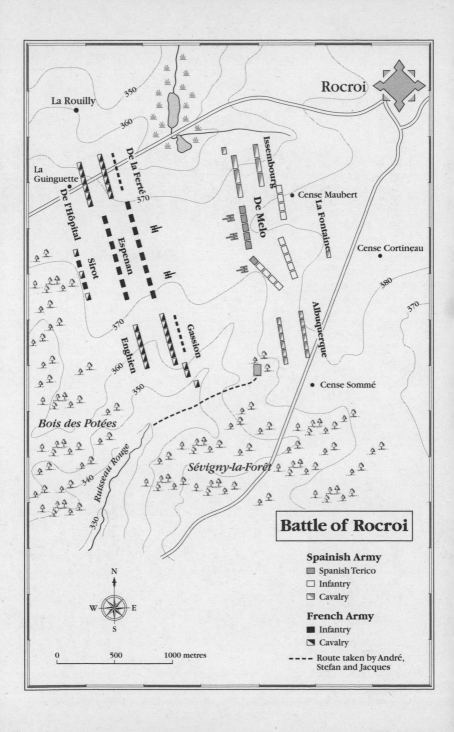

La Rouilly

La Guinguette

De l'Hôpital

De la Ferté

Espenan

Sirot

Enghien

Gassion

Bois des Potées

Ruisseau Rouge

Sévigny-la-Forêt

350

360

370

380

Rocroi

Issenbourg

De Melo

La Fontaines

Cense Maubert

Cense Cortineau

Albuquerque

Cense Sommé

Battle of Rocroi

Spanish Army

▨ Spanish Terico
☐ Infantry
◩ Cavalry

French Army

■ Infantry
◪ Cavalry

- - - - Route taken by André, Stefan and Jacques

N
W E
S

0   500   1000 metres

PART ONE

The Hero

One

Jacques Gilbert

From his interviews with the Abbé Fleuriot, 1669

I know what you're thinking. Sometimes I wake up sweaty from nightmares I can't remember and think the same thing.

But it's bollocks really, and I know that now. There's nothing I could have done to stop it happening, not the boy the way he was. For André to be safe it was the whole world needed changing, but you'd have had to be God to do that, and I don't think even God could have done much with France just then, back in the summer of 1640 and the middle of a war.

You can't blame us for not seeing it. We'd left Dax that morning with the crowds cheering because the Saillie was liberated and we were finally out of danger. André and I were travelling in triumph to his grandmother in Paris, with nothing to do when we got there but be looked after and made to feel important. The sun was shining, we were free and riding through Picardie with harvest starting all round us, fields of hops and golden barley and women with their skirts tucked up singing bawdy songs as they slashed. André was singing too, that slushy '*Enfin la Beauté*' de Chouy used to like, and I knew he was thinking about Anne. Everything felt exciting and full of hope, and it wasn't till we got clear of Lucheux I realized anything was wrong at all.

The landmarks were gone. I nearly missed the turning by Luchuel because the windmill had disappeared, and couldn't keep straight for Milly because I was looking for a spire that wasn't there. Then we came to the hamlet of Petit-Grouche, and I understood. I remembered it as a cluster of farm buildings, a wooden church, and a yard with a water trough and stone well where children used to play. Now the trough was dry and clogged with leaves, the well's rusty chain hung without a bucket, and the smell that drifted up was brackish and sour. There was nothing else but a circle of burnt stones where the church ought to have been and a field of sunken oblong patches with wooden crosses. The Spaniards had been through.

The war seemed to be everywhere after that. We kept passing soldiers on the roads, grim marching ranks stamping through lines of tall poplars, all heading for the border and the siege of Arras. When we reached Amiens there was a whole army camping in the fields and we couldn't even get in the gate. The guards said the King was there and half the court with him, they were mustering a force to break the blockade round our starving troops. 'Not a bed to be had anywhere,' they said. 'Everything's for Arras.'

I thought that was a bit much actually. I mean André was the Chevalier de Roland, the man who'd held the Dax Gate and opened the way to Spanish Flanders, they ought to have been chucking flowers and stuff, not leaving him to kip in the fields. I started to argue, but the boy touched my arm, said 'Stefan's at Arras,' and turned away.

I didn't give a stuff about Stefan, the one good thing I could see about Arras was him being stuck in it, but I sort of understood all the same. That night I looked at the campfires and listened to the men playing 'En passant par la Lorraine' on little tin pipes and got my first glimmering of the truth. We were using what felt like every man in France to take a single town in Artois, but there were Spanish and Imperial armies all over Europe, and us like a little tiny island in the middle. It was only a matter of time before they came again.

We'd fight them. We'd always said we would, and André was old enough now, just weeks off seventeen. The firelight was catching the side of his face as he sat watching the soldiers, and I remember noticing the little dark shadow that meant he needed a shave. He was ready.

We'd got a little respite while the Comtesse saw to his education and chose a regiment, but André obviously wanted it right now. We were getting breakfast next morning when trumpets started blaring and people came pouring out of the gates to line the road, so he just grabbed the bag of andouillettes and rushed to join in. Drums were rumbling in the distance, and beneath them the clatter of hundreds of hooves.

'The Noble Volunteers,' said a grizzled musketeer next to us. 'The Immortals. Fancy themselves, don't they?'

They did. They came prancing out with standards waving, not just those cavalry guidons but great flags with gold fringes and men specially to hold them. Their clothes were silk and velvet with so much gold in the fabric the sun flashed off it and hurt my eyes.

'The Grand Écuyer,' breathed a woman with a bosom so big it nearly blocked the road. 'Ah, how handsome he is, how young and beautiful.'

She was looking at the one in front, a fair-haired boy with a petulant mouth and dimpled chin who only looked about my age.

'The Marquis de Cinq-Mars,' said André, with a mouth full of sausage. 'Monsieur le Grand. He's the King's favourite, isn't he, Monsieur?'

'Favourite?' said the musketeer, and spat. 'That's one way of putting it.'

André looked confused. I was shocked myself actually, I mean I knew that stuff went on, but you don't expect it of the King when it's against the Church. I wondered what the other nobles thought about Cinq-Mars, and noticed a young one right behind who looked like he wanted to kill him. He was beak-nosed and nothing like as handsome, but held himself like the most important man in the world.

'D'Enghien!' cried the crowd as he passed. 'D'Enghien!'

André took another sausage, saw a pikeman watching him enviously and gave him half. 'The Duc d'Enghien,' he said, like I was deaf. 'Everyone's going to bloody be there, and all we can do is watch.'

I thought that was just as well. I don't mean I knew what was coming, I never thought Cinq-Mars or d'Enghien would mean more to us than they did right then, but I already knew André wasn't ready to take his place among them. He'd got the birth, he'd be Comte de Vallon when his uncle died, but you'd never have known it to look at him. His clothes were shabby, his manners rough, his voice had almost as much Picardie in it as my own. I'd done that myself, of course, I'd trained him to pass as a peasant in order to survive, but watching him mixing with the crowd, calling a musketeer

'Monsieur' and sharing our andouillettes with a broken-nosed pike-man, I wondered if I'd maybe overdone it. When the rest of the army came out and I saw him blowing kisses to a camp prostitute I was bloody certain of it.

I told myself the Comtesse would put him right, she'd undo what I'd done and teach him the way a gentleman ought to be. I didn't think it would matter for the moment, it was just a bit embarrassing, that's all.

It never occurred to me that it was dangerous. I never even thought of that till the third day, and by then it was already too late.

Bernadette Fournier

From her interviews with the Abbé Fleuriot, 1669

How trusting you are. You do not know me, yet appear sure you can believe everything I say. You seem as innocent as Jacques Gilbert.

Perhaps that is why I am willing to tell you my story. Perhaps in truth it will give me pleasure, for I like to remember the summer of 1640 when I was sixteen years old and as beautiful as your most forbidden dreams and as foolish as a mouse with no head. The war? No, Monsieur, I cared nothing for it. I was in Paris, and to us the war meant only higher taxes, that is all. I worked hard for my bread in those days, for I was the 'girl' at Le Pomme d'Or, and though there was also a 'boy' for the heavy work, it was I who cleaned the pots and pans and swept the hearth and made the beds, it was I who served the gentlemen who came.

It was not a bad life, for I had a kind master and a little bed all to myself beneath the rafters. It is true that sometimes gentlemen would find their way there, and sometimes I fought them off, and once or twice I could not, and once I did not choose to, for he was young and handsome and gave me a silver écu for myself when he went away. It is true also that the house was the property of Monsieur's wife, an ugly woman with an enormous goitre who sometimes beat me so hard I dreamed of running to my aunt who kept a house in Compiègne. Yet my life had comfort enough and

I had even a friend in the little cat that kept the rats from the horses' feed. At nights I took her to my own bed, where she would knead me with her claws and make deep rumbling noises that would have been a wonder for twice as much cat as she was. No, she had no name, she was a cat, that is all. So small a thing to change the future of France.

That there was danger in the house I did not think. There were politics, yes, but this was Paris, there were always plots, and still the Cardinal Richelieu kept his head on his shoulders and life went on. I knew only that Madame had a patron, a great lord called Fontrailles, who had lately taken to using our back room for secret meetings with his friends. It is true they spoke in front of me, for I was only the girl and of no more account than the cat, but I learned nothing from them beyond such names as seemed to be in code. They spoke of a 'Monsieur' as anyone talks of their master, and sometimes of a nameless 'M. le Comte', and sometimes of a man so important he was only 'le grand Monsieur'.

Some of these gentlemen came so often as to become familiar. No one could mistake M. Fontrailles for reasons you will under-stand, but sometimes there came also a shy young man of wispy beard and nervous manners, who wore many rings on his fingers and seemed constantly to count them lest one be stolen away. Some-times there came a languid army officer with thin moustache and cold eyes, who yawned a great deal and wafted his handkerchief as if to disperse a smell. But the one I liked least was a thick-necked fair man with odd eyes who strutted like a cockerel and kept his hand on his rapier as proof of his very manliness. The others spoke of him as a great swordsman, and gave him the name Bouchard.

They were there this day, Monsieur, everything as usual, but M. Fontrailles himself did not arrive and the gentlemen were most put out at the delay. I thought their concern due to a guest among them, a little dark man with a sharp beard who spoke not a word in my presence but was treated by the others with deference and seemed much annoyed by the absence of M. Fontrailles. Monsieur made excuses, he emptied the public room for them and offered wine for no charge, but it was his evening at the Guild and he could not stay longer.

'You must serve them, Bernadette,' he said at last. 'They seem well behaved and I am sure M. Fontrailles will not be long.'

So I remained alone and I served them, and so the damage was done, that day at the end of July when André de Roland came to Paris.

Jacques Gilbert

It was done anyway. We stopped at an inn outside Chantilly, and that's where it really began, right there.

The grumpy stablehand was busy with a load of soldiers' horses, so we rubbed down our own and gave them oats from our baggage. I didn't want anyone else looking after Tonnerre anyway, and it was good for André to bond with his new horse. I knew he still missed Tempête, but he was doing his best with the colt, he'd called him Héros and was using the name every minute, murmuring to him and fondling his ears.

The stablehand watched them and started to look a bit less pissed off.

'Wouldn't leave them there, if I were you,' he said. 'The army are commandeering everything for Arras. Stick them behind those officers' horses, no one'll touch those.'

André looked appalled at the idea of soldiers stealing, but we did it anyway and slipped the man a couple of sous for the tip. He looked down at the money, then sideways at the elegant dress swords on our belts, then up at the rest of us.

'You might want to tidy yourselves a touch before going in,' he said. 'Just saying.'

He was right. The rapiers marked us as gentlemen but nothing else matched. Our clothes were tatty from battles and things, we were covered in dirt from the roads and our hair was much too short for the fashion. We brushed each other off a bit, but we couldn't brush our clothes newer or our hair longer, we'd just have to do as we were.

We went in. It wasn't like the Quatre Corbeaux in Dax, with old men playing chess and drinking cider, this was the main road to

Paris, the customers were all strangers and it felt as friendly as a foreign barracks. Soldiers lined the walls and sat on the boards, the air was full of gruff laughter, and the only woman I could see was a big-breasted girl barging men out of the way with her hip as she swept by with bowls of steaming lentils.

We wriggled through to a counter at the far end and waited to get served. Other men yelled and banged their fists on the wood and got given jugs of wine and beer, but we stood politely and no one noticed us at all. I whispered to André 'I think we've got to shout,' but he said 'Isn't that rude when they're busy?'

I'd done this. I'd taken a young nobleman who used to shout and stamp with the best of them and turned him into someone as polite and humble as me. I said 'We'll starve otherwise.'

He shrugged and turned back to the counter, but someone else spoke first. A man's voice behind us said loudly 'Nice sword.'

Something flashed in André's eyes, and there it was, everything I'd been trying to wake up in him and suddenly wished I hadn't. He turned slowly, rested his elbows on the counter and said 'Thank you.'

Someone sniggered. A flabby-faced soldier said 'Whose is it?'

André let the laugh rise and die away. Then he let his hand drop casually to his belt and said 'Who says it's not mine?'

Everything went horribly quiet. The flabby-faced man looked him up and down, but André didn't move. Everything about him seemed relaxed except for the unnatural stillness of his face. His legs were slightly apart, his left hip thrust to point the guard of his rapier to the hand on his belt. He was a swordsman and looked it.

'No one,' said the flabby man at last. 'Just asking.'

André allowed a slight dip of his eyelids. 'As long as there's no misunderstanding.' He turned again to the counter and gave the man his back.

The chatter broke out again behind us, but the nape of my neck was cold with sweat. I hissed 'For God's sake, André, don't do stuff like that. What if he'd taken you up on it?'

He looked surprised. 'I'd have fought him. He insulted me, didn't he?'

I ought never to have brought him in here, not till he looked and sounded right and no one would dream of insulting him. He ought

9

to have had like a bubble of nobility all round him, but I'd gone and broken it and this was the result.

I said 'Sod this place, we'll eat in Paris.'

His eyes widened. 'But I'm hungry.'

I took his arm and bloody well pulled. 'Your grandmother will feed us, it'll look rude if we've already eaten.'

He was laughing in protest as I hauled him through the crowd. 'Oh come on, Jacques, I'm not going to start anything.'

Someone already had. I heard yelling and jeering down towards the door, a man protesting his horse had been stolen and soldiers saying he ought to be grateful for the chance to contribute to the war effort in Flanders. I kept dragging André past, and hoped to God our own horses were safe.

'Damn your Flanders,' said the man, with the kind of authority that makes you shuffle your feet and say 'Sieur'. 'I need another horse, and if there's a gentleman in this disgusting place he'll help me find one.'

André's head shot up at once. No one else responded, someone was telling the man to watch his language and others just laughed. It sounded bad, I was expecting to hear a sword rasp out any second, but then we were through the screen of bodies and I saw the man wasn't noble at all, just a huddled figure in the brown robe and hood of a Capuchin monk, turning this way and that to confront his tormentors. His face was shadowed by the heavy cowl, but his head was stooped anyway by the deep curve of his back.

I tugged at the boy's arm. 'It's just a hunchback, come on.'

'Tell you what,' said a soldier. 'Give us a rub of the hump for luck and I'll let you pat my horse, how's that?' The others howled with laughter.

André jerked his arm free and stepped forward. 'May I be of assistance, Father?'

The soldiers murmured and I saw it again, that up-and-down look and then the hesitation. There were more of them here, so I moved quickly to the boy's side to let them see I'd got a rapier too. The mumbling died away.

'Not unless you have a horse,' said the hunchback ungratefully. 'I've lost hours searching for a replacement and must be in Paris before dusk.'

'Bets, everyone!' cried a young arquebusier. 'Let's see how fast a *bossu* can run!'

André's eyes suddenly got thinner. He raised his voice over the cackling soldiers and said 'I can't lend you a horse, but you're welcome to ride with me if you wish.'

The cowled head moved as the hunchback studied us. He must have seen how shabby we were, but just said 'Thank you, Messieurs, I accept,' and began to shuffle purposefully towards the door. I whispered to André 'He's hiding his face, he might be a bloody leper,' but the boy said 'He's a monk, isn't he? He wouldn't put us in danger without saying so,' and walked confidently after him, ignoring the mocking grins of the crowd.

I suppose there was nothing really wrong with it. Héros carried the two of them easily, and we didn't even slow down. I didn't have anything against hunchbacks either, I mean I'd never minded Nicolas Moreau at home, but there's something sort of sinister about a man who won't look you in the face, and this one really wouldn't. He kept his hood right down all the time we were riding, and I felt more and more uneasy with every mile.

Bernadette Fournier

It was the wine, I expect, Monsieur, that and the heat of the evening. Some of the gentlemen remained both sober and civil, especially those beside the dark man with the little beard, but Bouchard and his friends drank without restraint and grew loud with merriment.

All this while my little cat lay curled contentedly in the hearth, for she liked the warmth of the stones and fancied she felt it even when there was no fire lit. She was no trouble to anyone until Bouchard chose to relieve himself in the fireplace, but then she sprang up and spat with protest, as who would not to be woken in such a way. Bouchard jumped back with an oath, while his friends laughed as at a farce by Jodelet himself.

Bouchard cried 'The devil!' and reached for my cat, but she backed into the corner, arching her back and bottle-brushing up her tail. He thrust his boot to prise her out of her corner, and I ran forward crying 'She is only a cat, Monsieur, only a little cat!' but he kicked her as if she had been a stone, he slammed his boot into her body so that she was crushed against the wall with a great crack and slid down into writhing contortions, crying most piteously. I struck out at his face and knelt beside my little one, but her back was broken, I could do for her now but the one thing. I put my hands to her neck and twisted the pain away until there was another crack then nothing but warm, limp fur and a dead cat and my heart that was too full even for tears.

There was silence about me, and I looked up and saw them staring down. Bouchard wiped his cheek with his handkerchief and stared in shock at the tiniest streak of blood on its folds. He said in disbelief 'You scratched me, you bitch. You *scratched* me.'

And then, Monsieur, oh yes, very yes, I was afraid.

Jacques Gilbert

We weren't much past Pierrefitte-sur-Seine when we first smelt it.

'Paris,' said the hunchback, snuffing contentedly. 'We can't be far now.'

You know what the city's like, but it was new to me then and even André recoiled. It had a dead animal stink like M. Gauthier's cottage, only a bit like someone had crapped in it too. The horses started sneezing and tossing their heads, and I felt like doing the same.

'We'll get used to it,' said André encouragingly, slamming a handkerchief over his nose. 'We must do, I don't remember it being as bad as this.'

I wasn't sure that meant much, it was five years since he'd last been there. I said 'We can't live in that.'

'Of course we can,' he said sort of heartily. 'The King does, doesn't he?'

I remembered the King was at Amiens and began to understand why.

The hunchback produced a little glass bottle from his robes. 'Sprinkle it on your handkerchiefs,' he said. 'It will help.'

He was right, the sharpness went zinging into my head like it was dissolving the smell in acid. I'd never seen a vinaigrette before, but couldn't help noticing how beautiful the bottle was or that the top was gold. I wondered more and more about that hunchback, and whether he was really a monk at all.

But it didn't look like mattering much longer, and within an hour we were approaching the Faubourg Saint-Denis. It was all right at first, just little stone houses and fields with sheep, and two distant windmills on a hilltop, but gradually everything grew bigger and bigger. Gardens stretched into the distance like farms, walled places with spires loomed like towns but turned out to be only hospitals. We rode in with Saint-Lazare on our right, the Hôpital Saint-Louis on our left, the walls of the city towering in front of us thirty feet high, and I felt we'd come to a country of giants.

The Porte Saint-Denis was open, and wagons were trundling out empty over the moat as farm people went home after selling their goods inside. I was all ready to announce the Chevalier de Roland and enjoy the guards' reaction, but a fat man in a short coat just said 'Come on if you're coming,' jerked his thumb rudely over his shoulder, then went back to guiding the wagons out behind us. We passed six feet's worth of double wall, emerged out of the tunnel of the gate, and that was it, we were in Paris.

The noise hit us at once, like being smacked with a sack of wet sand. Wagons were creaking and jolting all about us, wheels grinding and rumbling over loose cobbles, a man with two barrels on a hoop was clanking along yelling 'Water!' Women shrieked abuse, shutters banged overhead, dogs barked up a side street, a man bawled from a fish wagon, and someone shouted after a little boy who pounded up the road with a clatter of clogs and ducked under Tonnerre's belly to vanish up an alley the other side. A carriage rolled towards the gate with a man in front calling 'Make way for Mme la Duchesse!' while people bared their forearms to thrust fists in the air, and one shouted back 'Fuck off!' Crowds were flocking to the gate, scampering children were tumbling in the streets and begging pennies from the onlookers, people yelling and laughing in one great mush of sound and behind it all a cacophony of thousands of bells.

Colours blurred in front of me, dazzling clothing that looked almost shocking after days of green fields and white skies. I felt dizzy and sick. Tonnerre walked steadily beneath me, but Héros had never been out of the country, poor beast, he was tossing his head and his eyes were rolling white. André leaned forward to murmur to him, the colt's nose turned to his voice, and the boy rested his cheek against it like he used to with Tempête. The hubbub about us seemed to still for a moment, and I was aware of a gentler sound nearby, the tinkling of running water from the Ponceau.

André twisted his neck to speak to the hunchback behind him. 'We're for the Marais, Father, is that on your way?'

'Perfect,' said the hunchback. 'I'll direct you.'

I was glad of that, I wasn't sure the boy would remember after so long, but the hunchback guided us east like he knew every stone on the way. We followed his directions to the Rue du Temple, then down a tiny backstreet and up to a door with a semicircle of bobbly glass over the top and a sign on a chain saying 'Le Pomme d'Or'. It had a very narrow front, but went back a long way and had its own courtyard to one side. I heard men laughing in there and wondered if that was who the hunchback was meeting, but when the boy helped him dismount he just thanked us distractedly and disappeared through the door to the house in a flurry of brown robes.

We so nearly left then, André had his foot in the stirrup to remount, but the courtyard gate opened and a potboy came out, drawn by the sound of horses. His manner was furtive and he was trying to close the gate behind him, but I could still hear raucous laughter and sounds of splashing.

'The public room's closed, Messieurs,' said the potboy, looking the colour of cheese rind. 'I will enquire if . . .'

The laughter rose to a howl, and somewhere inside it came a girl's scream.

André thrust his reins at the potboy and strode forward. I said 'No, no, we can't interfere,' but he just smacked his palm on the gate and shoved it wide open. I slid off Tonnerre to grab at him, but he was already through the gate and gone.

I flung the servant money, said 'Look after the horses,' and bolted after him.

Oh, they found it so funny, Monsieur. They decided I was a dirty little beast and must be given a bath.

I would have run, but Bouchard scooped up my feet and his friends carried me between them to the courtyard door. The shy man did say 'I don't think you should,' but when Bouchard told him to run home to bed he meekly donned his cloak to leave. The silent dark man merely averted his eyes as if there were nothing happening and the rest followed his lead. I cried out for Madame and know she heard me, I saw her enter the room as we left it, but she only closed the courtyard door and went away.

They carried me to the horse trough, swung me over and dropped me into it with a great splash. The shock of cold water was frightful. Its filth invaded my mouth and nose as I tried to scream. I breathed in only water so that my head and chest swelled with the fear of it, then the weight was released, my head came again into the air, I was lying in a dirty horse trough spluttering and coughing and retching, and around me the gentlemen laughed until almost they were sick.

'Again,' said Bouchard, and I had time for only one cry before my head was forced back under. My hands flailed at the rim, but my shoulders were held down, my legs kicked at air. There was gurgling nothingness in my ears, the sky above me was rippled with brown water and dark shapes looming beyond it, I was clawing at emptiness and the panic forced me to gasp. The pain in my chest swelled, my throat burned, and my mind screamed that this was no game, they would keep me there until I drowned.

The pressure relaxed from my shoulders as an arm slid beneath them and hauled me up out of the water. My legs flopped down to touch solid ground, and through stinging eyes I glimpsed a man in a white shirt stepping back as I fell on my knees on the cobbles. My ears were filled with water, and I heard nothing but the rattle of my own breath as I vomited helplessly over the stones.

And not only the stones, for as I opened my eyes I became aware of a pair of boots in front of me spattered with brown streaks.

I allowed my gaze to travel upwards over the hem of a black cloak, full dark breeches, a belt and scabbard, the swept hilt of a grand rapier, a sleeveless blue doublet stained with wear, and a dirty white shirt unlaced at the neck. He was poor, perhaps, but certainly a gentleman – and I had been sick over his feet.

I cried out, but a hand came and rested on my head and a voice said 'All right.' I looked up fearfully, and saw the face of a young man perhaps seventeen or eighteen, with dishevelled black hair and green eyes that regarded me with the brightness of distress.

'All right,' he said again, and the touch of his hand was warm against the wetness of my scalp. I felt that he protected me, that as long as I stayed under his hand I would be safe.

Jacques Gilbert

I was terrified. There were four of them, all gentlemen, the kind of people I ought to be taking my hat off and grovelling to. Then the girl turned her face up to André and something inside me flipped over. Streaks of dirty water ran down her cheeks, her brown hair was plastered to her head, her eyes looked red and sore, but I was holding my breath all the same.

André kept his hand on her head, but he was looking at that blond bastard who was lounging against the trough with an expression of total boredom. There was something odd about his eyes, one seemed to be almost looking at his nose.

André's voice had a little shake in it. 'This to a woman?'

The blond practically yawned. 'What business is it of yours?'

André didn't hesitate. 'That of a gentleman.'

They looked at us, weighing us up. We wore the sword, but I knew that next to themselves we looked like nobodies.

The blond smiled. 'Oh come, fellow, a gentleman would know what happens to a commoner who strikes one.'

André looked down at the girl, but she shook her head and said 'They killed my cat.'

'Did they?' said André lightly. 'How brave of them.'

The blond suddenly stopped looking bored. André stepped back on one foot, hand going to his hip, ready for the challenge.

It didn't come. The blond glanced at his companions and said 'Here's another wants cooling off. What do you say?'

André didn't understand, he was standing waiting for the duel, but they were on him before I could move. The girl scrambled to her feet, trying to stand between them, but the blond smacked her out of the way, she reeled back dripping wet into my arms, and for a second her eyes were on my face.

'In with him!' the blond said. I tore my eyes off the girl and saw them dragging André towards the trough. His head went down, his elbows back, he wrenched an arm free and punched that blond whack on the chin. The man teetered backwards, his legs banged against the trough and for a glorious moment I thought he'd fall right in, but he just toppled sideways, bashing his head against the trough as he went down.

The others swung back to the boy and I heard a great *shing* of steel as they drew their swords. André shouted 'This is an affair of honour!' but he was in the wrong bloody world, they weren't after a nice fair fight, they were all charging him at once.

I shoved the girl away and yanked out my rapier. I'd never drawn it except to clean it, but it slid out smoothly to my hand, three good feet of shining steel. I shouted 'Come on, André!' and clashed my blade hard against the first sword I could see.

It was an older man with a red face wielding it, but he struck at me with a roar of rage. I was in and stamping with the front foot, blade up backhanded to deflect his thrust, then back to lunge at the throat. Only I couldn't, I couldn't, this was a Frenchman, I just scratched down his neck and jumped back.

At least André was drawn now, but he'd got two against him and I couldn't turn to help. Mine was at me again, trained as well as I was, he plunged in sharp at my face, and even as I sidestepped I knew he meant to kill. I slashed out desperately, using the edge, ripping his sleeve, but he twisted up to come at me overarm. I flinched away, feet tangling, and lost balance. His blade chopped down, then another flashed in to parry it, André of course, André, he'd pinked one man who'd dropped his sword and was clutching his shoulder, he'd got his other backing off to the inn and shouting for help, now he'd got mine, one, two and a stab in the thigh and the man was down and yelping.

'Run, Messieurs!' screamed the girl, as men came piling out of a door into the courtyard, drawing swords as they ran. A little dark man with a beard stopped and exclaimed '¡Madre de Dios!' but I hardly took it in because there beside him stood our hunchback. His hood was down, his head exposed, and for a second he and André stared at each other, then again the girl screamed 'Run!'

Bernadette Fournier

My gentleman turned to face them, so I appealed to the other, he with the blue eyes and the scar on his cheek, I cried 'Your master, get him out!' For one little second his eyes were on me, then he seized his master's arm and said 'Now, André, now!'

This was a servant, his voice more common even than my own, but the gentleman heeded him and ran for the gate. The servant said 'Our horses!' but I said 'Come back for them,' and pushed them both through. The gentleman protested 'Yourself, Mademoiselle!' I said 'I shall be safer when you're gone,' and turned to slam the gate behind them, but a weight smashed into my back, the gate was wrenched from my hands, and I was swept aside as our guests pressed through after them, shouting with the excitement of the chase.

I looked back into the courtyard. The dark stranger remained and the two wounded gentlemen who sat groaning on the stones, but at that moment I had eyes only for M. Fontrailles. He had a great temper, Monsieur, I had often heard him scream with fury, but now he stood utterly still with something in his face that frightened me more.

'It's all right, Monseigneur,' said one of the wounded, the older man with the florid face. 'It's only a bit of a game.'

M. Fontrailles said quietly 'He saw my face.'

Now it was the others who were still, and even the groans of the pale plump one ceased.

M. Fontrailles nodded savagely. 'That's what you've done with your games, Dubosc. That boy saw my *face*.'

Two

Jacques Gilbert

We sped round the corner and into another street. There were people carrying furniture back inside their shops at the end of the day's trading, so we slowed and sheathed our swords, but the footsteps behind never paused, and I turned to see six men charging right at us.

We put down our heads and kept running. No one was bothered, the traders kept moving, nothing to do with them at all. My sword was half in, half out, I was trying to wrestle it free and went crashing into a stack of wooden chairs crossing the road all by itself. A hideous old woman behind it gaped at me with outrage, but the boy gasped 'Your pardon, Madame,' and actually touched his hat. She stared, but we were through and past, and behind us came a great clatter as she pushed the stack over in front of our pursuers. She did it on purpose, she did it because of the boy.

Others felt the same. Two men were grappling a bedstead flat across the road, but one gave a jerk of his head and we leapt up and on it, springing down safely on the other side. The boy ran backwards a moment, panting 'Thank you, Messieurs!' and I did the same because I was beginning to understand a bit of what Paris was and how it worked.

But the men after us weren't bothered by things like bedsteads, they just shoved it out of their way and kept coming like they weren't going to stop till we were dead. Fear was drying my throat as we scudded round the corner and saw another long street in front of us, nowhere to hide and lots of people who didn't care. Carriages rattled past in the dusk, and a driver slashed at me with his whip for getting too close.

'Come on,' said André, tugging me round behind it. 'Cross into the Rue Vieille du Temple, my home's off there somewhere.'

We dodged across the street ahead of our pursuers but the next road was even longer and straighter. We paused at a gated archway with liveried servants outside, but when the boy said 'Your master, please tell him the Chevalier –' they just levelled their halberds and told us to piss off. The pounding footsteps were getting louder and harder behind us and when they chased us past a gate with flaming sconces I saw the bastards' shadows almost merging with our own. I imagined a sword in my back, I almost felt it between my shoulder blades, it was all I could do not to turn round.

'Any of the hôtels,' panted André. 'If we can just explain . . .'

The portes-cochères were all shut, we couldn't wait for admission. My feet hurt from the cobbles, I'd got a stitch in my side, we practically fell into the next turning and lurched blindly down it. It had great high walls that echoed the sound of chasing footsteps like a hundred men were after us, and roses on one side that tore at my cloak. Another opening loomed through a thick stone archway to our right, an alley half-blocked with piles of stacked crates. I shot through the gap, but André stopped in the archway, turned and levelled his sword.

I swivelled back, but the men were already hurtling round the corner and stopping dead at the sight of the boy. I was trapped behind him, and he was on his own.

The blond stepped forward, sword waggling loosely in his hand. He held his neck a bit stiffly, but otherwise seemed unhurt.

'Now then,' he said, and smiled.

André didn't move. The wall of the arch was to one side of him, the crates to the other, they'd have to take him one at a time.

'Would you care to make your apologies now?' said the blond. He flexed his blade in his fingers, then pointed it languidly at the boy. 'Perhaps I won't even kill you.'

André rested his elbow against the corner of a crate and I realized how tired he was. 'I'm sorry I treated you like a gentleman and not a cowardly bastard. Next time I'll know better.'

The blond changed colour, and behind him the others went curiously still. One in the shadows gave a little, soft laugh.

The blond changed grip on his sword. 'I'm afraid there won't be a next –'

I shouted a warning as his blade shot forward, but my voice was lost in the clash as André's flew up to meet it. The blond dropped quickly to reprise in the throat, but André twisted to let the thrust pass him, scything his own blade backwards to strike with the edge. The blond stepped back with a hiss of breath and I saw a fine scarlet line across his neck. His eyes looked hot with rage.

Then he was in again, hard and fast at the face, André whirling the blade to drive him back. The blond was older and stronger, the boy had to avoid close body and keep distance, but he couldn't step back beyond the crates, if he opened the gap they'd cut him down from all sides. And he was good, that blond, really good. He was drunk, of course, he hadn't got André's accuracy, but he was fast as well as strong, and he wasn't trying just to get a hit like the boy had done, he was looking to kill.

I looked desperately down the passageway beyond the arch. On one side the wall was just twelve feet high with no roof, but it was still too smooth to climb. After all those years of fighting Spaniards we were going to be killed in a stinking alley by a pack of noblemen looking for an evening's entertainment, we were going to be murdered by the boy's own kind.

André drove the blond back again, but now a thickset dark man pressed in, they were taking turns to have a cut at him. The boy was using the crates to guard his flank, but they were just boxes, they could be knocked over, kicked aside, then they'd be all round him, six against one. Then at last I saw it and knew what I'd got to do.

I grabbed a crate from the back of the pile. André was holding, the blades were clashing and I knew he was all right as long as I could hear that sound. I stacked three crates against the wall beyond the arch, two more in front of them, one in front of that.

I lifted another, but a man yelped behind me, the swords stopped, and I spun round with the box still in my hands. The thickset man was staring in disbelief at his ripped and bloodied sleeve, while André swung his blade in a rapid half-circle, watching for the next to make a move. I couldn't see his face, but the tip of his sword was wavering, and the panting of his breath seemed magnified by the echo of the arch.

I smashed my crate right into the stack beside him, toppling the whole lot down towards the mob. The stocky man dodged, but the others were jumping back and cursing, I dragged André behind me and shoved him at the makeshift steps. The dark man leapt forward, but I thrust my guard in his face, brought up my leg and bloody kicked him, sending him staggering back into his friends.

The boy was already clambering on to the wall. I jumped after him, got an arm over the top and kicked back down, scattering the crates below me. André hauled me to the top, then swivelled round and was gone. I dropped after him into the dark.

And landed on grass. I was expecting cobbles, but I landed on soft, sweet-smelling grass, like I was dreaming all of it and we were back in Dax and a world I knew. There were trees above my head and in front of me a fountain playing, water splashing and sprinkling like there was nothing in this world to worry about except getting wet. Ahead of us lay a silvery grey path with the oddest trees each side of it, tiny, stunted little things at the front but the further ones all bigger till I couldn't see their tops. Beyond them was a building stretching from wall to wall of the garden, and out of it were running a bunch of men shouting orders to someone I couldn't see. Then I spotted the great brown leaping things pelting towards us, and scrambled up in panic.

'It's all right,' said André, shaking his head groggily. 'I think we're –'

He stopped as he saw the dogs. I didn't, I shoved him towards the nearest tree, screaming 'Climb, climb, get off the ground!' but he pushed me aside and shouted to the men 'Call them off!'

It's no good trying to tell a dog you're the Chevalier de Roland, it could chew halfway through your groin before you'd finished. I tugged frantically at his sleeve, but he shook me off and shouted again 'Call them off, Guillot, it's me.'

The dogs came lolloping on, horrible great mastiffs with huge heads and about a million teeth, but one of the men gave a shrill, agonized whistle, and they stopped. They looked a bit fed up about it, but they stopped.

The handlers stayed with them, but one great giant of a man strolled calmly on. He reached us, peered down and bowed.

'Chevalier,' he said, his voice surprisingly gentle.

'Charlot,' said the boy, and stepped into his arms.

My head cleared. I looked at the other men and knew the crest on their coats, I'd seen it on the carriages at Ancre every day of my childhood. I looked again at André hugging the big man and told myself, 'Four years, four bloody years, I've done my job, he's home and safe and not my responsibility any more,' then the relief was washing over me in waves like drowning, and leaving nothing behind but an emptiness that felt like loss.

Bernadette Fournier

I, Monsieur? I was the 'girl'. I did as I was directed and undertook the care of the wounded.

M. Fontrailles took the dark stranger into the private room while I set myself to work. First was the red-faced Dubosc, who had helped carry me to the trough and now sat groaning with a sword cut to his thigh. I washed the wound tenderly and dressed it with linen, and beneath the salve I laid an even coating of salt. Oh, it was safe, Monsieur, the ointment must melt before the salt could penetrate, and when a surgeon examined it there would be nothing to see. Then I turned to the plump man who had a trifling cut to his shoulder which I served in the same way. Then I went out to the plot beyond the courtyard and buried my little cat.

When I returned the others were back, and I rejoiced to hear that my avengers had escaped by climbing the wall of a great hôtel. There was still much laughter at the thought of the drubbing they would undoubtedly receive for their impertinence, and Bouchard spoke of the whole event as a pleasant evening's sport.

The languid army officer lounged silently in his chair through all this, but now he studied his wine glass and remarked 'Only playing with the boy, were you, Bouchard? Do you know, for a moment there I thought he had you worried.'

Bouchard flushed red. 'What do you mean by that, Desmoulins?'

The officer smiled. 'I merely commend your humanity. The fellow struck you, didn't he? In your place I'd have wanted to do a little more than . . . play.'

'Had he been a gentleman, I would have done,' said Bouchard. 'As it is, I think making him run for his life through half Paris is sufficient of a lesson, don't you?'

Dubosc grunted. 'Not sure Fontrailles will agree. He thinks the lad saw his face.'

And there it was again, Monsieur, that strange uneasy silence as they looked from one to another but said not a word. I took advantage of their distraction to salt another dressing and began humbly to wash the scratches of Bouchard.

'Oh, what does it matter?' said he, twisting his thick neck irritably as I wiped. 'Why shouldn't Fontrailles visit an alehouse with friends?'

Desmoulins raised his eyebrows. 'Dressed as a Capuchin monk?'

'If he likes,' said Bouchard. 'He could be conducting a secret liaison.' He twined his fingers in my damp hair and said 'What about it, girl? Would you say no to a hunchback?'

The laughter stopped abruptly as the door banged open to admit M. Fontrailles.

'I'm glad you're amused,' said he, his face dark with anger. 'Our guest was not. I have placated him for now, but until this is resolved I decline to go further in the business.'

Oh, such uproar as they made at that! They insisted everything was going so well, they were so near success, it would be madness for M. Fontrailles to withdraw now.

He silenced them with a single savage gesture. 'The damage is done. If word should reach the ears of – someone we know, what will he make of my travelling about the country in this disguise? Next time I will be followed. Blois may not matter, but the Sedan? No, I must tell Monsieur my usefulness is at an end.'

Bouchard leapt to his feet. 'This is ridiculous. A fellow like that won't even know who you are. He's nobody.'

'Nobody?' said M. Fontrailles, giving me a curt nod of dismissal. 'The rapier was a good one, I observed it closely. His speech was rough, but his instincts are those of a gentleman. And if he is, Messieurs, if he is the kind of man who will be in society, then mine is not the only name he will learn.'

Bouchard stopped still and stared at him. 'Then, by God, we'd better learn his first.'

I closed the door softly behind me.

The 'boy' was in the courtyard, and I told him on no account to let anyone know about the horses in our stable. He asked a kiss for the service and I gave it him, for he was fourteen years old and in love with me, then I went to the stables myself. Louis had eased the beasts of their baggage before laying their blankets over their backs, but I found the packs in a corner and looked inside.

The contents, oh, Monsieur, they made me laugh. A burnt wooden horse, a tennis ball with its inners hanging out, why, I owned almost as much myself. But as I rummaged deeper I heard the familiar chink of coin, and there at the bottom were two leather bags, one containing jewellery but the other filled with money. There was enough to buy me Madame's house, enough to buy me a dowry and a husband of my own.

I dared not really steal it, but thought a man with so much might not know the exact sum, a man so rich might not miss three little coins. I took them and replaced the bags, but my hand brushed a bundle beneath them, and inside I found a dagger engraved with a crest I knew as well as anyone in the Marais. The Roland crest, Monsieur, and on the dagger of a man who used a sword as if he had been born with it in his hand. I sat back on my heels and began furiously to think.

Yes, I had heard of André de Roland, everyone in Paris knew that name. There had even been a play about him, Madame had seen it herself. She had come back with eyes like boiled gooseberries with love of the leading actor, but she told Monsieur the story, how a nobleman disguised himself as a peasant and lived with ordinary people to protect them from the invaders, how he spent his money to feed them and risked his life to protect them, and was saved in the end by the love of a Mlle Celeste, who was really some rich lady in Paris. It sounded foolish to me, Monsieur, and I knew no nobleman really does such things, but still I remembered the day the criers said the Saillie was liberated, I remembered how everyone cheered. Now I knelt in the straw and wished just a little that I had cheered too.

I did not doubt the identity of my gentleman, though I wondered about his companion, for if he had been in the play Madame had said nothing of him. I thought of these things and hesitated, then

I replaced two of the coins, keeping only one shining golden écu for myself, then repacked the baggage and returned to the house.

My room seemed cold that night, for my dress had been a long time damp against my skin and when I lay down to sleep I missed the warmth of my little cat. My heart was bitter at what was done to her, but I comforted myself with foolish thoughts and when I slept at last it was his face and no other that I saw in my dreams.

Whose face, Monsieur? You do not attend, or perhaps you do not know women. Whose do you think?

Jacques Gilbert

We walked down the silver track with the trees getting bigger all the way. Charlot said it made the path look longer from the house, but I didn't want anything to look bigger, I was scared enough already. We went in through huge doors with windows of flat glass, crossed a reception room with a ceiling so high it was like we were still outside, then passed into a hallway with a great staircase winding up to a railed gallery. Servants came crowding from all over, girls in pink dresses flocking round saying 'M. André, M. André!' and the boy kissed them all and made them giggle. No one tried to kiss me, so I stayed where I was and stared hard at my boots. They looked worn and grubby against the marble floor.

'You will want refreshment, Monsieur,' said Charlot, gently steering me away.

I looked behind to see the boy being whisked up the staircase by a footman. 'But the Chevalier . . .'

He smiled blandly. 'Madame la Comtesse has sent for him. Doubtless you will see him in the morning.'

I felt sort of flat. I knew it was fair, I mean André was her grandson, but she knew perfectly well I was too. I'd had a kind of idea she'd always wanted to know me, I'd even had this stupid picture in my head of her giving me a hug. I saw André disappearing along the railed gallery and felt suddenly desolate.

I said 'I'm his aide, I ought to be looking after him.'

Charlot's eyes crinkled at the corners. 'Indeed you are, and that makes you very important. Tonight others will attend the Chevalier while we look to your own needs.'

He didn't really mean 'we', he just clapped his hands and everyone else rushed about. They escorted me to the kitchens and gave me wine and a dish of veal liver they fried just for me, but it was difficult eating by myself while three maidservants watched with their hands in their aprons and smiled every time I looked up.

Charlot was giving orders in the background, and when I pushed away my plate he was at my elbow wondering discreetly if I might like to wash. I got up to go to the well, but two footmen sort of boxed me in and led me into a room with a stone floor and a huge bath with steam coming out like I was going to be made into soup. They wouldn't go away either, they practically ripped my clothes off and even helped me get in. I didn't seem to have any control over what was going on, my head was swimmy with wine and the steam from the bath, I was as naked as when I was born and felt like it was happening again right now.

They scrubbed till my skin was pink and sore, then I put my clothes back on and they suddenly felt stiff and dirty. At least someone had cleaned my boots while I was bathing, and one of the footmen started working them over my dirty hose while the other combed my hair. Then Charlot appeared again and said in a carefully unsurprised voice 'If you are ready, Madame will see you now.'

The footman's hands stilled on my boot. The comb stopped dead in my hair. The Comtesse was asking to see her grandson's aide.

There wasn't any question of keeping her waiting. Charlot swept out of the bathing room with me practically hopping after him, trying to tug the second boot up over my heel. My heart was suddenly banging and my skin all damp and prickly. André'd told her. He'd said we knew who I was, and she was furious, she was going to order me out of the house in the middle of the night.

We went up the sweeping staircase and down a long gallery, but I wasn't looking at anything but Charlot's back in front of me and wondering what I'd see when it went away. I followed him through a door with a footman outside, heard him say 'M. Gilbert, Madame,' and watched his back bend as he bowed and stepped aside. I was looking at a silvery coloured wall with shimmery blue curtains, then

I lowered my gaze and there she was facing me, Elisabeth, Comtesse de Vallon, my grandmother.

I'd forgotten how small she was. She was so tiny and perfect she made me think of an elaborately carved chess piece. She was quite old, of course, I mean she must have been over fifty, but her face was pink and her eyes bright, and her hair shone like silver in the candle-light. I hadn't time to take in more, I dropped my eyes at once, because she was nobility and I mustn't look at her face.

'Come nearer the chandelier, M. Gilbert,' she said. 'Let me look at you properly.'

She had the most beautiful voice I'd ever heard. It went up and down in little trills like a bird's, and she didn't just say the shape of words like other people, she said the whole word with all the letters in it. I stepped forward dumbly and kept my eyes on the floor.

'Head up, man,' said the voice, with a trickle of laughter in it. 'I want to see your face.'

I stared hard at the wall behind her head. Something moved to my right, and I saw André leaning against the mantelpiece, looking somehow taller and more elegant than I was used to. He caught my eye and grinned.

'Well, Charlot,' said the Comtesse. 'You know who this is, don't you?'

André's head shot round, and I had to work hard not to turn myself. Charlot knew. I wondered if everyone did, if me and André were the last people in France to find out.

'I would have known it anyway, Madame,' said Charlot, closing the door softly. 'The resemblance rather declares itself.'

'Yes,' said the Comtesse, and I felt her searching my face again. 'The blue eyes are the mother's, I think. She was a pretty child. My poor Antoine.'

My poor mother. I could see her as clearly as if she was in the room with us, her anxious face and shabby blue dress, the look of wonder in her eyes when she'd told me about my real father and how she'd always loved him. I couldn't speak.

André's voice had a sudden edge in it. 'Madame, this is my dear Jacques, my best friend and brother.'

'Half-brother,' corrected the Comtesse. 'Half and illegitimate.

We cannot quite sweep aside the sanctity of marriage, no matter how inconvenient it may be.'

André didn't waver. 'He's still your grandson. We have to acknowledge him.'

'Have I said I will not?' There was a kind of twinkle in her voice. 'Your uncle and I are fully minded to do it, Chevalier, we have thought it all this last year.'

He looked steadily at her. 'Truly?'

'Truly,' she said, and smiled. It was an amazing smile, it didn't make her face softer, just harder and more brilliant, like a diamond. 'While you continue to risk your life in this reckless fashion, surely you can see the value in a second heir to safeguard the estates?'

Colin's dad always said they ought to have a spare. Well, they did, they'd had one all along, and it was me. I felt too numb even to be miserable.

She turned back to me. 'You are silent, Monsieur. Have you no opinion on this?'

I said quickly 'I'm not asking for anything.'

She flinched at the sound of my voice, and I heard it myself, thick and very Picardie, as wrong in this room as a horse would have been. But she only said 'I know that, child, what I wish to know is whether you will accept it if it is given.'

I started to say 'Yes, of course,' but she flicked up her hand to stop me.

'Think what it will mean. You will be under my authority and your uncle's. You must subjugate your wishes to what is best for the family. We will control your career and marriage as we do the Chevalier's. Are you really prepared for this?'

André was studying the floor, determined not to sway me, and I knew it had to be my choice. I looked desperately round the room, then my eyes caught on something and sort of went back all by themselves. Above the fireplace was a picture of a man on horseback with his sword in the air. Whoever painted it knew bugger all about horses, it had a body so huge its legs would have snapped under it, but the man looked noble and heroic and exactly as I remembered him. He was laughing in the picture, there was a youth and excitement about him, and his eyes were right smack on mine.

'The Chevalier Antoine,' said the Comtesse's voice, and I thought she sounded softer. 'Your father.'

I looked at that picture and thought of all the other times I'd seen him. They were things that actually happened, but this was the first time I'd looked at him knowing I was his son.

My voice came out better this time. 'If it's what you want.'

She inclined her head. 'Bravo. We shall see what can be done.'

André took two quick paces across the floor. 'Jacques,' he said, and grasped my hands.

'All right, Chevalier,' said the Comtesse. 'Now go and have a bath or something, you smell like a stable.'

He gave me a little grimace and released me. 'My apologies, Madame. I have of course no excuses.'

'Oh, don't be pompous, André,' she said briskly. 'You have plenty of excuses, I never knew you when you didn't. But I need to speak with Monsieur without your pouncing to his defence at every imagined slight or I shall be here all night.'

He grinned suddenly and looked more like himself. 'All right.' He made her a beautiful bow, but when she gave him her hands he stooped and kissed her cheeks before she could stop him, said 'Good night, Grandmother,' gave me a little wave and walked out.

I thought she looked warmer for a moment, but then she turned back to me. 'Now, Monsieur, you would like to be Jacques de Roland?'

It sounded stupid and wrong. 'I suppose so.'

'Good,' she said. 'Now for heaven's sake sit down, you're giving me a stiff neck.'

I plopped down on a pretty little chair with curved legs. It creaked under my weight and I tried not to think what would happen if it broke.

The Comtesse started pacing round the room in an oddly silent way that was like a swan. 'To legitimate a baby is relatively simple, but a young man is quite another thing. You will have to be taught the ways of the nobility, and that is difficult when childhood is past.'

I said miserably 'I'll be twenty in September.'

She looked at me. 'I know when you were born, Monsieur. I know the very hour.'

I felt the first twinge of feeling towards her, but she was off floating about the room again and the moment went.

She said 'We'll keep you here discreetly for a time while Charlot teaches you to be a gentleman. The Chevalier will learn with you. You know he needs it, don't you?'

I admitted I did.

'Oh, I'm not blaming you, child,' she said. 'I'm aware there have been other, less desirable influences. This man Ravel, for instance, the Chevalier has written of him more than once. Is there danger of further contact?'

I said 'I don't think so.' I was sure, actually. Stefan was never going to forgive André for not killing d'Estrada, they'd hardly spoken since.

'Good,' she said. 'Then we have only to teach him how to survive his new life.'

I was puzzled. 'He's safe here, isn't he?'

'Safe?' she said, and stopped right in front of my chair. 'He has come within a feather of fighting three duels in a single day.'

It didn't sound very good when she put it that way. 'But he can win, he's really –'

'Duelling is illegal, Monsieur, surely you know that?'

I said 'It still happens, doesn't it?'

'Naturally,' she said, 'and I would be ashamed if the Chevalier failed to act when his honour demanded it. But every hour of every day? No, Monsieur, he must learn greater distance for his own survival. Will you help him?'

I looked at the empty hearth and silvery wallpaper, and everything felt cold. When M. Gauthier talked about nobility it was all swords and honour and glory, but this felt flat as stone. I said 'All right.'

'Well done,' she said, and extended her hand. I took it and sort of stuck out my lips till they touched her, then she took the hand away and smiled, and I knew I was dismissed.

Charlot escorted me along the gallery to a bedchamber, then bowed and left me alone. The room was huge, and the bed had velvet curtains like I was going to be lying dead in state. There was a bell and a fat beeswax candle on a chest by the bed, and a great white nightshirt and cap laid out on the covers. I put them on obediently.

The bed was soft and squashy with all smooth linen sheets, but it was horribly chilly when I climbed in. I supposed I ought to blow out the candle, but I'd never slept without even the horses for company and didn't want to face the dark. I felt a sudden longing for my old blue blanket that was still on Tonnerre's back at Le Pomme d'Or. I'd had that blanket since I was twelve. I wanted its familiar roughness and warmth, I wanted its old smell. Nothing around me smelt right just then, not even me.

I heard light footsteps outside, then a tap on the door. I said nervously 'Come in.'

The door pushed open and there was André. He was wearing a nightgown just like mine, but he'd obviously thrown away the cap and I suddenly wished I had too.

He said 'Hullo,' and leaned against the doorway. 'I came to see you were all right.'

I ignored the coldness of the bed. 'I'm fine, it's all lovely.'

'Good,' he said, not moving. 'I just thought you might be finding things a bit strange. You know, just at first.'

I started to say no, then understood. I remembered the Comtesse saying 'he must learn greater distance', then thought 'Sod her, I'll start tomorrow,' and pulled back the covers.

He brightened. 'Perhaps just the first night . . .' He climbed in beside me, then shot back up towards the pillows. 'Bloody hell, they've forgotten to warm it. Have you rung?'

I felt suddenly very stupid. 'No.'

I felt him looking at me. His voice said 'You're right, let's not bother.' He sucked in his breath, plunged down under the covers, said 'See? It's fine,' then shivered and said 'Fuck.'

I started to laugh. It was an odd kind of laughter, it felt almost painful, but it really was getting warmer, just having the boy with me helped. I said 'You mustn't say "fuck" now, you're a gentleman again.'

'Oh shut up,' he said comfortably. 'You sound like my grandmother.'

I blew out the candle without even thinking about it, and curled up with my pillow.

After a moment he said 'She's going to let me marry Anne, you know.'

'Is she?'

'I think so. But do you think Anne will want it herself? She might have forgotten.'

Women never forget anything, they just kind of hoard it up to use against you later. I said 'You'll have to remind her, won't you?'

'Perhaps,' he said thoughtfully, wrapping his arms round his pillow. 'Mmm.'

The darkness didn't feel frightening any more, it was warm and soft and so was the bed. My mind drifted and swam with pictures of the day, and I found myself thinking of that girl at Le Pomme d'Or, the way she'd stood with her wet dress clinging to her body, those seconds I'd held her in my arms. Another memory floated past, something I hadn't taken in at the time but was somehow waking pictures of an empty hamlet and a row of wooden crosses in an overgrown field. I snatched at the cause of it and forced it into sense.

I sat up and said 'That was a Spaniard.'

'What?' he said sleepily.

'That man in the courtyard, the dark one with the little beard. He said "*¡Madre de Dios!*" He was Spanish.'

'Was he?' He was silent a moment, then said 'Well, so's the Queen, come to that. This is the city, there are all sorts here. He's probably a diplomat or something.'

It seemed odd to me, having Spaniards about and not fighting them, but André knew more about these things than me. I shoved the memory aside, lay back down on the pillow, and went back to thinking about the girl.

Three

Extract from her diary, dated 2 August 1640

Last night I dreamed of André. I was back in the Forest of Verdâme, dressing behind the screen and listening to the sound of him riding away, but then his voice said 'Anne' just the way it did before he kissed me, and he hadn't gone at all, he was standing behind me and I had no clothes on. It made me feel very strange, and I am still a little shaky now.

I think it is Florian who prompted it. He came in early last night, and sat counting off the rings on his fingers like beads on a rosary, which is always a sign he is thinking back to our captivity. He seems still to live in constant fear of starvation, and insists on keeping as much wealth about him as he can. I might have given it no special significance, but when I retired he embraced me and said 'Anne, you know I'll always protect you, don't you?' with an earnestness I could not mistake. It has long preyed on his mind, that dreadful night when I cried for his help and he could not save me, but I believed him recovered from it and cannot think what could have recalled it to him now.

It will be to do with these vile friends of his. He was doing so much better before they came. This morning I plucked up courage to tell Father so, but he only hemmed into his beard and said that Florian is engaged in an important investment for our futures and I should not question a connection he himself approves.

But I do question it, I *do*. I am not the child they think me, I am sixteen years old and know there is something wrong. I do not understand why Father tolerates these people, for Bouchard and Desmoulins are openly contemptuous of our humble origins, and if the others are like them then they are simply abominable. Bouchard treats Florian like a stupid child and the servants like dirt. Everything they hand him has to be polished on his handkerchief before he deigns to touch it. Once I asked if we had given him a dirty glass, but he slammed it down with annoyance and refused to drink at all. Father reproached me with discourtesy to a guest, but when I asked about discourtesy to our servants he pretended not to hear. He always does when I speak about the servants as people.

I wish Father were easier to talk to. He seemed kinder when we first arrived, but I cannot help wondering if that was only because he hoped for a betrothal with André. As the days pass and still André does not come to Paris, Father is becoming cooler and cooler.

He is wrong. André would never have forgotten me. He will have had a lot to do in the Saillie before he could leave, but I know he'll come soon. It is only fifty-two days since he sent me the rose and I must learn to have more patience.

Jacques Gilbert

The Comtesse kept us hidden like lepers till we were fit to be seen in public. André wasn't even allowed to write to Anne, and the Comtesse sent servants in plain livery to Le Pomme d'Or for the horses. I was disappointed about that actually, I wanted to make sure the girl was all right, but the servants said she seemed fine. I'd still like to have seen her, just looked at her one more time, but we weren't allowed to see anyone till we'd been groomed like horses ourselves.

André couldn't understand it, he said the Comtesse had never bothered what other people thought before, but he couldn't marry Anne without her blessing so he hadn't much choice. We had our hands oiled and nails trimmed, and our skin rubbed with perfume till we smelt like cat's piss. We were dressed in breeches so full it was like wearing a dress, and shirts with so much lace at the wrist you couldn't find your fingers. The Comtesse even wanted us to wear wigs, but André threw his out of the window and said if she tried it again he'd burn it. 'Very well, Chevalier,' said the Comtesse. 'Then let us hope for your sake your hair grows quickly.'

Then Charlot did his best with what was left. He taught us how to sit and stand and even how to walk. He got in a dancing master who made us twirl round slowly while he hummed dull music between dried-up lips. I used to like dancing in Dax, everyone leaping and whirling together, but Charlot said it was different at court, we might have to dance one couple at a time with everyone looking and making snotty remarks if we got it wrong.

Even harder was learning about literature and stuff for the salons. André didn't mind the poetry and I liked the battles in Corneille, but that didn't matter, Charlot was trying to teach us to say the right thing. One day we had these foul verses about how beautiful Mlle de Bourbon was, but Charlot said they were fine poetry because they'd been commissioned by Cardinal Richelieu himself. He smiled when he said it, but André sort of growled.

There were politics wherever we looked back then, like smoke from a bonfire that left little black specks on everything. André was always poring over the *Gazette* for news of the war, but that stunk of it too. They had this piece praising the heroism of Cinq-Mars at Arras, which Charlot said was the editor trying to please the King, but when Arras fell there was another account that hardly mentioned Cinq-Mars at all, which Charlot said was him trying to please the Cardinal. The whole thing was just mad.

But the worst were lessons in what Charlot called 'society', learning who was important and who wasn't. Even our own title was complicated because we used to have a province of our own, which apparently put Comte de Vallon right up there with ducs. The Comtesse even had something called the 'tabouret' which sounded really grand, but Charlot said only meant that she could sit on a stool in the Queen's presence. It didn't affect me, of course, I mean bastards can't inherit titles, but actually none of it felt real. It might have helped if I'd met the Comte himself, but he never went out much because of being poxed and having no nose, and that summer he was ill and not seeing anyone at all.

The one thing I was good at was the fencing. Our style had got a bit unconventional through learning on our own, but Charlot seemed pleased with my progress. He was a real artist himself, of course, he'd fenced our father and uncle before we were either of us born, but André could still beat him. I was starting to think he could beat anyone, but when I said that he slanted his eyes at me and said 'Not quite.'

He hadn't forgotten d'Estrada. He was mastering the *main-gauche* so he'd be better prepared when he next encountered a left-hander, and I knew who he had in mind. He asked Charlot to show him Spanish techniques, and I knew what that was about too. He was even determined to join a regiment on the Flanders front, because that's where d'Estrada had been. He just wasn't going to be happy till he'd fought the man again and beaten him.

But the fencing gave me something familiar to do, and the rest gradually got better. I got used to being waited on and actually had a valet of my own, a handsome young Gascon called Philibert who was desperately proud of the promotion. He wouldn't let me be familiar, but was fascinated by anything to do with battles and listened to my experiences with his mouth wide open. He'd tell me heroic stories out of books as if they were just as real, and to him I think they actually were.

André found it harder. He was chafing to see Anne, of course, but I had an odd feeling he'd been happier in Dax, living in the Hermitage with his friends and taking his turn to sit guard on the roof. I told myself it was only the being cooped up he couldn't stand, he'd be fine once we were allowed out, but weeks went on by and the Comtesse gave no sign.

Then September came. We were fencing with Charlot in the courtyard one afternoon when a familiar voice shouted 'Chevalier!' and an elegant young man with blond curls and a coat of turquoise silk came running towards us. It was Crespin de Chouy.

You remember de Chouy. He was the fashionable officer who brought despatches from Châtillon, the one who was always singing and thought war a great game, and judging from the enthusiastic way he hugged André he hadn't changed a bit. He even embraced me too, but then he'd known us in the old days when we all mucked in together, he'd thought it delightfully eccentric and fun.

Charlot said sternly 'Do you wish to see Madame, M. de Chouy?'

'Already seen her,' said de Chouy, beaming. 'Only a message from my mother, you know, wanting to know why she's not been seen about, wondering if she was ill, all that. It's been dead in town this summer, everyone at Arras.'

André said gently 'Didn't you go, Crespin?'

De Chouy's face fell like a scolded child's. 'My stupid back, you know. They sent me home.'

I remembered he'd been racked by those bastard Spaniards. I didn't want to look too obviously but he seemed all right, I guessed it was muscles inside that got torn.

'Rotten shame,' said de Chouy. 'I'm perfectly all right really, and to miss Arras! De Bergerac was wounded, did you hear? Santerre was there, Monsieur le Grand, the Duc d'Enghien, oh, everybody, and they sent me home.'

He had the most innocent eyes I'd ever seen, round and blue and so trusting it was horrid to think of anyone hurting him. André grasped his arms and said 'I bet they're jealous of you, though. The man who saved the Saillie by keeping silent, I bet they wish they'd done that.'

De Chouy gazed at him sort of mistily. 'I say, do you think so? I think they think I'm an awful fool. But just wait till they hear you're back, we must show you the town.'

Charlot coughed delicately. 'The Chevalier is resting after his labours, Monsieur. Madame would wish you to be discreet as to his return.'

'Oh, absolutely,' said de Chouy, looking blank. 'Discreet, yes, absolutely.'

I think 'discreet' meant something different in Paris, because only a week later we found a paragraph in the *Mercure François* announcing André de Roland had returned to the city the previous August. It said coyly the information would be gladly received on the Place Dauphine and wondered if at last Mlle Celeste was to be reunited with her Apollo. It added poisonously 'After so long a delay, no doubt Mademoiselle will be wondering too.'

'Anne,' said the boy. He crushed the paper in his hands as he stood. 'That bloody bastard play. They're getting at Anne.'

He strode across the salon and the servants took one look, threw the doors open and flattened themselves against the wall. I rushed after him, saying feebly 'It's not for much longer . . .' but he said

'You think I'm going to let them laugh at Anne?' and spun off down the gallery. I followed quickly, and heard the soft unhurried steps of Charlot coming up behind me.

The Comtesse was having her hair done. She didn't even turn when André came crashing in, just looked at him steadily in the mirror.

'Good morning, Chevalier,' she said exquisitely. 'Thank you, Barbe.'

The maid dropped a hurried curtsey and legged it.

André smacked the *Mercure* on the dressing table. 'Have you seen this, Madame?'

We watched her read it. After a moment she turned round on her stool and looked at us. 'People talk, Chevalier, someone was bound to hear in the end.'

'I have to see her,' said André. 'I must see Mlle Anne.'

'Mlle du Pré,' she corrected. 'The elder girl is married now.'

'You know who I mean.'

'And you know what I said.'

'It's been two months now, it's my duty to call, and you have to let me do it.'

I'd seen him in a temper loads of times, I'd seen him yell and stamp and go red in the face, but this was different. His voice was quieter and deeper, and he stood very still.

The Comtesse rose. 'That is good, André. At last you are beginning to sound like a gentleman.'

'Then have the goodness to let me act like one.'

She inclined her head. 'I shall write to the Baron and arrange a visit.'

'No,' said André. 'This is yesterday's paper, it won't wait. I'm going now.' He bowed, turned and walked out.

Charlot said 'You wish him stopped, Madame?'

'No,' said the Comtesse, and she sounded tired. 'It's my own fault, I pushed him too hard. But go after him, won't you, Charlot? Keep him safe.'

I tried to be reassuring. 'He's learned a lot, he won't do anything silly.'

'He's already done it,' she said. 'He made how many, eight, ten enemies on his first evening? I had hoped to keep him here until no one could associate that rough lout with the Chevalier de Roland, but now . . . ?'

Then I understood. All that stuff about waiting for us to grow our hair and get nice manners, it was complete bollocks, she'd been thinking about this all along. She was doing exactly what I'd been doing myself the last four years, using anything and everything she had to protect the boy.

I bowed to my grandmother with a new respect, and went out after Charlot.

Anne du Pré

Extract from her diary, dated 30 September 1640

I know it was wrong to hope so desperately for something that was never promised, but it was still a shock to read that paper and realize how foolish I had been. André had been in Paris two months and never once called.

I needed a proper Mass today, so Florian took me to Notre-Dame. He wouldn't stay for the service itself, but I had my dear Jeanette for company, and I do find Notre-Dame beautiful. Jeanette says it is too dark, but I love the sun filtering through the stained glass to paint colours on the battle flags, I love the smell of incense and the way the muttering echoes from wall to wall. I prayed hard for Florian and Father and really did feel better for it, for Notre-Dame is a place for miracles.

We had another this morning, for it was announced the Queen has indeed given birth to a second son, and joybells were rung after the service. When we stepped down on to the parvis the air was wild with their voices: Marie, Jacqueline, Gabrielle, Guillaume, Pasquier, Thibaud and the dear Sparrows, all ringing gladness in glorious, tumultuous thanks to God.

'Mademoiselle,' said Jeanette, and her hand clutched my arm. 'Mademoiselle.'

I could not at first see what she stared at, for the sunlight was bright after the darkness inside and my eyes are not good. Crowds of people mingled about the square, but one figure stood out because it was motionless, a young man, tall and dark, and when he saw me looking he removed his hat.

A carriage rattled between us and I could have cried out with vexation. I stepped forward blindly, then the carriage was past and he was there in front of me, his hat in his hand and his head on one side, it was him after all, it was André.

I never imagined it like this. I had thought he would be announced, we would sit and speak politely with Father, and I would have time to compose myself. Now I was standing like a fool with my hair blown by the wind and not a word in my head, and he bowed and said 'Mademoiselle,' and it was his voice.

I was ashamed of the way my legs trembled in the curtsey, but managed to say 'Ah, Monsieur, we heard you were back in Paris,' and waited to hear his excuses.

He said wretchedly 'I know, I'm so sorry. I gave my word not to call until my grandmother thought I was ready.'

His expression was so sad I could not for a moment speak.

'Have you a carriage, Sieur?' said Jeanette, sounding wonderfully brisk and normal. 'Mademoiselle will need to sit down.'

'No,' he said, dragging his eyes reluctantly from my face. 'Oh, hullo, Jeanette, how lovely to see you. No, I'm sorry, I ran.'

That seemed as ridiculous as my dream, but Jeanette sat me firmly on the parapet that divides the parvis and I made a determined effort to appear calm. I said 'What an extraordinary chance we should meet like this!' and immediately *hated* myself for saying something so stupid.

'Not really,' he said. 'I've been round every church on the Île de la Cité.'

I had to look away again.

He said 'I had to see you somehow, you do understand that, don't you? I'd have done it weeks ago but for two things.'

I said 'What things?'

His eyes dropped. 'Because my grandmother's right. Look at you,

Mademoiselle. I'm an ignorant country *hobereau*, why would you even look at someone like me?'

He seems more substantial in daylight. There is more colour to him than I remembered, and the sun has tinged his face an unfashionable light brown. There is a fine dark stubble shadowing his jaw I'm sure was not there before. Then he moved to avert his face, the hair shifted on his shoulders, and I saw it stopped short where it lay.

His cheek reddened. 'I know, that's part of it. The Spaniards cut it.'

The thought of their laying hands on him overwhelmed me with a desire to *hit something*. I know I stood up, I remember doing it, but I think all I said was 'How dare they?'

He looked at me again, but seemed suddenly as inarticulate as I. I remember a touch on my fingers, then he was lifting my hands and holding them so tightly I caught my breath. 'Anne,' he said. 'Anne.' I felt the warmth of his breath on my face.

'Mademoiselle,' said Jeanette warningly. 'Monsieur your brother . . .'

Florian was approaching to escort me home and I had only seconds left. I whispered 'What was the second reason?'

'You know it,' he said. He lifted my hand to his lips and over it his eyes were fixed on mine. 'I need her permission for something. You must know what.'

I needed him to say it himself. 'Tell me now. My brother is coming, tell me now.'

He had not realized, and I should have guessed it, for with his affliction he could never have heard Jeanette's whisper. He spoke very quickly. 'Marry me. Please, Anne, please say you'll marry me.' For a second his lips touched my skin.

'Mademoiselle!' said Florian, his voice high with disapproval. I was sorry to see he had two of his vile friends with him, but refused to be discomfited while something inside me was singing like the bells. I said 'Why, Florian, you remember M. de Roland?'

He clearly did, for the suspicion left his face at once. He said haltingly 'Your pardon, Chevalier, my memory of those times is a little faulty.'

André said 'You were not well, Monsieur, but I remember your courage.'

Florian's eyes brightened with astonished gratitude, then he recollected his manners and turned to introduce his companions. I recognized them both as they doffed their hats, but the look on their faces I did not know, for Desmoulins' smile seemed almost frozen beneath his moustache while Bouchard was so pale his eyes seemed red by contrast. I looked at André, and saw that he too was standing still and taut, with an expression so dark I was afraid.

He said 'I believe, Messieurs, we have met before.'

Jacques Gilbert

We'd traipsed round all the churches after him, but couldn't burst in on his first meeting with Anne. I knew her at once, her hair shone in the sun like red gold, but it felt wrong to be even watching them, let alone go barging in to interrupt.

We saw the men approaching, but Jeanette curtsied and Anne smiled and I recognized the skinny one with the feeble beard as Florian. It wasn't till they took their bloody hats off that I realized and plunged at once into the crowd.

'Those are the men?' said Charlot, working his way beside me.

I wasn't sure about the dark one, but couldn't mistake the thick bull-neck or mane of fair hair on the other. 'The blond is.'

Charlot parted a group of gossiping women with swimming motions of his arms. 'A pity. Henri Bouchard is a swordsman. He has killed twice already this year, one a boy of fifteen.'

'I thought duelling was illegal.'

'So it is,' he said. 'Unless it is unpremeditated and there are no seconds involved, when it is merely an "encounter".'

I could see them all clearly now, Anne with her hand on her breast, Jeanette moving anxiously to her side, André standing just as he'd done in the alehouse at Chantilly, and facing him two men doing exactly the same.

'Like that, you mean?' I said savagely.

He quickened his pace without another word.

The bells were still ringing, and their raucous clamour confused my thought.

Bouchard finally replaced his hat. 'Forgive my failure to recognize you, Chevalier, but you will remember I had mainly a view of your back.'

André replaced his own. 'If you consult your shoulder it might recollect me better from the front.'

Bouchard's head flicked back. 'Perhaps we should refresh our memories.'

'Perhaps we should,' said André.

I said 'Florian, stop this, speak to your friends,' but he seemed as confused as I.

Whatever was happening, Desmoulins was part of it. He said 'And me, Monsieur? Do you include me in your . . . memories?'

André bowed. 'You were no part of the original insult and I can't blame you for supporting your friends.'

Desmoulins inclined his head and retired a few steps, but as he passed Bouchard I heard him murmur 'All yours,' and saw them both smile.

Bouchard turned back to André. 'Now, Monsieur, we have something –'

Someone called 'Chevalier!' Two men were pushing through the crowd towards us, one dark and somehow familiar, the other an enormous sandy-haired gentleman who muscled his way past everyone to stand at André's side. I heard him ask deferentially if he could be of assistance.

André scarcely looked at him. 'I have private business with this gentleman, Charlot.'

'Of course,' said the man called Charlot. 'But I'm sure it can be discussed amicably. No one would wish to distress Mlle du Pré.'

I stepped forward immediately. 'Yes, please, Chevalier, I should be grateful if you would take me home.'

André hesitated, but Bouchard did not. He raised his voice that the whole parvis might hear and said 'Hiding behind the women, Chevalier? Hardly the act of a gentleman.'

Jacques Gilbert

André whirled round so fast he nearly knocked me over. He faced Bouchard, and suddenly the elegant clothes didn't matter, he was the same grubby little boy I remembered throwing himself fists first into a fight. 'Do you say I am a coward?'

Bouchard exchanged a triumphant look with the slim dark man, and I realized he'd been playing for just this. 'Obviously.'

André took a deep breath. 'Then I say you're a liar.'

Charlot stepped back smartly and I had to do the same. André had given the démenti, and there's no way out after that. What I couldn't understand was why Bouchard pushed for it.

The dark man said 'Church land, Bouchard. Do you want to . . .?' He jerked his head at the low wall dividing the parvis.

Bouchard slapped his hand on the stone and simply vaulted over it. There'd been people sitting there a moment ago, but the whole crowd had drawn back to leave an open space like they were at the theatre and this was a stage. The nobility were going to fight, and they weren't missing it for anything.

André took off his coat and thrust it clumsily into my hands. 'Get Anne away.'

But Anne wasn't a piece of baggage. She reached for the coat herself, and said 'If you must do it then I must stay, because the answer to your question is yes.'

He looked at her and something shot between them. He said 'My God, Anne . . .'

'When you're ready,' said Bouchard, bored. He was pacing up and down, and I saw it again, that oddly jubilant look exchanged with the dark man, like they'd actually planned it, like they wanted the boy dead.

André vaulted over the wall. 'I'm ready.'

Charlot said quickly 'First blood, Messieurs?'

'Of course,' said Bouchard, but there was a gleam of amusement in his eyes that said first blood would be all he'd ever need.

André faced him and drew, but Bouchard didn't take conventional guard as I expected. He pulled back the scabbard with his left hand in the usual way, but then lifted his right foot, hooked out the sword, spun it in a semicircle to point backwards over his shoulder, then swung it round to face the boy.

'Thibault-trained,' said Charlot. 'This should be interesting.'

It wasn't, it was scary. I watched the first tentative exchange of blows and knew I'd never seen anything so controlled. Bouchard's sword moved with scientific precision, perfect arcs of a circle, his body in tune with the blade like two parts of the same instrument. The man we'd fought in the alley had been swiping and inaccurate, but of course he'd been drunk. Now he was sober and it was André who looked clumsy, beating him off but no more. I turned anxiously to Charlot, but my fear shot into panic as I saw even he was alarmed.

'Spanish!' he called hoarsely to André. 'It's like Spanish!'

André nodded, and up came his elbow as he raised his rapier to eye height, but there was still something wrong with him, some-thing stilted I couldn't understand. He put in a strong attack at the face, but Bouchard's blade swept his aside, followed the circle through and slashed into André's right sleeve. The crowd shouted, but André flapped his arm to show his body wasn't touched and Bouchard looked actually relieved. He wasn't after a prick in the arm, he was looking to kill.

André stepped back, raised his hand for a pause, and furiously pushed back his sleeves. The madness of it was suddenly overwhelm-ing. It was so polite and civilized, the people watching, Bouchard giving time for the boy to adjust his dress, it was bollocks, all of it, André was going to be killed right in front of me over nothing at all. He shot a quick glance at Anne before resuming guard, and that was part of it, like he was worrying about his audience instead of his bloody life.

Bouchard approached again, and I knew he meant to finish it. He'd probed the boy's weaknesses and knew exactly how to hit him, I saw it in the calculation on his face. An elegant sweep to confuse, then a stamp and lunge, André would have been skewered clean through if he hadn't swivelled so fast he nearly fell over. He stumbled against the crowd as he righted himself, but then he shoved his hair out of his face in the same old way and suddenly my mind cleared. All these years he'd been fighting his own style, learning in battle, doing what felt right, but now he'd been filled with all these diagrams and techniques and that's what was screwing him. He'd forgotten about just beating the man in front of him, he was trying to do it right.

I jumped on the parapet and shouted 'Fight him, André!' Everyone was staring, but I'd got to get through. 'Sod the rest of it, just bloody fight him!'

He heard me, and for half a second our eyes met. Then he hefted his sword more comfortably and turned again to meet Bouchard.

Bouchard smiled complacently, tilted his body sideways and presented the horizontal blade, but André just smashed it down, ducked in close and lunged at the bastard's foot. Bouchard skipped back nimbly, but it was his turn to be off balance, he riposted at air as André twisted sideways, flicked up his blade to envelop Bouchard's, winding the steel together before sliding up sharp underneath at the bastard's belly. Bouchard dodged it, but he had to bend in two to do it, he was staggering backwards out of his own circle, his sword flailing at nothing. André assessed the danger of the whirling blade, and plunged his own clean past it, straight into Bouchard's left arm. Then he stepped back.

The crowd howled with excitement. Charlot shouted 'First blood!' and we could all see the red on Bouchard's fingers as he clutched his arm. I suddenly realized I was standing on a wall, and jumped down on legs that went wobbly when they hit the ground.

But there was another sound under the crowd roaring, someone shouting 'Stop!' I saw movement thrusting like a red arrow in the press of people, two men with crimson tabards elbowing their way roughly towards us.

'Put up!' said the dark man, leaning urgently over the wall. 'Cardinal's Guard, put up!'

Bouchard hurled his coat over his injury and they both quickly sheathed their swords. I looked nervously at Charlot, but his expression was back to its usual calm.

47

'Duelling, Messieurs?' said one of the Guards, arriving in the space on the other side of the wall. 'In the precincts of Notre-Dame?'

Charlot laughed. 'Indeed not. M. Bouchard requested an impromptu fencing lesson, and with the help of the Chevalier de Roland I have obliged him.'

The crowd picked it up at once, I heard the name 'de Roland' whizzing all round. The first Guard gave André a respectful nod, but the younger one was looking at the blood on Bouchard's hand.

'Someone's hurt,' he said. 'That's public disorder.'

'I should have used rebated swords,' said Charlot sadly. 'I fear we overestimated M. Bouchard's skill.'

The crowd gave a great shout of laughter and the older Guard suppressed a smile. He knew the truth as well as we did, but there were no seconds, no one seriously hurt, and Charlot had given a perfectly good excuse. He said just 'Is this true, M. Bouchard?'

Bouchard's face was scarlet with fury but he'd got no choice. He muttered 'Yes,' and looked away.

The Guard grinned, put a hand on his keen companion's shoulder and steered him firmly away, the crowd parting for them with laughter and exaggerated bows. Bouchard let it all wash over him for a moment, then lifted his head and looked at the boy.

My breath caught in my throat. I'd seen anger, I'd seen André look at Spaniards in the Saillie, but there'd always been a sort of skin over it to keep it human and understandable. What I saw in Bouchard's face wasn't just naked, it was red raw, a kind of scorching hatred blazing out through the skin, and all of it, every bit of it, directed at André.

Bernadette Fournier

There had never before been a meeting on a Sunday.

First came Bouchard, demanding messages be sent at once for M. Fontrailles. Then came Desmoulins with a thickset man I had heard called d'Arsy, then the red-faced Dubosc, then the plump one whose name I did not know, and last came the shy young man with the wispy beard. He seemed in a condition of pitiable fear, but

Bouchard was kinder to him than usual, sitting him by the fire and calling him his friend. Finally M. Fontrailles arrived in very ill humour, at which the door of the private room was shut and I saw no more.

No, I did not listen, I have told you I had no interest in such things. Nor was it possible, for the plump gentleman had brought with him his valet, an animal called Pirauld, and stationed him outside the door. I did not like that man, Monsieur, I did not like his yellow teeth or the way he looked at me, I would not even pass along the corridor while he was there. So I occupied myself in scrubbing the floor of the public room, and the meeting was no more to me than a rise and fall of voices as a background to my labour.

Yet even as I reached the brush to the bucket I heard a name I knew, and my hand was arrested over the water. 'De Roland' someone said, and as I listened I heard it again. Nothing else could I make out, only those words of which I already knew the pattern, but I guessed the gentlemen had finally learned what I already knew. How they reacted I could only guess from M. Fontrailles' parting words, which were most forcefully spoken from the passage. He said 'Understand this, Bouchard, understand, all of you. Under no circumstances will I condone murder,' and then I heard his footsteps passing angrily down to the kitchen. The others were quiet a moment, and then I heard another voice, so low I could not be sure whose it was. It said 'On the other hand . . .'

Four such little words, Monsieur, you will laugh that they should frighten me. I hoped to hear another voice say 'Don't be a fool,' but the only sound was a shuffle of feet and a closing door, and I knew they were resuming their meeting after all.

I, Monsieur? What should *I* do? For a girl of my kind to speak against her employers is to be whipped and imprisoned and perhaps worse. So no, I will not tell you a story of my heroism, I shall tell only the truth. I finished scrubbing the floor, I replaced the bucket and brush in the kitchen, and then, Monsieur, I went to bed.

Four

Anne du Pré

Extract from her diary, dated 1 October

Florian stayed out very late last night and returned shaking and sick. I wished to send for a physician, but he insisted that he was fine and I simply did not understand.

He spent hours closeted with Father this morning, but at noon the Comtesse de Vallon was announced and I could scarcely contain my excitement. Jeanette changed my dress and tidied my hair while we waited for my summons, but an hour passed, I heard the Comtesse leave, and still no word came from Father. Jeanette said 'Perhaps he keeps it as a surprise, Mademoiselle. You know he wants this marriage as much as you do.'

Then tonight came this terrible dinner. The first course passed in silence but for Father's rhythmic sucking of soup, and it was not till Clement served the goose that I dared ask about the visit. Then he said 'We can do better than that marriage now, Mademoiselle. I had thought of M. Bouchard.'

I could not think straight for fear. 'But I want to marry André.'

He continued chewing. 'What's that got to do with it? Name one person of quality in Paris who can pick and choose who they'll marry. Mlle de Scudéry tells me even the Duc d'Enghien is to marry a niece of the Cardinal's and is most unhappy about it.'

She did not tell him, she said it at the Samedi Salon and Father was in the crowd like everybody else. I said 'I know, Monsieur, but Mama always said –'

He coloured violently and looked quickly at Clement. 'Mademoiselle, you will not speak of your late mother in this childish way. Our circumstances have changed since then.'

Sometimes I think we were happier in those days before Father made so much money and bought the title. I said 'I'm sorry.'

He stroked his beard. 'I can make allowances for the unfortunate experiences of your childhood, Mademoiselle, but your brother has recovered from them and does us all credit. It is time you did the same.'

Florian glowed with pleasure and said not one word to support me.

I was so upset I challenged him when Father had retired. I said 'Why won't you stand up for me, Florian? André saved you too, don't you think you owe him something?'

He jutted his chin. 'There's no need to go on about it. How do you think it makes me feel to have been rescued by a mere boy?'

I *must* remember it is not his fault he is as he is, it is because of what the Spaniards did. I said 'Then for my sake. Don't you want me to be happy?'

He hesitated, and lowered his voice. 'That's why it's better if you don't marry him.'

I said 'How could it possibly make me unhappy to marry André?' but he only whispered 'You'll understand one day,' then patted my arm and hurried out.

Jacques Gilbert

We didn't realize anything was wrong. The Comtesse said the Baron was just stalling in the hope of a lower dowry, but he'd never resist a chance to join the real nobility. André was furious about the delay, but he couldn't go breaking into the Baron's house and snatching Anne out of it, we were in civilization now and had to do things properly like everyone else.

I didn't even guess there was danger till de Chouy came. He was our first visitor, of course, Guillot found him waiting outside the porte-cochère when he opened it next morning. He'd brought his best friends with him too, the dazzlingly fashionable Raoul de Verville and the aristocratic half-Spaniard Gaspard Lelièvre, who seemed to spend most of the visit with his eyes closed. De Chouy whispered that he never normally got up before noon and we ought to feel awfully honoured he'd done so today.

'It's this Bouchard business, you know, Dédé,' he said as we sat over chocolate. 'You're absolutely the talk of the salons. I simply had to bring the chaps to meet you.'

'But why?' said André. 'Is Bouchard important?'

De Verville answered. He scared me at first, he was dressed in purple silk and smelt of flowers, but he was as friendly as de Chouy and had a smile like a little boy's.

'Oh, my dear!' he said. 'Don't you know he claims to be the illegitimate son of the Duc de Montmorency? It's quite ridiculous, everyone knows the late duc was *far* too boring for such a thing, but Bouchard's rich and a bastard, he was baptized with a Montmorency name, and of course there's that squint. There are respectable people who perfectly *swear* he's genuine.'

I thought it was an odd thing to pretend, I mean Montmorency got his head chopped off for treason, but André said that was only politics, Richelieu needed a scapegoat for the last rebellion and the duc paid for the lot of them.

'It's a respected name, Jacquot,' said de Chouy. 'All the malcontents flock to it. It's awfully sad really, when he's just a bastard pretending to be someone he isn't.'

The sweetness of the chocolate came back sickly into my mouth and I had to choke it back down. André reached over for a macaroon, and his hand brushed casually against mine.

'That's not his fault though, is it?' he said. 'What he was born.'

'Of course not,' said de Chouy, shocked. 'Nobody minds those things these days, Dédé, bastards are romantic. It's only that he's frightfully touchy. He killed a man last year for hinting his hair was the wrong colour for a Montmorency.'

André considered. 'Maybe it's a pity I called him a bastard to his face.'

De Verville went into peals of laughter, but Lelièvre opened his eyes fully for the first time. They were very clear and very grey, and there wasn't a hint of sleep in them at all.

'Then you will need to be careful, my friend,' he said. 'You must watch where you go and with whom. That man is capable of murder.'

There was a little silence, then de Verville laughed uneasily. 'Don't mind Gaspard, this is his first season in the city. You've never even met Bouchard, have you, Gaspardine?'

'I've seen him at the theatre,' said Lelièvre, unmoved. 'The man is an oaf with a thick neck, and he has nasty friends.'

The others laughed, but I remembered that look on Bouchard's face and wondered if Lelièvre might be right.

The Comtesse seemed to share the feeling. She knew there was no point hiding us any more, but when we tried to go out that evening we found Charlot and three big footmen waiting to go with us. André scowled at the sight of them, but they just swept off their hats and smiled back and we knew we'd got no choice. Charlot said 'It's only till things have died down, Chevalier, Madame will be reassured in a week or two,' but the boy just said darkly 'She'd better be,' and set off so fast the footmen had to run to catch up.

It was all quiet when we got home. The footmen went to get the gate opened, and for a moment the street was clear, nothing but the two of us and the huddled shape of Jean bent over his brazier. Charlot was talking to Guillot, I remember the murmur of their voices and the clink of lanterns being lifted to light us inside. A horse snorted, and across the street I saw the black shape of a closed carriage, but there were tall shadows next to it, men huddled together and starting to move. Among them glinted suddenly a long orange streak, and it took me a second to realize the fire of our brazier was reflecting off the blade of a sword.

I jumped as something bumped my leg, and there was one of the dogs with Guillot holding its lead. Another panted and strained at the leash, claws scrabbling on the wet flags.

'Come inside, Chevalier,' said Charlot gently. 'It's cold.'

The gate closed behind us with a reassuringly solid bang. I wasn't sure I'd really seen anything, I might have just imagined it, but it was good to know Charlot had thought of everything. At least nobody could get André in here.

Anne du Pré

I worked myself into the most *foolish* state this evening. I heard Bouchard's voice in Florian's apartments as I retired to my chamber, and the thought of what they might be discussing filled me with terror. I resolved that if I could not elope with André then I would enter a convent and be done.

When Florian came I backed away as if from an enemy and said 'I won't marry Bouchard, brother, I will die first.'

He jerked his head. 'There's no need to be like that, we only want your good.'

'You don't,' I said, and felt the tears coming before I could stop them. 'How can it be my good not to marry André?'

Florian put his arms about me quickly so as not to see me cry. He said 'It's only that you don't know him very well, that's all. We'd like you to see more of him before we decide.'

The relief was so wonderful I could scarcely believe it. I said just 'Oh, Florian!'

'Silly,' he said, pressing my head back into the thinness of his chest. 'Now, we go to the Cardinal's gala on Saturday, don't we? To celebrate the birth of Philippe d'Orléans? How would it be if you write and invite the Rolands to join us?'

I stared at his shirt-front. 'You think perhaps Father . . .?'

'Perhaps,' he said. 'But it would be better if the two of you had some time alone.'

To see André alone! I said 'How could we do that in a party?'

He knocked my head gently against his chest. 'I know the Luxembourg. They're still working on the hedges of the labyrinth, and there's a temporary gardeners' hut nearby. Suppose you and André were to meet there?'

I said 'I can't wander off alone with André. Father would never allow it.'

His beard tickled my forehead as he smiled. 'He will this time, Anne. I guarantee it.'

Jacques Gilbert

I've got no excuses, I know what I did. But it did look safe, I mean André was escorted everywhere, it never occurred to anyone that the person they should have watched was me.

It was all because of the betrothal. André was still simmering with frustration, and the minute he heard the Comte was up to visitors again he insisted on seeing him to get his support. I wasn't going, of course, I mean the servants didn't know who I was yet, it would have looked odd for André to take his aide to see the Comte. I wasn't ready yet anyway, I wouldn't have wanted to be an embarrassment. I did understand.

I still felt flat when I saw the carriage trundling out of the portecochère with a load of grooms surrounding it like guard dogs. I thought about André marrying Anne and being happy, and that was good, of course, it's what I wanted for him, but I did just wonder a bit where it left me. I wandered round the house with servants bowing and going out of rooms as soon as I went into them, and it felt like I was looking for something without knowing what.

So I went out. I didn't think it mattered, I wasn't needed anywhere, and sort of wanted to be somewhere I might be. I walked out into the Rue du Roi de Sicile, turned right towards the maze of streets we'd come in by, and set off towards Le Pomme d'Or where it all began.

Bernadette Fournier

When Louis said one of the strangers wished to see me you can imagine what I assumed. As I entered the room the gold coin seemed to burn inside my dress to brand me for what I was.

It was the servant of the two, but dressed so like a gentleman as to frighten me with his magnificence. He thanked me for my care of their horses and asked after my health, and I curtsied and thanked him, and waited for him to say what I knew he must.

He looked up at the rafters and down at the floor, but could not seem to say a word.

I wished it over with. 'There is something you wish to say, Monsieur?'

'Yes,' he said at once, seizing on my words as if they would help him. 'Yes.' At last he looked at me directly, but there was no accusation in his eyes. 'I ought to have brought you something, oughtn't I?'

I was confused. 'Something?'

He nodded vehemently. 'I thought about flowers. I passed a stall, they had beautiful roses, pink and orange. Only then I thought . . . I thought . . .'

I took pity on him. 'What would a girl like me do with flowers?'

'Yes,' he agreed, and smiled anxiously.

I could not help but smile back, but then I heard Madame shouting at Louis in the yard and remembered who and what I was, and what the world was too.

I said abruptly 'Why do you come here, Monsieur?'

His smile faded. 'I wanted to see you.'

Oh, you did not know him then, you do not know what he was, but listen, this was Jacques Gilbert. He was tall and straight and handsome, and the scar on his cheek made him so much a man as to take my breath away. He wore fine clothes and carried a sword, he should have been strutting like a very peacock, but he stood and looked at me with a face as red as sunset and fumbled his hat round and round in his hands.

I took the coin from my dress and held it out. 'There, Monsieur, that is what I am.'

He looked as if he did not understand what it was. Then his eyes lifted again and this time it was I who flushed. 'You only took one?'

His mistrust scalded me. 'You may search me if you like, that is all I took.'

He shook his head in distress. 'That's not what I mean.'

I thrust the coin at him. 'Take it, Monsieur, it is yours or your master's.'

'He'd want you to keep it. So do I.'

I flung it to the floor at his feet. 'I do not need your charity.'

He did not move. 'It's not charity.'

56

I thought I understood. 'As you wish, Monsieur. I have a little room upstairs, we can go there if you want.'

He stepped back as if I had struck him. I thought 'Good, that is good, now he will go away and never come back.'

But he did not go. We stood facing each other, he and I, with a coin worth six livres on the floor between us and neither willing to pick it up.

At length he said 'I'm sorry, I'm doing this so badly.' He put on his hat and gave a smile so tentative my heart moved. 'Can you forgive me?'

Me, Monsieur, girl at Le Pomme d'Or. I said 'Perhaps.'

His hand stole down from his hat, and I saw hope brightening his face. He took a step forward, stopped as his foot met the coin, then stooped and picked it up. I watched warily as he wiped it on his breeches then held it out to me.

I said 'You might need it yourself, Monsieur.'

'Jacques,' he said. 'I'm just Jacques.'

I opened my hand and he placed the coin gently on my palm. 'I will keep it for you then, Jacques. Come back when you need it.'

He smiled such a wicked smile. 'Maybe I'll need it tomorrow.'

A sound behind alerted me to the entrance of Madame. At once I slipped the coin into my dress, but Madame's eyes turned into little hard stones of suspicion, and I guessed she had caught the glint of gold.

My poor Jacques was as shy of her as I was. He bowed, bade her good day, and almost backed from the room in his haste to be gone. I followed him to the door and watched him down the road, cramming down his hat against the rain, but walking with exaggerated carelessness as if he knew I was looking.

But I was not the only one who watched. A figure sheltering in a doorway turned to look after him, and my head returned abruptly into cold sense, for it was one of M. Fontrailles' gentlemen, the plump one with the monstrous valet. He strolled across towards me and said curtly 'I wish a word with your mistress.'

I left him with Madame, but noticed how quietly they spoke together, and when I next passed the door they both glanced up, then looked away.

No one asked where I'd been. André never even noticed I was wet with rain, he was too busy bubbling with excitement at a letter from Anne. It didn't sound much to me, she was only suggesting we join her family for Richelieu's party, but André was waving the letter around like a flag.

'Don't you see?' he said. 'The Baron wants us there, and that's got to mean something. The Comte's going to ask him about the betrothal on Monday, and he's going to say yes, I know he is, he's going to say yes.'

I don't remember ever seeing him as happy as he was that evening. He came bursting into my room while I was dressing for dinner, sprawled on my bed and talked about Anne, stroking his foot up and down the bedpost like he'd already got her in his arms and no one was getting her out of them. It irritated me a bit at the time, but I feel bad about it now. I think of him lying there saying 'We're going to live here, of course, I'm not going anywhere without my brother,' I think of that now and it hurts. He hadn't had much in his life for himself, not really, nobody could grudge him this one little moment of happiness. It didn't occur to either of us that it might be all there was ever going to be.

Bernadette Fournier

I knew my danger. I knew the gentlemen feared M. de Roland, and could not imagine they would welcome the sight of his companion in the very house, or indeed his giving me money.

Yet I did not run. I had the protection of my master, and was confident both of the authority of M. Fontrailles and the strength of my own innocence. So I held my nerve and continued my duties just as usual, but I observed how long Madame was closeted with Monsieur when he came home, I noted that a servant of Bouchard's called on them a long time in the evening, I watched and I listened, and my unease grew.

When I went to bed that night I pulled the ladder up after me and quietly closed the trap. Then I sewed my golden écu safely inside my dress, removed my shoes, and laid myself on the bed to wait.

My bedroom faced the courtyard so the sounds from the road were muffled, but as I lay with my ears open I heard even the late carriages rattle by in the Rue de Braque, splashing up water from the puddles as they passed. When Louis shut the courtyard gate the crash of the bolts seemed loud as a gunshot. I listened for the familiar bang of the side door as he came in to bed, then the squeak of hinges as the kitchen door closed. After that should be silence, for so it always was, but this night there were still faint voices from the public room and I knew Madame and Monsieur were waiting up.

I wondered what for.

I do not know how much longer it was before I heard horses, but if I had dozed I woke in an instant. I climbed quietly from the bed, found my cloak in the dark and fastened it round my shoulders. Below me I heard the front door open and close, and again the murmur of voices. Then the stairs began to creak. I crept to the trap, and watched its edges begin to shimmer with faint light as someone carried a candle from below.

I pressed my head to the crack and heard Monsieur whisper 'The ladder's gone.'

Another voice murmured, then Madame said 'But not here, he promised, not here.'

A reassuring mumble, and then Monsieur spoke again. I caught only the one word, but it was enough to make me start back at once from the trap. The word was 'window'.

I dared not risk shoes. I gripped the windowsill and lowered myself until my arms would stretch no more, then dropped quickly to the stable roof below. My bare feet made only the softest thump below the drumming of the rain, but the bolts of the side door were already rattling and I had time only to swing myself over the side of the roof, drop hard to the cobbles and conceal myself behind the trough before the door opened and a man walked out. Monsieur was with him, and I saw him point towards my window before going to unbolt the courtyard gate.

The man looked up at the window, shook his shoulders and

walked towards the stable. I saw him quite clearly as he passed, a stocky creature with a face scarred by smallpox, a man I was certain I had never seen before. He patted the stable wall as if puzzling over the climb, then pulled open the door and used it to scramble his way up. His mind and eyes were fully engaged with the effort and Monsieur had returned to the house, so I waited no longer but ran silently for the unbolted courtyard gate.

But it was opening of itself, it pushed in towards me, and revealed a gentleman entering behind it. I should have remembered I had heard more than one horse, but my mind was too full and now it was too late, for he seized my wrist and called to his companion who was now scaling the ivy 'Here she is, you fool, she's right here!'

I tried to pull away, I even brought his disgusting hand to my mouth and bit, but he simply grappled me round, then lifted me clear off my feet to sling me over his shoulder like a sack of grain. My fists beat helplessly against his back, but he only chuckled and held me tighter, while behind us I heard his lackey jump back to the stable roof.

Then my hand touched a wooden handle, and I knew what it was. They call it a *main-gauche*, Monsieur, the dagger gentlemen use when they fight, and it is carried on the back of the belt to be drawn with the left hand. I snatched it and stabbed as hard as I could into the man's back, I punched it in as if it had been my fist, and then I wrenched it out.

He made a deep soft grunt, which did not sound much for so great a blow, but then his knees buckled and his grip slackened, he was folding to the ground and I was able to jump free. Behind came a cry and a crash as the other man jumped from the stable, and I ran at once out of the gate. Two horses waited, but I swerved past them, my feet slipping and sliding on the wet cobbles, and turned fast into the Rue de Braque.

I could not outrun the man, I must lose him and quickly. The road was paved and my feet ran more securely, but my hair was slapping wet across my eyes and I had much to do to keep the cloak from entangling my legs. The Rue de Braque is long and straight, Monsieur, it was death to remain on it, so I hastened down a side street, then again down another and into a little alley by the graveyard of the Chapelle de Mercy. I climbed its low wall, ran to crouch behind the tallest gravestone, and waited, cold and wet and trembling in the dark.

After a moment came hooves down the Rue de Braque, but they were slow and indecisive, and in a little while I heard the rider turn back. I allowed my breathing to slow, but dared not move yet. The man could not follow me down every street and byway in this whole great city, but he might perhaps guess I had hidden, and lie in wait for me to reveal myself.

I tried to think what I must do. The streets were dark and empty, but we had a night watch even in those days and I could not hope to escape through the gates. I had stabbed a man, perhaps killed him, and the evidence was plain upon me, for there was blood down my arm and on my dress. Not even a church would take me in, for the man I had injured was a gentleman. I would be handed over, I would be taken and hanged, there was nobody who would give sanctuary to such as me.

Then the idea came that there was perhaps one. I bathed my hands and arms in the wet grass of the graveyard, rearranged my cloak to hide the stains on my dress, and set out to find the Rue du Roi de Sicile.

The walk was not far, but I dared not go openly for fear of the watch. From doorway to doorway I crept, ducking into side streets at the faintest sound of footsteps or voices. There were few people about, gentlemen spilling out of a cabaret, a pair of ruffians swaggering with clubs, a group of soldiers who cried 'What's your hurry, sweetheart?' but I did not turn and they did not come after me. The darkness was my greatest protection, for my cloak was full and black, and the great high walls of the Marais are full of stone bornes and niches which provided cover for one small woman creeping like a mouse towards safety. Some of the grand hôtels had lanterns outside, and these I passed on the other side of the road. Some had servants about the doorways, and those I passed with head averted, but the sight gave me hope, for what I would do if I found the doors of the Hôtel de Roland both shut and unmanned I could not think.

They were shut indeed but a liveried servant stood outside

warming his hands by the fire of a brazier. I approached boldly, dropped a curtsey, and said 'Your pardon, Monsieur.'

He shook his head. 'I'm sorry, lass, I haven't the cash.'

I said 'You mistake me, Monsieur, I wish to come in. I need to see Jacques.'

You will laugh, but it was not until then that I realized I had no idea of his other name.

'Lot of Jacques in Paris,' said the porter. 'Would a Jean do? You can call me Jacques if you like.'

I almost turned away, but then recollected there was one name I did know, and if there was a door in Paris it would open it was surely this one.

I said 'Then the Chevalier de Roland, fellow. I need to see him now.'

His eyes widened, but he said 'Of course you do, darling. Now be a good girl and try it on somewhere else.'

I sprang past him and banged on the gate with my fists, I shouted 'Chevalier!' as if certain he must know me. I cried 'It's me, Bernadette, let me in!'

The porter swore and pulled me from the gate, but it was opening and another servant came out, an older man with a kind face. I grasped at his coat and said 'The Chevalier knows me, you must tell him now, this minute, that the girl from Le Pomme d'Or is here, and I swear to you he will come, I swear it by all the saints.'

The first man was saying 'I'm sorry, Guillot, I couldn't stop her,' but the older man only detached my hands from his coat and looked in my face. He said 'You know the Chevalier?'

His eyes were honest and I saw his uncertainty. I said 'I know what he will say if you throw me out into the night when I have pleaded for his protection.'

He laughed. 'You know him all right, Mademoiselle.' He placed his hand under my elbow and steered me in, they were letting me in, and the one called Jean closed the gate behind us. My legs felt weak beneath me, but Guillot sat me down on a bench and ran across the cour d'honneur calling for servants, and almost I wanted to be sick with relief.

Moments passed, and there were people running and doors

banging, and then a firm tread across the stones and a voice I remembered saying 'Wake the kitchens, Pierre, and send someone for Jacques, I want him *now.*' My head was stupidly heavy, but I managed to lift it to see him standing in front of me, André de Roland himself. His shirt was open, he was without belt or sword, he had the flushed, tousled look of a man suddenly woken from sleep, but they had said it was me and he had come.

I said 'I'm sorry, Monsieur, but they came for me, and I stabbed one, I had to, he was taking me . . .' and to my horror I felt myself starting to cry. I wished to apologize, but it was too late, his arm was behind my back, the other scooping beneath me, and next moment I was in his arms and being carried across the courtyard. My cheek was against his chest, still warm and damp from sleep, and above me his voice was giving orders, he was asking for hot water, I think, and blankets, the word I remember most clearly was 'now!' I took in little of it, Monsieur, what I knew then and what I remember now is the warmth of his chest and the strength of his arms and the unbelievable feeling of being safe.

Five

Jacques Gilbert

I hurled my breeches on over my nightshirt, belted down barefoot
to the kitchens, and there was my girl of Le Pomme d'Or in André's
arms. He was laying her on a chair with servants milling round
bringing wine and heating water but she saw me through the crowd,
stretched out her hands and said 'Jacques.'

I walked awkwardly towards her, the maids all gawping and Charlot's expression stuck sort of rigid. André straightened to face me,
then his eyebrows lifted and he gave me a funny little smile. He said
'Stay with her, will you, she's had a terrible shock,' then stepped
aside.

I knelt down beside her. There was a smudge of blood on her
forehead and more round her fingernails, and her eyes were even
bigger than I remembered. She muttered something I didn't catch,
then looked me full in the face and said 'I killed a man.' She was
shivering with cold and something else. I stopped caring about the
servants and wrapped my arms tight round her. Her dress was
clammy against my skin, but inside I felt hot and almost savage, I
wanted to hit someone and do it hard.

Somewhere behind me André was talking. He said 'Charlot, stop
looking like a nun in a brothel and get that bed sorted out. Robert,
where's that wine? Well done, Guillot, you and Jean did absolutely
the right thing.' Then he bent down and whispered 'What's her
name?'

I felt unbelievably stupid, but the girl said quickly 'Bernadette
Fournier, Monsieur,' then gave me a little smile of conspiracy. Something inside me bubbled up like laughter. I felt it wouldn't matter if
the whole roof fell in as long as I could go on kneeling on that hard
kitchen floor with Bernadette in my arms.

I couldn't, of course, she had to sit up while Perette dressed her torn feet, but she told us her story while it was happening and I stopped wanting to laugh about anything. André was brilliant. He never blamed her for not warning us before, he didn't even blink when he heard I'd gone and visited, and when she told him about stabbing that man he just squeezed her hand and said 'Well done.' When she finished he stood up and told the servants Mlle Fournier was in danger because she'd helped save our lives, and they couldn't do enough for her after that. They got her washed and fed and put to bed in a little guest room for visitors' maids, then André threw himself down in a chair by the kitchen fire, kicked the grate and said 'The filthy, cowardly bastards. I hope she did kill him, Jacques, I hope it really *hurt*.'

I sat beside him. 'It's my fault, isn't it? It's because I went to see her.'

He nudged his shoe against my bare foot. 'At least we're warned now, we know what we're up against.'

'Do we? She doesn't seem to know much.'

'Enough,' he said, and I wondered what I'd missed. 'It's too big for us, Jacques, we'll have to talk to my grandmother. I must warn Anne's family too, they mustn't be involved with people like this.'

Agnès hadn't put much wood on the fire. The last log collapsed and sprayed ashes all over the hearth.

I said 'I'm sorry I never said . . .'

He stooped to brush ash off his shoe. 'Why should you?'

Because he told me everything. Because I loved him. I said 'I don't know.'

He stretched and stood up. 'Don't be sorry. Anyone can see what she feels about you.'

I thought about that when I got back to bed. I'd had women before, you know I had, but I'd always had the feeling they only really wanted to get close to André. This girl didn't want my brother, she wanted me. I thought of her lying just one floor below me, and when I finally went to sleep I was happy.

We went into the Comtesse before the hairdresser next morning and she received us from her bed. She was perfectly calm about it, she got Suzanne to bring breakfast, then sat up straight against the pillows while André told her everything we knew. When he'd finished she took a little sip of bouillon and said 'The girl is sure of the reference to the Sedan?'

André nodded. 'She heard it quite distinctly. That's why I think we can work out the names.'

'Quite,' she said, almost dismissively. 'Quite.'

I still didn't see it, we'd only got code names like 'Monsieur' or 'M. le Comte' to work on, but the Comtesse said they weren't code, they were protocol, and then she explained.

She told me about the Comte de Soissons, who was a prince of the blood and so important he was called just 'Monsieur le Comte' like there weren't any others. She told me about Gaston d'Orléans, the King's brother, who was First Gentleman of France and known simply as 'Monsieur'. She said they'd got caught plotting to assassinate the Cardinal in 1636, but while Orléans had just been ticked off and was sulking in his estate at Blois, Soissons had had to leg it to the Sedan and the protection of the Duc de Bouillon. He'd been lurking there ever since, but everyone knew he was only waiting for another chance, and the fact these gentlemen were visiting him suggested the time was now.

'We still need names,' she said. 'The Sedan is out of reach, we need the names of their allies in Paris.'

I said 'There's Bouchard.'

She gave a graceful little shrug. 'A figurehead, valuable only for the name of Montmorency. He hasn't the power to drive a conspiracy.'

'There's the gentleman we helped,' said André. 'He's the one they were afraid I'd recognize. Bernadette gives him the name Fontrailles.'

She turned so abruptly a little splash of bouillon flew out of her cup. 'Fontrailles?'

The boy nodded dumbly.

She took a napkin to the speck of bouillon on her chemise. 'Then we are on a different battlefield altogether. Fontrailles, Marquis d'Astarac, is a *créature* of Orléans and formidable opposition. He has no religion and fewer morals and dislikes the Cardinal intensely. More to the point, his closest friendship at court suggests the identity of your girl's other mysterious lord. Not "le grand Monsieur", but "Monsieur le Grand", the Grand Écuyer.'

I pictured that young pretty face I'd seen on the road outside Amiens. Cinq-Mars, the King's favourite. André was right, this was too big for us.

I said nervously 'It's politics then, isn't it? It's nothing to do with us.'

The Comtesse returned to her bouillon. 'I might agree, if they were not so eager to annihilate my grandson.'

'It's our business anyway,' said André. 'They're going to use Spanish help, they'll bring Spanish troops back into France. We can't just let it happen.'

She turned to me. 'This Spaniard you saw. You could not be mistaken?'

I thought about that little dark man with the pointy beard, I heard him saying '¡Madre de Dios!' and remembered voices like that in my own village, men with scarlet plumes on their helmets swaggering into our homes. I said 'No.'

'No,' she said, and put down her cup so delicately it made a tiny sort of *ting*. 'Then we cannot allow it. But it will be difficult with Cinq-Mars against us.'

André stared. 'The King will never be swayed by a mere favourite.'

The Comtesse gave a tiny snort. 'He will by this one. No, the only man we can trust is Richelieu, and we must speak to him at once. There is a long wait for appointments, but we might manage to see him at tonight's festivities.'

The idea terrified me. 'I thought we needed more names.'

She picked up a little bell and tinkled it. 'This girl of yours knows faces. I can turn them into names.'

We looked blankly at her.

She sighed. 'These celebrations will draw all the quality in Paris. Do you not realize these gentlemen will almost certainly be there too?'

Bernadette Fournier

I felt such a fool you would not believe. They dressed me in silk and ribbons, and a woman to whom I would normally curtsey dressed my hair, then they gave me into the care of this Charlot and said for tonight I was lady companion to the Comtesse de Vallon. I showed myself to Jacques and said 'Now see how safe I shall be, for no one in the world would know me like this,' but he said 'I would know you anywhere,' and kissed my hand. And there I was, giddy with his kiss and warm with the love of him, dressed like a lady and going to a party in the Royal Gardens where there would be fireworks, and the world seemed a great and glorious game, for I was sixteen and a woman, and that is how it is and will always be.

We were driven across the Pont-Neuf to the Place Dauphine, where I saw a carriage with bright gilt on its panels as if there were no such thing as a Sumptuary Law. A linkman lit the way to our own carriages, and behind him strutted a short gentleman with an important beard and magnificent clothes. Beside him came a young lady, and oh, she was pretty, Monsieur, her neck so slender you would not think it could sustain the weight of red-gold hair piled above it, and her skin as pale and smooth as china. I watched the short gentleman hand her into our lead coach with M. de Roland and the Comtesse, and became very aware of the redness of my hands and the brownness of my hair and the ordinariness of my face.

'That's Mlle du Pré,' said Jacques. 'That's Anne.'

A second group entered the gilt coach, attendants like ourselves, and lastly an elegant young gentleman whom I recognized at once, for he was the shy man with the wispy beard.

I said 'That is one of them,' and pressed back in my seat to allow Jacques a clear view.

'Her brother,' he whispered. 'He's a friend of theirs, that's all.'

'He is more than that,' I said. 'He left early on the evening you came, but he is as regular at these meetings as Bouchard himself.'

Jacques Gilbert

It was chaos outside the entrance, with loads of carriages arriving all at once, and horses snorting and bumping into each other, and footmen all yelling for everyone else to make way. The guards were trying to weed out the scruffy ones and forbidding entry to anyone in livery, but the linkmen had sort of given up, they were huddled in a lump near the gate and you could see them looking at the crowd and thinking 'Sod that.'

André was waiting by the entrance with Anne tucked safely in his arm. I told Bernadette to hold on tight and barged through the mob to reach him, but by the time we got there the Baron had joined him with that bloody Florian, and I couldn't say a word. They were right by the linkmen too, it was like broad bloody daylight and I had to whisper Bernadette to keep her head down. She could fool a casual glance, but Florian was only feet away and no one who'd ever seen it would forget Bernadette's face. Then a dark shadow fell over her as Charlot planted himself between us and the torches, and gave me a tiny reassuring nod.

October's not the best time for the Luxembourg, but it was still the most beautiful scene I'd ever walked into. Candles formed shining lines down the straight paths, hanging lanterns turned the spray from the splashing fountains into great arcs of sparkling jewels, and a warm spicy perfume wafted up from copper braziers glowing on the lawns. An orchestra was playing nearby, violins and flutes and aerophones, lilting music sort of melting into the evening air. I couldn't actually see them, they were probably hiding in the bushes, but that made it somehow more dreamlike, and Bernadette hugged my arm with pleasure. I wanted like anything to just give in and enjoy it with her, but could only say 'For Christ's sake keep your head down,' and fix my eyes on Charlot's back.

He didn't let us down. He stepped discreetly to the Comtesse's side, said 'Excuse me, Madame,' and bent like he was untangling her dress from something on the ground. The Baron politely turned to chat to Florian, but I saw Charlot's head close to my grandmother's and knew he'd got the message over. A moment later and I saw her whispering to André. He wasn't as good an actor as she was, the shock sharpened his whole face, but after one glance at Florian he pulled himself together and turned back to Anne. She looked wonderingly up at him, but he managed a smile and folded her hand tenderly back in his arm.

The Comtesse was superb. She kept leading us along, chatting brightly to the Baron and Florian, and leaving us free to do our job.

Charlot dropped to the back so we could report what we saw, but we didn't spot anyone till we came to a huge white marquee in a chained enclosure with Cardinal's Guards patrolling the perimeter.

'That's one,' said Bernadette, tipping her head at the officer in charge. 'I think they call him d'Arsy.'

I hoped she'd got it wrong, but then the Guard turned his head and I saw him myself, a thickset man with heavy brows, the dark man I'd kicked back in the alley. I said 'She's right.'

They were everywhere after that. Bernadette saw one in the uniform of the Maréchaussée, one of the Garde Française, and another Charlot recognized as an officer who worked on the Porte Saint-Antoine. I only spotted one myself, the plump man in the courtyard André had spiked in the shoulder, but Charlot said that was bad enough, his name was Lavigne and he was in Cinq-Mars' own entourage.

We started to wander back the way we'd come, and then another face sprang into focus, Bouchard himself sitting at a crowded table opposite the marquee. Bernadette began dutifully picking out his companions for Charlot, but I wasn't listening, I was looking at Bouchard. He was watching André, following every step of his progress through the crowd, and to my surprise he was smiling.

Bernadette Fournier

The Comtesse was a fine actress. She told the Baron so charmingly that we had a prior engagement for the fireworks that even I who knew she was lying was almost fooled. The du Prés departed at once, though I noticed M. de Roland kept hold of Mademoiselle's hand even when he had kissed it and wondered what she was saying to bring such light to his face.

But there was no time for such things now, and we hastened to tell the Comtesse all we had discovered. There was still one regular I had not seen, he with the florid face called Dubosc, but she only shuddered and said 'Thank heavens we are spared that. But I dare not delay, the fireworks will start any moment and His Eminence will doubtless leave straight afterwards.'

M. de Roland hesitated. 'You won't tell him about the du Prés?'

She regarded him with severity. 'Chevalier, duty is duty.'

He stood his ground as a lover should. 'Florian is feeble-minded, he can't realize what he's involved in. Anne knows nothing, but she's already begged me to extricate him from his dreadful friends.'

'It's too late for that,' said the Comtesse. 'The friendship is known, and our honesty will be impugned if we suppress it. I shall say we believe him an innocent tool, and if the facts support it I am sure no action will be taken against him. Will that satisfy you?'

M. de Roland bowed.

'Good,' she said. 'Now get me into that marquee, my feet are freezing and I want to sit down.'

And there was the problem, Monsieur, for we had first to convey her past this d'Arsy, who as Cardinal's Guard might deny entrance to any but the King himself. But M. de Roland made a plan, and we gathered near the chain of the private enclosure while he walked alone to the opening. Bouchard and his companions watched warily, for though they could not know what he had learned from me, they perhaps feared he had guessed the identity of M. Fontrailles and was about to disclose it.

D'Arsy squared his feet more firmly as M. de Roland announced himself, then said 'I regret, Chevalier, but His Eminence wishes no more guests tonight. I will pass the message to his secretary, who will make you an appointment for another day.'

Across the path I saw Bouchard smile.

M. de Roland tilted his head to one side and regarded d'Arsy through half-closed eyes. 'Don't I know you?'

D'Arsy must have expected it, but perhaps he hoped the darkness and his hat would disguise his features. He said 'I don't think so, Monsieur,' and looked away.

'But I do,' said the Chevalier, 'and we have business between us, you and I.'

Charlot said 'That's it, Madame', and the Comtesse slipped from my side to stand behind the great bulk of her valet.

I did not hear d'Arsy's reply, but then M. de Roland spoke again, with his voice pitched louder. 'Do you say I am lying?'

Heads turned all over the enclosure, and Bouchard half rose from his seat.

D'Arsy made a great effort to maintain his dignity. 'Monsieur, these are the Royal Gardens of the Luxembourg, and this is not the place for such a discussion.'

I heard the Chevalier's smile in his voice. 'So will you appoint one or will I?'

A gasp sounded all round us, and Charlot said *'Now.'* There was a faint movement behind him and the merest clink of the chain, but I dared not look, I must do as everyone else and keep my eyes on the Chevalier and the Guard.

D'Arsy appeared suddenly to relax. 'All right then, I'll call on you tomorrow.'

Someone at Bouchard's table laughed, but I did not care, for I saw a little group on the other side of the chain standing to watch the fracas, and among them was now our own Comtesse, as dignified and elegant as if she had never scrambled under a chain like a little girl playing *cache-cache*. Jacques at once began to walk towards M. de Roland.

The Chevalier began to say 'I would rather discuss it now,' but saw Jacques approaching and knew our business was done. He added 'But noon tomorrow will be acceptable,' then bowed and turned away. Beyond him I saw the Comtesse making herself known at the marquee, and a moment later a Guard came to escort her inside.

M. de Roland walked back to us with Jacques, their heads together as if in conference. He smiled as he reached us and said only 'Well, she's in.'

'And you have an engagement for the morning,' said Charlot, with a hint of reproach.

M. de Roland shrugged. 'He took me by surprise there. I didn't think he was that good, did you, Jacques?'

'No,' said Jacques bluntly. 'I wonder what made him change his mind.'

Oh, we should have seen it then, Monsieur, but M. de Roland had no interest in the question and I soon understood why. He announced casually he was off to keep an appointment, and there was not one of us but guessed with whom.

Charlot said 'Perhaps you might take M. Gilbert with you. There are people here who might be only too pleased to encounter you unprotected.'

We looked towards the table where Bouchard sat with his friends. They appeared more relaxed now the Chevalier had been refused the enclosure, and were passing a bottle between them in high spirits. The others we had seen had all by now joined them, but the red-faced man was still not among them and I wondered if perhaps his wounded leg kept him home.

'They're safe enough there,' said M. de Roland. 'If they wander off then I've told Jacques where to find me. But I'm sorry, Charlot, I need to do this alone.'

If he had in mind what I believed I could not but agree. Jacques merely said 'I'll watch them, André,' and fixed his stare on Bouchard as a dog guards a bone.

M. de Roland thanked him, bowed to us all, then set off among the crowds towards the distant hedges of the labyrinth.

Beyond the marquee I saw movement in the dark, where men in green bustled almost invisibly among the towers and racks of rockets. There was a large shrouded mass at the front, and as the men hauled away its covering there was revealed a great stone lion with wide-open mouth. The crowd murmured with expectation, while within the enclosure servants emerged from the marquee and set up chairs on a square of gold cloth so their occupants might face the display. Somewhere out of sight a great gong was sounded, and the orchestra began a new and grander theme.

The fireworks were about to start.

Anne du Pré

Extracts from her diary, dated 13 October 1640

The hut is tucked away beyond the hedges of the *dédalus*, concealed within a bosquet of cypress. I have heard people wonder how the Luxembourg gardens are maintained when no gardeners are ever visible, and was amused to discover so ingenious a solution.

Florian seemed uneasy. I thought perhaps he was concerned by the isolation, but he said King's Musketeers were protecting the gardens and there would be no footpads or ruffians to worry about tonight. Still he hesitated, and as we reached the path through the cypress he stopped and said 'I don't know, perhaps I shouldn't do this.'

I said 'Surely you know you can trust André? He would no more let harm come to me than you would yourself.'

He explained quickly his concern was more for my reputation. 'You mustn't stay more than twenty minutes, that would be most improper. The first part of the firework display ends with the firing of a giant rocket, and when you hear that you must leave at once and alone. You can't be seen with him, Anne, there must be at least ten minutes between you.'

It seemed foolish to me, for I had been walking arm in arm with André all evening, but he said what was done in the company of my father and brother was different from what was done alone, so I gave him my word and he left me. I walked down the gravel path, pulled open the door of the hut, and went in.

It was dark, but I had taken a candle from the rose garden as we came, and now planted it in the soil of an earthenware pot by the door. As the flame flickered and grew strong I saw more of my surroundings and wanted to laugh at their unromantic nature. The hut was large, but a table displaying a map of the labyrinth occupied most of the floor, while the walls were almost covered by the array of implements standing against them: spades and forks with their business ends caked in dry, grey earth, a red-handled axe propped in a corner, and a great pair of shears hanging from a rusty hook. In one corner lay discarded remnants of broken statuary, a lion with no head, and the grey stone arm of a lady all by itself, flung out eloquently with open palm and fingers that pointed at nothing.

I heard footsteps outside.

Almost I hoped it was Florian returning, but my mouth was dry and my heart seemed to kick inside my chest as if my body knew who was really there. I backed stupidly against the wall, and the handle of a spade dug into my back.

The door juddered open, but no one came in. A voice said 'Anne?'

I came further into the candlelight, then a dark shape stepped forward, his arms went about me, my face was pressed against the soft, cold wool of his cloak, his hand was twining in my hair, his voice murmured 'Anne, Anne,' my hands met behind his neck to pull his head down, and then he kissed me.

It was not like the kiss in the forest. There was a year of hunger behind it, mine as well as his, and I was standing on tiptoes to get as much as I could. And now I knew how, my mouth opened to his without even thought, then his tongue was inside and I gave him mine back, and there was nothing but the strength of his arms, the pressure against my back as he pulled me deeper into him, and my need to have him closer still. His hand slid down the line of my back to the curve of my buttocks, and then he was crushing me against him so that my body opened all by itself until I was trembling and my feet unsteady on the ground. I pulled back my mouth, and at once he lifted his head, pulled in a sharp breath, then curved his hand round my head to lay it against his chest. I felt the hammering of his heart slowly subside and his breathing grow soft. After a moment he said 'I'm sorry, I shouldn't have done that.'

I butted my head lightly against his chest.

He stroked my hair. 'But I shouldn't, my darling, there's something I have to tell you, and you might hate me afterwards.'

I tried to imagine hating André. 'What is it?'

He did not answer at once. I looked up and said 'André, what?'

He put me gently away from him. 'Florian. And perhaps your father.'

Fear licked me inside. 'What?'

He took a deep breath. 'Your brother's friends, Bouchard and some others, they're involved in something dangerous. My grandmother has to speak to the Cardinal.'

I had a sinking feeling as if this were something I had already known. 'You think they've involved Florian?'

He did not answer directly. 'She won't blame him, she's promised me. I've said I'm sure he's innocent.'

The fear did not leave me. I groped blindly at his doublet, frantic to make him understand. 'He's not responsible, you know he's not. Even my father would never do wrong deliberately. Please, we must keep them out of this.'

He seemed almost as desperate as I. 'I will, I'll go to the Cardinal myself if I have to. Oh God, Anne, please don't cry.'

He held me again to his chest, and I leaned my head against him and closed my eyes. After a moment I felt brave enough to ask 'Is it so very dangerous, what they've done?'

He kissed the top of my head. 'No one's done anything yet, it's only a conspiracy.'

Relief rippled through me. I knew about conspiracies, Jeanette said they were everywhere you looked. 'You mean it's just politics?'

'Just politics,' he said. 'Please, you mustn't worry.'

Politics could not worry me, Father speaks as if intrigue is natural since so many of the nobility do it. Everything felt peaceful again, and the soft explosion of distant fireworks seemed nothing to do with us.

He said 'I must let you go, your family will be concerned.'

I laced my hands behind his back.

He drew in his breath. 'Be careful, Mademoiselle.'

I did not want to be careful. I wanted to feel again that it was just the two of us together, and I strained upwards for his kiss.

He did kiss me, but only lightly, then pressed his cheek against mine.

I was confused. 'You've told me, and you know I don't hate you.'

I felt his cheek move as he smiled. 'No.'

'Then why won't you . . .?'

He lifted his head. 'Because if I kiss you again I might not be able to stop.'

His eyes were intent on my face, and as I looked at him his breathing quickened.

I tugged his head down towards me and said 'I don't care.'

Jacques Gilbert

It started soon after André left.

We saw the Comtesse being escorted out of the marquee, but Richelieu obviously wasn't finished talking to her yet, the footmen placed her right by the biggest chair where she stood looking sort of

76

smug. I felt even smugger when I looked at d'Arsy standing forbid-
dingly at the entrance, with no idea André's grandmother was just
behind him.

Then the Cardinal himself came out. I couldn't see much of him,
there was just a great lump of guards with this little streak of scarlet
hiding in the middle. Charlot said it was always like that, he thought
everyone was out to get him, but I looked over at Bouchard's mob
and thought he maybe had a point.

Light flashed down towards the palace, then the sky split in a
crash like twenty muskets firing together. For a second my knees
quivered with the urge to drop, then I took in the white streaks
whooshing up into the sky like lightning going backwards and saw
them burst into sparks that fell gracefully to earth like flakes of
snow. The fireworks had started.

I'd never seen anything like it. It was like someone was scribbling
light all over the sky, making clusters that burst like flowers opening
and fountains that showered down like glittering rain. There was
stuff on the ground too, they'd got wooden frames that suddenly
broke into whirls of whizzing light, a castle burning, a volcano with
fire coming out, something new every time. It was like magic.

'They are good tonight,' agreed Bernadette. 'We have them every
year on the Place de Grève, but these are quite good.'

I felt like an ignorant peasant, but then she squeezed my arm and
said 'Tonight they are magical to me too.' Her eyes glistened with
the reflection of a thousand stars.

The excitement was all about us. Every face was turned up in
wonder, men with hardened faces and swords on their hips suddenly turned into children. I thought of Bouchard and felt a stab of
panic as I remembered I was meant to be watching him. There was
still a bunch of men at his table, but my eyes were half-dazzled, I
was seeing white spots and couldn't be sure. I said to Bernadette 'Are
they there? Has anyone gone, are they all there?'

'All,' she said. 'There is still no Dubosc, but I do not think our
Chevalier need fear one man.'

My eyes began to adjust, and I saw Bouchard sitting safely in the
middle. The relief was so huge it took a moment before the oddness
struck me. He'd seen André try to get into the enclosure, he must

know we were on to him, he ought to have been dashing home and trying to get a boat out of France, but he was just sitting there with the same complacent smile I'd noticed before.

Something in my head felt suddenly cold. I thought of d'Arsy agreeing to meet André tomorrow, and that didn't make sense either. Everyone knew André had beaten Bouchard, so what made d'Arsy confident enough to risk it? Nothing I could think of, unless tomorrow was never going to come.

I still couldn't see how, I mean they were right there in front of me. My brain whizzed round trying to find something I'd missed, then I looked down at Bernadette and it hit me.

I said 'That man last night, you'd never seen him before.'

She shrugged. 'He was a lackey, a hired assassin, Paris is full of such people.'

I had a horrid feeling the Luxembourg might be too. I tried telling myself they'd never get past the gate, then remembered what the elegant lady beside me really was. Clothes, that's all it came down to, bloody clothes.

I turned to Charlot. 'I'm going after the Chevalier.'

His eyes moved to Bouchard's table, then back to me.

I said 'I don't care, I know something's wrong.'

He nodded. 'Then you must not waste time talking. Go now. I will look after the ladies.'

I heard Bernadette's gasp but couldn't afford to wait, I just plunged into the crowd without looking back. André had said beyond the labyrinth, I saw the tall green hedge in the distance and headed straight for it.

As soon as I saw clear space in front of me I began walking faster and faster. Behind me I heard an almighty great bang, like the biggest firework we'd had yet, but I didn't so much as turn round, I put down my head and just ran.

Six

Anne du Pré

I guessed what the explosion meant but did not care. He was wrapping my body into him, his head stooped to kiss the back of my neck, my sleeves were sliding down and my feet unsteady, but he held me firm and I could not fall. His hand caressed my shoulder, then down to stroke the curves of my breasts, and I could not help but arch my back with wanting him to take them in his hands.

His fingers slid at once to the top of my bodice, but the wretched splints would not admit them. He lifted his hand, but a second later I felt his touch on my back, a tightness then release of pressure, then cool air on my skin as the gown began to part. I felt his fingers on the next button and knew I should tell him to stop, but I loved the sensation of the dress brushing over my breasts, the warmth of his hands behind me, and the urgency of his breath on my neck.

Something flickered on the edge of my awareness, a sound took shape in my mind, and I froze at the recognition.

He stopped and looked at my face.

I whispered 'There's someone outside.'

It came again, the faint crunch of gravel, but the door was to his left side and he did not hear. Still he did not doubt me, although the flush of his cheek betrayed his disappointment. He began to refasten my gown at the back, but his breathing shook a little and his fingers trembled against my skin.

I said 'What if they come in?'

'They won't,' he said. 'We're only making you respectable for when we leave.'

I thought I heard the murmur of voices. 'I must leave alone, I promised Florian.'

His fingers stilled. 'He knows we're here?'

I smiled. 'It was his suggestion.'

He hesitated, then slid my sleeves back into place. 'Well then, I'll go first and draw these men away, and when I've done that you can leave.'

I said 'Can't we just wait till they go?'

He smoothed my bodice. 'No, my darling, because I think I know what they're after and they may come in.'

'But you said . . .'

'I know.'

Then I understood. 'You cannot think that Florian –'

'No, but others he might have told.'

'He would never tell anybody, he worries about my reputation.'

He gripped my shoulders. 'I need you to do what I tell you now, Anne, will you do it?'

I looked at him and said 'Yes.'

He kissed my forehead. 'In a moment I'll open that door, but I need you out of sight, I want you to hide. You must stay there no matter what, do you understand?'

I said 'Yes.'

'Good,' he said, and began to tidy my hair at the back. 'Come out when it's all quiet. If I'm there, we'll do as your brother said and you'll leave first. If I'm not, go at once to the enclosure by the lake and tell Jacques what's happening. Can you do that?'

His eyes flicked to the door, and I felt his urgency. I went to the corner behind the stone lion, and said 'Will this do?'

'Admirably,' he said, then turned to face the door. He eased his blade in the scabbard, then muttered something that sounded like 'Fuck it' and drew it clear out. He glanced round, smiled, and said 'If I'm wrong, I'm going to look very, very stupid.' Then he lifted his foot, kicked the door wide open, and leapt out.

At once came a shout, then another, then the clash of swords. The shock numbed me into uselessness. My instinct screamed 'Go, go to him,' but my feet did not move, and I stayed trembling against the wall with a voice in my head saying 'Coward!' André had fought against great odds in the past, but there were so many voices outside and not one of them his.

A man yelled in pain, and I thought 'Good, that's one down,' but others were calling 'Behind, behind,' 'Get his arm,' then 'Now!' and suddenly a short cry. I heard laughter then shouting and knew I must get to him, but my dress caught on the stone hand, and I had to rip it to wrench free. The lion statue jarred my shins, but I scrambled past and stumbled to the door.

I ran blindly over the gravel on to the grass and I think I was crying 'Stop!' Even the air was frightening as if filled with unseen swords, and I turned round and round, my dress tangling in my legs, and my head confused with pain and fear. Something grasped my ankle, I snatched it away in terror, and saw a man lying writhing on the ground. I stared in panic, but it was not André. The two of us were quite alone.

The man's hand pawed weakly at my shoe. I knelt beside him, and at once he clutched at my gown, crushing its folds in a white-knuckled fist.

I said 'Where are they? The Chevalier, have they taken him?'

His lips moved, but only to cough out blood. I began again 'Where are they?' but a faint shout from the darkness brought my head up sharply, and ahead of me I saw my answer.

Two great green walls of box hedge loomed before me, and between them yawned the black gap of an entrance. It was from there the voice had come, and now I caught another calling in answer, the sound muffled by layers of many hedges. They had run into the maze.

André was alive, for whom else would they be pursuing? Hope cleared my head, and now I remembered his instructions. I tried to rise, but the man still clutched my dress and as I tried to detach his grip I heard footsteps thumping over the grass, someone running round the outside of the hedge and coming this way.

I hesitated, unsure whether to flee or cry for help, but a man was already skidding round the corner and when he saw me he stopped dead. Candlelight was spilling out from the open door behind me, and in it I saw the face of Jacques.

Jacques Gilbert

Anne was dishevelled and desperate with blood on her dress, I could only think to draw my sword. I said 'Where is he?'

She said 'They chased him into the *dédalus*. I think he may be wounded.'

My legs almost turned and went by themselves, but I forced myself to say 'Are you . . .?'

She shook her head. 'Please, go after him.'

It felt unchivalrous, but the boy was hurt, I couldn't wait. I said 'Stay there,' and belted after him into the maze.

The entrance was a straight pathway through a tunnel of thick green, but it was blocked at the end, and I nearly smashed into a hedge. The tunnel split in two to form an outer path like a giant circle, I could go round either way but didn't know which. It was dark, there weren't footprints or bent branches to follow, just two paths exactly the same, but André might be caught any minute, I'd got to just pick one and come back if it was wrong. I half-turned left then thought 'No,' and turned right instead. Even as I went I was certain I'd got it wrong.

I'd only gone a few steps when I saw an opening to the left that would get me off the outer ring and into the maze. I plunged through it, followed round a lot of bends, turned a corner and almost jumped at a figure right in front of me. My sword was up in an instant, but it was only a statue, a horrible grinning thing with goat legs and horns and a pipe in its hand. Behind it was nothing but hedge. Dead end.

I ran back to the outer ring, shot up the next turning, saw a path off and took it, found I was doubling back on myself, took a side turning and hit another dead end. The sweat was wet on my forehead, I spun round to go back, then stopped short as I heard footsteps on the other side of the hedge.

I opened my mouth to call André, then shut it again fast. There were too many steps for one man. The hedge was a solid mass of greenery, but the bottom looked more spindly where the trunks went into the ground, so I dropped to my knees and peered through.

I caught a blur of grey hose as the first man went past, then someone else in brown. The next legs had smart yellow hose but worn black shoes, someone just pretending to be a gentleman. He was carrying a naked sword, the point flicking to and fro as he passed. Three. I'd known the boy fight that many before, we could take them between us.

Someone shouted ahead of me, a word like 'Venus!' which didn't make sense, but it was another of them, there were four. Someone else yelled from the other side, something like 'Clear Mars!' Five. I gripped my sword harder and walked cautiously back the way I'd come. The men I'd seen weren't shouting at all, and I wondered how many others were just prowling round silently. The maze might be full of them.

A bang and whoosh overhead made me jump before I saw the white flash and realized the fireworks had started again. The light washed over the hedges as it passed, making the grass turn pale grey and flicker with white tips, but it was broken by a splodge of black, by several, a trail of little dark dots on the ground. I crouched and put my hand to the biggest. The light had gone, but there was damp under my fingers, the stickiness of blood.

I was suddenly calm. André had come this way, he was wounded and hunted and needing me, all I'd got to do was keep my head and get him out. I followed the way the blood had been leading before the light went, and I wasn't scared and lost any more, I felt like a soldier. Another dead end, two more statues, then one went and bloody moved, and it wasn't a statue at all, it was a man with drawn sword and his mouth open to yell.

I didn't think, my hand came up in the old way, lunging clean, no armour to worry about, straight in the chest. No noise came out his mouth, nothing but a spray of blood and an odd coughing noise, then he was down on his knees, on his face, he was down. Behind him the statue loomed taller, a man with a jagged chunk like lightning in his hand, and a memory stirred, lessons with Charlot, a lot of guff about Roman gods, then I understood what all that shouting had been about. Venus, Mars, Jupiter, there were statues all over the maze, the bastards were checking every corner and moving towards the centre like a tightening net. The man at my feet retched and died, and I didn't so much as look. He was the first Frenchman I'd ever killed, but I stepped over him and never looked back.

I was torn whether to stay as Jacques had ordered or run for help from his friends. I could never go and come back in time, yet it seemed impossible to do nothing while every second my mind said 'If you had gone when you first thought of it you would be halfway there by now.'

The wounded man choked, and his eyes fixed in an agony of pleading on my face. Here at least was something that would not wait. I hope I didn't do wrong, but I took his hand and said what I could remember of the *Dominus reget me et nihil mihi deerit*. He knew it, his hand tightened on mine and the pupils of his eyes grew bigger and blacker. His face was terribly disfigured with smallpox and the cheekbones sharp with hunger. I am sure he would not really have wanted to kill André, but perhaps they offered him money and he had a family.

I went on with the psalm. I was so afraid for André I dare not allow myself to think, but I heard myself saying the words and it helped us both be calm. There was only the sound of my voice and the roughness of his hand as we waited together for death in the dark.

Jacques Gilbert

I was running through darkness, on and on, and when a hedge came in front of me I just swerved till there wasn't one and went on running to find the boy.

There was a yell ahead of me, then the ring of swords. André was fighting somewhere within feet of me, I hurled myself round the bend and found another bloody hedge. The path curved away from it and was going the wrong way.

Answering shouts came from all round the maze, they knew where he was and were coming to finish him off. I threw myself at the hedge, but the branches were thick and tangled, I couldn't even work an arm through. I tried to climb, but the branches bent under me, the hedge was swallowing my foot like sponge. I clutched at the hedge and shook it, I shouted 'It's me, André, I'm here!'

A voice behind said 'So you are.'

I spun round. A big man in a brown coat was standing in the mouth of the path I'd just come from, and another coming up behind.

I ran at him, but he was already lunging. I twisted so sharply my ankle bent over, but I stayed upright and my left hand grabbed his wrist as he plunged past. I brought my sword up and in him, right in the side, got the bastard, got him, pull out and spin for the next. I heard others coming, but was suddenly almost drunk with fearlessness and went at the next like André himself. This one was an ogre with squashed nose and jagged teeth, but he wasn't trained, I parried him high, my forte to his faible, felt his blade give, slid out and up for the lunge in the armpit. He dodged back, my thrust wasn't deep enough, but I turned for the edge as I came out and sliced his upper arm.

Something flashed in the shadows behind him, then a pain so excruciating I think I shrieked. A blade was biting into my knee, I had to pull my leg back off it, sickness shuddering through me as I stumbled away. Another man was lunging past his wounded comrade, I blocked him but reeled back from the power of the parry and bumped into someone behind me. My leg wouldn't turn properly, I whirled my blade wildly and hit only hedge.

'Steady,' said André.

Something soft brushed my sleeve as he stepped past, his cloak bundled in his left hand. The nearest man sprang, but André thrust the cloak in his face and whipped his sword clean in the body. But something was wrong, one side of André's shirt looked deep black, and as he twisted to get his blade to the man behind I saw the glistening wetness of blood.

My mind froze into clarity, even my knee went cold. I lurched forward and took the last one in a kind of frenzy, slash, slash and out, and there we were with three men down, but others coming towards us. I heard yelling and the pounding of feet.

'Come on,' said André, and I turned and ran after him, my knee making odd screwing sounds in my head as I went. We pelted round the next bend and shot up the first path we saw, but it opened on to nothing but another of those statues and a bench with a bloody bird bath.

'Here,' said André, pulling me towards the bench. 'I'll help you.'

He stood on the seat, spread his cloak over the top of the hedge and scrambled clumsily on to it, reaching down his hand to haul me up. It was easy from the bench, I was with him before anyone even showed round the corner. He slid down the other side, I followed and was immediately aware of open ground. I heard tinkling water and thought we were out at last.

We weren't. We were standing in a big space, but there was box hedge all round in a perfect circle and just a fountain with a great copper dolphin in the middle. There was something odd behind it, a big wooden construction with bits sticking off it, but I didn't take that in, I was looking all round and seeing just a wall of hedge broken only by more dark slots of entrances. We were in the centre of the maze.

'Good timing, Jacques,' said the boy, straightening awkwardly. 'Where's Charlot?'

I felt flat. 'There's just me. We didn't know . . .'

He turned his face towards me, white as the fireworks. 'But didn't Anne . . .?'

My hand shot up to hush him. Footsteps on the other side of the hedge, thudding round the bend and stopping short, then a voice said 'No,' and I heard them moving away. They'd never thought of us climbing, and for a moment at least we'd lost them. André leaned against the hedge and began to massage his side.

Another firework flew overhead, but the light didn't quite go as it faded. Something else was blazing nearby, yellower, more fire-like, I was glimpsing it in bits through the hedges. It was coming towards us at hand height, and I realized it was an ordinary torch.

I said 'They've got lights, we'd better go.'

He swivelled at the hips and went on massaging. 'Just give me a minute.'

André never said stuff like that, never. I stared in shock, then saw the lopsided way he was standing and understood. I said 'I'll get you out, André, it's all right.'

He made a kind of hissing noise through his teeth. 'Sounds good to me.'

It would have to me, if I hadn't been the one who'd said it. I sat him down on the rim of the fountain and turned to face the approaching light but he saw me wince at the movement, forced a grin and said 'Pair of crocks.'

I said 'It's only one man,' and hefted my sword in my hand. It was certainly only one torch, but it was coming confidently towards us like the man knew exactly where we were and how to get there.

'Wait a bit,' said André. 'Look at this.'

He was studying the wooden frame behind the fountain. It was a rack of metal poles pointing at the sky, all of different lengths to round the whole thing like a blunt arrow. Each pole had a cylinder with a pointed cap like the cones on the château roof at Lucheux, and thick string sticking out the end like a match. I'd seen things like this not twenty minutes ago, my brain clicked on to the right cog and I said 'Fireworks.'

Light flooded through the entrance as the torch rounded the corner, and with it came a sound I knew, ridiculous and impossible, someone whistling. I even knew the tune. It was 'En passant par la Lorraine'.

Anne du Pré

The man closed his eyes at 'I will fear no evil' and died before I could finish.

My fear for André was now almost choking me, and I could no longer be obedient and wait. I wished to run straight into the labyrinth after him, but knew it would not help him to have me to worry about too. I ran instead back into the hut and stared at the map of the maze.

I was hopelessly confused by it, and only two points impressed themselves on my mind. The first was that it was symmetrical, with a great opening in the centre and easy routes radiating away to the outer ring. The second was that the outer ring did not run clear all the way round, but cruelly tapered into dead ends, so that only the last segment of the circle ran true to the exit. A man might reach the outer hedge but be no nearer freedom than in the thickness of the middle. I thought of André and Jacques trapped in such a cage, and thumped the map foolishly with my fist.

I looked up in despair at the walls, and only then did I see the answer.

Jacques Gilbert

André slid off the fountain to stand beside me, sword levelled firm towards the sound of whistling.

The light spread into the clearing in a widening pool, but the man who strolled in behind it was short and wiry, dressed all in dark green, and with a face that looked wrinkled as a walnut. He had the torch in one hand, a long stick in the other, and nothing that looked like a weapon at all.

He walked cheerfully up to the frame, stuck his torch in a wire basket, then pulled on a lever so the whole rack came down to point horizontal, the strings of the rockets dangling invitingly in a row. He looked at them lovingly, then lifted his pole, a linstock with a bit of slow-match wound round the crook.

'Monsieur,' said André.

The man jumped back with a yelp. 'Fuck me to Freiburg, what you doing there?'

André raised his hands. 'Please, speak softly.'

'What do you mean, speak softly?' yelled the green man. 'What you up to? That's the Cardinal's fleur-de-lys, going up right after the starburst.'

André flapped his hands frantically to silence him but I heard a voice yell 'In the centre!' and others answering, the sound of running feet. They sounded horribly close.

I grabbed André's arm and turned for the nearest entrance, but a man was already coming out of it. I jerked right, but there were two emerging from that one. Across the clearing the dark holes of the last two openings thickened and blurred as a man appeared in each. Five of them, and the torchlight glittering off their swords as they advanced.

'Hey,' said the green man with a hint of unease. 'Bugger off out of it, will you? Take your games outside and let me do my job.'

They kept coming. Two looked wobbly, and one I recognized as the ogre whose arm I'd cut, but they were still too many for the state we were in.

André faced them. 'In front of a witness?'

'What witness?' said the one in front, and lunged straight at the green man.

André's blade whipped out to deflect the blow, but the sword still scraped down the green man's belly as it was knocked aside. He stared down in shock at the blood on his coat.

André slashed back at the leader, but couldn't twist properly, the man dodged and brought up his sword with a grunt of triumph, then suddenly I was roaring with rage and snatching the burning torch out of the basket, I whirled it round like a thunderbolt, and the man reeled away in fear of the fire.

'The rockets,' said André, stumbling back towards me. 'Jacques, the rockets!'

The green man was quicker than me, he screamed 'Not with the rack down!' and then I understood. The other men were almost up to us as I swept the torch left-handed against the trail of slow-matches, one, two, three, four, a man coming at me but André's there, knocking the blade down hard. I keep sweeping, five, six, seven, step along the rack, eight, nine, ten, matches sizzling behind me like spitting snakes, eleven, twelve, thirteen, fourteen. None have gone off yet, but as I light the last four I see the matches are shorter and realize they're timed to go together. The green man's yelling 'The lever, get the rack up!' but I don't want them shooting in the air, I want them where they are right now. The nearest man knows, he's trying to get past André to stop me, but the boy's still fighting, wounded or not, he'll fight till the world ends, and then suddenly it really does.

It wasn't a bang, just a kind of hiss and whizz, then the rockets blazed forward with such force the whole rack kicked and swung back at me, knocking the torch out of my hand. They didn't all go straight either, the poles were curved and rockets going everywhere, we didn't dare move from behind the rack. One smashed into the front man, hurling him back against the hedge then blowing up in his clothes, and I had to look away. The rest exploded round us, everything blanked out with sudden whiteness then the yellow of fire, a blue-grey choking smoke, and the familiar smell of gun-powder in my mouth, my nose, my lungs. I groped for the torch but the grass was burning round it, I snatched back my hand.

André pulled at my arm. 'Leave it, come on!'

I came. The explosion was fading from my ears only to be replaced by the savage crackling of flame where rockets had lodged in the hedges. I couldn't see our attackers, I guessed they'd just run and couldn't blame them. We'd set fire to the whole bloody maze.

Bernadette Fournier

I could not say what I expected, Monsieur, perhaps a rush of guards from the enclosure to drag Bouchard and his friends away to have their heads cut off. That is what *I* would have done, but then I am only a woman and what do I know of politics?

Instead there was only Madame escorted back by a servant of His Eminence, and d'Arsy never even glancing at her as she passed. She returned to us with a look of quiet satisfaction, then looked and said 'Where is the Chevalier?'

No one answered directly, for at that moment the great lion was lit, and oh, a great spray erupted about it like a halo and out of its mouth spewed a light that was golden, not merely white, Monsieur, I swear the sparks were bright yellow. In the distance came a great boom, then another, and we all looked expectantly upward, but there was only whiteness as if something glittered below, while plumes of grey smoke coiled up to the night sky. That this was a mistake I was not alone in guessing, for a sigh of disappointment rippled through the crowd, and as I looked towards the source of the smoke I glimpsed in the distance orange flickers of flame.

'Don't bother,' said the Comtesse, the triumph faded from her face. 'I can guess.'

So could Charlot, for he started at once towards the fire. And I too, for if the Chevalier was there then so was Jacques, so I tucked up my skirts and ran.

What saved us was the hedges being damp from yesterday's rain. They fizzled and smouldered, but it was only where the rockets had actually lodged that went up in flames. It didn't stop the smoke though, thick and grey with that bitter green smell that catches in the back of your throat. Patches of grass had caught too, flames licking up the rocket frame, and I heard a crash as it collapsed behind me. André's hand slipped out of my arm.

Smoke drifted past my face, and through it I saw a slot of blackness, an opening in the hedge. I shouted for André, but his voice came back muffled 'Just a minute!' Metal poles clanked, I flapped away the clouds in front of me and saw André hauling the green man from under the frame. I was coughing now, my eyes stinging, my throat closing up, I yelled 'Come *on!*' but the boy went on dragging till the poles rolled off with a clang and the green man stumbled to his feet. He didn't even look grateful, he was swearing worse than Stefan, I heard him say 'Sweet Jesus and Mary. Fucking saints and all.' I grabbed André's sleeve and pulled.

The smoke was thinner on the path, and it was easier to breathe. I didn't worry about where we were going, what mattered was getting away from that burning centre. I just kept taking whichever path had least smoke and guessed we must at least be getting closer to the outside, but André was pulling at me to stop, and the green man said 'Whoa there, boys, this don't look right to me.'

It didn't look bloody right to me either, we'd got another hedge in front of us and smoke all round, but talking about it wasn't going to help. Then I remembered that torch floating confidently towards us through the winding paths, and felt a sudden jolt of hope.

'You know the way out?'

'Course I do,' he said, affronted. 'Now, which path did we take out of the centre? Needs to be north or south, see, them others are going nowhere.'

My little bit of hope curled up again. 'I don't know.'

He rolled his eyes. 'All right, we'll see.'

He wheeled off down a side turning and we followed him meekly.

He was amazing, really. He'd got a sword gash across his belly and a lump coming up on his forehead, he'd been stabbed and crushed and half blown up, we'd ruined his firework display and probably lost him his job, but he was calmer than we were, I think he was even whistling as he walked. But I could hear something else too, a woman's voice shouting nearby, muffled through hedges and smoke.

'All symmetrical, see,' said the green man, leading us into a clearing with another statue in it, a big man with a hammer who made me think of Colin back home. 'Nah, ruddy Vulcan, we're in the wrong part. Back to the centre, boys, we'll take the next exit.'

The woman's voice was calling 'André!' and this time we all heard it.

'Anne,' said the boy, looking round like he expected to see her standing in the smoke. 'Anne!'

She called back. 'I'm here. Can you get to the outer ring?'

André turned to the green man. 'Can we?'

'No way out there,' he said, turning back towards the centre. 'It's the middle or nothing.'

Anne called again, her voice breaking and desperate.

The boy grabbed the man's coat and practically shook him. 'The outer ring, please, now!'

'All right,' said the man, shaking him off and staring. 'Steady, that man. I'll take you.'

He turned off jauntily and we limped after him. André was holding his side all the time now, shaking the man had just about done for him. My knee was throbbing like things were grating together inside it, I hoped to God it wasn't far.

We were there in less than a minute, but the green man was right, the outer path tapered into another dead end. He said 'See?'

André ignored him. 'Anne, we're here!'

She was only feet away, I heard her running on the other side of the hedge. Then her voice said 'Can you stand back?'

André's arm pushed me away from the hedge. 'We're back.'

The whole hedge suddenly shook, there was a loud cracking sound, then the fluttering of agitated leaves. I caught a glimpse of flashing metal, then the hedge shook again, more violently than before.

'Mind your heads, boys,' sang out the green man. 'Female with an axe!'

The next blow cleft the hedge wide open at the top, I could see her on the other side tugging the axe free for another go.

André stepped at once to the gap. 'Give it to me, sweetheart, we'll finish it.'

She didn't argue, I don't think she'd got any breath left, she just passed it through. I took it myself, André was in no state to swing, I took it and chopped down twice, wrenching the axe out of the splinters of the last trunk, and there was a space a man could climb through.

I shoved André to the gap, and for once he didn't hesitate, he saw Anne on the other side and practically leapt. I stood back for the green man then started to follow, but my leg was dragging, I caught my foot on a shattered trunk and fell headlong, crashing heavily on to the grass on the other side. I levered my face up out of the turf and saw something coming towards me, smart yellow hose above a pair of shabby black shoes. Anne was crying out, I scrabbled up on my knees and there they were, four of them, and us in no state to fight a fly.

A hand reached down to the grass beside me and picked up the axe.

'I'll have that,' said the green man.

André pushed at Anne, his voice high with panic. 'Run! Get help, *run!*' She was off at once in a rustle of skirts, and then he was calm again, turning to face the enemy with his sword steady in his hand. I clutched at the hedge and hauled myself to my feet.

They approached us warily but I didn't think they needed to. The boy was done in, I was half lame, the green man was a gardener, we were fucked.

Bernadette Fournier

Others ran as we did towards the fire. Ahead of us hurried a group of Musketeers, swinging their grand blue cloaks so the crosses on their backs flashed their self-importance.

The hedge of the labyrinth rose up before us, and the Musketeers ran down the side where the smoke billowed thickest. I followed with Charlot, but towards us came running a girl in a pale dress, her cloak flying wildly behind her, and it was Mlle du Pré, alone and in fright and with blood on her skirt. She seized the sleeve of the leading Musketeer and babbled that there were men attacking the Chevalier de Roland and they must come at once to his aid.

Charlot and I pressed forward, but the leading Musketeer drew his sword and turned back to face us. A great firework exploded high above us, a magnificent ball of stars which erupted into a fountain over the whole gardens.

'Stand back there,' commanded the Musketeer. 'Stay back, in the King's name.' He turned to lead his men down the side of the maze and I stopped indeed, but only in shock, for the starburst flicked a white light under the brim of his hat and revealed to me a face I knew. It was the last of those gentlemen, the red-faced Dubosc, and we had sent the Chevalier only more enemies.

Jacques Gilbert

We hadn't a chance of fighting our way out, we were just trying to fend the bastards off. André's left hand was pressed constantly to his side and my leg was creaking under me, a trained swordsman could have had us in seconds. It was the green man who really saved us, he was whirling that axe in great sweeps, shouting 'Keep back, you buggers,' and none of them dared come near.

Footsteps charged towards us, voices shouted 'Put up!' and 'Stop in the King's name!' I swivelled sharply, and that was it for my knee, it shot a slicing pain up my leg and dropped me in a heap on the grass. I peered up and saw Musketeers coming towards us with drawn swords. Two of our attackers turned and legged it, the others backed off like they couldn't decide, but their weapons went down and I knew it was over.

André lowered his blade and leaned against the hedge. 'Sorry about all that, Jacques.'

I said 'You and your women,' and watched him smile.

The Musketeers came panting up, and the last two attackers turned and fled. But the lead Musketeer kept his sword levelled, he was still charging at the boy and a woman's voice cried 'Look out, Chevalier!' Then I saw, I bloody saw, he was one of the men we'd fought that day, and his blade thrusting full at the boy's chest.

I shouted 'André!' I think I bloody screamed it. The boy scrabbled up his sword in a frantic parry and the Musketeer's blade slid harmlessly over it, but he'd been lunging even as he charged and his body crashed on to André's sword with the force of his own thrust. The boy struggled to withdraw but his elbow had been smashed back into the hedge and the man was already stuck through. He collapsed on his knees, blood pouring thickly out of his mouth on to the grass, then he pitched forward on his face and was silent.

Feet came towards us, more Musketeers, but they weren't running any more, they were staring in horror at their officer dead on the ground. So was André, I heard his shallow gasp as he took in what he'd done. Other voices were round us now, I heard a woman's little scream and a man saying 'Killed a Musketeer. Did you see? Man's killed a Musketeer!'

André's head came up, and there he was, stood with bloody sword over the man's body, then I saw what other people were seeing and was suddenly sick with understanding.

The leading Musketeer cried 'Seize him.'

André's sword lifted in feeble defence, but he couldn't fight them, he couldn't kill another. The woman's voice came again from the crowd, Bernadette yelling 'Run!' The boy stared round wildly, at the crowd, the advancing Musketeers, the dead man at his feet, then seemed to grasp what was happening, spun round and bolted into the dark.

The Musketeer was sending men after him, I was struggling up to stop them, but a hand clamped firm on my shoulder and Charlot's voice said 'Stay where you are, Monsieur, it is your safest course now.'

He was right. The only reason they weren't grabbing me was because I was down, not even those Musketeer bastards could pretend I'd been fighting them. But the unfairness was unbearable, I kept saying 'The man was going to kill him, it was self-defence.'

Charlot's grip tightened on my shoulder, but the senior Musketeer stood with his arms folded and his lip curling, and I guessed he was another of them. When a young Musketeer said 'I don't understand, why did Dubosc . . .?' the senior told him to shut his mouth. I remembered suddenly there was another witness, but when I looked round to where the green man had been there was nothing but that red-handled axe lying on the ground.

Seven

Albert Grimauld

From his interviews with the Abbé Fleuriot, 1669

Never mind the 'Monsieurs', laddie, Grimauld's good enough for me. A name's not where the respect is, see, it's who a man is. You know what they call me in the Vieux? Old Gappy. Boys look at my teeth and call me Old Gappy, but there ain't a man in the regiment they'd rather have next them than me. I'm the man can blow up anything, the man who mined the gate at Hesdin in '39. Steel? War's about the walls and the black powder, that's where it's at, that's the future.

Ah, but it's the past you want, and I won't say no to a bit of that. You're thinking 'An old man, what can he tell me about the age of honour and a young man called André de Roland?' Well, pour us another goblet of that wine and you'll see.

1640. I was out the army for a while, and never you mind why, maybe I'll tell and maybe I won't, let's just see how we suit. I was out the army and in stinking Paris where there's no work for a man without his nose up the arse of the guilds, and nothing and its bastards for a man like me. Then this firework business comes up, so it's back with the old powder and making things go bang, but not for its natural purpose of ripping a man to pieces, this was for making pretty sparkles and to get the gentry going 'Ah!'

There was a bit more than 'Ah' in it that night. Rockets sizzling into men's bellies, whole ruddy maze on fire, *not* what His bleeding Eminence had in mind at all. Not the brightest of lookouts for me neither. Job up the devil's chimney, people killing themselves all round me, bunch of Musketeers yelling 'murder', and when a gentleman's accused for no more than defending himself, what chance for a man like me? Trust me, I was out of it, off and over the back wall in less time than it'd take you to pour me more wine.

But one handy thing about the Luxembourg is where it is, see, because the minute I was over that wall I was safe and solid in Saint-Germain. Ah, use your head, boy, it's abbey land, the King's law doesn't reach there. There's bankrupts moved in, there's cutpurses and footpads and all sorts know how to nip in smartish when things get hot, and never you mind how I know them things, I knows them, that's all.

So I ain't worried when I hear someone scrabbling up the wall after me, I just duck in a doorway for a discreet look-see. Over he comes like a cat with a dog after it, lands heavy on the stones, then straightens up to lean against the wall. It's the young gentleman that spiked the Musketeer, but pale as a mushroom and that much blood down his breeches I couldn't say which bit of him's punctured. He wipes his arm across his face, takes one deep, shuddering suck of air, then sets off down the street, weaving like a dockside drunk.

Well, that gave me a qualm. Saint-Germain was a poor lookout for any gentleman straying in after dark, specially one reeling about with 'wounded and helpless' round his neck like a banner. He was worth the stopping too. He'd lost his hat and cloak, but the baldric on him was enough to feed a man's family for months, to say nothing of whatever purse he'd got. I wasn't thinking that for myself, see, I'm only saying others would. Left to himself the lad was sausage meat by morning.

I strolled after him, but he was turning down the Rue Taranc when I saw a couple of figures in a doorway already giving him the look. Their heads never moved, but their eyes went slowly round with him till he was past, then they looked at each other and that's it, the hitch of the shoulders and out they come, solid and soft-footed as cats in the dark. Well, I knew the bigger one, fellow named Menoult, Molin, something with an 'm' in it, so I kept myself to the shadows and followed.

He sensed them fast. Round he came, hand on hilt in a heartbeat, and I thought maybe he'd more savvy than I gave him credit for, but not a bit of it. This is a gentleman can take a Musketeer, but the minute he sees a couple of roughs lurking after him with 'footpad' like it might be branded on their foreheads he relaxes like there's nothing to fear. He takes his hand off his sword and actually speaks to them, he goes and asks the way to the bleeding abbey.

They can't believe it neither, it's not often you get the bird asking you where on the lime you want it to sit. The 'm' one, oh call him 'Molin', it'll do, he gets a grip on himself and says 'We'll show you, Sieur, it's right in our way.'

So in they come, close either side, steering him off of the middle of the street. There's a lantern on this road, see, a little house opposite does the business with the women if you get me, and they want him safe in the shadows before they start to work. The gentleman doesn't like being crowded, he's saying 'I'm all right,' and trying to shake them off, but Molin says 'You're hurt, Sieur, let me just help you.' He realizes at last, struggles back and goes for the sword, but Molin's out quick with his foot, trips him neat as neat, then it's in with the old one-two jabs in the guts, down he goes and it's done. They pause a second, caught in the lamplight, faces up and listening for the watch, but they don't see no one, so it's hand under each armpit, lug the gentleman into the alley and that's him cooked.

I could have walked away. Mark that, I could have looked the other way, but I crossed the street and into the alley after them.

They hadn't wasted time. They were tossing him a treat, shoes already off, feeling down the body for the purse and found it too from the sound of it, I heard the chink of coin. I stepped up and said 'Whoa there, boys, that's a friend of mine.'

Ever caught a cat with a bird? Their hands were down smack on the body, faces sharp as knives with suspicion. Molin said 'Fuck off, Grimauld, we found him first.'

The other's fumbling at the baldric. 'Turn him over, will you, I want the sword off.'

They roll him on his back, and his face is that white I think he's popped it, but when Molin starts undoing the scabbard there's suddenly a hand groping out to the hilt, and the laddie mutters 'My sword.'

'You can keep the sword,' says Molin soothingly. 'We just want the baldric.'

The other says nothing, just slides his hand in his coat. I snatch his arm and tell him to leave off, but he don't want to hear it, see, he's up and swiping with the knife, so I sock him one to teach him better, then curl round the old leg to trip him down smack on the stones.

Molin springs up while I'm still off balance, he's whipping out his own dagger and it's all I can do to duck the slash, but then comes the slide of steel behind him, and there's the gentleman propped up on his elbow, his eyes wide open and the sword in his hand.

'Get back,' he says. 'Drop the knife and get back.' The voice ain't up to much, but the sword's something can prod holes in you before you get near knife range.

Molin hesitates. He was a Marseilles water rat if I remember right, all cunning and no balls. He looks at the gentleman sliding himself up the wall, he looks at his mate on his hands and knees, he looks at me with my fists up, ready for him and his mother, and he sees it's not worth it. He says something I won't repeat, sticks his knife in his belt, and turns to go.

'Stop,' says the gentleman, full upright now. I ain't sure what's holding him up, tell you the truth, the only steady things about him are the hand and the sword. He says 'My purse.'

Molin's eyes measure the distance between them. He says 'Fuck you,' and turns away. Next second the gentleman's lunged with the sword, and there's Moulin yelping like a girl, blood pouring down the back of his hand.

'My purse,' says the gentleman.

Moulin throws it down on the street, coins spilling out and bouncing away. He says 'Buy yourself a good piece of armour, friend. You'll need it next time I see your back,' then swaggers himself off, his friend hobbling after him like a broken-backed spider.

I chase up as many coins as I can see in the dark and give him them back, yes, the whole lot, what do you take me for? I say 'You make friends wherever you go, don't you?'

He looks at me and smiles. 'Maybe I do,' he says.

Jacques Gilbert

When we got home the authorities were waiting. There were Gardes-Françaises because of it happening in the Royal Gardens, Cardinal's Guards because of it being his party, Musketeers because it was one of theirs who was killed, *prévots des maréchaux* because of it being a crime, we'd got half Paris crashing round the courtyard and wanting to search the house.

But she was strong, my grandmother. She got a surgeon to stitch up my knee, sent Bernadette to her room with Robert and Jean to guard her door, then graciously admitted the whole invasion and instructed the kitchens to offer them wine. By the time I was bandaged and carried upstairs it was starting to feel like a bloody party. None of us could sleep through it, so the Comtesse took Charlot, Suzanne and me into the big salon with the sky ceiling and sat us down at three o'clock in the morning to play *triomphe*.

A whole stream of people poured in to search round us, but the Comtesse still kept us playing. Just the sight of those pictures now, David, Charles, Alexander, Caesar, I can't see them without remembering how they blurred into a mess of colour in front of my eyes and hearing the Comtesse saying teasingly 'Now, Monsieur, you do not concentrate.'

None of us were, and trumps changed from spades to hearts in the middle of a hand without anyone saying a word. The second the guards moved out of earshot the Comtesse said under her breath 'The Chevalier, how seriously is he hurt?'

She was fumbling the deal, a card fell face up. I flipped it back over and said 'He was well enough to run, he'll be all right.'

Charlot gave me a tiny nod of approval. 'Will His Eminence help us, Madame?'

'If he can,' she murmured. 'He was certainly grateful for our information. But it will be difficult now the King's Musketeers are involved.'

I said 'We've got witnesses.'

She ordered her hand. 'And who are they, Monsieur? A serving girl compromised by her friendship within this household, and an engineer of fireworks who has disappeared.'

'And a stable boy,' I said bitterly. 'Don't forget him.'

She glanced at me over the top of her cards. 'Naughty temper,' she said, but there was a flash in her eyes that was almost warm.

I declared the ace of trumps and went to pillage the pack. 'There's that young Musketeer, I'm sure he saw.'

The Comtesse nodded. 'I shall speak to de Tréville in the morning.'

A couple of Cardinal's Guards came muscling in, so we played in silence till they went down the far end to poke behind the tapestries. I said 'There's Anne. Even if she didn't see the end of it, she saw us being attacked.'

The Comtesse studied her cards. 'And will she say so, I wonder?'

I said 'You don't suspect Anne?'

'Do I not?' she said. 'Who made this appointment at which the Chevalier was ambushed?'

I remembered walking André back from the enclosure, his whisper of 'She loves me, Jacques, she wants to see me alone.' I remembered what I'd seen outside the hut, Anne comforting one of the enemy. I said 'She got us out. I told you, she fetched the axe.'

'And brought you out where assassins were waiting.'

'We were shouting, they followed the noise, that's all.'

'Hmm,' she said, and played a card.

I tossed another on top of it. 'And she went for help, you know she did.'

'She fetched another assassin.'

'How could she know?'

The Comtesse took the trick. 'Aren't they her brother's friends?'

The Maréchaussée were coming in for their turn, but I couldn't answer anyway. The truth was banging in my head like a bell and nothing I could think of would make it stop.

It was nearly dawn when I got back to my room. It was strange thinking how happy I'd been last time I'd slept here, almost like remembering myself as a child. The bed felt as cold as it had that first night.

The door creaked open. A girl in a long nightdress came in with a candle, and when she put it down I saw it was Bernadette.

I said 'You're meant to be guarded. Where's Robert and Jean-Luc?'

She sat on the bed beside me, careful not to disturb my leg. 'I climbed out of the window and came back in through the courtyard.'

I couldn't say anything, but she reached out her arms and leaned me against her chest, and I think maybe I cried a bit. But it was all warm and soft in her arms, and she was kissing my head, then after a while she opened her nightdress and gave me her breasts. They were as beautiful as I'd imagined, but I'd still got to be fair, so I made myself draw back and say 'I'm going to be a gentleman, I won't be allowed to marry you.' She giggled, then kissed me so hard I felt giddy and said 'That is because you even thought such an impossible thing.' So I slid back the covers and rolled her into bed, then she straddled me so as not to hurt my leg, and I made love to her and she to me. She was soft and moist with wanting me, she made joyful little squirming movements and funny little noises like pleasure, she was innocent and lovely and loving, there wasn't a thing she wouldn't let me do.

Afterwards, when we lay side by side, exhausted and slippery with sweat, she said 'Say it again about not being allowed to marry me.' I asked why, and she looked at me so seriously and said 'Because it is the nicest thing anyone has ever said to me in my whole life.' I looked at her face, all pink and flushed and trusting on the pillow, and said 'I'm free to love you, Bernadette, no one can stop me doing that,' and she caught her breath and reached for me, then we made love again and it was even better than before.

I held her snuggled into me, and the warmth of her helped when I thought about the boy. Last time I'd lost him he'd just come back like nothing had happened, and I was sure in my heart he'd do it again now. So I slept at last, but I dreamed I was back searching for him in that maze, calling his name over and over, but there was never any answer, just silent hedges and dead ends, and paths that wound into nowhere in the dark.

Anne du Pré

Extract from her diary, dated 14 October 1640

I can't believe I have been so slow. When Florian hurried me away to our carriage I thought he wished to save me further distress. When Father ordered me not to say what I had seen I thought he feared others would wonder why I had been there at all.

I said 'André's life is at stake, Monsieur, we must forget reputation and tell the truth. You too, Florian, you must say who else knew about our meeting.'

He coloured dreadfully and insisted that he had told no one. He said 'Why should you think you were attacked at all? De Roland would start a fight with anyone, look how he challenged Bouchard.'

I said 'It's Bouchard who's behind this, André said so. Did you tell him, Florian?'

The noise of the gardens receded behind us and everything seemed suddenly very quiet. The seat creaked as Father leaned forward across the carriage.

'What else did de Roland tell you?'

My words seemed to dry in my throat and I looked at my father as if he were a stranger.

Florian said pleasantly 'It's important, Anne.' He was swaying gently from side to side with the movement of the carriage, but his eyes stayed on my face.

I forced myself to speak. 'He only said it was dangerous. And it is, isn't it?'

Father sat back. 'Not if one has the right connections. Has he told anyone else?'

I said 'Only his grandmother. Please, Monsieur, he is our friend. We could go together to the Cardinal and put things right.'

'The Cardinal?' said Florian.

The wheels rumbled as we entered the Porte Saint-Germain and the swinging lanterns flicked light through our window, casting fleeting shadows over both their faces.

Father said 'Attend me, Anne. André de Roland is not our friend, and you will have nothing to do with him ever again. Do you understand?'

I said 'But you invited them tonight. It was Florian's idea and you . . .'

My own words gave me the truth. They are not merely embroiled in this, they actually planned it. There is nothing innocent about their involvement, and the only dupe in this whole affair has been me.

Albert Grimauld

They patched him up in the abbey's infirmary. Fr. Anselm and Fr. Dominic were proper Christians, they never asked no questions, just sewed him back up like new.

He needed it too, oh my word, there was enough blood gone out of him to float a barge. Still he was tougher nor he looked, that laddie, and been in the wars before if the musket hole in his back was anything to go by. Some not very classy language we had out of him while they was stitching, but never a bleat, not one.

'He'll be fine,' says Fr. Anselm. 'Nothing vital's pierced. He needs to rest to let the blood make itself up, but he'll heal with time.'

'Ah,' says I, 'but that's just what we ain't got, see? This ain't your everyday in-and-out-thief, this is your actual murderer, or so they'll say. The provosts won't hold off for ever, we've got to move him on.'

Fr. Dominic and Fr. Anselm look at each other, and even the gentleman sees their doubt.

'I'm all right,' he says, looking like a day-old corpse. 'I'll leave now if you like. I can go back tomorrow anyway, my grandmother will have sorted it out by then.'

Green? You could have ate that boy as a salad. I said 'Not unless she's the bloody queen, she won't. You need a horse to the coast and a boat out of France.'

What little blood he'd got left in his face faded clean out of it. 'I can't go home?'

'Not unless you want them took for harbouring,' I said briskly. 'Now about that horse . . .'

He shook his head. 'I'm going to be married.'

'Not this year,' I said. 'Maybe your friends can get you brought back in two.'

He was quiet as he took it in. I braced myself for the weeping and wailing, but he rummaged in his clothes, said 'Can you get me a horse?' and offered me his purse.

I don't know, I'm not a bad man, there was something I couldn't understand holding me back. I said 'Listen, laddie, you don't just go handing purses of money to strangers. How do you know I ain't going straight off with it and you'll never see me again?'

He looked at me smack on, and bugger me to Breisach, it was like taking a kick off a mule. He said 'I've already cost you your job. You're not even safe here now you helped me against those foot-pads. So you can take the money and run, or you can help me and trust I'll take care of you afterwards, but either way I owe you and at least you'll get paid.'

You ever heard a gentleman speak like that? No, nor likely to neither, and if you were to pass over that bottle I'd drink my life on it.

I stowed the purse safe and said 'What do I call you anyway?'

He said 'My name's André.'

Real names in a business like this? I said soothingly 'Right you are, my poppet, André it is.'

'No,' he said. 'André's fine, but call me "poppet" and I'll kill you.'

The monks twittered with alarm, but I saw the glint in his eyes and couldn't help but laugh. He laughed too, only a little, but a sight better than the dying girlie look he'd been giving me earlier. I gave him my hand on it, and he took it like a man my own kind and said 'You might want to make it two horses,' and I said 'You might be right.'

I knew just where to get them, but by the time I got there it was sun-up and the situation changing fast. Drouart the salt smuggler was ahead of me waiting to change a broken-winded animal he'd bought earlier and saying 'You want to ride out of Saint-Germain you'll have to wait a week, they're beating the bounds all round.'

I said 'Why's that then?' and he said there was cavalry ranging all over the roads, stopping and searching travellers to find a fugitive.

'Big one too,' he says wistfully. 'Gentleman defied the King's own orders in his mother's own gardens, went and killed a Musketeer stone dead. That'll be an execution worth watching, Grimauld. They're saying it's André de Roland himself.'

That set the old brain whirring, oh my word it did. Everyone knew de Roland was the gentleman who'd disguised himself as a peasant and lived like one of us. They said he was a swordsman too, and I'd seen a bit of that myself, some very pretty rapier work he was dealing out in that maze. But I still weren't fool enough to see it getting us past a whole regiment of cavalry, so I gave the horses the go-by and put my mind to something else.

I went to a little place I know that deals in . . . well, never you mind what, it was the kind of place people like Molin found handy, that's all. I got what I wanted, then it was back to the Abbey to break the news to the laddie.

He took it like a pro. 'Then we'll go the other way. We'll go back till it all dies down.'

'Bang in the gold,' says I, chucking him one of my parcels. 'They won't be watching for people going *in* the city, we'll stroll in with the traders and no one'll pay us no nevermind. Get yourself in that lot, and no one won't know the difference.'

It was a motley lot of clothing I'd got us, a man didn't like to think too careful who it had come off of, but it was just the business to make him look the roughest kind of artisan. I'd some for myself too, I wasn't walking about in a green uniform screaming 'fireworks engineer' to anyone with more hearing than a mule.

Poor Fr. Anselm looked like I'd pissed in the chapel. 'You can't ask a gentleman to dress like this,' he said. 'He could never pass, the distinction in bearing would be far too great.'

'So it might be, my poppet,' says I, 'for any gentleman but this one. But I think this one can do it, am I right?'

The gentleman looks at me sharp and he sees I know. He says 'Yes.'

'Good,' says I. 'But have you got a friend you can go to ground with till the heat's off?'

'Yes,' says André. 'I think I have.'

Jacques Gilbert

The Comtesse set off for Richelieu first thing, but they told her His Eminence was too busy to speak to the family of a criminal. She said he might just be pretending in front of everybody else, but I wasn't sure she really believed it.

It was hard to stay hopeful, the atmosphere was just foul. The servants were going round subdued and red-eyed, and we'd got guards on the gates waiting to pounce on André if he tried to come back to his own home. I couldn't even ride into Saint-Germain myself without them following me. We couldn't do a thing but sit and wait.

Then de Chouy came. We were back in the sky salon when he arrived, I could still see the cards on the table that no one had bothered to clear away. No one had cleaned yet either, it smelt of dust and early morning defeat. Then the door whooshed open so vigorously it banged against the wall, and we heard someone saying 'Whoops!' Robert announced 'M. de Chouy' in the kind of voice you use when there's plague in the house, and in he bounded, sweeping off his hat and apologizing before he even reached us.

He said 'I'm sorry, Madame, but it's about the Chevalier,' then noticed Charlot and said 'Oh.'

The Comtesse said 'You need not mind Charles, Monsieur. If you have news we shall be only too pleased to hear.'

'Of course,' he said, clutching his hat and looking down at her with anxious eyes. 'But I've come from him, you see. The Chevalier.'

The Comtesse didn't speak, and I suddenly realized she couldn't. I said 'Is he all right?'

He turned to me with obvious relief. 'Hullo, Jacquot, isn't this terrible? But he's quite all right, I've left him tucked up in bed and the servants won't talk, he's quite safe.'

The Comtesse looked at him steadily. 'Are you saying you have taken the Chevalier into your own house?'

'Well, yes,' he said in a small voice, like he was scared he'd done something wrong. 'It's André. I mean it's the Chevalier.'

There was a moment's silence, then she glided across the room and said 'M. de Chouy, perhaps you would have the kindness to allow an old woman to embrace you.'

He did, and his whole face went pink. But at least it made him more coherent, he sat down and told us the boy had arrived a couple of hours ago, dressed like a common artisan and with some kind of working man in tow.

'Oh, not like you, Jacquot,' he said hastily, 'this man was really *rough*. But he helped the Chevalier out of Saint-Germain, so naturally we've taken him in too. They're quite safe.'

The Comtesse inclined her head. 'Not, I fear, for much longer. Once the authorities draw the covert of Saint-Germain they will realize the Chevalier has escaped and turn their attention to his friends. I'm afraid we must get him out.'

De Chouy looked anxious again. 'I'm not sure we can. The gates were all shut at noon, the Chevalier must have been one of the last in.'

We were all silent. Paris wasn't like Dax, the city walls were thirty feet high with little sentry boxes all round.

'The Seine?' said Charlot. 'Perhaps a boat.'

De Chouy shook his head apologetically. 'There are guard boats all along the boom.'

We went quiet again, and I became aware of clattering and voices outside, something happening down in the courtyard. I went to the window and saw a load of armed guards coming through the gate surrounding a grand sedan chair. Our own guards actually bowed.

'Naturally,' said the Comtesse, peering out to examine the livery. 'That is the Secretary of War, M. de Noyers himself.'

'Odd,' said de Chouy. 'I heard he was indisposed. He wasn't at the party, was he?'

The Comtesse glanced sharply at him, then turned casually back to the window. 'Perhaps, M. de Chouy, you would retire with M. Gilbert while I receive this visitor?'

I understood then and practically dragged him under the tapestry into the Comtesse's apartment next door. I listened at the gallery and heard servants down in the hall and the heavy-footed arrival of the men with the chair. I heard the servants ordered away, and guessed the visitor wanted privacy in order to get out. I heard the stairs creak as he came up alone, slow and painful till he reached the top. I heard Charlot saying deferentially 'Monseigneur,' then the salon door closing and Charlot leaning against it with a deep sigh.

'I say,' said de Chouy, 'do you think . . .?'

I said 'Shh, yes.'

We crept back to the door under the tapestry and squashed our heads right up against it, but could only hear the low rumble that was him and the light up-and-down trill that was her. The gallery door opened again, a mumble of voices, then footsteps coming towards us, and there was Charlot standing in the doorway.

He didn't show any surprise at finding us listening, I bet he'd been doing the same at the other door. He said 'He would like to see you, Monsieur.'

My throat clenched in panic, but Charlot was already turning and I'd got to follow him. He practically shoved me into the salon, said 'M. Gilbert,' and closed the door.

He was a blaze of scarlet in a high-backed chair like a throne. There was the red skull-cap, the white collar, the short, flat silver hair, the pointed face with stumpy moustache and little grey imperial, the long nose and cold eyes half-hooded with heavy lids. Everything was just as I'd seen it in the paintings, and I didn't need anyone to tell me I was looking at Armand Jean du Plessis, Cardinal-Duc de Richelieu.

He was hunched slightly forward, grasping the chair arms with long, thin hands, and for a moment he looked me up and down in silence. Then he said 'So you are the young man who spoiled my little fireworks party?'

I said 'Yes, Monseigneur.'

He smiled. It was an odd smile, sort of watery, like sunshine on a wet day. 'Then unless you wish to pay for the ruined display, perhaps you would like to explain what happened.'

He shifted in his chair, and I realized he wasn't leaning forward to be intimidating, he was actually in pain. It showed in his eyes too, a wariness that was almost like fear. Somehow that made me less frightened, it helped me get through my story right to the end.

He said 'You realize you're accusing Lieutenant Dubosc of the Musketeers of an attempted murder?'

I swallowed. 'If that's his name.'

He nodded, and there it was again, that watery glint in his eyes. 'Good.'

I said 'Then you'll support him. The Chevalier de Roland, I mean.'

He brought his hands together like somebody praying and touched the tips of his fingers to his lips. 'No.'

'But you know he's innocent . . .'

He gave me a tiny smile over his fingers. 'I know a great many things.'

I felt he knew what I'd done in the privy that morning. 'You've got the power to do it.'

He kept his hands together but brought them down to point at me like an arrow. 'You forget yourself, Monsieur. I am but a humble servant of His Majesty. His will is mine – in most things.' His hands opened slowly, and I almost saw the world sitting in them like a globe. 'But I am powerless in this. The Musketeers are the apple of His Majesty's eye, and he already believes me hostile to them.'

I remembered the glint in his eye and thought the King was probably right.

I said 'But if one of them speaks out. There's a young one, he saw it . . .'

'So I understand,' he said. 'I would guess his name was Darnier.'

'Then you can get him to speak for us.'

'Not even I,' said the Cardinal. "That is the name of a young Musketeer whose body was taken from the Seine this morning. They say he bore the marks of twenty-seven cuts.'

I saw his face flashing up in front of me, young and keen and truthful. Twenty-seven cuts then the filthy water of the Seine, and all for knowing even less than we did.

I said 'Then there's no hope.'

'There is if we prove motive,' he said. 'But for that we need to prove what the Chevalier suspects is true.' He heaved forward again, and I realized he was actually going to stand. He waved away my assistance, paced to the window and looked out over his world.

He said 'Some does not need proving. His Majesty and I have been interested in the Sedan for some time, and have little doubt some form of rebellion is planned.'

He touched his finger to the glass and began to trace little circles on its surface. 'But the Chevalier has discovered the conspiracy reaches even to Paris. That Fontrailles is involved. That the figurehead here is someone on whom His Majesty and I are not of one mind.'

There was only one man he could mean. My grandmother's eyes warned me to silence, but we were all thinking 'Cinq-Mars' so loudly we might as well have shouted.

'But to convince His Majesty I will need documents, treaties, signatures,' said the Cardinal. 'Without those I cannot act.'

I tasted disappointment in my mouth like flat wine.

He turned round slowly, a featureless black shape against the light of the window. 'Unless nobody knows that I know. Unless nobody knows you do either, as that would amount to the same thing. Unless they continue to believe you know only the names of

Fontrailles and Bouchard with no idea of their significance, and they are in no danger at all.'

I thought that was stupid. 'But there'll be an investigation, we'll have to explain to defend the Chevalier.'

'You must not defend the Chevalier,' he said. 'You may speak of what happened in the gardens, but of nothing else.'

Not speak in the boy's defence. Stand by and say nothing. I said 'I can't not –'

His hand flicked up instantly. 'A man can do anything in service of the state. But this will serve your Chevalier too.' He prowled away from the window, his robes sliding over the floor in great swirls of cloth. I wondered how much they weighed on him, and how thin he was underneath.

'Consider,' he said. 'We speak now and gain nothing. Anything the Chevalier says will appear only a wild story to cover his crime. Anything you say will be seen as a lie to protect him. If I speak without evidence, I forfeit the trust of His Majesty and alert his enemies to my knowledge. They go to ground, I learn nothing further, and we lose everything.'

It was like being back in that maze, banging into hedges everywhere I turned. I looked miserably at my grandmother, but she kept her eyes on Richelieu and seemed calm.

'Now suppose we stay silent,' he said. 'Consider that. These people continue to act, I watch and learn, and when I have evidence I go to His Majesty. The conspiracy is destroyed, these people exposed, and your Chevalier cleared. Does not that seem a better outcome?'

I said 'If he's not executed first.'

His eyelids fluttered in mild reproach. 'I shall of course ensure his escape.'

'Escape, Monseigneur?' said the Comtesse. 'But surely he is already out of Paris?'

The smile he gave her was almost flirtatious. 'Oh, my dear Madame. He is in the city, and you know it as well as I. He was in Saint-Germain last night with one of my green men, and today he is in the city and we must get him out.'

You can't pretend with someone who knows everything. I said 'How?'

He gave me a nod of approval. 'There are circumstances in which a gate might be left open. If a regiment needed to leave, for example, the Chevalier might depart in the train.'

I said 'Is there one?'

'There will be if I order it,' he said. 'Say the Porte Saint-Martin. Wait in the cooper's yard near the Lapin Gris at nine tonight and an officer will bring you into the corps. There is a woman too, is there not?'

I nodded.

'She can travel with the wives and followers. Keep her safe, Monsieur. She and my engineer are witnesses as much as your Chevalier.'

I hesitated. 'But if it doesn't happen? I mean if we're all in the cooper's yard . . .'

He straightened his robes and nodded my dismissal. 'Really, Monsieur,' he said. 'Who can you trust if you can't trust me?'

Eight

Albert Grimauld

Ah, that's how it goes when you know the right people, see? André cheered up like wine to hear we'd the Old Devil on our side, he was certain sure of our escape now. He'd been lying in bed moping, saying no, he didn't want no soup, no, he didn't want no nothing, and suddenly he was sitting up saying 'Where's my soup, Grimauld, you've bloody eaten it, haven't you?' Course I had, and very good it was too.

So he chucked his pillow at me and a pretty girl went to get him more, then he scrounged paper and a quill off young de Chouy, scribbled away with ink flying, then asked if I'd deliver a letter to a house on the Place Dauphine.

I said 'Got no choice, have I? Still waiting for payday.'

He said 'One day it'll come for both of us.'

Ah, I know, thinking of it now makes me want to spew. But not at the time, see, I went off thinking nothing but good. I found the house, banged at the kitchen door and told the stunted little maid I'd a letter to go into her mistress's own hand.

The maid looked at me with lower lip flopping and said 'The mistress is sick of a brain fever, the master says she's not to be disturbed.'

'Ah, but my letter will cure all that,' says I, oozing charm like a monk with a collecting box. 'You fetch her for me, my poppet, you'll see.'

'I'll get her companion,' says she, not being up to anything harder, nor likely to meet it with a face like that. 'Jeanette will know.'

Ah, now Jeanette was more like it, wide smile, plump where you like it, altogether nice-looking piece. There was no messing with her either. She says 'Is it M. de Roland?' I says 'Yes,' and she says 'Right,' then she's off again and back in a moment with a poor wilting creature it takes me a second to identify as the woman I last saw hacking at a hedge like a Lyons executioner. She rips open the letter and reads it, and oh my word, the difference. When she looks at me again, she's a lovely thing, ripe and blushing, I wouldn't have said no to it myself, always providing there weren't no axe in the vicinity.

'Is there an answer?' says I.

'Yes,' says she. 'That's the answer. Yes.'

It was all over her, that 'yes', like blossom on a tree. I found myself thinking of it all the walk back, and for a little time the world looked shiny and bright-coloured to me too, just the way the laddie saw it and it never ever was.

André de Roland

Letter to Anne du Pré, dated 14 October 1640

My very dearest,

You know what has happened. I dare to hope also that you know me innocent, for so I am, my darling, I give you my word before God.

I must, however, leave Paris until the truth can be established. I do not ask you to come with me, for I can offer you nothing but the life of a fugitive and a husband your family may not care to own. I do not ask, but if you were to be in the back room at the Lapin Gris by the Porte Saint-Martin at half after eight tonight I have a way out of the gate with a departing regiment and we could leave together and marry the next day.

I do not ask, my darling, because I have no right. If I did, I would beg.

Forever yours, whatever you decide,
A

Jacques Gilbert

My grandmother would have made the most brilliant general. She looked at the whole picture then went bang and bang at the weak points till there was nothing left to resist.

She knew we were bound to be followed, so she got a pass from the Cardinal for the Porte Saint-Antoine and appointed herself to be the distraction. While she was having the carriage prepared with as much fuss as possible, me and Charlot and Bernadette simply nipped over the back wall.

We needed horses on the other side, of course, but she'd fixed that too. She'd been out visiting the most irreproachable people she knew, and not one of the guards noticed she'd gone out in a coach-and-six and came back in a coach-and-four. Tonnerre and Héros were left in the stables of the Comte de Vallon, where we found them saddled and ready, complete with pistols and our baggage. I took Bernadette on Héros because Charlot would have just flattened him, then the three of us galloped straight for the Porte Saint-Martin.

It was gone eight when we found the cooper's yard. The gate was ajar, we were obviously expected, but there were no lanterns or torches inside, just great high walls and rows of barrels stacked in towering pyramids. I left Charlot and Bernadette with the horses, and stepped cautiously into the dark.

A bony hand smacked round my mouth, an arm jerked tight round my neck, I was bent back so violently I nearly lost my footing. I kicked out behind, but there weren't any legs there, the bastard was an expert, and my wounded knee just collapsed under me. I was being dragged helplessly back towards the barrels when a voice said urgently 'Leave him, Grimauld, it's Jacques.'

The pressure relaxed and I turned to see the green man from yesterday. De Chouy was there too, beaming with relief, and standing beside him was André. He was dressed as a cavalry officer but otherwise he was just the same, the boy like I'd last seen him. He was standing all right too, he didn't look hurt on the outside, but when I looked at his face I felt like I'd been kicked in the stomach.

He said 'Hullo,' in a tight sort of voice, then stepped forward and grabbed me. His clothes were cold but nothing else was, he hugged me like he used to when he was a little boy and me not much more. It was good to remember that afterwards.

He stepped back at last and introduced me to Grimauld, who

grinned cheerfully and said 'You want to watch your back more careful, I could have had you for dinner.'

'I doubt it, fellow,' said a voice, and there was the great shape of Charlot looming up in the dark. 'M. Gilbert did not walk into danger without reserves.'

Grimauld gawped at him. 'Sod me to the Sedan, where'd you grow *that*?'

'Never mind,' said André quickly. 'Is the street clear, Charlot?'

Charlot wrenched his eyes off Grimauld. 'Yes, Chevalier. I'll fetch Mademoiselle and the horses.'

'Good,' said André, and turned to me. 'Can you look after them while Crespin checks the gate's clear? I just need to nip off to the Lapin Gris.'

I stared. 'You're a bloody fugitive, you can't nip off anywhere.'

'It's only a hundred yards away,' he said, sticking out his chin in that way he'd had since he was ten. 'But Anne might be there, and I can't send anyone else.'

I was so shocked I could hardly think. 'You've told her we're leaving tonight?'

'Of course,' he said. 'I've told her everything. Why not?'

Anne du Pré

Extract from her diary, dated 14 October 1640

My chance came at dusk. Marie reported the way through the kitchen was clear, so Jeanette and I crept down the back stairs as cautiously as if this were a prison of the enemy. And so indeed it was, for at the bottom stood Florian, and behind him Bouchard.

I gave them good evening and made to pass, but Florian did not move and Bouchard stuck his leg across the passage as if we might try to run. I said 'Florian, I will be late for Compline,' but my voice faltered, for I saw by his face he guessed the truth.

'Compline?' he said, and dragged my hand from my side so that the bundle slipped beneath my cloak and slithered out on to the floor. 'With your luggage?'

I said 'You're hurting my wrist.'

'Come down then,' he said, and jerked me off the step to the floor. Behind him Bouchard retrieved my bundle, laid it on the chest and began to rummage inside.

I said 'Florian, you cannot allow –'

'Here it is,' said Bouchard. He was holding out André's letter.

Shock and hopelessness hit me both together. 'So now I am spied on by my own maid?'

Florian did not even flush. 'Marie acted as a loyal servant should,' he said, unfolding my letter as if it had been his own. 'I'm disappointed Jeanette has not done the same.'

Jeanette glared fearlessly at him. 'Monsieur, when I think what your sister has done for you . . .'

'Leave us, Jeanette,' I said quickly. 'This is not your affair, please go.'

She hesitated, but I whispered 'Please,' and she turned reluctantly back up the stairs.

'Have her watched,' said Bouchard absent-mindedly. He was gazing into my bundle as if something there absorbed all his attention. 'She's no more trustworthy than her mistress.'

Florian finished my letter and stared at me in sickening reproach. 'How could you, Anne? You betray us all.'

'She hasn't lied, anyway,' said Bouchard, and I saw with a horror I cannot describe that he was holding my diary. 'It's only the grandmother who knows, and she's no threat. D'Arsy swears she never got near the Cardinal last night, and no one's going to believe her now.'

He *read my diary*. He read the whole entry too, for as he lifted his eyes from the pages he allowed them to drift over my body with an air of amused curiosity. He did not in the least mind that I saw him do it, but met my revulsion with an insufferably familiar nod.

'Here,' he said, passing the diary to Florian. 'See what you're keeping under your roof.'

Florian began to read. I said wretchedly 'I haven't lied. I mean you no harm, neither does André. What harm can it be if I go to him? Please, just let me go.'

He looked up, eyes dark with shock. 'You wrote this? My sister wrote this?'

His hypocrisy was unbearable. I said 'I kissed my fiancé, Florian, I'm not colluding with murderers.'

'Neither am I,' he said at once. 'De Roland was only going to be abducted and kept out of the way, it's his own fault people got killed.'

But his voice trailed away, and I saw the beginnings of doubt. I seized his hand and said 'Florian, you know you can trust me, I've always defended you.'

Bouchard cut across me at once. 'Like you did in your diary? Poor feeble-minded Florian?'

Florian's weak little mouth hardened and my hope died. He said 'Go to your room, Anne. I'll decide what's to be done with you later.'

'Better lock it,' said Bouchard. 'We wouldn't want her slipping out to see her lover, would we?' He clapped on his hat and gave me a mocking little bow. 'Don't worry about de Roland, Mademoiselle. I'll see he's not kept waiting.'

Jacques Gilbert

She knew the time and gate, she even knew we were going with a troop column. Our only hope was she'd be in the Lapin Gris after all and the Comtesse had got it wrong.

We sent Grimauld. Anne would remember him, and if there were any kind of police about he'd spot them at once. André was sure there wouldn't be, he insisted Anne was innocent of everything and the ambush was all down to Florian.

I said 'And it was him kept you in that hut so long, was it? Or was that you?'

He hesitated. 'I was going to leave but –'

'She stopped you?'

It was too dark to see his face properly. 'You don't understand, a woman can't fake something like that.'

I said wearily 'If you say so.'

Footsteps running, one man, maybe two. Charlot took position by the gate, with me in the shadows opposite. André steered Bernadette behind the barrels.

The gate banged open, Grimauld shot skidding into the yard, and Charlot pounced on the stranger running behind. I sprang into the entrance, but there was no one else, I closed the gate and turned to see Charlot laying the man gently down on the stones. Even in the dark I could see the distinctive red breeches and blue coat of the Garde-Française.

'Crawling with them,' said Grimauld. 'The whole tavern packed with police, and these buggers prowling round outside.'

I helped Charlot lug the unconscious Garde away from the gate. I didn't want to look at André's face.

He said 'She must have been followed. She's trapped inside, I've got to get her out.'

Grimauld spat. 'She's not there, laddie, not unless she's grown a beard and put on eighty pounds. That's all that's waiting for you in that back room, I saw it through the window.'

The Garde seemed all right, he was breathing steadily. Behind me André said 'They must have intercepted the letter.'

'Christ in a chandelier,' said Grimauld in exasperation. 'I give it her myself, didn't I?'

'Then they can't know,' said André. 'She'd never tell them, never . . .'

Grimauld hushed him, and then we all heard it. More footsteps, slower and quieter, one man in shoes. Charlot crept back to the gate, but this time it opened cautiously and the man who came in was de Chouy.

He looked subdued. 'I say, I think there might be a problem with the gate.'

'Shut?' I said.

He shook his head. 'They've just opened it. But a lot more fellows are turning up to join the sentries, I saw Garde-Française and Musketeers with lanterns. It looks awfully as if they're going to check the column.'

'They are,' I said bitterly. 'We're expected.'

André was standing with his head down, and when he lifted it I had to look away. Anne was the one little bit he'd been able to salvage from his life, and now he'd lost that too.

He said 'You're right. I can't go out that way.' He didn't even sound like he cared.

In the distance we heard the hooves of the approaching column. None of us moved, we just stood and listened to a rescue operation that had suddenly lost all point.

Bernadette brushed down her dress. 'What must I do, Chevalier?'

He dragged his head round to look at her. 'Jacques can still take you. They're not looking for you, you'll be quite safe.'

'No,' she said. 'I mean what must we do to help you escape?'

He stared at her, but she looked back quite calmly, waiting for him to tell her his plan.

The van of the column was approaching the yard, and a moment later the gate pushed open to admit an elegant regimental officer.

'All here?' he said briskly. 'Good. I'm Danthan. The domestics can travel with my own, the gentlemen will ride with me, and I've another wagon for the woman. Everyone ready?'

André was still staring at Bernadette. Then he took off his hat, chucked it to Charlot and gave Danthan a little bow. 'Not quite,' he said. 'There's been a change of plan.'

Bernadette Fournier

The officer was clearly embarrassed at placing a woman of my apparent station with prostitutes, but in truth it did not trouble me. I was born in the army, Monsieur, and my mother had been happy there. I knew about such things.

These were the common women, not personal whores as my mother had been, but they did not seem to resent me. One even said 'He must love you very much, your man, for such measures to be taken,' and her face shone with happiness that a fellow woman should enjoy such fortune. I realized they believed me to be part of an elopement, and wished with all my heart that I were.

The wagon stopped as we neared the gate, and an older woman pulled back the canvas to see the cause of the delay. I was glad to see how close I was to the driver, for the Chevalier had said it was all down to me. I thought what little cause he had to trust any woman ever again and felt nothing but determination as I stroked the pistol hidden in my wrap.

'Why, they're searching us, girls!' said the older woman. 'Lanterns to every face. Imagine when they reach Mme de Mauban!'

There was much laughter at this, but then one woman said in a voice suddenly hushed 'It's de Roland, isn't it? Why else would they go to such lengths? Your man is André de Roland.'

I said quickly 'Is it likely, Mesdames, a woman like me?' but no one laughed. Then the older woman reached out and twitched aside my cloak, revealing the fine gown of last night underneath.

'Perhaps it is,' she said. 'Or perhaps there are two noblemen in this city pursued by every guard this side of the Seine?'

Further denial would have been foolish when they knew the truth as well as our enemies who were searching outside. I said only 'He is not in the train.'

Their eyes seemed to glisten in the dark. Then a little dark woman leaned forward and whispered 'So it's true? He cares about people like us, as they say? It's true?'

I would not pretend to women my own kind. I said 'He is not my lover. But let me tell you how I first met the Chevalier and you shall tell me if he cares.'

So I told the whole story of that first day and what he had done. They listened with mouths open, and all the while I watched through the gap in the canvas and saw how every man was scrutinized under the lantern before he was allowed to pass. As I finished we were almost at the gate, and there was our officer being examined, the one who was Richelieu's *créature*, and after him came my own Jacques. The guard clearly recognized him, for a smile of satisfaction appeared on his bony face as he guessed the Chevalier must be nearby. The lantern was swung with eagerness to Jacques' neighbour, but it was only Charlot and the light passed to the next man with a droop of disappointment.

'You're fortunate, Mademoiselle,' said the older woman. 'I've lived thirty years in this world and the most a man's ever given me is pox.'

The back canvas was ripped aside and a lantern shone among us as it came our own turn to be searched. They were serious about it too, for one of the guards climbed clear into the wagon for a better look, despite the abuse he had of us for his reward. The little dark woman thrust his hand down her dress and said 'What do you think,

Sieur, you think I might be a man?' There was much laughter and ribaldry, but through the open canvas at our back I glimpsed the servants' wagon stopped behind our own, with Grimauld himself sat boldly beside the driver. He was watching our search, and across the heads of the cackling women our eyes met.

Our guard left us in embarrassed haste, our wagon moved on, and beneath us the wheels changed to a deeper rumble as we crossed the moat. My hand grasped the pistol, for now was when it must happen. We were far enough away for a watching man to see what the crush had so far concealed, and my body tensed with expectation.

My heart jumped at the shout, and I strained my neck to look again through the rear canvas. The servants' wagon behind us blocked the gateway as it was searched, but to one side stood a figure in the uniform of the Garde-Française pointing his sword at our retreating vehicle. He shouted again 'There! Man under that wagon!'

Guards ran from the gate in pursuit, and our wagon slowed as the driver looked behind. I reached through the canvas, dug the pistol into his side, and said 'Drive faster.'

His eyes dropped to the gun then lifted to my face in astonishment. 'They're telling us to stop.'

I prodded the gun into his ribs and said again 'Drive faster!'

He hesitated, but behind me the opening was now crowded with other women, and the oldest said 'It's de Roland, Jean. Do as she says.'

He turned again to face forward. 'Put your gun away, *fifille*. Drive faster it is.'

Jacques Gilbert

She was only just in time. The guards were halfway over the bridge when the wagon gave a great lurch and started to rattle faster down the Faubourg, scattering our cavalry to either side. But it couldn't last long. As Grimauld's wagon cleared the gate, the bottleneck opened behind it and mounted guards began to clatter through after those on foot, all waving and shouting 'Stop!'

A church, we needed a church, André had said the first we came to. A spire was coming up behind houses on our left, I couldn't see an entrance but it would have to do. Bernadette's wagon was already slowing, I let Grimauld's draw closer behind it, then turned to Danthan and yelled 'Now!'

Danthan nodded, then urged his cavalry to close round both wagons, screening them from the pursuing guards by a thick ring of his own men. I saw with relief Bernadette was staying put, and knew her companions had decided to help.

But the servants' wagon was slowing, and Danthan's cavalry beginning to overtake it, we'd got to get clear before our screen disappeared. Charlot was already wheeling in tight to the driver's box, I dug hard in the stirrups and leaned over behind him, then Grimauld rose to a crouch on his seat, Charlot reached out his arm and –

Albert Grimauld

– pulled me off like a giant lifting a baby, he hoiked me over his horse's neck and down on the ground, hooves and wheels pounding all round me, oh my word. Gilbert dragged me tight to his horse's flank, then 'Now,' he says, and makes the animal up and ruddy rear, shoving me smack under it to the side of the road. I'm clear of the cavalry, clear of the wagons, but here's them mounted guards pelting up to join the party, so it's whoops and the old quick turn then I'm off and running, head down and legs pumping to get me to that church.

'There he goes,' yells Gilbert, and others take up the cry like hunting noblemen. I hear some taking off after me, but they're no match for a man used to be in my line of work, and never you mind what that was, what matters is I know how to run. I spring over that wall and into Saint-Laurent, and that gives the buggers pause, thank you, I'm in sanctuary and thumbing my nose and they knows it.

So I'm up and along the whole length of the ruddy building, then there's a handy side door and I'm shooting sharp out of it, round the front, over another wall, then it's off with the black cloak and hat and stroll round the corner back to the column, Grimauld the harmless artisan coming to gawp at a bunch of soldiers playing silly games on the Rue Saint-Martin.

Many of the guards turned off straight after Grimauld, but others hastened to surround us and demanded angrily of my driver why he had not stopped. We had a plan for this, Monsieur, I was to have dropped and fled with Jacques so my driver could claim he had been threatened, but he said he was more than equal to a pack of red-legs, and so indeed he proved.

'How could I stop with you spooking my horses?' he said, sounding quite as angry as they. 'Running after us and shouting, no wonder the poor beasts legged it. I stopped as soon as I could, didn't I?'

The guards were ill content, and still insisted on poking beneath our wagon, but it was obvious to everyone that the fugitive had already escaped into the church, and after only a brief inspection they left us to join their fellows surrounding Saint-Laurent. Only one seemed unconvinced, the Garde-Française who had first given the alarm and now reached up to mount and join us inside.

The women gave groans of derision, and the small dark one said 'How many times, boy? Would you like to search my fanny in case your fugitive is hiding inside?'

The Garde said gravely 'You honour me, Madame,' then turned to me and said 'Well done, Bernadette. Do you think your driver might go on now?'

I asked Jean to continue, but when I turned back to the interior the women were all staring in total bewilderment.

I said 'Mesdames, it is my honour to introduce to you André, Chevalier de Roland.'

Jacques Gilbert

We left the column just north of the Faubourg, picked up Grimauld at the crossroads, and rode together to the farmhouse where we were to meet my grandmother.

It was only a small farm, fields of parsnips and straggly artichokes, and orchards of apples and pears, but it belonged to the

Rolands and was where our vegetables came from every day. The people were certainly welcoming, and when André introduced himself they threw the door open for all of us, even Grimauld, who looked like something you'd want to chuck stones at till it went away. It was a pity de Chouy had stayed behind, he was much the most respectable, but André wanted someone to make sure that Garde was all right when he came round and found himself stuck in a cooper's yard without his uniform.

They were good people, the Porchiers, a middle-aged couple with three strapping boys who all had the same hair and voices so it was hard to tell them apart. They didn't ask any questions, not even with André dressed like a Garde-Française, they just gave us bowls of leek soup and sat us down by the fire to wait for the Comtesse in peace and quiet.

It was the oddest sort of lull, like waiting between one life ending and another beginning. André gazed into the fire with eyes that didn't blink, and I don't know what he was seeing, he'd lost too much for me to guess. I remember saying 'You've still got me,' and he gripped my hand and said 'I know.' Bernadette sat on the floor leaning against my legs like a cat, and I remember thinking none of the other stuff mattered really, I'd settle for this, what I'd got right now.

Then the Comtesse arrived. She raised her eyebrows at André's uniform, blinked at Bernadette's informality, and recoiled at the sight of Grimauld, but otherwise she was her usual self and not in the least surprised or impressed that we'd made it. She dispatched Bernadette and Grimauld to assist in the kitchen, then sat down with determination and we knew she'd got something to say.

She got straight to the point. 'His Eminence has spoken to the King and the situation is as we feared. There are formidable witnesses ranged against us, condemnation is inevitable, and the sentence can only be for death.'

André sat with his elbows on the table, the sleeves of the Garde's coat flopping down his arms. He laced his hands together tightly and lowered his head.

I said 'What charge?'

'Murder,' she said, with a kind of bitter lightness. 'They claim the

Chevalier killed a Musketeer who tried to stop him duelling. Bouchard's friends have volunteered evidence to that effect, and it is given credibility by the fact the Chevalier has already publicly issued two challenges in Paris. You are said to have been his second, but no one blames an aide for defending his master. The Chevalier has no such excuse, and will lose both his life and his property.'

André's head was still down. 'Then it's lucky I don't have anything. Even Dax is in my uncle's name.'

'Now it is,' said the Comtesse. 'But do you not realize he could die at any moment? If it happens while you are under this sentence then everything will be confiscated. His house, the Auvergne estates, the farms, Dax, everything. You are his sole heir.'

There was a little silence. A log hissed in the grate.

André lifted his head. 'Not quite. There's an alternative.'

She nodded. 'Exactly. The Cardinal has agreed to support M. Gilbert's legitimation, and if we can keep him clean of this business there is no obstacle to his inheritance. But of course he will have to remain in Paris, and we must disassociate him from you in every way.'

The words blurred, it was only André's sharp intake of breath that was real. I said 'I can't. You can't ask me that.'

She smiled tightly. 'You asked for the rights of a gentleman, these are the responsibilities that go with them.'

I said 'I don't want it, I'm not having it.'

She sighed. 'It may not be for long. These people will act, the Cardinal will obtain his evidence and the Chevalier will be cleared. But we cannot count on it to happen in time, which is why I must rely on you.'

I stood and blundered over to the fire. 'I won't, I'm not leaving André.'

'You must,' said André. He came and put his hands on my shoulders. 'Think what it would mean if you don't. It's not just my grandmother or the servants. Think of Dax. If the Crown takes it they might give it to one of my accusers. They might give it to Bouchard.'

My mother was there. My mother, my little sister, my friends, everything we'd bloody fought for those four long years. I looked blindly round the room, trying to wipe out the picture of Bouchard strutting round Ancre, treating my mother the way he'd treated Bernadette. I turned desperately back to André, and saw there were tears in his eyes.

'It's not for ever,' he said, and tried to smile. 'My grandmother's right, I'll be cleared somehow. But you must do it, Jacques. Please.'

I said 'You've got nowhere to go. You'll be alone.'

His grip tightened on my shoulders. 'Then you'll do it?'

I said 'Yes, all right, bloody yes if I've got to,' and I think I was crying too.

Bernadette Fournier

No, Monsieur, I did not blame him. Yes, he had said he was free to love me and now he was not, but he parted from me with great tenderness and I knew he did not do so willingly. When they drove him away in the carriage with Charlot and Madame, his face was wet with tears.

'What now, laddie?' asked Grimauld cheerfully. Madame had given the Chevalier gold before she left and Grimauld was clearly happy to stay with him till it ran out.

The Chevalier had difficulty wrenching his mind back to our situation. 'We'll stay here tonight, and then tomorrow . . . tomorrow . . .'

I said 'I have an aunt in Compiègne, she will take us in while you decide.'

'Yes,' he said, and nodded firmly. 'Compiègne. Thank you, that's what we'll do.'

He walked back to the farmhouse with Grimauld, but I stood a moment and looked back towards Paris. There were fewer street lanterns in those days, and to me she seemed a great black monster in the distance, smelling of evil and corruption in every way there is.

I was no one to judge it, Monsieur, I was a girl in a borrowed dress and nothing beneath it but my naked self, yet I looked at the city and spoke as if it could hear me. I said 'You think you have beaten him, but one day he will come back and you will tremble at what you have done.'

Above me the nightbirds called, and a fresh wind stirred the apple trees, but Paris was silent as stone. 'Do you hear me?' I whispered again to the darkness. 'He is *coming back*.'

PART TWO

The Fugitive

Nine

Jacques Gilbert

They hanged him in effigy, did you know? I had to stand on the Place de Grève and watch them read a long denunciation then hang a dressed-up straw figure they pretended was André de Roland. When the judges had gone Bouchard and his friends batted the figure about between them to make it swing.

It was meant to stay hanging for a week, but I sneaked back that night with de Chouy and his friends to cut it down. We took it home, removed the clothes to make it just straw again, then burned it in the courtyard on a kind of pyre. I gave away the clothes too. It was a shame, André loved that doublet, but I could never see him wearing it again.

They were good friends to me that night, de Chouy, Lelièvre and de Verville. They said I was one of them now, they made me call them Crespin and Gaspard and Raoul, and came to see me every day. Even the Comtesse liked them. They were young and silly, but they brought a gaiety to the Hôtel de Roland I think she'd missed. She mocked them sometimes and called them 'the Puppies', but they thought that was the most wonderful joke, and started using it themselves. They'd greet each other with 'Good morning, M. le Puppy,' like it was an exclusive society anyone would want to join.

It made the loneliness less awful having them around, but really we were just passing the time while we waited for news. Every day we hoped the conspirators would move, the Cardinal would pounce, then André would be cleared and come home. Nothing ever happened.

We knew he was all right, he sent a letter under cover to Crespin to tell us he was at Compiègne, but it made me ache to read it. He tried to sound brave, he said he was growing a beard and moustache that made him very handsome, but I could see the pain in every line.

At the end he just wrote 'I miss you', and that was the only thing that felt real. I went into his room that night to feel him sort of near, but it was all still and silent, there was dust on the bedcover, and his water jug had dried till there was nothing in it but a dead spider. It was hard to believe he was ever coming back.

Anne du Pré

Extract from her diary, dated 12 February 1641

I am locked in my room again. It is my own fault, I know how rigidly Florian insists on my courtesy to his friends, but I simply could *not* keep my temper.

Bouchard provokes me on purpose. He has no need to come to the salon, he always conducts his business in private with Florian, but he loves to see me sitting quietly in the corner, compelled to smile and make polite responses he must know are insincere. Today was worse than ever, for he had just heard the news that Jacques is to be legitimated and decided to relieve his bitterness by abusing André. He laughed at his being brother to a stable boy, and said had he known it he would never have sullied his sword with such filth.

I said 'Then it is fortunate it was only the Chevalier whose sword was sullied.'

The look on his face was almost worth it. Florian apologized so effusively I almost blushed myself, but I said 'It's true, isn't it? What can be wrong with saying what is true?'

I should have known better. Florian compelled me to make a humble confession to that loathsome Père Ignace, who I know perfectly well is Bouchard's friend and will undoubtedly tell him everything I was forced to say, and now I am confined to my room for a week. There was no point appealing to Father. He never even speaks to me these days, and the only reason he hasn't sent me to a convent is that he still hopes I can give him an advantageous marriage.

Jeanette thinks he might do it yet. She was allowed in to braid my hair for bed, and was insistent I should be more careful. She said

'It's a miracle you get away with what you do, Mademoiselle. I've known a lady put away just for speaking to the wrong man.'

I said 'I don't care. What kind of life is this, Jeanette? I can't even stir outside without Florian or my father, how can anything be worse?'

But it could, for then she gave me her own news and with it the death of my last hope. My letter to the Comtesse has been returned unopened, and Jeanette's messenger said they'd asked nicely for me not to trouble them again. I cannot blame them, I know what they must think me, but tonight the unfairness *hurts*.

'Oh, it's not so bad, my lamb,' said Jeanette, brushing out my hair with long, soothing strokes. 'The Chevalier will know the truth one day, he'll come and help you in the end.'

I said 'I'm not asking his help, Jeanette, how can I? It's we who should be helping him.'

For a moment there was only the purr of the brush. Then she said 'Perhaps we can. What would the Chevalier give, do you think, for a friend to be living right in the house of the enemy and learning their secrets?'

I said 'They'll never trust me enough for that.'

She started to plait. 'Well and perhaps they won't, Mademoiselle, with you sitting glaring as if you wanted to eat them. But now I ask you, what harm would it do to make yourself a little more pleasant? If you were to hint to M. Florian you were coming round to his way of thinking, mightn't that make it easier for him to confide in you?'

I said 'That would be dishonest.'

She jabbed in the first pin. 'And what would you call it when your brother reproaches you for disloyalty, or sends you his confessor to tell him what a bad girl you've been? What would you call it when their friends tell lies about our Chevalier and get away with it because nobody finds the means to bring them down?'

I thought of André driven into hiding in some faraway country, and all because he trusted me and met me when I asked. If anything in my useless life can help him then suddenly it would have both purpose and meaning. I said 'Just tell me, Jeanette. Tell me what I can do.'

She looked up from the braid and in the mirror our eyes met. 'Lie, Mademoiselle,' she said. 'You must learn to lie.'

Nothing's worse than doing nothing. The Comtesse kept saying 'Leave it to the Cardinal,' but I needed something to fight.

The Puppies were the same. They'd come bouncing round every morning asking if we'd got orders from André and obviously we never had. Raoul used to pass on every scrap of gossip he heard at court, saying 'Does it help, Jacquot?' so yearningly I was desperate to say 'yes.' Crespin and Gaspard even took to visiting Le Pomme d'Or, but they never saw any of the people we were interested in and guessed they were meeting somewhere else. We weren't getting anywhere at all.

My only hope was my uncle. He was poxed, of course, but he'd got battle experience, he'd been the deadliest swordsman in Paris in his day. I thought he'd be like an older and wiser André, and just the person to guide us. He spent most of the winter in the Auvergne having a new kind of mercury treatment, but he came back that February and my grandmother finally arranged for me to meet him. It was only meant to be about getting his permission for the legitimation, but what I wanted was a leader and a plan, and as I set off for the Place Royale I was hoping to find both.

I'd been warned what to expect, but it was still a shock when I was finally shown into his room. It was kept warm and very dark, the walls rippling and flickering in the light from the enormous fire. There was sweet apple wood burning on it, but it couldn't quite disguise the other smell, a faint, sickly sort of rottenness like badly cured pork. The Comte sat in a padded chair by the hearth. There was a little table beside him with a decanter of carved glass that twinkled and sparkled in rainbow flashes in the firelight, but he himself was in shadow.

I made polite noises and waited.

He leaned forward and I saw the mask. It wasn't a full one, just a thing like a bright blue bird's head with a big beak where his nose should have been, and ending abruptly at his upper lip. His mouth and chin looked quite normal, he could have been just an ordinary person at a masked ball.

He said 'Sit down, Jacques, it's good to see you at last. I was beginning to think you were avoiding me.'

The shock snatched my breath away, because it was my father's voice. This great hunger I hadn't even known was there leapt almost babbling into my throat.

'Don't be nervous,' he said, pouring us both wine. 'I'm not going to refuse you, am I?'

His beard even looked the same, I wanted to snatch the mask away and see my father's face. I sat down quickly and said 'It's a lot to ask, to make me your heir.'

'Is it?' he said. His hand trembled as he passed me the glass, and a little drop of wine spilled on to his black glove. 'Poor André seems to have ruled himself out, doesn't he?'

It was one of those Spanish fortified wines, a kind of Jerez, and it walloped through my head in a warm buzz. I said 'It wasn't his fault though, was it, Monseigneur?'

'Wasn't it?' he said, and his mouth smiled. 'Tell me, would you have handled this the way André did?'

Of course I wouldn't, but I was going to be a Roland, so I said 'I hope so, Monseigneur.'

'A pity,' he said. 'This family could do with an injection of common sense and I rather hoped you might be it.'

The wine caught in my throat and sprang back out again. I wiped my chin furiously, but when I looked up he was still regarding me with courteous attention. I said cautiously 'You don't think André's sensible?'

He looked into the fire. 'I think he's a very fine young man.'

It wasn't an answer. I didn't think I could say that, though, I mean he was Comte de Vallon, so I sipped my wine and tried to look wise.

He said 'I knew André was doomed as soon as I met him. Honour's a great thing, but not when it blinds you to your own survival.'

It was all right for me to think that sometimes, but I felt uncomfortable hearing it said in my father's voice. I said 'You think he should have left the whole thing alone?'

He sighed and rumpled his hair. 'I would have. So I think would you.'

I remembered saying to the Comtesse that it was nothing to do with us, and quickly looked away. 'But we've got to beat them now, haven't we? It's the only way to save André.'

'Oh yes,' he said. 'We've no choice now. But how are you going to do it?'

I'd hoped he'd tell me. I said 'I don't know. I thought of going to see André –'

'Don't do that,' he said quickly. 'Do you want to lead them on to him?'

I stared. 'The guards aren't following us any more.'

He got up and went to the window. I went after him, and was oddly disconcerted to find he was taller than me.

'Look,' he said, and jerked his head out at the Place Royale. 'What do you see?'

There were loads of people wandering about outside, but I noticed one man standing still, holding a horse's bridle like he was waiting for someone. His mouth was shut so I couldn't see the jagged teeth, but I knew the squashed nose and mottled face, I'd seen them close enough when I stabbed his arm in that bloody maze.

'His name's Pirauld,' said my uncle. 'He's valet to your friend Lavigne and a very unpleasant character indeed. Rumour has it he brings his master whores from the streets and they're never seen again. He hung about here when André was in Saint-Germain, and I had the servants make enquiries.'

I said 'But if it's you he's watching . . .'

'It's not,' he said. 'I saw him arrive when you did.'

He'd been looking out of the window. He'd been watching for me like he really wanted to meet me. Then I realized what he was implying and said 'Why . . . ?'

He shrugged. 'My guess is Bouchard. André's no danger to them now, but that man has a personal grudge he'll want paid in blood. Visit André and you'll bring it on him.'

I said 'Maybe Crespin . . .'

He was already turning back to the fire. 'De Chouy? No. He stood next you at the mock execution, don't use him for anything. Have you other friends they don't know about?'

I said 'Yes, there's –'

His hand came up so fast it was like André in a parry. 'Don't tell me. Trust no one. Don't make André's mistakes, Jacques. If you want to survive you've got to forget honour and loyalty and doing anything openly. Stay quiet and out of sight.'

I said miserably 'Then what can I do?'

He sat back down. 'Get André out of France.'

'He won't go. He wants to bring down these conspirators.'

'He can't,' said my uncle bluntly. 'Neither can you, neither can I. Forget about saving the state, you've got to think about saving yourselves.'

I hated him for being right. 'But I want to fight.'

For a second something gleamed in the dark eyeholes of the mask, then he turned back to the decanter. 'There's only one way to fight this one and that's on the battlefield. Richelieu's right, the rebellion's coming, it's only a matter of months.'

'Good,' I said. 'When they're out in the open we can expose them and André can come home.'

'Amen to that,' he said tiredly. 'But don't you see the flaw in that reasoning?'

I looked doubtfully at him. He reached for my glass and began to refill it.

'They're everywhere,' he said. 'Outside your house, outside mine, in the bed of the King. They're in the Sedan. They're in Soissons territory in Champagne. They're among the Huguenots, itching to avenge La Rochelle. And beyond the borders lies the Empire and Spain.'

He handed me the glass. 'That's your flaw, Jacques. You're assuming we'll win.'

Carlos Corvacho

From his interviews with the Abbé Fleuriot, 1669

Now, this is nice, isn't it, Señor? Quite missed our little sessions, I have really. It's been a pleasure talking over old times, remembering my gentleman and yours, and now here we both are again and the story still going on as if it never stopped.

No, no more it did, Señor, nor for my Capitán. We'd had a quiet few months, but that wasn't my gentleman's choice, he'd have been up and back where the action was if it weren't for the surrender terms after the Battle of Dax. We weren't to take up arms against the French for a year, if you remember, and that's a long time in a war.

But there are other ways, if you understand me, and my Capitán was still the Don Miguel d'Estrada whether he'd a sword in his hand or no. We were set to work in Madrid, Señor, in Rome, in London and in Brussels, but our purpose was always the same, and that was to cause an insurrection in France.

But you know how it is with the French, Señor, the business was on, off, on, off, every month a different story, and at the end of 1640 they were jumpy as cats. The Cardinal had his eye on the Sedan all right, he'd caught a courier from England, tortured him too, would you believe, and was looking at Bouillon very beady indeed. But much worse for us was a silly brawl that gave away our main contact to a passing nobleman, and looking like to uncover our whole network in Paris.

Now that's serious, Señor, there's no chance for the rebellion without Paris in our pockets. Old Louis wasn't going to chop his First Minister and sign away territory to Spain because Champagne was ablaze, we needed insurrection within his own gates and men at court to guide it. My Capitán said we should reason with this nobleman, show him peace with Spain was best for France, but our courier said 'I don't think so, Señor. It was André de Roland.' My Capitán looks at him a moment, then rolls up our map of France without a word.

It wasn't often he was wrong, Señor, but next news comes de Roland's discredited and on the run, that he can say what he likes and no one will believe him. My Capitán demands all the details, but when he's got them he just walks out and bless me if he doesn't come back drunk. Not a word of a lie, Señor, I find him in his chamber that night doing point exercises against his shadow on the wall. Never mind the state he's in, the sword never wavers, he holds it as steady as if he's all of a piece with the steel. There's a moth on the curtains, and he twirls to go at it overhanded over his shoulder, and there it is skewered on the tip of his rapier. He says 'You see, Carlos? You see how clean that is?'

I say 'Of course it is, I oiled it only this morning.'

He sits on the bed and rocks with laughter. 'Dear Carlos,' he says to me, and he does, Señor, he says 'Dear Carlos.' Then he looks at the wall as if he sees pictures in it and says 'To hell with politics. Why can't we just go back to war?'

Well, I thought we would, Señor, I thought all these upsets would scare off our temperamental French allies for good and all, but my Capitán says no, if there's one thing can make a flock of birds start flying in the same direction it's fear. And he was right, Señor, they were all frightened now. Soissons, Bouillon, Orléans, all the big ones, yes and young Cinq-Mars too, it seems to them their only hope is to band together and make the revolt happen. 1641 comes and we're looking a lot more like business.

The Conde-Duque likes it, he says we can promise seven thousand troops and as much again in a joint Imperial Army, to say nothing of fifty thousand pistoles for the campaign. That's more than enough, Señor, what with the Sedan's own army and the promised uprising in Champagne. My Capitán's only fear is it starting before the 8th of June when our year runs out, and him not able to fight himself.

'There's no danger of that, Señor,' I tell him. 'Look how slow they've been so far. You don't think it'll happen before the autumn, do you?'

He smiles and says 'I think you should pack a bag.'

Anne du Pré

Extract from her diary, dated 26 March 1641

I suspect their business is coming to a head. Bouchard, Lavigne and d'Arsy were closeted with Florian for quite two hours today, murmuring in low, important voices. Father never attends these meetings, I think he prefers not to know what they discuss, but today even he joined them briefly before going to the Chambres des

Comptes. The others came into the salon afterwards and I hoped they would speak of their affairs, but all I heard was d'Arsy saying 'June's not so long, we can wait, can't we?' before Bouchard stopped him.

He still does not trust me, and I'm not sure what more I can do. I have disgusted myself with the submissiveness I have shown to Florian. I have had Father take me to the Couvent de la Visitation to ask spiritual help for my womanly errors, although the hypocrisy of it makes me *sick*. I have voluntarily confessed to Père Ignace, and the lies I have told that abominable man make me blush at the memory. All of this *must* be going back to Bouchard, but he seems determined only to force me into a reaction that will prove me a liar. He is rude to Clement, he makes disparaging remarks about Jeanette, he even manages snide references to garden sheds, and I can do nothing but smile and endure it.

But today was the worst. I thought myself safe at first, for he seemed to have other things on his mind, and scarcely acknowledged my presence before announcing to the others that Gondi has received a letter from the Duchesse de Chevreuse.

D'Arsy frowned. 'That's a devil of a risk. Doesn't she know what happened to la Vigerie? All our couriers are watched.'

Bouchard waved dismissively. 'I expect she found some lovesick English boy to take it. There was nothing incriminating anyway, only a little society news.'

His eyes slid casually round to me, and I felt my mouth suddenly dry.

'Oh, do tell,' said Lavigne eagerly. 'La Chevreuse has the best nose for gossip.'

'Her eyes aren't bad either,' said Bouchard. 'And she says de Roland isn't in England.'

There was a moment's silence, then d'Arsy made an exclamation and sat up straight.

'But he must be!' squeaked Lavigne. 'He can't be in Rome, Gondi would have heard. He's an exile, he couldn't be anywhere else without Guise knowing.'

'Oh, he could,' said Bouchard. 'Has it occurred to you he could have stayed in France?'

He was watching me, I knew he was, I felt his eyes on my skin.

D'Arsy gave a sudden grunt of amusement. 'God, I wonder. He could have, you know, he's audacious enough.'

'That's one word for it,' said Bouchard.

Lavigne emitted a shrill peal of laughter. Bouchard turned to look at him, and for a moment they shared a smile.

Florian watched them wonderingly. 'But, Monseigneur, why does it matter? He isn't any danger to us now, is he?'

'Oh, hang the danger,' said Bouchard. 'I'm talking about honour. D'Arsy has a little something to settle with him too, don't you, d'Arsy?'

D'Arsy looked up. 'I owe him a fair fight, which is what I engaged for, God help me. What's your excuse?'

Bouchard's face darkened crimson. 'He murdered Dubosc, didn't he? Doesn't friendship mean anything to you?'

It means everything to Florian. He said at once 'It's justice, d'Arsy. Monseigneur is thinking of us all. I should have seen that. His interest is only in justice.'

My poor brother. Bouchard patted his shoulder as if he were a favourite spaniel, and said 'You see, d'Arsy? Justice. Now how shall we see about getting it?'

It was clear something vile was intended, yet my heart pounded harder and firmer as I realized my opportunity. Bouchard may have staged this conversation to test my reaction, but for the first time I had a chance to learn something important.

I affected to be quite untroubled, and served them myself with wine and sweetmeats so they need not be restrained by the presence of servants. I smiled at disgusting Lavigne, I polished Bouchard's glass, I even allowed d'Arsy to flirt with me, but none of them seemed to know their next move. Jacques has never left Paris, neither has that nice M. de Chouy. The Comte has been to the Auvergne, but d'Arsy is quite sure that means nothing. He said they'd watched the place in case the Comte led them abroad, and if André had been hiding there his men would certainly have known.

'Then where?' said Lavigne. 'It's too ridiculous. He's a gentleman, he can't go to ground like a rabbit.'

Bouchard's hand was arrested on its way to the sweetmeat tray.

Then he picked up a honeyed almond and tossed it in his palm. 'Maybe he can. Maybe we should forget the drawing rooms and start looking in the gutter. You forget, Messieurs, he has friends there too.'

'Not that we'd know,' said Lavigne disdainfully.

'Oh, I don't know,' said Bouchard. 'The one I'm thinking of might rather appeal to you. Someone we know he befriended. Someone we know disappeared only a couple of days before he did. Someone we wouldn't mind seeing again on our own account.'

It may have been a trick of the candles, but I thought Lavigne's mouth looked suddenly wet. 'But you said it yourself, she's gone. You said it didn't matter, no one would listen to a slut like that. You said she wasn't worth looking for.'

Bouchard threw the nut in his mouth and smiled as he chewed. He said 'She is now.'

Albert Grimauld

Ever looked after a powder store? Trust me, it's a piece of cat's piss compared to looking after André de Roland. Stick him in the remotest place in Europe and he'd still find a way of drawing trouble like another man draws breath.

And remote is right, oh my word. We were in a little village called Saint-Jean aux Bois, buried deep in the Forest of Compiègne with nothing and its bastards for miles. It was built round the old Abbey, see, proper-walled and fortified with gates, but nothing worth the nicking inside, nothing but a church, a bakery, a smithy, and one little inn for the comfort of the lucky buggers who were passing straight through. Even the monks had scarpered for the city, and I couldn't blame them.

The inn itself now, that wasn't so bad. Bernadette did the serving, me and André did the heavy work, and a softer billet I've never had. It was old, I'd say, half-timbering and thatch, but good stone floors against the damp and all kept clean as a bride's dress. There were flowers in baskets and climbing up the walls, shutters done up blue and yellow, it was pretty as a painting and twice as snug. Set the thing down in Amiens or somewhere worth living and I'd of been ready to marry the widow and move right in.

Ah, now, pass the wine and I'll tell you about Martine. Sweet-tempered lady, soft little voice, put you in mind of a plump wood-pigeon. She was the wrong side of forty, but then I was more than thirty myself, and that's when you want the older ones, see, you want a woman won't rob you blind and run off with your junior officer. But she was sweet with it too, Martine. She'd a weak chest and maybe that had to do with it, but there was nothing harsh about her, never raised her voice to me, not once. There was times I thought 'Sod Amiens and anything like it, a man could go further and fare worse.'

It would have been all pudding that place if it weren't for André. We kept him out of sight while his wound was mending and his whiskers growing, but once he was out we were stuffed six ways to Stralsund. He could make his voice rough and his walk humble, he could do everything people said he could, but he was different in his head and it showed. He was opening doors for people, he was bowing and calling them 'Madame', he was looking at them bright-eyed and perky, and drawing attention like a nun in a whorehouse.

And we couldn't do a thing with him. Bernadette used to fair yell at him, she'd say 'Chevalier, you are going to get yourself thrown in prison or killed,' and he'd try his heart out for days afterwards, but next thing there'd be the wheelwright's wife fretting about her son in Germany, and there'd be André sitting down to help her write a ruddy letter. He never meant no harm, no, nor saw it neither, but he had 'gentleman on the run' writ over his head like fireworks in the sky.

Ah, but a man's real self has to come out somehow, and he'd worse things fermenting inside him nor nice manners. Poor little bugger, he'd been shafted from here to Hesdin, lost his reputation and everything he owned, and nothing to be done about it but wait tables. He was twisting and turning in on himself like a sizzling fuse, and looking every which way for something to fight.

We kept his sword hid in the stable, but he was forever nipping into the woods to do what he called his 'exercises', and I reckon he was hoping to run into the bandits we'd got swarming all over the forest. He never did, they'd the sense to avoid anywhere with walls and people, but he took the threat of it very serious and made us take guns whenever we went out. He was worried for the women too, the inn being stuck away near the old abbey and nothing but the smithy within call, so he bought a wheel-lock musket in Compiègne and taught Bernadette to load and fire it herself.

But the danger was a sight closer to home nor that. Having the gentlemen notice he was a cut above the usual mutton didn't do no harm, they weren't going to get talking about an inn servant, not they. But the females? It weren't so bad when his whiskers was on the way, he'd that callow moth-eaten look didn't do him no favours at all, but once he'd got himself a neat little beard and moustache he was turning heads to Honnecourt. He was young and tall and straight, and there weren't so many of *them* in Saint-Jean-in-the-Middle-of-Nowhere. They were over him like mould.

It was the visiting ladies needed watching, especially them old ones, the hags with blond footmen and predatory eyes. He called himself 'Gauthier' back then, and them ladies, it was always 'Oh, perhaps Gauthier might bring me a posset in bed,' or 'I'm so frightened of bandits, perhaps Gauthier might sleep outside my room.' Bollocks in spades, and spades trumps. If I hadn't shared his bed they'd have been climbing right in it with him.

He never touched them, not one, he'd learned a healthy distrust of women his own kind. He didn't mind the local girls, I'd see him at the well of an evening helping them with their buckets, and he was that relaxed you'd think him a different man. He'd sit casual on the parapet with his sleeves rolled up to the elbows, chatting and laughing and joining in the village talk, and I'd believe it then, the things they said about him and the life he'd led. But there was danger in it and I should of seen it, a man ought never let down his guard with a female. They had him picked for gentle-born by Christmas, and by March I reckon there were folk getting close to a name.

Martine said it didn't matter. She said 'They like him, Grimauld, they won't say nothing to do him harm.'

'Ah,' says I, 'but what about them visitors, my poppet? What's to stop them picking up the gossip and passing it on as it might be at Compiègne?'

'Silly old fool,' she says, laughing so much it sets off her wheezing. 'This is Saint-Jean aux Bois you're in now. These are gentry folk in Paris you're worrying about, why in the Lord's name would they be poking about down here?'

Anne du Pré

Extract from her diary, dated 10 April 1641

I must act. I have almost forgotten how, but I *must act*.

Florian's friends were in boisterous mood tonight, and I could have learned even more but for Bouchard's mistrust. Lavigne boasted openly how he had learned from a girl's former employers the whereabouts of her family, and might even have named the place if Bouchard had not turned the subject. It must be a big town, for Lavigne's spies have spent some days searching there without result, but today they reported back a rumour of a young menial so noble in his behaviour he returned a visiting lady her jewels which she had hidden for safekeeping and was about to leave behind. They are quite certain this must be André, but still they would not say where, and there could be no possible reason for me to ask. I could only sit in utter frustration while they talked about the theatre.

Then a tap at the door introduced Lavigne's frightening lackey. I have never seen him closely before, and truly he is a nightmare of a man, his face shot with broken red veins and his mouth crowded with pointed yellow teeth. No one can understand why fashionable Lavigne bears with so vile a servant as Pirauld, but today I was glad of him for he asked when the horses were needed for tomorrow's journey and Lavigne told him at daybreak.

The urgency is therefore acute, and I must act now, tonight. *How* is harder, for Jeanette is watched as well as I and our only hope of sending messages is by the fish boy, but he may not call until mid-morning, which may be too late.

I must try anyway. Jeanette shall write it so my hand will not be recognized, and we shall not sign a name. Perhaps the Comtesse will trust it. Perhaps it will reach her in time. Perhaps at last I can do something *to help*.

Ten

Anne du Pré

Letter to Elisabeth, Comtesse de Vallon, dated 11 April 1641

Madame,

Those who mean your grandson ill departed today on a journey to seek him. I cannot tell you where, only that their destination is to do with the family of a girl he knows and that somehow the Chevalier has given himself away. If you wish to help him, you will ensure he is warned and has support.

Believe me, Madame. I am only a servant in their employ, but like many in Paris I have great sympathy and respect for the Chevalier de Roland and would dare much to help him.

A Friend

Jacques de Roland

We knew it was her right away. It wasn't her writing, but there wasn't a maid in the city could construct a sentence like that, let alone write it without a single mistake. The fish boy even admitted he'd got it from a woman in the Place Dauphine.

'I thought better of Anne,' said the Comtesse. 'To betray the Chevalier to save her brother is one thing, but this is a clear attempt to find and murder him for no reason at all.'

I'd got to agree. There was no place mentioned, they didn't know where the boy was at all, they were just hoping we'd go dashing off and lead them right to him.

We put the letter aside, then in the afternoon we went to the Hôtel de Ville with my uncle and I was legitimated. It was only a formality, a bunch of people nodding their heads and a load of papers to sign, but I came out with a new name and was suddenly a new person. When we got home the servants lined up in the court-yard and bowed. Philibert was swanking unbearably because now he was valet to M. de Roland himself, and I'm almost sure he spent the night with Agnès.

The Comte actually stayed to drink wine with us before going home. As he left he squeezed my arm and said 'You're giving the family a second chance, Jacques. You won't be a fool and waste it, will you?'

I said 'No.'

Armand Jean du Plessis, Cardinal-Duc de Richelieu

Note to Elisabeth, Comtesse de Vallon, dated 11 April 1641

Madame,

Our friend B left Paris this morning in the company of d'A, L, and one servant.

I regret he did so sufficiently early to avoid the attention of my agents. I have, however, obtained information from his household that their destination is Compiègne, so you may choose to act yourself.

Be careful.
R

Jacques de Roland

The first I knew was Charlot's fist smashing against my bedroom door. Years of sleeping in the Hermitage listening for the roof-guard came walloping back like living a dream. I was out of bed and grop-ing for my breeches before he even appeared in front of me, a huge black shape behind a lighted candle.

'A note from His Eminence. Madame wishes to see you at once.'

I reached for my boots, but they skidded away over the floor. 'He's caught, isn't he, they've got him.'

'Not yet.' He explained while I dressed. I couldn't take it in properly at first, my head was screaming questions louder than his voice.

I said 'How can they possibly know he's at Compiègne? We've been so careful.'

'Who knows?' said Charlot. 'Perhaps they have intercepted our letters.'

I followed him out into the gallery, my mind whizzing round in panic like a squirrel in a cage. 'But they've all gone through Crespin, and they can't know about . . .'

I stopped as I remembered. My uncle had said not to use Crespin and I hadn't listened. He'd told me to get André out of bloody France, and I hadn't listened to that either.

I said 'Will they kill him, Charlot?'

He opened the Comtesse's door without knocking. 'Mlle du Pré seemed to suggest so.'

Someone else I hadn't listened to. 'Oh God, were we wrong about her too?'

A voice said 'That is possible, and we shall consider it when there is time.' My grandmother was coming towards me, her hair arranged in a neat plait over her nightgown.

I said helplessly 'I don't know, I don't understand.'

Her hand was on my arm, white and delicate, but steady as a man's. 'Charlot, wine for Monsieur. The boy is shocked.'

I said 'Never mind that, I need a horse saddled, I'm going after them.'

Her hand curled round my arm and actually held it. 'Robert is already seeing to it. Charlot goes with you.'

I'd guessed that. She'd called him first as usual. I said 'It's all right, I'll save him.'

'If you can,' she said, as Philibert came dashing in with my cloak. 'But if you can't you must keep your distance. You must not be involved in an escape that fails.'

I grabbed the cloak, thinking 'Sod that, I'm not leaving him no matter what.' I bowed and turned for the door, but her hand was still on my arm.

She said 'Be careful, Jacques.'

I said 'Yes, yes, all right,' and went out after Charlot.

It wasn't till we were out the gate that I realized she'd actually called me 'Jacques'.

Bernadette Fournier

It is strange, but of all the times in my life I would wish to recall, the day I know best is this one I would rather forget.

I woke early. We needed no cock, Monsieur, we were in the forest and the singing of birds makes a great chorus while the sky is yet dark blue. I waited until the grey light formed pale lines about the edges of the shutters, then rose and dressed myself for the day. My aunt slept soundly on the bed, for she had been busy with Grimauld half the night, and there he still lay, on his back and snoring with a smile on his face like a child. I was not sure of Grimauld back then, I knew he spent the Chevalier's money as if it were his own and took from my aunt all she had to give, and yet I sometimes thought he gave her something too. The Aunt Martine I remembered from my childhood was a sour thing with tight lips, but this one had the laugh and pink cheeks of a girl and I knew it was he who made her so.

I revived the kitchen fire. The wood was piled ready for me, beech as I liked it, for my aunt found the oak too acrid for her chest. André always remembered these things. I heard the clanking of buckets in the yard, and knew the familiar sounds that would follow. Why must men make such a performance of their washing, Monsieur? A woman dips her hands in the water and pats it on her cheeks and round her neck, but a man scoops up great handfuls so that it splashes through his fingers and sluices down his chest, he slaps it on his face as if he would hit himself, and blows air through his cheeks in a determined gasp. This morning I leaned against the doorway to watch the Chevalier put himself through his ritual. He shook his head so vigorously the water sprayed off his hair in a great arc of tiny droplets, and I laughed, Monsieur, for he looked like nothing so much as a wet dog.

He became at once self-conscious and gave me a little shamefaced grin. 'Good morning, Bernadette.'

I said severely 'Where is my cooking water?' and watched him smile. I used often to speak so, Monsieur, it was a foolish game we played, and I only recall it now because it was the last time we ever played it. The morning was already waking, the shutters opening in the guests' window, and Grimauld coming out for his morning piss. I returned to the kitchen and prepared the breakfast, everything as I did it every morning and would never do again.

In the afternoon André and Grimauld went to the woods to trap rabbits, but it did not trouble me as those were our quiet times. The guests would be gone and new ones not yet arrived, for travellers passing by the village at this hour had still time to reach Compiègne before night. Sometimes people came just for refreshment, and for them we were always prepared, for Adam the smith's son was within call to help with the horses.

My only worry this day was my aunt's shortness of breath, for it was lately giving her a troublesome cough of which I did not like the sound. I propped her with pillows in a high-backed chair and prepared an infusion of coltsfoot, but as I brought it from the kitchen I heard the distant clopping of approaching hooves. It was a sound I half expected, yet even as I gave my aunt her cup I noticed a difference. Our guests usually arrived slowly, for the inn was remote and travellers had always to stop and enquire for lodging, yet these riders came fast and with purpose, like men who have swept in at the gate and not slackened their pace as they drove to their goal.

'Is it the Chevalier?' asked my aunt, struggling to sit higher in her chair.

There seemed too many, and the hooves did not fall silent as they would if the riders crossed the grass to our stables at the back, but clattered instead on to the cobbles of our front yard. I went to the window and saw two men reining to a halt outside, although I had thought they sounded twice that. The horses were fine beasts laden with saddlebags, each with a musket slung alongside, while the masters wore swords on their hips and wide-brimmed hats that shadowed their faces. The boots of the first smacked loudly on the cobbles as he dismounted and turned to face us, regarding our house with as much calculation as if it were an enemy fort and not a simple country inn.

I heard the quickened wheezing of my aunt's breath beside me. 'Go you to the smithy, Bernadette. I think I would like a man about the house.'

I said 'Do not open up until I am back,' went swiftly to the kitchen and through the back door. The yard seemed exactly as it had been that morning, yet still I felt relief when I went to the gate and saw Adam already strolling down towards me. He must have seen the horsemen passing for he lifted his arm in casual salute and shouted 'Coming!'

The sight of him calmed me, but as I crossed the yard back to the house a muffled crash ahead told me my fears were all too justified. We were being attacked and the front door broken in, and I had left my aunt alone. I dashed for the stable to fetch my gun.

The door was already ajar, but I was thinking only of my aunt. I darted inside and was brought short only at the sight of two horses in front of me, laden with baggage like the ones out front. The truth struck me at last and too late, for a shadow was already closing on me, a rough hand grasped my arm and yanked me skidding across the straw, another tangled in my hair and jerked back my head so that I looked into the face of a nightmare, a half-remembered ogre with terrible teeth and bulging nose, whose muscular arms held me with the strength of some monstrous animal.

I screamed 'Adam!'

His hand cracked into my face, spinning me away so it was only the grip on my hair that kept me from falling. I clawed upward for his eyes, but he gave a short grunt and drove his fist into my belly, so that a tearing pain ripped through my womb and wrenched away my breath. I crumpled to the floor and as his feet moved away I heard a rasp of steel. Beyond him came the gate banging and running footsteps, then Adam appeared in the doorway, peering into the gloom and saying anxiously 'Bernadette?'

I had not the breath, Monsieur, nothing came out but a gasp of warning and then it was too late. The sword flashed out of the shadows, a great white blade smashing down on the bare neck of a country boy who had heard me scream and come to my help.

I heard the bite of it and Adam's hoarse cry, the scrabble of his feet and thud of his fall. I forced myself to look, and there was Adam lying against the wall, his head impossibly sideways and more blood than I had seen in my life pouring down from the great cleft in his throat.

The feet trod back towards me, and beside them swung a massive edged blade, red blood dripping down its runnels and on to the straw. The sword began to lift and I closed my eyes.

'No, Pirauld,' said a voice behind me. I turned on my knees and saw a pair of bucket-top boots and above them full mauve breeches. I looked higher, and there was a face I knew, one I had seen many evenings in a life I thought I had long left behind. He was the plump gentleman Charlot had given the name Lavigne, and I knew we were found at last.

'Hello, Bernadette,' he said. 'Is there anyone else you want to call?'

Jacques de Roland

We changed horses at Senlis. The post ones weren't as good as our own, but we couldn't stop to rest them. Bouchard had nearly a day's start, our only hope was to catch up while he slept. Charlot said 'He'll have stopped at least one night, Monsieur, he doesn't know we're behind him.' I wasn't even sure of that any more, it felt like everyone knew everything except us.

Charlot made me drink soup while the horses were saddled, but it was hard even to sit down. All through the night we'd been pounding along, nothing but the rhythm of the hooves and my own voice praying desperately in my head, 'Please, just this once, I'll never ask again.' Now all that stopped. I was sitting in an alehouse courtyard in the morning sun, with a bowl of soup in front of me and pretty brown hens pecking round the cobbles for crumbs of food. It's all mixed up in my head now, the smell of asparagus and the sound of Charlot arguing with the ostler, church bells nearby, and a fat child playing with a blue hoop round the courtyard, sending it spinning and spinning on the stones.

Familiar voices drifted into my head like they do in your dreams, and it was the Puppies arriving, they'd managed to catch us up. I'd sent to them last night, but hadn't dared wait, they must have ridden even harder than us to be here now. They looked quite rested and cheerful and didn't want to bother with soup. I remember Crespin just snatching a chunk of bread and leaping on his post horse with it still sticking out of his mouth.

Then we were off again, five horses together, twice as much clatter as we galloped through the morning streets to the gate. Through the arch and back on the road, Charlot's brown travel-coat in front of me, the Puppies a blur of colour either side. The pace picked up to the old rhythm as the road lengthened ahead of us, people in the fields looking up as we passed, a windmill, a church with an old man outside, and the voice back in my head saying 'Let him be all right, let us be in time, please God, please God, I'll never ask again.'

Bernadette Fournier

They led me back into the house and there was my poor aunt wheezing dreadfully in her chair while over her stood Bouchard with a drawn sword.

I ignored his smile of triumph and said 'This man of yours has committed murder, and you will all be hanged.'

He preened himself, a man in his prime intimidating an old lady who could not breathe. 'Lavigne, you must tell Pirauld that is very wrong of him. But since he's to be hanged for one he may as well be hanged for two, so let's hope these ladies will now cooperate.'

Another man brushed past me from the passage, the Cardinal's Guard called d'Arsy. He said 'Old woman's room with a cot, but another looks as if it's been occupied recently. The bed's rumpled, and there's a man's cloak in the press.'

'You have a man here?' said Bouchard reproachfully to my aunt, and prodded her foot with his sword.

'Adam,' I said. 'That's Adam's room. The man this creature of yours has murdered.'

'Really?' said Bouchard. He swung his rapier round to point at my chest. 'And what is Adam's other name?'

My aunt attempted to speak, but Bouchard said 'Pirauld, if this hag opens her mouth I'd be grateful if you'd shut it.' The monster grinned and went to stand over my aunt's chair.

Bouchard said 'Well, Bernadette?'

Only gossip could have led them here, and I could think of only one person whose behaviour would have attracted it. 'Gauthier.'

He gave a little crowing laugh. 'Oh, good girl, *clever* girl, but too slow by far. Describe him, Lavigne.'

He described poor dead Adam, a curly-haired and rustic young man no one could mistake for the Chevalier.

Bouchard said 'Then this famous Gauthier is still alive some-where, isn't he, Bernadette?'

I did not answer.

'He's not here,' said Lavigne. 'There are no horses in the stables.'

Bouchard sighed, turned to me and said 'Where is he, girl?'

I would like to have spat, but my mouth was dry.

'Very well,' said Bouchard. He slipped his blade under the shoul-der of my dress and jerked up hard so that the cloth parted and the sleeve fell away. I backed away at once, but Lavigne was behind me, his plump white hands closing softly about my arms.

Bouchard said genially 'That's right, man, hold her there.'

It was disgusting, Monsieur, disgusting. That Lavigne was excited by it I did not need to be told, for I felt his arousal digging hard into my back.

Bouchard said 'I'm going to keep asking questions, Bernadette, and every time your answer doesn't please me I'm going to cut away something else. Do you understand?'

I said nothing.

He slid the blade under my arm and sliced neatly through the seam. The sleeve fell away entirely and pulled down half my dress as far as the hip, but my chemise underneath was intact. Lavigne's breath was warm on my neck.

Bouchard said 'Where is de Roland?'

My aunt heaved forward in her chair, but Pirauld smashed his fist into her face and she collapsed back, her breath rasping in high and terrible gasps of panic.

I said 'You're killing her,' and tried to wrench away. I could not believe they would murder a woman who had done them no harm. 'Let me go to her, you're killing her.'

Bouchard signalled the monster but he only jerked my aunt upright and tried to pour the coltsfoot down her throat. It was not enough, she needed a doctor and the fear to go away, not to be handled by a creature out of nightmare. Her face was turning pale blue.

I screamed at Bouchard 'Go away, go away, André is not here, you're killing her for nothing.' I tried again to tug free, but Lavigne's fingers bit hard into my arms.

Bouchard addressed his point to the top of my chemise and sheered it right down to the navel. '"Not here" is a start, but would you care to elaborate?'

D'Arsy's voice sounded uncomfortable. 'The woman needs a doctor, Bouchard. Leave the girl, it's time we went.'

Bouchard snorted. 'And where's the fun in that for Lavigne?' He flicked his rapier between the halves of my chemise and opened them like curtains to expose my body. He studied it for a second, then brought his blade to circle my breasts, first one, then the other, finishing each with a delicate touch on the nipple.

He said 'I think you'd like these, Pirauld.'

With a lady it would work perhaps, the terror of being touched by a menial, but Monsieur already knows I was no lady. I made no reaction as Bouchard stepped back.

Then Pirauld appeared in front of me, without the sword but with his large hair-backed hands in their place. He squeezed my breasts, and I told myself it was no more than a young man does before he learns better. His hands shoved between my legs, his nails scraped my skin, and still I told myself 'It is a man, that is all, just another man.' Then I heard an exclamation of distaste from d'Arsy, and it was that, I think, that woke me. I opened my eyes and saw the mottled face that advanced towards me with spittle glistening on its open mouth, I heard the grunt as his probing fingers pushed me apart, and suddenly I was the child I had perhaps never been and the thing that groped me was an animal. I could not help a little cry.

Bouchard smiled and leaned back against the wall. He said again 'Where is de Roland?'

We saw horses tied up outside the front door, but it didn't bother us beyond wondering where Adam was to see to their stabling.

'Perhaps they've only just arrived,' says André. 'Let's do ours, then we'll go and help.'

The yard gate's open, but we don't think nothing of that neither, we're in and dismounting when André stops dead like a deer on a gun. I look where he's looking, and there's a great splodge of blood on the cobbles and a trickle leading back to the stable door.

We grabbed the guns off the horses, and pushed the door right open. Ah, sweet saints, that was bad. Young Adam's head was half off his neck and the floor sticky-wet with red blood.

Something cold's pressing into my hand, and there's André passing me his pistol. I said 'You're going to need it, laddie,' but he went to the back of the stables, uncovered a canvas bundle and took out his sword. His face when he turned was grim as I've seen, and he strode for the house without one more word.

The pistol was primed and loaded, but I left the musket, a matchlock's no good in a point-and-shoot, and judging by the horses we'd four against us somewhere. We heard voices ahead, two at least in the public room and one laughing, time to stop and use the old brain, but not André, he was kicking that door open and bang through it before I could stop him.

I'd no choice now, nothing but in and after him. First thing to do's check the room, but André sees two men struggling with a naked girl and he's straightway charging at them, blade out and screaming 'Get away from her!' in a voice I don't hardly recognize. For a second he might be a little boy.

They spring round at once, and ah Christ, that's a horror of a thing that's pawing at Bernadette. He's off and yanking out a great broadsword, but André's stopping for nothing, he's bashing it aside like it's no more than a stick and thrusting forward with his rapier, down to one knee as he lunges after the man and spits him clean through the middle.

The plump one's snatching for his own sword, so I punch the

pistol wallop in his gut and hook his legs out from under with my boot, but there's another out my reach, a well-set-up blond fellow who's already drawn, he's straight after André while the laddie's still trying to wrench his blade out the monster, striking to skewer him where he stands.

I yell the warning, André twists side-on to dodge the lunge and pulls desperate fast to get his sword out the thug's guts. Too late, the blond's already turned and whipping in at his face, but then a flash of something gold, a loud clang, André's snatched a candlestick and smashed the blade back with it like a second sword. That's as much as I see before something comes leaping at me from across the room, and here's the fourth man come to play.

I've nothing to swing but that pistol, but it knocks his blade wide a whole half second before it comes whizzing back in. Blue light in front of my face, then white in my mind as the shock of the cold blade opens up my neck. I'm buckling, waving wild with the pistol to keep the blade back, but something else blocks it, a rapier's whistling past my face, André's left the blond to come for me.

The man backs away, but André stabs deep in his arm and I hear the cry and clatter as the sword falls. There's blood sprayed in my eyes, but I hear the man scraping up a chair as defence and backing off, thank you, Mary and the rest of them, I hear him backing right off, then André's hand's on my arm and his voice says 'Grimauld!' and I say 'I'm fine as Friday, now watch your fucking *back*.'

He's already doing it, already turning and swiping for the blond, but he's not there, is he, the bastard's used the time to back himself cosy to the wall with Bernadette, and when he sees André coming he whirls her smack in front of him, blade tight under her throat.

André stops dead to the line, and I get ahold of myself quick. I whack my handkerchief to my neck, give a kick to the plump man on the floor to keep him down, snarl the pistol round to the one behind the chair to make sure he ruddy stays there, whirl it round again like what I should have done when I first come in, and see we're all clear but for the blond.

But there's someone else down the far end and that's my Martine, slumped in a chair with a face like dark cloud and a body not moving at all. André sees her too, and if I'd thought he couldn't look grimmer, well I was a lot wrong. He looks back at the blond, and everything's suddenly very quiet, nothing but the fire flickering in the hearth, and everyone staying right where they are. It's maybe one minute since we walked in the room.

The blond looks back at André, or I think he does, it's hard to be sure with eyes that crooked, but either way he don't move his blade from Bernadette's throat.

'Hello, Chevalier,' he says pleasantly. 'They hanged you in effigy, did you know? Your brother cried.'

I gather this is an old friend we've got here, but I'm keeping my eyes on my own chicks. That rough one with the nightmare face, he's flat on his back and the blood stopped pumping, he's as dead as I like them. The plump man's crouching feeble as an old maid and I think he's safe enough. The dark one's still behind his chair, trying to bandage up his arm, but I don't trust the look in his eye. That's two of the buggers I've to watch with one gun and one ball.

'Drop your sword, Chevalier,' says that blond, twitching his blade under Bernadette's chin. 'Drop your sword or I'll slit her throat.'

I flicked my eyes round, and oh Christ in a carriage, André was actually hesitating. Murderous bastard in front of him, two more waiting, and he's looking at dropping his sword. Well, not on my watch he wasn't, I socked up my forearm, levelled the barrel over it and said 'No, you drop yours, straw-head, or I'll put one in your eyeball.'

The blond didn't doubt me, but he knew André was softer. He jerked Bernadette's head back another inch, touched the edge up against her skin, and said 'The sword, de Roland.'

André looked from him to me and back again, stewed up like last week's mutton. Something was driving him I couldn't make sense on. Every time he looked at that poor naked girlie his eyes came over with that same madness I'd seen when he leapt in.

I said 'She's dead if you drop it, laddie, raped and dead. Now stand back.'

I don't know what got through, seemed like that word 'rape', but whatever it was he heard it. He blinked like coming out of a dream and slowly stepped back.

The blond still knew his weakness. He said 'If I put it down you'll murder me.'

I said 'Yes, if he ruddy wants, now fucking drop it.'

They went on staring at each other, hate fizzing between them like fireworks.

'I won't murder you,' said André. 'Let her go.'

The blond hesitated, then very slowly he smiled. He lowered his sword, shoved Bernadette away with his knee and stepped smart back.

She was up in a second, never even bothering to draw the rags of her chemise round her, she was up and running to her auntie, taking her hands and trying to talk to her, but I knows a dead woman when I see one and it was giving me an anger hot as André's own. I kept that pistol hard lined on the blond's skull and I'd have given a year's pay to pull that trigger. I reckon he knew it too, he gave me one quick glance and placed his rapier on the floor.

Bernadette stands and walks over to him. He don't look so happy now, and I can't say as I blame him, she's got that ball-breaking look that's a bad sign in a female. She looks at him a moment, then reaches out and rips the cloak off his cringing shoulders. She wraps it round herself, dignified as a queen, then says 'Thank you, Chevalier. I knew you would come.'

Bernadette Fournier

Grimauld went straight to my aunt, and no matter what he tells you, Monsieur, there were tears in his eyes. He touched her poor dead face with his finger and I heard him say 'Sleep well, lass.' He was bleeding from his neck and a drop landed on her face, but I did not think she would mind it and saw the clumsy tenderness with which he wiped it away.

André said 'You murdering bastards.'

Bouchard did not like that word 'bastard', Monsieur, his hand twitched as if it ached for the sword that lay by his feet. He said thickly 'Not us. Lavigne's servant killed her.'

I said 'But they allowed it, these men who brought him here.'

André said 'Then we will see them hanged.'

D'Arsy was inserting his bloodied arm into his baldric to create a sling, but now he looked up and gave a short laugh. 'Go near the authorities and you'll be the one to swing.'

André hardly glanced at him. 'You murdered the smith's son, you assaulted this lady, the people of the village are free to act.'

'And when we denounce them?' said Bouchard. 'What do you think happens to peasants who harbour the King's enemies?'

André's hand tightened on his sword. 'They knew nothing, I can explain . . .'

Bouchard laughed. 'You can explain nothing. Don't you understand, you're outside the law.' He was right, Monsieur. Grimauld and the Chevalier held the weapons, but it was this man and his friends who held the power.

'All right,' said Grimauld. He straightened and moved away from my aunt's chair. 'Forget the law, just kill them like the filth they are.' He held the pistol in one hand, d'Arsy's sword in the other, and the grooves of his wrinkled face had sharpened into dark, hard lines.

Lavigne scrambled up in alarm, and d'Arsy's hand fell slowly away from his sling.

Bouchard turned to André. 'That's murder. You can't kill unarmed men.'

André hesitated, then said softly 'You're right.' He stooped to pick up Bouchard's rapier, reversed it and offered him the hilt. 'Take it, we'll fight fair.'

Bouchard made no move. Outside I heard the faint rattle of the woodcutter's cart as he drove past towards his home.

'You can't refuse,' said André.

Bouchard moistened his lips. 'I can. You're an outlaw.'

'And what are you?' said André. He thrust the sword again at Bouchard, his face suddenly desperate. 'Take it, haven't you any honour?'

D'Arsy stepped forward, a new seriousness in his expression. 'You must, Bouchard. We all must.'

'No,' said Bouchard furiously. 'Don't you understand? He'll kill us one by one.'

André glared in frustration. Then he laid down the sword and slapped Bouchard full across the face.

The crack of it was shocking, and d'Arsy winced as if he had been struck himself. Bouchard stood with his cheek scarlet from the blow, then raised his hand to his mouth, looked at the tiny spot of blood, then stuck out the tip of his tongue and licked it clean away.

He said 'You have no idea how much you are going to regret that, Chevalier.'

'Then make me,' said André. He tried to force the hilt into Bouchard's hand, but he only opened his fingers and let it fall. The rapier rolled noisily on the stone floor then bumped into a chair leg and was still.

André bent to retrieve it, weighed it in both hands, then broke it savagely across his knee. He threw the pieces away from him and lowered his head in a silence of defeat.

'Just stick him,' said Grimauld wearily. 'Make the earth cleaner and –'

He was looking at Bouchard, Monsieur, he was looking the wrong way. Lavigne threw himself at his back, jerking the pistol from his hand so that it struck the floor and fired with a great bang. Grimauld swung round, but Lavigne was already running for the back door, d'Arsy fast after him, while in two strides Bouchard was at the front door and out of reach of André's sword. André leapt after him, but the door was broken, Bouchard had only to kick it and slip past. They were all fled and we had not so much as the pistol to bring them down.

André smacked his fist against the table and bowed his head. I will not repeat what Grimauld said, Monsieur, but I understood what he felt. I remember listening helplessly to the horses moving away outside.

'I'm sorry, Bernadette,' said André. 'I've brought all this on you. Your aunt. Adam.'

Grief is for later, I needed him to act. 'Do not think of this now. Those men will bring troops, we must get away while we can.'

He shook his head. 'This is your home now, there's your aunt to see to. I'll go alone.'

'She ain't staying here, laddie,' said Grimauld. 'Nor me neither. They'll say we harboured you, we're all on the run now.'

His roughness did what my words had not and seemed to wake André into urgency.

'Yes,' he said, straightening and ramming his sword into his belt.

'Yes. Bernadette, do you have another dress to put on? Grimauld and I will pack saddlebags for the –'

He stopped. He had started to be the Chevalier again, and now he stood still with a face suddenly grey. He said 'Grimauld, when we arrived, there were guns on those horses, weren't there?'

Grimauld looked at him, and now his face too was becoming ash. 'Muskets.'

André turned quickly to the first window, looked outside, then pulled the shutters closed.

I said 'What are you doing? We need to go now.'

Grimauld went to the other window and peered cautiously through.

André said gently 'What would you do if you were those gentlemen, Bernadette? If you knew where we were and that we would have to come out? And if you had guns?'

Grimauld pulled the last shutters closed. The room was darkened but for the fire, and I was looking at two pale faces lit only by the flicker of flame.

Eleven

Bernadette Fournier

I ran upstairs to dress, and even then I was afraid. We could not watch all places, I could not be sure a man had not entered while we talked and was now waiting in the shadows of my aunt's room or creeping towards me up the stairs. My aunt had a long mirror, and I dressed in front of it that I might see what lay behind me as I worked. The single second while my dress was over my head seemed the longest I have ever lived.

When I came again down the stairs the house was secured and dark, and Grimauld was holding a candle to light André's passage to the kitchen. I thought they would barricade the back door as they had the front, but Grimauld took up guard while André pulled it open.

I said 'You cannot, Chevalier, they may be round this side.'

He peered out. 'We've discharged the pistol, I need the muskets and ammunition from the stable.'

He leapt out into the yard, my view of him lost as Grimauld pushed the door half-closed behind him. I heard his footsteps pelting for the stable.

I said 'You should not have let him.'

Grimauld kept his eyes fixed on the gap in the door. 'I'd like to see anyone stopping him. There now, he's in.' I heard the distant thud of the stable door.

I said 'They might be too, that's how they got Adam.'

He took his hand off the sword hilt, flexed his fingers, then grasped it again. 'They'd have had to think quick for that, my poppet. They'd got to move the horses, get the guns, come up with a plan, and they weren't in the best of states to start with.'

I could not see round his body to what was outside. 'Is the gate open?'

'We never closed it when we come in.'

I stared at his shoulder, hunched and tense against the wall. 'If they shoot him . . .'

He shifted his weight to the other leg. 'Do me a favour and shut up.'

There came again the little thud, and Grimauld's voice seemed lighter. 'He's got them.'

I felt myself relax. 'Perhaps we are wrong, and they –'

He straightened so quickly his elbow struck my arm, he wrenched open the door and bellowed 'Run!' Evening light washed in, Grimauld thrust me back, I heard running footsteps then the bark of a musket. The pounding feet faltered but kept coming, someone shouted, then a dark shape hurtled through into the kitchen, a musket clattered across the floor, and Grimauld slammed the door shut so that the bang and the darkness came as one.

As my eyes adjusted again to the gloom, I heard the rattle and clunk of the bolts sliding home, and then the most extraordinary sound, Monsieur, for someone was laughing. André was sitting on the floor clutching his leg and laughing like a boy, and I distinctly heard him say 'Ow, fuck,' before he turned and said hastily 'Sorry, Bernadette.'

His boot was gashed and the hose bloody, but he ran his finger over the grazed skin and showed me how slight a smear it made. 'Look,' he said, grinning up at me. 'It's nothing.'

Grimauld retrieved the musket from the floor. 'How much powder?'

André tossed him a flask and sat cross-legged to load the second musket himself. 'We can hold here for half an hour. We can't wait longer in case one of them's gone for the troops.'

They seemed quite unperturbed, the two of them, soldiers performing a task that was quite routine. I said 'Then we are trapped. We cannot go for fear of the guns, we cannot stay for fear of the troops.'

'It's nearly dark,' said André. He slid out his ramrod and gave me a quick smile. 'When the woodsmen come by for Vespers we'll just stroll out among them. Not even Bouchard will risk picking us off in front of a dozen witnesses.'

Ah, but there was other things they could do and I ought to of seen it, but I'd a few other things on my mind just then. Me and Bernadette were laying out Martine nice with flowers from the baskets, because we might not be here when they buried her but I was fucked fifty ways to Freiburg if I was having people think no one cared.

So we lays her out and Bernadette says a little prayer, then suddenly *bang* there's this ruddy great thump above our heads. Whatever it is goes rolling down the roof and bumping over the bindings, then I hear another hit overhead in the passage. Something's crackling right above us, and a smell a man in my line knows as well as his own sweat. Naphtha, laddie, naphtha, the quickest way to make a fire there is, and that's just what it's doing not two feet above my head.

I grab Bernadette out of it sharp, because that's the weakness of thatch, see, snugger and drier by far nor slate, but not what you want to be standing under when it's going up like a bonfire. I yank her down the stairs and there's André calling for us, smoke oozing out the public room behind him. They've forced a shutter somewhere and chucked a torch inside, they're after smoking us like so many eels.

'I think we won't wait for Vespers, Grimauld,' says André. 'I think we'll go now.'

Bernadette says 'We can wait. People will see the smoke, someone will come.'

He puts his hand on her arm very gentle, like closing the lids of someone dead. 'That's why we must go now. It won't be a crowd, it'll be only one or two at first, and you know what these people will do then. We don't want another Adam.'

'No,' she says. 'No. But if we leave now they will shoot us.'

'No, they won't,' he says. 'Not if you shoot them first.'

Bernadette Fournier

It was true he had taught me to fire the musket, but I had done it lying down, not on my feet and with a stand. I said 'Perhaps if I had the pistol,' but André explained the pistol was the only gun that could be fired one-handed, and Grimauld must take it to provide a second shot as they ran for the horses.

'It'll only take seconds,' he said. 'The horses are saddled and waiting, we'll be back before you know it.'

'It's easy enough, my poppet,' said Grimauld, checking the gun's action with smooth, professional movements. 'Those are matchlocks they've got, I seen one fire. You'll see the glow of the slow-match, just point at that and pull the trigger.'

I said 'What if there is more than one?'

'There won't be,' said André. 'D'Arsy's wounded in the arm, there are only two who can shoot, and they must have one to watch the front. It's just that one shot we need to stop.'

Grimauld passed me the musket and folded down the gun-rest to hold the end of the barrel. 'You've to keep it rock-steady, see. Wobble by an inch here, that's four feet off by the time the ball hits, you got that?'

I looked down the barrel and held it firm. 'Then I will miss, and perhaps may hit you.'

'Right as rabbits, girlie,' he said, and grinned.

We could delay no longer. Burning thatch was already falling in upstairs, for smoke now issued through the cracks in the beams above our heads. André settled his pack, adjusted the grip on his sword, said 'Over in a minute, Bernadette,' and pulled open the back door. He was gone in an instant, Grimauld after him, then the doorway was clear. I steadied the musket, and looked about the yard.

The flames of the burning thatch cast a yellow flicker over the dark space, but there was no one there. André and Grimauld were running hard for the stable by the gate, but at them I must not look, I must keep my eyes and the barrel on the bushes opposite and at the little privy behind which a man might hide. The trees stirred in the evening wind but I ignored them, for I had only the one shot and must save it until I was sure. And I was not sure, I saw nothing, and then my mind said, They will not try to shoot a running man, they will wait until they are mounting the horses, so they will be by the . . .

I saw it then, a glint of glowing red in the bushes closest to the gate, and the branches twitching with something that was not the wind. My finger squeezed the trigger, the calm of my mind exploded in a bang and crack of flame, the gun bucked in my hands and smashed into my shoulder, and ahead of me came another bang and flash that said I had fired too late.

A horse neighed shrilly, hooves raced across the yard. I ignored the pain in my shoulder and the sulphur burning in my lungs, I dropped the musket and stepped out through the doorway, and a horse appeared almost on top of me, its rider leaning down with outstretched hand. I reached up and caught at his coat as his arm gripped my waist and lifted me clean from the ground. My shoulder tore with pain as I slid over the horse's flank, then I was safe on its back, André was tucking me in close to him, and we were turning back for the gate.

I saw it ahead of us, and beyond it Grimauld struggling to control the big warhorse, which was turning violently round and round with much stamping and snorting. 'Come on,' he yelled, waving his pistol wildly in the air. 'Come *on!*'

Another beast was already driving towards us over the grass, a man riding round from the front. André kept us steady for the gate but I saw it closing against us, pushed by another man in the bushes. Our horse checked and reared, and I dug my hands frantically into its poor mane, but André's arm tightened me into him, while his other came up and with it the sword.

I snatched the reins as the horse shied, then André leaned down behind me, sword slashing the air in a blaze of firelight, and I caught only a glimpse of d'Arsy's face before it disappeared beneath us with a cry. We bumped the gate, I reached down and pushed, and the horse stumbled through. The last of our attackers charged to meet us, but Grimauld's pistol cracked and the horse screamed and fell, spilling its rider to the grass. Even then the man was so desperate in his hatred he snatched at my foot as we passed, but I kicked out with my heel and he fell back cursing. I did not need to see the fair hair to know it was Bouchard.

Our hooves passed from the softness of grass to the rumble of the track as we pounded past the forge and towards the village gate. People were hurrying towards us, drawn by the shots and the sight of the flames, and they were men I knew, the wheelwright and the furrier, but we had to ride on past and not involve them, we galloped by as if they were nothing to us nor we to them. As our horses passed beneath the shadow of the gate and into the forest, I heard faintly behind us the distant bell for Vespers.

Jacques de Roland

We saw smoke rising out of the trees ahead of us, a thick purple cloud in the night sky, big and soft and silent. I'd seen it before, something like that, I'd seen it standing on the back meadow at Ancre with a twelve-year-old boy by my side. That's when I knew.

We followed the smoke through the gate, into the village, up the track, and there it was, a whole house burning. Villagers were watching in silence, a few carrying buckets from the well, others forking down burning thatch, but it was pointless and they must have known it. The walls were alight and half the roof fallen in, it was over and done. An elderly man was on his hands and knees sobbing on the grass, while two women tried to comfort him.

I dismounted slowly. The people nearest shrank away as if we were dangerous, and I realized suddenly what they were seeing. We were finely dressed gentlemen with swords on our hips, people who could get them flogged or hanged if we didn't like what they said. For a second I felt like one of them, looking at myself and being scared.

'What happened here?' said Charlot.

The curé stepped forward, a little man with a face like a frightened baby's. 'Bandits, Monsieur, we are much troubled with them here. We have sent to inform the authorities, we reported it at once.'

'And did you see them, these bandits?' asked Charlot.

The curé's eyes flickered with alarm. 'Not closely, Monsieur, only glimpses, or we would not be alive now. But they have stolen the horses from the inn, they have murdered the people, who else could they be?'

I knew who they were all right, I knew who they bloody were. 'Have they killed everyone?'

The curé flinched. 'Everyone, Monseigneur. Even the son of our blacksmith, who did nothing but help in the stables.'

The crowd murmured in sympathy, and a couple glanced over at the man crying.

I felt helpless and sorry but had to keep asking. 'Someone might still have got out, you might just not have seen them.'

One of the younger man stepped to the curé's side like he thought I was going to hit him. 'This is a walled village. We have gates. How could we possibly not have seen them?'

Their faces blurred in front of me. I wanted to yell at them, shake them, but it wasn't their fault, it was ours. This time it was us who'd been the Spaniards, coming to an innocent village bringing swords and fire and death.

I said wretchedly 'I'm sorry.'

The curé's face softened. 'You've been here before, Monsieur? You knew these people?'

Charlot's hand scrunched tight round my arm. I tried to think of the Comtesse saying 'You must not be involved,' but all I could see was André. My head was filled with pictures of him, a little boy yelling and stamping with temper, a bigger one laughing as he fenced me, an older one sprawling on my bed while he talked about marrying Anne. Other memories clamoured in on top, a ring on my finger, a kiss on my cheek, a sword in my hand, I saw them in flashes like lightning, all the things he'd ever given me, the home I'd never had, the meaning I'd never looked for, a name and a person to be.

I said 'No, I didn't know them,' and turned away.

Bernadette Fournier

He became quieter as we rode deeper into the forest. The excitement of action was fading from him, and he had nothing left to do but lead us into the dark trees, and nothing left to hope for beyond a place that was not here.

We had nowhere to go. We had not even much in the way of money, for what was left of the Chevalier's had been concealed in the roof which was now ashes behind us. We could not appeal for charity, for we were now all fugitives. Even I had fired at one of the gentlemen and Grimauld assured me I must have hit him, for his shot had gone wild and done nothing but scare the horses. I had no other relatives who might take us in, no friends outside Paris, and those André had in Picardie were the very people who would be most closely watched. There was nowhere but the endless trees with no hope of sanctuary on the other side.

It was Grimauld who stopped us in the end, insisting his arse was sore and we must make camp and rest. Indeed he was not a great horseman and had never much cared for the great steed he rode now. This was Tonnerre, Monsieur, a magnificent stallion André insisted was Jacques' own. Grimauld ought to have been happy with the loan of such an animal, but in truth he feared him and when André was not by would often call him 'the Fucking Thing'.

So we chose a small clearing among the oak trees and did what we could to make it home. Grimauld had a tinder box to make a fire, André found a stream for fresh water, and I had brought a cooking pot and herbs, so we had all we needed for supper, as the horses were still festooned with rabbits from the day's trapping. No, Monsieur, not one of us questioned the propriety of such a meal on a Friday, it was the idea of eating at all that concerned us now.

That André himself was worried I knew, for I saw him counting carefully the remaining coins in his purse and putting it away without a word. He did his best to stay cheerful and poured us out a mug of wine to share, but at last there was only the crackling of the fire and the silence of our own thoughts.

André poked a twig into the flames and watched it burn. 'Still waiting for payday, Grimauld?'

Grimauld sucked his last rabbit bone. 'It had better be a bleeding good one.'

André stared down at the fire. 'It certainly needs to be.'

I said 'We can trap more animals, there may be fish in the streams, we can survive here many days.'

He shook his head. 'The horses need oats, rough fodder, they can't live long on grass.'

'Why don't you write your grandmother?' said Grimauld. 'Bit of cash'll see us through.'

Still he did not look up. 'I'd have to tell her where to send it.'

'So?' said Grimauld. He reached again for the mug, but it was empty and he set it back down. 'You trust her, don't you? And de Chouy?'

'I don't know everyone in his household. There may even be someone planted in mine. How do you think they found us this time?'

I was afraid he was right, Monsieur. Saint-Jean Aux Bois is a beautiful village, but it was not somewhere those gentlemen would have chosen to visit for themselves. I retrieved from my handkerchief the one thing I had kept by me all these months, and handed it to André.

I said 'This will help, won't it, Chevalier? If we are careful we can surely make it last a month.' It was my gold écu, Monsieur, worth six whole livres.

He said 'But it's yours.'

It was his, but I did not need to say so. 'Jacques gave it to me in case I needed it, and I think we need it now.'

He could not deny it. He squeezed my hand then kissed it, and was silent a long while. Then he said 'I'm sorry. Your aunt, your house, what those men . . . It's my fault, all of it.'

Grimauld's eyes slid round to meet mine. He said 'Never mind that, laddie, let's get these guns reloaded. We don't want them bandits taking us by surprise, do we?'

The Chevalier rose at once to help him, while I did what I could to make our patch of ground more comfortable. We had little baggage and no blankets, but I arranged bracken into soft heaps and dragged a fallen branch across two trees to make a break from the wind. In truth there was none, but it was something to do. To sit still was to think of my aunt, burned in her bed without so much as the burial of a Christian, or to think of our future, which was bleaker than any I had ever faced.

Grimauld sat by the fire to take first watch. I wrapped myself in my cloak and lay down on the bracken, but André only leaned against a tree trunk with his head bowed and his arms rested loosely on his knees.

I tried to sleep. The forest seemed quiet at first, but really there were tiny sounds all about me. The twigs in our fire crackled with sap, the owls and nightjars called in the trees, and the undergrowth seemed alive with the scuttering of small creatures. There was the furtive clink of Grimauld refilling the mug from the wine bottle and the noisy slurp as he drank, the stirring of dead leaves with his boots, and the rustling of bracken beneath my body as I breathed. I looked over at André. He alone was silent and still, but his eyes were wide open and staring hopelessly into the dark.

I rose from the bracken and went to him. Grimauld glanced up from the fire, then looked down again and stirred it idly with a stick.

André looked up only when I knelt down beside him. 'What is it, Bernadette? Are you thinking about your aunt?'

I said 'I am cold, Chevalier.'

The darkness went out of his eyes. 'I'm sorry,' he said. 'Here.' He raised his arm that I might huddle in next to him, and arranged his cloak to wrap it about both our shoulders. 'Is that better?'

I rested my head on his chest and curled my hands into his coat. 'Much.'

'Good,' he said, and tightened his arm about me. 'Good.'

A nightjar called above us, but we did not move. The forest seemed gradually to recede about us as his head slowly drooped against mine, until at last I was aware of nothing but the warmth of his body, the softness of his breathing, and the steady beating of his heart.

Jacques de Roland

We hung around till the fire was out, but the roof had collapsed and crushed everything, the only corpse we saw was dragged out in black pieces. I was stumbling back to the horses when I saw a villager chuck away a pile of burnt rubble, and among it was a rapier, broken in two.

Gaspard touched my arm. 'Do you want it, my Jacques?'

I thought of M. Gauthier bringing it out of the Manor all those years ago, clean and whole and bright. I said 'No.'

The numbness stayed with me all through the ride back. Raoul was saying the villagers might be lying to protect themselves, but I couldn't listen, I couldn't feel anything at all. There was just one thing burning away at the edges of the blankness, and it wasn't grief, it was anger.

None of this need have happened. That blacksmith's son could still be working the forge, Bernadette could still be alive and André right beside me, everything like it ought to be if it hadn't been for the boy's honour. It wasn't his fault he'd come here, he'd had no choice, but I began to think he hadn't had one since he was born.

Honour. If it wasn't for that we'd never have helped that hunchback. We'd never have gone in the courtyard of Le Pomme d'Or, we'd never have met Bouchard at all. They wouldn't have killed Bernadette if we hadn't turned up, it was our own bloody honour that had done that. It was honour made the boy fight Bouchard, honour took him to the Luxembourg gardens to try and save the whole of France. Honour had done it all.

It was my fault too. André was trained to the idea of honour, it maybe wouldn't have mattered if I hadn't taught him to start caring about people as well. Stefan had warned him, he'd always said he couldn't do both and survive, and now I knew he was right. So was the Comte. Everything he'd told me was right, everything I'd believed in was wrong, honour was stupid and I was even stupider because I'd wanted to believe it.

It was early morning by the time we got back to Senlis. Everything was the same, the courtyard, the brown chickens, I almost expected to see the fat child with the hoop. Everything was just like it had been, but ugly and different because there wasn't anything to pray for any more, there wasn't any meaning and never had been. My world was a black smoking ruin and André was dead.

Twelve

Anne du Pré

Extract from her diary, dated 16 April 1641

Bouchard is back. He said André deserved to be broken on the wheel for wounding d'Arsy and murdering Lavigne, and I bore it all gladly because he was saying André was alive.

That, of course, did not please him. 'You may smile, Mademoiselle,' he said, though I was careful to do no such thing. 'I smile myself when I think of him being brought back to Paris in chains.'

Florian looked up. 'You've reported him, Monseigneur?'

'Of course not,' said Bouchard, looking at him uneasily. 'Gentlemen can't be involved in such things. We told the authorities there'd been bandits, and they're sending a regiment to search the forest. It'll be a nice little bonus for them when they catch a fugitive from the King's justice while they're at it. More wine, Mademoiselle? You appear to be a little dry.'

He is cruel, really cruel, and I wish I understood why. When at last I escaped to my chamber I picked up my lavender bowl and smashed it against the wall.

'That's right, Mademoiselle,' said Jeanette, picking up the pieces. 'Better in here than down there. You're doing very well these days, they trust you more all the time.'

'And what good is it?' I said, only wishing I had something else smashable to throw. 'The Rolands don't trust me, they can't have taken notice of my letter or Jacques would have been there when Bouchard arrived.'

'This time, perhaps,' said Jeanette. 'Next time they'll pay more attention.'

'I can't bear a next time,' I said, which was feeble and wrong of me but I couldn't help it. 'Tonight I sat and heard André slandered and did not spit in their faces. How is that possibly helping him?'

'It will one day,' she said. 'You've chosen your road, Mademoiselle, and you know it's the right one. You have only to stay on it to the very end.'

Albert Grimauld

We kept moving. All we could do, see, just get our heads down and keep moving, even if we hadn't the glimmer of an idea where.

Soldiers, that's why. The woods were full of them, they'd of had us the first day if it wasn't for André. He was an old hand at this woods game, he knew about leading the horses down the streams and keeping to the hard paths to stop anyone tracking us, he knew about stifling our little bits of fires. But we couldn't dodge them forever, not that number. They was going to catch us sooner or later without we spent the whole day in trees like ruddy birds.

So out we come and on to the roads to bluff it out. It seemed safe enough, the laddie wasn't so recognizable these days, and soldiers weren't going to stop law-abiding folk riding open about the country. We'd find a farm every couple of days, get fodder for the horses and bread for ourselves, then it was back to the woods, a bit of fire, and another meagre mouthful of rabbit. We hadn't the money for more, see, we were stretching Bernadette's bit of gold all we knew. Sometimes a farm would give us a day's work weeding the winter corn, but there's not much that time of year and we weren't the only vagabonds abroad by a long stretch.

What we were was the most noticeable. Two men and a woman, that's nothing, but them horses, oh my word. There we are hats in hand begging for a day's work in the fields, and behind us two war-horses worth a thousand livres apiece. We had 'thieves' writ round our necks like placards on the pillory, and after three weeks we was going to sleep hungry.

André handled it like a soldier. He'd had good training in that past life of his, someone had toughened him like ox-hide. He'd work in the fields, he'd take the cussing and doors shut in our faces, he'd skin rabbits and gut fish like he'd done it all his life. The one time I saw him angry was when a farm set dogs on us, and that was only for Bernadette. She was knocked clear off her feet by one of they mastiffs, and André turned back, flattened the farmer, and made him apologize for abusing a woman.

He was still smouldering inside. I'd see him sometimes of an evening, stripping wood to make a spit for supper, and know he was thinking of it then. There he'd be, cutting down with knuckles white as the blade, knife slicing savage down the bark, *t'chunk*, then again sharp hard, *t'chunk*, and all the while that darkness in his eyes.

Ah, but there was something else darkening over that spring. We were seeing soldiers again, more every day, thousands of them and on the march. There's a muster somewhere north and things is waking up in Flanders, rumours buzzing all over. We did a day's work near Lassigny, and heard the Comte de Soissons had been ousted as Governor of Champagne. 'It's coming, Grimauld,' says André. 'This is it, it's coming.'

I'd have known it anyway, even without his talk of conspiracies. If there's one thing a man like me can smell it's war.

Jacques de Roland

It was coming, we were sure of it. Bouillon and Soissons were making warlike noises, and when it was announced Châtillon's army was off to join la Meilleraye in Flanders I wasn't the only one betting he'd end up in the Sedan instead.

Everyone in Paris knew about it now. They were calling themselves the 'Princes de la Paix' by then, Soissons and Bouillon and Guise, and coming out with a lot of guff about wanting peace with Spain so people wouldn't have to pay such high taxes. They didn't mention more power for themselves, of course, or inviting Imperial forces into France, that sort of got lost in the general enthusiasm. And there was a lot of it, actually, someone was stirring things up in the city, and we'd a pretty good idea who.

I didn't care much now André was dead. The Comtesse still

banged on about clearing his name for the honour of the family, but all I knew was it was my chance to bloody fight. The Comte made sure I got it, he went to see Châtillon himself and had me and the Puppies all signed on as Gentleman Volunteers attached to a cavalry squadron of the Orléans.

We spent the last day getting ready. Charlot was coming with me as my aide, but I chose Philibert as my lackey. He wasn't a brilliant cook but he'd always wanted to be in the army, he kept clippings from the Gazette and could tell me every single regiment at every action France had fought in the last ten years. He went all Gascon with ecstasy when I told him, he kissed my hands and promised to serve me 'to the death, Monsieur, to the very death!'

That night the Comtesse took me out to show me off. I hated going out those days, we kept bumping into people I wanted to kill. Desmoulins was in all the salons, soaking up attention because he'd got a new regiment and was off to war any day. I'd seen d'Arsy too, but at least he'd got a stiff arm and a bloody great scar down his neck, and I just knew in my heart who'd given it him. We never saw Lavigne, and Raoul heard a rumour he'd died of a chest complaint, but I bet I knew what kind.

But that night we went to the Hôtel Rambouillet, and when we walked into the Chambre Bleue the first person I saw was Bouchard. I was so shocked it took me a second to notice he was chatting to Florian du Pré, and even longer to realize that the woman with them was Anne.

I shouldn't have been surprised really. We'd been making enquiries ever since her letter, I'd worried she might be a prisoner or something, but people said she'd been around at church and stuff, and I'd begun to think it must have been Jeanette sent the letter herself. Now I knew it. Anne seemed perfectly happy to be where she was, and when Bouchard said something she even gave this gay kind of laugh. Anne du Pré, who André had loved since he was a child, standing laughing with his murderer. She was part of it too, all the things André had believed in that turned out to be worthless and wrong.

Then I looked again at Bouchard basking in the light of the copper chandelier, and everything else got swamped with the hate. The Marquise brought him over to be introduced, and I remember the tiny lift of his eyebrow and tucked-in smile at the corners of his mouth as he said 'Delighted, M. de Roland,' while his eyes said 'I killed your brother, stable boy, what are you going to do about it?' I already knew what I was going to bloody do about it. We were going to beat the rebel armies, then I was going to come back and kill him.

We left the next day, Tuesday the 7th of May. I'd pooled the money for a baggage wagon with the Puppies, and they came to the Hôtel de Roland so we could leave together.

I remember Raoul was all excited because people were lining the streets to see us off. 'You'll see, Jacquot,' he said. 'The ladies won't look at anyone who doesn't fight this season. They want a man of war, warm and sweaty from the battlefield.'

'How disgusting,' said Gaspard. 'Personally I do not intend to sweat. I shall look magnificent on my new mare, and the ladies may throw flowers as I pass.'

Philibert led me out Guinevere, the best horse in the Roland stable, and the servants cheered as I mounted her. I felt self-conscious and wrong, but then Crespin whispered 'You're doing it for André, you know, Jacquot. He'd be awfully proud.'

I wasn't sure for a moment, then turned to see Charlot formally presenting me with my new battle sword. I hadn't held one like it since the Battle of Dax, and just the touch brought it all back in a shock of blood and musket fire and screaming horses. Crespin was right. This was André's fight, clean and free of politics, the only kind that really mattered. When I slid the sword into the scabbard it made a decisive *click* that was like a door shutting on Paris.

Albert Grimauld

There weren't much spring where we were, and that's a fact. It wasn't just the being hungry and the money running out, it was the bone-aching endless weariness of it and the not having nothing to hope for next day nor the next.

But it wasn't even that stuffed us in the end, it was my own ruddy neck. The thing wasn't healing, see. André had this notion it needed to be kept clean, said he'd heard it off a friend of his called Stefan, so every night Bernadette was washing and dressing me, and very discreet she was too, she never said one word about what she found there. But the wound's getting puffy, and one night André says 'That's it, we've got to get you to a surgeon.'

So what he did, if you'll believe, what he did was take me into Beuvraignes, find me a surgeon, get us a room, and put me to bed till it's healed. What he did was sell his shirt, his hat, and the buttons on his coat, and when that wasn't enough he sold his ring. He didn't even get much for it, the crest made it dangerous, he had to deal with a dodgy customer in a cabaret to get it off his hands at all. But that's what he did, he went round with his coat held together with a belt and left himself nothing but his knife and sword.

It was only just enough even then. Bernadette rationed our food all she could, but it still took more than two weeks before we were on the road again and down to our last sou. André said we'd keep heading north and his own people would hide us, but he was reckoning without a little something that puts the pox on a man's prospects like nothing else. Rain, boy, I'm talking about rain. Kipping under the stars on a fine evening's one thing, huddling on a mudbank with half the Seine down your neck's another. We were cold, wet and hungry, we'd no money and no means of getting it, the only thing missing was plague.

We spent the last night outside Roye. The rain hadn't let up since daybreak, we was breathing it as well as feeling it, and the ache in our bones was telling us time to call it a day. We found a wood to bivouac, but the rain had wheedled its way into my tinderbox, I couldn't have got a spark out of it in the devil's own drawing room. André got a handful of tinder under his coat and chafed it and breathed warm air on it, he kept saying 'That's done it, try again, I'm sure it's dry now,' but his hands were wet and so were mine, we were flogging a horse so dead it was rotting. I said 'It's not going to happen, laddie, give it up and let it go.'

There was a spark then all right, it flashed up in his eyes like a powder-pan, and then slowly I saw it fade and go out. He sat back on the sopping ground and said 'You're right.'

I said 'Come on, one night in the cold's not going to kill us, is it?'

'Not us,' he says, and there's his eyes sliding over to Bernadette wiping her sleeve over her cooking pan, bravely confident there'll be meat for it and a fire to cook it on. 'She can't go on like this, Grimauld, I'm killing her.'

Females. That's what drags a man down in this life. There she was, shivering wet in her rag of a cloak, and André's spirit dying out of him just looking at her.

There's no arguing with him neither, and in a minute or two he's got himself a plan. He'll take us into Roye and sell the big horse called Tonnerre, then me and Bernadette will get lodgings on the proceeds and sit it out while he goes on alone to this place called the Saillie where he says he'll get help.

Yes, yes, a-course I told him, what do you take me for? I said 'All right for the girlie, but I'm coming with you, you'll need someone to watch your back,' but he says Bernadette's got to be looked after and the only one to do it is me. I says 'She'll never let you go alone,' but he says 'So we don't tell her. I'll give you the money and slip off once she's settled.'

It wasn't just his back wanted watching, it was his front as well. I said 'Give over, you'll get yourself killed.'

He grins at me. There we are, sopping wet in a patch of nettles with no food and no fire, and he goes and ruddy grins. 'No, I won't,' he says.

We went into Roye good and early. The rain had stopped, we was drying out nice, and there's the city smell about us again, bit of colour, bit of life, bit of anything other than mud and trees and rain. We scraped together our last deniers to buy a loaf of rye bread and a mug of bouillon, and leaned against a wall in the sun to share our breakfast. Ah, burn me to Bremen, but that bouillon was good. Hot and wet, and the meat tang in the back of the throat, it even put colour in Bernadette's cheeks. Life looked brighter after that.

Not for André. It was a sad old business for him, leaving his friends, not to mention selling his dad's old horse. He was soft over that animal, kept stroking it like telling it sorry all the walk into Roye. But we'd ate our last meal, there was no more for no one till the horse was traded, so off we went to the livestock quarter to do the deed. And that, my poppet, is where things started to turn turnip.

We found a place with a big yard and the coper looks proper impressed. This ain't your ordinary animal, see, it's what André calls a Mecklenburg, and the fellow's eyes are popping just at the sight of it. He goes running over its points, having himself a good look under the saddle in case there's something we're not telling. André's scowling at the floor, but I'm watching, I'm on to it, and when the coper's hand stops sudden in mid-air I see it right off.

'Wonderful animal,' says he, face gleaming with sudden sweat. 'I'll talk to my partner, see how high we can go.' He backs out the yard, wiping his hands on his apron and leaving a smell of fish worse nor Marseilles.

I'm in and up with the saddle, and there it is, plain as paper, a crest on the cloth with a big gold 'R', same as the one on the ring. Call me a fool for not seeing it before, but I never had the saddling of that horse, never, the fucking thing would have had me in seconds. I grabbed its bridle, jerked it round, and said 'All of us, out now.'

As we nipped out the yard I saw a boy already pelting up the street for a provost. Maybe they guessed he was de Roland, maybe they thought we was horse thieves, but it was the gallows either end of that question. I was up on the big stallion and yelling André to up on the other to get somewhere healthier fast.

But the coper comes running after us yelling 'Stop!' and others take up the shout all round. A couple of bored soldiers at the end of the street hear it and go to put the chains across, they're a-blocking of the road. Round we go and fast, but the other end's got a huge carriage fat-bellied in the middle of it, footmen scurrying round and yelling at whatever poor honest tradesman's got in the way. I'd maybe slip past on foot, but we've two ruddy horses laden with baggage, we're good and trapped.

'This way,' yells André, turning down a cobbled passage and near scraping his leg off as he goes. It's narrow all right, and me on the bigger horse, I have to flip the saddlebags atop the beast's back to get us through at all. Behind us I hear yelling and the pounding of feet.

We squeeze through into a bigger road but you'd never know it, we're wedged in a crowd of people and carts, hardly room to get a hoof down nowhere, and down the far end a block of soldiers marching right this way. I can't think what's up, but I know what to do about it, and so does de Roland, he's off his horse and lifting Bernadette down with him, and I'm on the ground already. When people are looking for you in a crowd, the place to be is in among it, see, not stuck on the biggest horse around.

We struggle forward together. There's others leading horses in this mob, even a couple leading oxen, I'm feeling a touch less like a spire sticking out of a village, but the whole crowd's shuffling slowly on like one big stream and us with no choice but to go with them. We're being squashed together, see, there's market stands either side narrowing the passage, then I get a glimpse of the square a-front of us and see why. There's soldiers lined up, one on a box reading off a bit of paper, men and horses clustered to one side, and above the crowd babble I hear the sound of a drum.

Recruiting. The street's blocked because the military's took over the square, they're on the *racolage,* and looking to lure some nice new men to the flag. They may be more than luring them too, the soldiers behind are herding vagabonds and driving them right this way. We've got a hue and cry after us, troops behind us, soldiers in front, we're trapped like rabbits and not a hole to run for.

'Leave the horses,' I yell at André. 'We can dodge in a cabaret and out the other side.'

He backs up against a wall, arm round Bernadette to keep her safe in the press. 'We need the money, they're all we've got.'

I say 'You've still got your life, laddie.'

He knows it, he's looking this way and that for a way out, seeing nothing but crowds and soldiers and the girlie needing protecting. Then he thrusts his reins at me and says 'Take Héros. They didn't see him, he's safe and nearly as valuable. Sell him, Grimauld, everything as we said. I'll take Tonnerre and ride my way out.'

But Bernadette's on it now, she's clutching at his arm like a blind woman. 'You can't, André,' she's saying. 'You can't, they'll shoot you.'

He tries to unpeel her fingers. 'Stay with Grimauld, you'll be all right, I promise.'

No one's going to be all right, he'll be caught or dead in a minute. His foot's in the stirrup, then the drum starts another roll, I see it at last, and grab him back down.

'Whoa there,' I tell him. 'Whoa now, boys. There's maybe another way.'

Bernadette Fournier

It was everything we needed. It was safety and food and shelter, it could give André the chance to fight the very enemies we now fled. Grimauld too was eager to return to the life he knew best, while Monsieur already knows the army had been my own first home.

There was no time to lose, for the troops were marching closer and we all saw the militia heading purposefully towards a man who led a horse. But the crowds were slow, we could only take the tiniest steps for fear of treading on the heels of the people in front and drawing the very attention we wished to avoid. It was like the horror of a nightmare, when one tries to run and does not move. Then at last there were smooth, hard flags beneath our feet, we were in the square, and the crowd thinning and spreading as they went about their business. We walked so quickly to the recruiting enseign I think we almost ran.

He looked at the horses, said 'Awfully sorry, this is for infantry,' and waved us back to the crowd.

I felt a great wave of panic, but the Chevalier said quickly 'Infantry's fine,' and explained our horses were only for baggage.

The enseign brightened. He was perhaps fourteen, with a freckled face and squeaky voice, and I guessed he was simply new to his job. 'Oh, jolly good then,' he said. 'But we can't have whores, the capitaine's *very* particular about that.'

André's hand pressed tighter round my arm, but Grimauld said 'No, this is his wife, see. Proper lawful wife. By the Church.'

The enseign's face cleared. 'Oh, jolly good, I know we're short. Now let's see, we'll need to find the caporal.' He looked vaguely about him.

I heard shouting behind, and risked a quick glance back. It was only some vagabonds escaping into the crowds, yet I saw now the buff coats of the Roye militia approaching the square itself, and knew we were out of time. The enseign began to lead us towards a man waiting by the Hôtel de Ville, but we had not even reached him when I heard a shout of 'Try the square!' and the sound of marching feet.

The caporal seemed to feel even less urgency than his officer. He was a great, tall man with a little scar on his cheek, lounging against the wall with an air of great boredom, his legs thrust out quite careless of who they might trip. His beard was rough, his appearance unkempt, and he was cleaning his nails with the tip of a broad, jagged knife.

'Look, Ravel,' said the ensign importantly. 'Our first recruits! Can I leave them with you?'

The big man sighed. 'I expect so.' He waited for the ensign to turn away, then uncoiled himself from the wall, straightened, and looked at us.

His eyes rested on me a moment, the look of a man who knows exactly what to do with a woman and wishes her to know it. He smiled slightly, then slid his gaze to Grimauld, took in the sight of an ex-soldier and gave a short nod of recognition. Then he looked at André.

His expression did not change, Monsieur, it seemed almost to fix exactly as it was. Perhaps the lines about his mouth deepened a little, I could not say, but when his lips finally spoke, it was only to say the single word 'Fuck.'

The Chevalier looked back at him, and to my astonishment there was a brightness in his eyes I had not seen for many days.

'Hullo, Stefan,' he said, and smiled.

Thirteen

Stefan Ravel

From his interviews with the Abbé Fleuriot, 1669

What the fuck did you think I'd been doing? Knitting?

Strange as it seems, M. l'Abbé, I'd somehow managed to reach the giddy rank of caporal all by my disreputable self. The fact all our NCOs got blown to fuck at Arras may have had something to do with it, but that's the grand truth of the army and you may as well learn it now. Talent will out in the end, as long as your entrails don't get there first.

Mine wasn't the only unit shredded at Arras. New regiments were formed every week: the Lermont, the Montecler, Lannoy, more than some of our new officers could count. The same old faces, though, and it was my old sergeant from La Mothe who recruited me into the brand new Aubéry when it was settling into winter quarters in Roye.

Oh, I'd had a comfortable enough time, lounging around waiting for our officers to prise themselves out of the Paris salons, but that was all over and done with now. It was May and a war to be fought, even if it wasn't the one we'd been expecting. We should have been gone a week ago to the siege of Aire, but no, our bastard lieutenant had arrived with new orders, and they were enough to make any man think. Rebellion was brewing in the Sedan, and we were to march every recruit we could find to the muster at Rethel.

That's what it was about those days, Abbé, more men. The civilians weren't exactly falling over themselves to join our little party, and we were peering under any stone we could find. We were taking them off the fields and waylaying them in the cabarets, one company marched into a church at Mass and took the whole congregation. None of it was enough. So there we were on our last day making one final appeal to the reluctant manhood of Roye, and who should turn up but André de Roland himself.

Well, now. Young André. Sorry to disappoint you, Abbé, but I hadn't given him a lot of thought that last year. Oh yes, I'd heard all about his little fall from grace, but can't say I was bothered. The last time I'd seen him he'd refused to shoot an enemy soldier who was trying to kill me, and oddly enough that wasn't a decision I agreed with.

And now here he was in front of me, a year and a beard older, maybe a little sadder and wiser, but still the same André, utterly confident that good old Stefan would rush to his rescue. Oh yes, I saw the militia striding purposefully across the square, I knew the kid was up against it, and you know what? That suited me just fine.

I spread my legs, folded my arms, and said 'Trouble?'

He didn't blink. 'Yes.'

'Need my help, do you?'

A muscle twitched in his cheek. 'Yes.'

The militia sergeant was walking over. I leaned against the wall and said 'Give me one good reason why I should help you.'

'There isn't one,' he said truthfully. 'I'm asking anyway.'

I said 'I asked you once – remember?'

He said 'I haven't forgotten any of it, Stefan. Have you?'

He had balls, that boy. The sergeant was up to us, the scrawny companion was edging furtively away, but André never took his eyes from mine. I broke the look firmly, but then noticed a little something else that gave me pause. That was a nice coat he was wearing, belted up tight round his waist, but there didn't seem to be any buttons on it, and all I could see at the neck was a little triangle of brown chest. André, Chevalier de Roland, didn't seem to own so much as a shirt.

I shoved myself away from the wall. 'Hullo, Coullart, what's up?'

'Horse thieves,' the sergeant said bluntly. He was possibly the dullest militiaman in Picardie, which is quite an achievement in its way. 'Suspected, anyway, they tried to sell one at Prédelet's place. Could be that beast there, mind if I look?'

I recognized it at once. They called it Tonnerre, it was the one Jacques used to ride.

I said 'Come off it, man, that's a regimental animal. If one of our officers needs to flog his own horse is that something we want to stick our noses in?'

Coullart's face went blank. 'Prédelet reckoned it was the Chevalier de Roland's. He saw the crest.'

Only André de Roland would try to sell a horse on the quiet and leave his fucking name on it. I said 'Their property was confiscated, wasn't it? Why shouldn't my officer buy it?'

I could see his sluggish brain churning. 'It's definitely his then? And these are your men?'

I let my eyes linger on André a moment. He was standing quite still, head up, and his eyes steady on my face.

I said 'Definitely.'

Bernadette Fournier

He did it, Monsieur. The militiaman walked clear away, and we were safe.

André moved at once to his friend. 'Stefan, thank you, that was –'

'When you're spoken to, soldier,' said M. Ravel, brushing brusquely past him. 'Now against the wall, the pair of you, I need to see you're fit to serve.'

The hurt in André's face was quite terrible. I was confused myself, for was this not the Stefan Ravel he had told us of so often and admired so greatly? Yet there was no affection in his manner, and when he examined André he did it with the detachment a man uses when he values a horse. He tested the strength of his arms, made him bend and stand, looked in his mouth, then said dismissively 'Good enough,' and turned to Grimauld.

Grimauld was apprehensive, Monsieur, and I understood why, for it was I who had seen to his dressing this last month. He said 'I've served before, caporal, I'm all right.'

'Graveyards are full of men who've served before,' said M. Ravel. 'What's under the dressing?'

Grimauld twisted his neck uneasily. 'Ah, it's just a clean cut, see, healing nicely, you won't get no surgeon's bills off of me.'

'Fuck the bills, man,' said M. Ravel, backing him against the wall.

'You think I want to pay recruitment money to someone who'll drop dead of gangrene in a month? Get your hands out the way.'

He was very much man, Stefan Ravel, and Grimauld could only stand helplessly as the caporal pushed the hair off his shoulders to examine the wound. And there they were, Monsieur, his ears exposed, each harshly slit through the lobes.

M. Ravel regarded him with contempt. 'What was it – stealing?'

'No call for that, caporal,' said Grimauld, and his bony hands were clenching at his sides. 'No fucking call. You weren't there, see, you don't know.'

'I know,' said M. Ravel. 'I know what robbing your comrades means, and we don't mutilate for that in this regiment, we hang.' He swung round again on André and for the first time I heard anger in his voice. 'For Christ's sake, look what you've taken up with. How much money has he had off you?'

'None,' said André, as calmly and coldly as if he had known all along. 'This man is my friend, and the wound in his neck came from protecting my back.'

They stared at each other a moment, then M. Ravel said 'Well, let's hope he never wants the same favour in return.'

I understood then we had a grudge to deal with, but at least the outburst seemed to curb M. Ravel's anger. He said no more about Grimauld's past, informed the men they were now musketeers in the Aubéry Regiment, and led them into the Hôtel de Ville to receive their recruitment bounty. It was to be twenty whole livres each, Monsieur, I could buy a new shirt for the Chevalier and food for many days, we could even send a letter to Paris to reassure Jacques. I thought of these things as I waited in the sun, and felt hopeful we might at last put the feeling of being hunted behind us and enjoy a little respite from our troubles.

Then they came out and I saw André's face. I said quickly 'What is it?'

He glanced around him. 'We're marching tomorrow against the Sedan.'

I said 'Are not these the people you most wish to fight?'

'Oh yes,' he said. 'But our commanding officer arrives this afternoon. They say it's a Capitaine Desmoulins.'

Oh, you know me, Abbé, always ready to give an officer the benefit of the doubt. This one invited the senior men to his room and even gave us wine, which was at least a promising start. What I couldn't work out was why he was doing it, since he spent the whole time lounging disdainfully on his desk, wafting a vinegar-laden handkerchief against the stench of common soldiers. I watched him, Abbé, I saw him scrutinizing each of us in turn, and wondered what he was really after.

He only had five of us to work on, the company being dismally under strength. There was a second caporal, Charpentier, a handsome, well-set-up brute on the outside, but with an ugly habit of pressing his attentions on those who couldn't fight back. I found a new recruit crying his eyes out one morning and gathered Charpentier had had him his first night. Well, I don't like to bother authority with these things, I just took Charpentier out to the privy and stuck his head down the hole to acquaint himself better with his own kind.

We'd a good sergeant, though, my old friend Jean Sury from La Mothe. Oh, he wouldn't have appealed to you, Abbé, he'd been in the Croquants' Rebellion and was as hot against injustice as I was myself, but he was a good soldier, solid as Burgundy stone. It was Sury who'd pleaded with my old capitaine against the running-the-gauntlet that day, and if he'd had his way my brother would have still been alive.

Then there were what you'd call the proper officers. Poor Michaud couldn't do his boots up without help, but I'd a soft spot for the kid all the same. You go on the *racolage,* you say 'Yes, this is for cavalry,' and by the time they find the nearest they're getting to a horse is to march through its shit it's all a little late. I heard Michaud telling recruits 'Sorry, this is for infantry,' and something inside that leathery thing I call a heart grew that little touch warmer.

Our revered lieutenant was enough to shrivel it entirely. I'd like to be charitable about Fauvel, given how things turned out, so I'll just mention he was a cousin of Desmoulins and a first-class bastard. There were only two goals in Fauvel's life, licking the arses of the men above him and kicking the shit out of the ones below him. He'd a curiously flat face, as if someone had had the sense to smash it against a paving slab where it belonged. Even his eyes were flat, like a lizard's.

It wasn't much of a staff for our new capitaine, us and twenty-four men out of a company that ought to have numbered fifty-five, but Desmoulins didn't seem bothered.

'It's not the quantity that matters,' he said, pressing his handkerchief to his nose in defence against our quality. 'We shall still show the enemy our mettle. Are the men properly dressed?'

'Of course, M'sieur,' said Fauvel.

'No, M'sieur,' said Sury at the same time.

There was a lovely little silence. I took advantage of it to grab another goblet of wine.

Sury said 'Some are in rags. We're sending men out to face the enemy half-naked.'

Desmoulins stretched out his elegant legs and admired his spurs. 'Not any more. I've arranged for a clothing issue this evening, along with boots for every man who needs them.'

Now that did get my attention. Infantry wore clogs back then, Abbé, but having a reprehensible desire to arrive at our destinations uncrippled, most of us grabbed boots wherever we could get them. A little thing like that could make Desmoulins the most popular officer I'd ever known.

'The whole regiment's to have them,' he said, snapping his fingers for more wine. 'The coats are the same colour, of course, to save money on the cloth, but that has its advantages. We'll need a lot of esprit de corps in this regiment if it's to fight fellow Frenchmen.'

'Damned Sedanaise,' said Charpentier. 'The men won't mind fighting them.'

Desmoulins looked at him through narrowed eyes. 'M. le Comte de Soissons is a prince of the blood. It will be difficult for a true Frenchman to regard him as the enemy.'

Michaud said hesitantly 'But then what's it –?' He caught Fauvel's eye and stopped.

'What's it about?' said Desmoulins. 'A fair question, enseign. Monsieur le Comte is concerned with the burden of taxes on our people. He desires the removal of Cardinal Richelieu and an honourable end to the war.'

The silence this time was even more interesting. I thought 'Fuck it,' had another slug of wine and said 'Sounds reasonable.'

Fauvel spun round with the nearest I'd seen him come to passion. 'Treason,' he hissed, spraying my cheek with spittle. 'That's *treason*.'

Desmoulins regarded him with distaste. 'Oh, come, Fauvel, our nation is known for independent thinkers, is it not?'

Fauvel's eyes almost bulged out of flatness. He was probably struggling with the concept of independent thought. 'Of course, M'sieur, but –'

'Oh yes, yes,' said Desmoulins, flapping his handkerchief. 'Duty must come first. His Majesty does not agree with Monsieur le Comte, and so – we fight.' He smiled disarmingly, and offered us more wine.

Fauvel cornered me as soon as Desmoulins looked the other way. 'I'll not forget that, Ravel,' he said, breathing hot in my ear. 'I'll be on your shoulder every day after this.'

It was an unattractive prospect, but fortunately Desmoulins turned again and said 'Ah, Fauvel, it occurs to me, should we not have two sergeants in this company?'

'Absolutely, M'sieur,' said Fauvel, snapping his neck back up to attention so fast he nearly broke it. 'But our strength is so low . . .'

'That discipline is the more important,' said Desmoulins. 'I believe Ravel is the senior caporal, is that right? Let's make him up, shall we, and see how it goes.'

A sergeant's pay isn't to be sniffed at, Abbé, and neither was the chance to stick two fingers up to Fauvel. I took both, and was understandably feeling a little pleased with myself when I strolled back to my quarters that evening. André was waiting for me, as I'd known he would be, but I said 'Later, soldier,' and walked straight past.

There's little more depressing than a field company's last night in quarters. Everything was already bundled up to go, nothing left but bare palliasses and miserable NCOs eating their last hot food for God knows how long. We messed together in our room, it stretched our supplies out longer, so I took my mug and helped myself to soup from the pot.

'Man outside to see you,' said Bonnier, our anspessade. 'Been there quite a while.'

'Has he?' I said, and took a drink of soup.

'Oh, don't be such a bastard, Ravel,' he said. 'It's one of the new lot, name of Thibault. He didn't think I could help.'

I thought I'd helped him quite enough already, but didn't want anyone to start wondering why only Ravel would do. I said 'All right, all right,' and headed for the door.

André was still waiting and looking pleasingly pissed off, so I took another sip from my mug and said 'Go ahead, Thibault.'

He said 'I want to thank you for what you did today.'

'All right,' I said. 'Anything else?'

'Yes. I've met your capitaine before, and it's possible he might recognize me.'

I laughed. 'Not with that beard.'

He looked at me. 'You did.'

I straightened to go. 'Our capitaine isn't likely to get within sniffing distance of a recruit, you're safe enough there. Just don't make yourself conspicuous, all right?'

'Of course,' he said, offended. 'But there's more to it than that.'

He was obviously going to haunt me till he got it off his chest, so I stood and drank soup and let him tell me the whole thing. It was a disturbing little story, especially in view of what Desmoulins had said about Soissons, but it didn't seem enough to worry about.

I said 'Look, if he's a sympathizer, fine, lots of men are. He can't do much harm here.'

'Can't he?'

'Well, if he orders us to go and stand naked in front of enemy cannon I'll be sure to let you know.' I finished my soup, but something in the way he watched me made me suddenly uncomfortable. 'Have you eaten?'

He looked away. 'I had to see you first. Bernadette will have got me something.'

It was dark in the corridor, but his face looked more drawn than I remembered and his cheekbones more prominent. I swore at him, went back into the room and brought out another mug. 'Get that down you,' I said, and thrust it at him. 'That's an order.'

He drank it slowly, and I noticed the thinness of his wrists. He leaned back against the wall when he'd finished, and I realized he needed the support.

I said 'Jesus Christ, André.'

He shrugged.

I said 'Where the fuck's Jacques anyway, why isn't he looking after you?'

'He's fine,' he said, and there it was, the old soft look he always had when he talked about that thick-headed stable boy. 'He's in Paris, he's fine. He's my brother, Stefan, did you know? My grandmother's accepting him, he'll be Jacques de Roland by now.'

It figured. 'So he's your brother and he's in Paris. I see.'

'You don't,' he said at once. 'He knows I'm all right, I've got friends.'

'I've seen them,' I said. 'Sod the beard, André, you're the same bloody fool underneath.'

He kept his voice expressionless. 'Same bloody fool.'

I took the mug back off him. 'Well, I won't give you away. But there aren't going to be any more cosy little chats like this one, and I'm not getting involved.'

He nodded. 'I understand, caporal.'

'I understand, *sergeant*,' I said smugly, and went back to my room.

It was only when I was dozing off to sleep that it finally occurred to me to wonder about the suddenness of that promotion. Looking back over the conversation, I began to wonder if there mightn't be a reason for it I didn't like at all.

Bernadette Fournier

We were in married quarters, Monsieur, for I was now Mme Thibault and must keep the pretence for my own safety.

The other wives were older and rougher and inclined to be unfriendly, but Mme Bonnier's husband was drinking with the NCOs so she was glad of my company and gave me much helpful advice. I had been worrying how to manage our horses, but she said our cooks would be delighted to ride like gentlemen, and since their mother Francine was our sutler, she would surely be willing to carry me in her viviandière's wagon in recompense.

I said 'There will be two places then, so perhaps you would ride with me,' but she laughed and said 'I'm an old hand at this, my dear, I'll not be shaming Bonnier by riding while he walks.' I was then afraid I might shame André if I did not march, but she squeezed my hand between two strong brown ones and said 'A pretty little thing like you? Your husband will be wanting you to save your strength for something very different.'

She was a kind, motherly woman who meant nothing but good, but I was afraid others would share her expectation, and could not help a slight uneasiness when André returned. We had at least a palliasse to ourselves, while Grimauld had told me he must share with two others, but the nearness still concerned me. I had slept in André's arms before, but now he must strip and I must at least undress to my chemise. Our situation was not helped by the boisterous activity of the others or the encouragement of a dreadful man with a loud voice who kept saying 'Last night in comfort, boys and girls, there'll be some hay made tonight.' I looked nervously at André, but he seemed quite unembarrassed and gave me only a little conspiratorial grin as he unbuckled his belt and began to undress.

I waited until he was under the sheet, then removed my dress and slipped quickly in beside him. He whispered 'It's all right, sweetheart, I won't do anything,' and I said at once 'I know,' and could not understand why a part of me felt sad. I settled beside him in my old position, with my head on his chest and my arm around his waist, but it was hard to ignore the unaccustomed warmth of his naked skin and the sensation of my breasts against his ribs, for he clearly felt the difference as much as I. After a while his body grew warmer and his breathing quicker, while a faint movement of the sheet suggested he was in discomfort below. I kept my arm steady where it was, for if I slid it any lower I knew well what I would touch.

His whisper carried a tiny vibration of laughter. 'I think perhaps I'd better turn over.'

I began to withdraw, but my arm brushed lightly against his belly as it passed and I heard the involuntary quiver in his breath. It was unfair, Monsieur, unfair and cruel, for he had every right to demand my body if he chose. He had lost everything through defending me, and all I gave him back was torment.

I laid my hand on his chest, tilted up my head and whispered 'You don't have to.'

His heart beat harder beneath my palm, and I knew he understood. He whispered 'You don't really want to, Bernadette.'

It was true I did not. I had been granted something denied so many richer women, the chance to give my heart with my body as if I were a single whole person, and nothing less would ever content me again. For me then as now there was only Jacques. I knew he had abandoned me for his duty, I knew by now he would have forgotten me, but I knew also he was my man until he died.

But his brother had never abandoned me, and here was a debt to be paid. I looked in his eyes and said softly 'You can if you like.'

'If I like?' he said, and cradled my cheek with his hand. 'Bernadette, do you really not know how beautiful you are?'

To him I was at that moment, and I saw it in his eyes. He was seventeen and a virgin, the woman he had waited all this time for had betrayed him, and my limbs felt suddenly weak as I realized the depth of his hunger. For perhaps two breaths we looked at each other, aware of every tiny place our bodies touched, then he bowed his head and rubbed his nose gently against mine. 'Only Jacques would never forgive me, and neither would you.'

I drew back to see him better. 'And perhaps you think also of Mlle du Pré?'

He touched his finger to my lips, said 'Good night, my darling girl,' then turned over and laid himself as if to sleep.

I remember lying with his back warm against me, and wishing to laugh at my earlier folly. Here I had been pitying Grimauld that he must sleep three to a bed, but it seemed to me we had four in our own.

Albert Grimauld

Stefan Ravel? Ah, don't get me started. And it's sergeant he was next day, if you please, a-swaggering round with them great long legs of his, bawling at everyone 'Line up there, slope your pieces regular, stop that shuffling, Grimauld', picking on men near twice his age, oh my word. André wrote his brother to say we were safe in the care of a good friend, but it didn't look much like it to me.

It started at the review that morning. That's the line-up for the *étapes*, see, to give the intendants the numbers to feed as we march through their territory, but there's some very funny characters among us and I know we're doing the old business with the *passe-volants*. Ah, it's common enough, most capitaines stick a few extra men in the line to pad out the numbers and pay, but I'd never seen a do like this, never. We had sutlers and cooks in the line, we had the capitaine's bootboy, we even had one of the rejected vagabonds with a long coat to disguise him only having one arm. Our capitaine was making good and sure people thought we'd a full complement and us only half the number.

André was muttering all through. 'It's not right, Grimauld. How's the Maréchal to order a battle if he doesn't know how many men he's got?' I'm trying to shush him, but it's no good, Ravel's already caught him at it.

'Silence in the ranks!' he bawls, waving his cane towards André.

The laddie starts to say 'But –' and Ravel lifts the cane to point right at his face. 'You have something to say, soldier?'

André glares back, and you could have fired a culverin off the look burning between them. Then he lifts his chin and says 'No, sergeant.'

'No,' says Ravel, 'I thought not.' And off he strolls, slapping his cane against his leg, pleased with himself as a cradle of cats.

But the next day, that's something else. We stopped at Ham that night, and by the time we gets there all the *logements* have gone. Bernadette's all right, she sleeps snug in the wagon with Francine the viviandière, but most of our company gets put up in halls in the château itself, nothing but hard floors and a ruddy draught. Ravel requisitions sacks and straw and gets a few of us sat stuffing palliasses, nice easy work, everyone sitting round chatting, then I see that big Caporal Charpentier's gone and wheedled himself next to André.

Ah, trust me, I'd had him pegged from the off, but I hadn't seen

André was just the type to appeal. He was young, kept himself clean, nicely spoken, oh just what they fancy, and Charpentier's eyeing him like a dog that's spotted dinner. But I hadn't seen it and hadn't warned him, and there's not a thing I can do now with the man right next to us. The laddie don't know no better, see, the caporal's speaking him nice so he speaks nice back, and I don't like how it's going one bit. Next thing they're both on their feet and Charpentier telling Ravel he's going to take young Thibault to look for more straw.

Ravel hesitates and I see he knows. I wait for him to tell the caporal to bugger off up his own backside, but he only says 'All right, off you go.'

Now that's not right in any language, and as soon as they're out the door I'm up to follow them, but Ravel tells me right off to stay where I am. There's stirring all round the hall and I'm guessing everyone knows, so I say 'Come on, sergeant,' and stand my ground.

For maybe the first time Ravel looks at me like I'm not just shit on his shoe, but all he says is 'The kid can look after himself. Now go back to your work.'

Ah, don't you give me that, couldn't go against an officer, could I? It don't make no nevermind anyhow, as two minutes later the door crash-bangs open and there's André back all by himself, straw down his front, shirt ripped at the collar, blood on his knuckles, and murder in his eyes. Ravel glances briefly up at him, and a moment later I see he's grinning. André stamps back to his place and starts stuffing his palliasse like he's trying to choke it, but in a little while he slows and looks up again more thoughtful. Ravel's watching him, and when they look back down to their work again it's both of them with that little smile. I was smiling myself next morning when I sees Charpentier with a fat lip and eyes so swollen he can't see beyond his own nose.

Ravel maybe had it right that time, but it was still him the real trouble came from and I saw it brewing very early. It was our lieutenant, see, he had it in for Ravel good and proper, always putting him down in front of the ranks. So much so ordinary, but Ravel was giving it back with sugar on and what's more he was getting away with it. When Fauvel threatened to report him to the capitaine,

Ravel would just say 'Thank you, M'sieur, shall I send to tell him now?' And there was the rub, see, because no matter what Ravel did, the capitaine always supported him. None of us could understand it, noblemen stick together tighter than herrings in a box, but it was the same with Sury, whatever them sergeants did the capitaine was right behind them. That's unnatural and Fauvel knows it, the man was going round in a tizzy of bewilderment, and sooner or later he was going to break.

Something was wrong, and I'm speaking as a man who knew the army all through. Ravel was wrong, Sury was wrong, and wrongest of all was our capitaine. No one was complaining of him, all just the opposite. He give us boots to our feet and warm coats to our backs, and them things meant a lot in the worst campaign weather we'd seen in years. The streams was swollen, the roads was muddy, and when we reached Champagne we'd got half Picardie sticking to our boots, but still our little company was warm and dry. By the time we got to Rethel the men were talking of Desmoulins like a holy saint.

It weren't just the clothing neither. After the muster we were marched off to Douzy by the Sedan, and that was a bugger if you like. There was near seven thousand of us to camp in the fields, but our capitaine got us a nice site by the river, all the company together and others of the Aubéry nearby. We had the regiment's sutlers and cooks right there, Mass every morning, the women doing our laundry, it was like having our own little village. Discipline was tight, but the men would have died for Desmoulins them days, he could of ordered them to war against their mothers and they'd of gone.

We talked about it one evening, the three of us. The rain had let up for a miracle and Bernadette sat scraping mud off our boots while me and André cleaned our muskets and watched the rest of the army arrive. That was Sourdis' lot, that was, back from their little tour in the Luxembourg, and ready to muck in with the rest of us. It was cavalry first as usual, well fed and clean, I was looking forward to them seeing the churned-up sludge that was the only free bit left of the fields.

'Desmoulins is plotting something,' says André, spitting on his handkerchief to clean round the serpentine. 'He's not the kind of man to treat people well with no reason.'

'What can he do, Chevalier?' asks Bernadette, banging a boot on a stone to shake the caked mud off of it. 'He is only one man and we are an army.'

'But it's not just him, is it?' says he. 'The whole Aubéry are being looked after.'

'A good thing too then,' says I, and meaning it. 'No one else is.'

'No,' says André thoughtfully, flipping open the powder pan to give it a blow. 'Morale's very low, isn't it?'

He was right there. There were some cavalry still owed their fifty écus bounty for a start, and if anything can make ill feeling quicker than that I'd like to see the nose on it. The little word 'mutiny' comes floating up into my mind, and I don't like what it's doing there one bit.

'All right,' says I. 'Say the capitaine's looking to make himself popular for a reason. But if he is, he's not alone. What about they sergeants, eh? What about Sury and Ravel?'

His head's up in a second. 'Stefan would never touch something like that.'

'Whoa there,' says I. 'If you say so. You know who you can trust and who you can't.'

He glares at me a moment, then bites his lip and looks down, and I know who he's thinking on now. So does Bernadette, she looks at me reproachful as a nun.

'Ah, don't you worry,' I tells him. 'What's one regiment in all this lot? If they was thinking of making trouble, they've missed their chance, haven't they?'

He looks up at the cavalry going by, men doing his job, the place he ought to be. 'You're right,' he says, something wistful in his voice. 'We're all here now.'

—

Jacques de Roland

I remember that evening.

We'd taken some forts with Sourdis, none with a garrison more than fifty, and we were all desperate for proper action. Philibert kept asking when we were going to fight some real Spaniards because he'd promised Agnès he'd bring her back a helmet. By the time we rejoined Châtillon's army to rebuild the bridge at Douzy I was starting to think war was just about mud and being bored.

The fields were horrible, you couldn't ask cattle to sleep in them, so we spent the night in an alehouse in Douzy. It was stuffed elbow to elbow with moaning officers, all complaining about the weather, no support from Lorraine, the King not being here, it was worse than a village at taille time. The people of the house served us like we were evil invaders, and Gaspard wouldn't touch his wine in case someone had spat in it.

Crespin just thought it was all jolly camaraderie, and was soon in conversation with an elegant officer he introduced as François, Chevalier de Praslin. He was really friendly actually, as soon as he heard my name he clasped both my hands and practically kissed me.

'Got to meet my brother,' he said. 'Served with your father, be thrilled, really.'

I said 'Wonderful, where is he?' but Charlot's foot nudged mine and he whispered 'Marquis de Praslin, Lieutenant-Général of Champagne, Soissons' former deputy, be careful.'

'Right here,' said François, and swivelled on his stool. 'Roger! Look who I've got!'

I turned in panic and saw a tall, dark-haired man sitting at a table nearby. He wore a buff tunic like an ordinary soldier, but beside him sat a grandly dressed man with a white moustache and ridiculous nut-brown wig who Charlot said was the Comte d'Aubéry, Colonel of one of the new regiments. Next were a couple of officers I didn't know, but at the end of the table sat an elegant figure I certainly did. Desmoulins, here with the army of Châtillon.

'Roger!' called François impatiently. 'Over here!'

The tall man rose to join us and I got the impression he was glad to move. He stood over François, tweaked his hair, and said in a deep voice 'What is it, Bébé, is your dinner cold?' I suddenly missed my brother so much it hurt.

'Jacques de Roland,' said François importantly. 'Thought you'd want to know.'

The Marquis looked at me, and I couldn't remember when I'd

seen eyes so unhappy or a face so strained. But he sat courteously on a barrel opposite and said 'La Rochelle. Then Trèves in '34. Your father was a fine man, Monsieur. I was sorry to hear about your brother.'

He'd been Soissons' deputy, he'd been sitting with Desmoulins, but I still believed him. He talked about my father and what he was like in action, then he said 'You were at the Saillie, weren't you? Will you tell me what it was like under Spanish occupation?'

I tried. I was determined to be fair at first, I said how honourable d'Estrada was and how they never really burned anything except the Manor, then I got warmed up and told him the rest of it, soldiers taking all the food, people getting raped and robbed and killed, what it was like grovelling to people who'd taken over your own land. Then I told him about André, and the difference it made having someone stand up for you. I described the raid on the gibbet and how he saluted the crowd, I even sort of gestured it, and Praslin's eyes followed the movement like he could see the sword in the air. When I'd finished he was quiet a long time.

'Thank you,' he said at last. 'It's good to hear these things from . . . Thank you.'

He smiled at me out of that haggard face, then abruptly got up to go. There was a screeching of stools as everyone stood out of respect, but he just patted his brother's arm, said 'I like your friends, Bébé,' then turned and walked away. He never even said goodbye to Aubéry and his table, and I was glad. If there was something going on there I didn't want him to be part of it.

He invited us to join him on a patrol next morning, and of course we went. We had to get permission from de Lancy at the Orléans, but he just said 'Believe me, if I could ride with the Marquis de Praslin I would do it and write a letter home. Go with my blessing.'

The rain had stopped, there was a kind of thin sunshine, and it felt good to be riding free of the column. I remember Gaspard was wearing this crackly green cape he'd got to keep off the rain, and Raoul was being all sniffy about it, he said 'My dear, it makes you look like a *tent*.' Gaspard replied serenely 'And which of us will look better this evening, do you think?' Crespin was singing and gazing happily round the countryside, while Philibert stared fiercely at every hedge in case there might be Spaniards hiding behind it. Beside me Charlot was silent and watchful, but everything was quiet. It was Friday the 21st of June.

We were almost back to camp when it happened. There was distant banging I suddenly realized was gunfire, then someone shouted 'My God, the Pont de Douzy!' The Marquis hesitated maybe half a second, then dug in his heels, yelled 'Come on!' and set off at full tilt for the bridge.

I dug in my heels to bring Guinevere to the gallop. The ground was squelchy and mud spraying everywhere, but I heard the muffled thunder of horses gathering pace behind me, and reached down for my sword. Others were drawing too, the hard *shing* of steel rising high above the rumble of hooves, and ahead of me Praslin pointed his sword and charged.

We hit the track to the river then swept round the bend to the bank. The repairs were finished, and only a small infantry advance guard left, but three hundred cavalry were galloping straight at them from across the bridge. They didn't look like Spaniards, but then I recognized the yellow banner and black eagle of the Holy Roman Empire, which came to the same bloody thing.

Our pike were frantically forming a line, our musketeers already firing, but the volley was ragged and only a couple of horsemen fell. The first were already on our bank and hacking into our musketeers as they struggled to reload. I rode harder and heard myself shouting, and men all round me were doing the same. I felt my mouth tighten in a stupid grin.

The enemy heard us and turned. Those on the bridge stopped indecisively, but the others swerved to face us and we crashed right into them. One minute I was galloping at full speed, the next second Guinevere was rearing and bumping into the horse in front, and I'm half over her neck with the jolt. There's a bang and the smoke of a pistol, a horse is screaming, Philibert's sliding off his mount and I'm struggling to stay seated myself. Charlot's great bulk passes in front of me, scything down with his sword, then there's another rider facing me, yellow and black of the enemy, my arm's slashing forward, and there it is, the familiar jarring of the collar bone against the blade, and he's down and screaming. Guinevere's bolting into the gap, we're into the next rank, a pistol facing me, smash it aside with the forte, back and slash for the gap between collar and helmet, he's falling away and I'm through the line.

And it's clear. There's space all round me, just knots of skirmishing and horses turning to hurtle back across the bridge. Praslin's still ahead, sword bloody and face stern as he cuts right and left about him, Charlot's thrusting one man clear out of the saddle, horses are bolting riderless and I glimpse bloodied bodies between the waving shafts of pike. Philibert's staggering through after me, dusty and furious but there's no one left to fight, the riders behind me are wheeling round and round in frustration.

We can't even chase the bastards, that's like invading the Sedan, we just rein up in silence as the rumble of hooves dies away over the bridge. Then there's nothing but the infantry slowly regrouping and helping each other up, the bodies on the track and a man in his shirt sleeves lying face down in the river. I remember the gentle rippling of the water.

There was a little metallic clank below me, and I saw Philibert furtively removing the helmet of a fallen cavalryman. I bent down to whisper 'But you didn't kill him,' but he said 'Ah, but how is Agnès to know that, Monsieur?' and went back to securing his prize. There was something familiar about the helmet, that shaping to a point, the gap like an inverted 'V' at the back, and suddenly I was back in a world where I saw hundreds of them, some plain like this, others with the red tuft or plume of an officer. Spain.

It shouldn't have made any difference, all our enemies were on the same side, but the memories came crowding in like they'd done the first day we stood by the ruins of a village in Picardie and knew what we were up against. Spain and d'Estrada and all the old horrors, then a man in a courtyard saying '¡Madre de Dios!' and it all coming back.

Now it really had. The politics were blown away by the gunfire and I saw where I was standing, on the edge of a hostile country on the brink of war. I tried to imagine André beside me, saying 'This is our chance, Jacques, we're going to drive the bastards back,' but the boy was dead and the picture wouldn't come. Instead I saw the ale-house of last night and heard the mutterings and complaints, I saw fields full of mud and men looking up at us with weary, beaten faces, and all I could hear was my uncle's voice saying 'You're assuming we'll win.'

Fourteen

Carlos Corvacho

Naturally we were there, Señor, where else would we be? Our year was up, and you wouldn't catch my Capitán missing the start of something he'd organized his own self. We were in the Sedan even before the Baron de Lamboy arrived with his Imperial troops, and were only waiting for our own.

Now that's just it, Señor, things were a little tricky at Aire at that time, and someone decided they couldn't be spared. Not that it mattered, there were Spanish troops in with the Baron's Germans and Westphalians, but my Capitán still took it hard. He said 'It's a matter of honour, Carlos. We promised the Duc de Bouillon troops and money, and here I am sitting at his board like a guest who can't pay for his lodging.'

Now the money was another thing, we needed cash to take the campaign to Paris, but the Duc said 'The Maréchal de Châtillon is our treasurer this time, d'Estrada. Our agents report he has a war chest twice the fifty thousand you offered and all we need do is take it.'

He was the best of them to my mind, the Duc de Bouillon. The Comte de Soissons now, we couldn't do without him, he was the figurehead to open Paris, but really, Señor, the man couldn't keep his mind steady for two minutes together. My Capitán's offered the chance to ride beside him, but when it comes to it he decides to go with the Duc's own cavalry instead.

Why, for the battle, Señor, what else? That little skirmish by the bridge, that was just a wee probe to see what we had facing us. I won't say it wasn't a blow finding Praslin supporting the King after all, and the Comte de Soissons most unhappy about it, but in the scale of things it was no more than what you'd call a gnat. We had the men and the will, we'd a year's waiting behind us, we were ready for that battle right now.

A couple of days later it was official. A Sedanaise force billeted itself in Torcy, and for once Châtillon took decisive action to boot them out of it. We heard the warning shots back in our little mudbath at Douzy, and knew the time for pissing about was over. Border skirmishes are one thing, but once the cannon speak, it's war.

We were ordered on to Remilly with morale down in our boots. A number of men just disappeared on that march, Abbé, deserted and slipped away, or so I thought at the time. One was appointé in our own company, a man as loyal as even the slavering Fauvel could desire, but when we got to Remilly he simply wasn't there.

He also left me a man down on the roster. I went for Bonnier, but found him at his wife's bedside being comforted by Grimauld. We'd a lot sick just then, cold and relentless wet tend to have that effect, but Bonnier's wife was expecting and he'd worked himself into hysterics over it. She'd got that intriguing so-called wife of André's nursing her, but he still said 'Oh, come on, Ravel, I can't leave her now.'

'Ah, I'll do it, sergeant,' said Grimauld, nobly clambering up on his scrawny legs. 'I don't mind standing a trick for a friend.'

Well, it was all one to me, so I let him make his heroic gesture and packed him off to patrol the perimeter. I didn't see anything wrong with him. Even when I passed André bringing in a jug of wine from Francine it never occurred to me it might not be the first. Yes, Abbé, that's right, it's called making a mistake.

I've no idea what blew it up, maybe the fresh air going to his head. The first I heard was someone bawling on the road, and by the time I'd strolled out to join them Charpentier was already hauling Grimauld in front of Fauvel. Poor Bonnier was trying to explain, a sympathetic crowd was gathering, and the situation had the makings of a nice little explosion before I even saw the one thing that would guarantee it. André was heading purposefully towards them, shirt-sleeved and barefoot, but with the gleam of suicidal chivalry in his eye.

I intercepted him in two strides. 'Stay out of it, soldier.'

His voice rose in outrage. 'But it's Grimauld!'

I said patiently 'I can see it's fucking Grimauld, now do what you're bloody told.' I put him firmly aside, and shoved through the crowd to see the damage for myself.

Grimauld was managing to stand upright and say 'M'sieur' in the right expressionless voice, but there was a tell-tale flush of red on each cheek, and Fauvel was positively exultant at the chance to put the boot into his favourite NCO.

'You know what you've done, Ravel?' he said, in a voice hushed with horror. 'You've put a *drunk man* on duty! I'll see you broken for this.'

'It wasn't Ravel's fault, M'sieur,' said little Michaud bravely. 'Bonnier says the man volunteered. How could Ravel know?'

'That's right,' said Grimauld, with the stupidity of a man clearly drunker than he looked. 'Volunteered, didn't I? Nothing wrong with me. Perfectly capable. Perfectly.'

Fauvel turned away with an exclamation of disgust. 'Michaud, take this creature to the Piémont and have the archers put him under guard.'

André had followed me through, of course, and at the mere mention of military police I saw him open his bloody mouth. I planted myself in front of him and said 'Oh, you won't want the provost involved, M'sieur, won't the capitaine prefer it kept in the regiment?'

I was damn sure he would, Desmoulins seemed unusually keen to avoid outside interference, but Fauvel recoiled as if from blasphemy. 'The man is *drunk* on *guard* at a time of *war*,' he shouted. 'How could you not notice it, Ravel? Are you *blind*?'

He really did have a problem with his spitting. I said mildly 'No, M'sieur, nor deaf.'

He saw Sury only just not sniggering and turned as red as Grimauld. I braced myself for a rant, but then he seemed suddenly to gain control of himself and became ominously quiet.

'I might have known you'd sympathize,' he said, his slit of a mouth curving into a smile. 'Your brother, wasn't it, who ran the gauntlet for it? Naturally you'd defend a drunkard.'

All right, yes, that shook me. I didn't talk a great deal about what happened to Alain, and the only people who knew were André and the men who'd been with me at La Mothe.

Fauvel laughed. 'Nothing to say? I thought you were the man with all the answers.'

I had one for him, Abbé, I had it right in my fist, but I'd just enough sense of self-preservation to keep it there.

Fauvel nodded in satisfaction and turned back to Michaud. 'Since Ravel seems to have no further objection, I suggest you do your duty.' He swept triumphantly back to his tent and I was glad of it. If he'd stayed another minute I'd have dropped him.

There was the usual burst of chatter when he'd gone, but I pushed through the crowd and walked away. It's possible I fancied a little privacy, but André followed me anyway, bleating 'I've never told anyone, you must believe that.'

I did, actually, it would have upset his precious sense of honour. 'Yes, all right, you're spotless as usual, now fuck off and leave me alone.'

I walked on, but a second later I heard footsteps and he was pushing right in front of me.

I said 'Get out of my way.'

'No,' he said. 'You can't have changed that much. I heard you try to help Grimauld.'

'Self-preservation,' I said truthfully. 'I picked him, some of the blame's mine.'

He shrugged that aside. 'But you'll stand up for him, won't you? He did it for Bonnier, he was helping a friend.'

'So?' I said. 'We're at war. How many lives would it cost if a drunk sentry missed something? I'll explain the circumstances, they'll maybe just flog him.'

'No,' he said, visibly shocked. 'I can't let them . . .'

I said 'You won't just let them, you'll stand and fucking watch.'

He shook his head violently. 'I can't. You can't either, Stefan, how can you . . .'

I grabbed him. I snatched his collar in both fists and yanked him up to face me. 'I've done it, haven't I? What are you saying, I'm less of a man for it?'

'No,' he said, wrenching clear. 'No!' He tugged at his twisted collar and glared at me. 'You know I didn't mean . . . You know I understand.'

I was sick of it and sick of him. 'No, you don't, it's the Saillie all over again. You'll muck in the dirt with the likes of me and Grimauld, but at heart you think you're better, don't you? You despise the lot of us.'

A gust of wind set the tents flapping with a crack of canvas, but André didn't move. His face was very white in the dark.

I said 'Well, you're wrong. We understand your finer feelings, we just can't afford them. And right now neither can you.'

I walked away and left him, and no, Abbé, I didn't look back.

Sury was alone in the NCOs' tent when I reached it. I gave him my best smile and said 'You bastard.'

He lifted his hands in surrender. 'It came up, that's all. Fauvel was whining to the capitaine you had a problem with authority, I explained about your brother, so what? Desmoulins quite understood.'

'That's nice of him.'

He passed over his flask. 'I should have guessed Fauvel would use it. He's really got it in for you, hasn't he?'

I drank his brandy and passed it back. 'One way of putting it.'

He started rummaging for our bread ration. 'You considered doing something about it? Getting rid of him?'

I looked at his back. 'In a battle, maybe. Officer falls to a stray bullet, I've seen it done. But in camp?'

'There wouldn't be an enquiry,' said Sury. 'The capitaine wouldn't care too much.'

'His own cousin?'

He turned round with what was left of our damp loaf. 'Let's say the appointment isn't working out how he hoped.'

I was tired of it suddenly, the hints, the politics, all the balls that have nothing to do with soldiering. 'Because Fauvel's loyal to the King and our capitaine wants rebels, you mean? People like you and me?'

'Like you and me,' agreed Sury, getting out his knife to cut off the mould. 'There's a few of us in the regiment, it's time you belonged.'

Oh, I knew what he meant, but we were at war now. There'd been people thought Praslin was suspect, but faced with a load of dons attacking our men he'd made a choice and the right one. I'd been hoping these others would do the same.

I said 'Not if you're planning on anything that endangers the men.'

He passed the bread. 'You know me better than that.'

I did, as it happened. 'What then? Going over? Deserting?'

'Maybe,' he said, watching me. 'Maybe not. You in?'

I liked him, Abbé. He cared about the men he fought alongside every day, I had a fuck sight more in common with Sury than I did with André de Roland.

I said 'No.'

He bit off a chunk of bread. 'Shame. I used to know a man who thought he could change the world if he stood against it passionately enough. What happened to him, do you know?'

Oh, they were all at it. I said 'Maybe he didn't want anyone letting dons back into France. Stupid, but I think I understand it. You don't?'

He was still watching me. 'I understand who my friends are.'

I said 'You don't need to worry about me, if that's what you're thinking.'

He was, I knew it, he'd still got his knife in his hand. I said 'Come on, think about it. If I wanted to do you down I'd pretend to go along then tell the Maréchal first chance I got. I'm just not interested, Sury, I'm staying right out. Fair enough?'

I could have counted maybe to ten while we looked at each other. Then he inclined his head and slid his knife back in his belt. 'All right,' he said. 'Fair enough.'

Albert Grimauld

You think the army would have listened? Capitaine Fabert came from the King to get our Maréchal to shove us on to the high ground at Frénois, but we just went on sitting on our arses dealing with important business like trying defaulters. André came haring straight round when he heard, fizzing with plans for whisking me out under the noses of them archers, but I wasn't for deserting, not me, I've a tougher hide nor that comes to.

So the day comes, and up goes a whipping post right by our tents. The capitaine's pleaded an officers' conference, but Fauvel's there like sodding Solomon, Ravel's there to keep the men facing front, Bernadette's there with her bowl of vinegar water, and André's there, white as he's going to puke, fists screwed into balls by his side. I'm worried he'll do something daft, so I tip him a wink, shake off the archers, and step up to the post myself.

The executioner ties my wrists, I turn my cheek to one side of the upright, and close my eyes. Charpentier wedges the strap of leather in my mouth, and I bite down hard. Tastes like dried shit.

The drummer boy gives his roll. Fauvel reads the sentence, two dozen lashes, 'Executioner, do your duty.' Ravel's voice behind me, steady as a priest, 'Keep your head up, Thibault.' I take in a half-breath and –

Stefan Ravel

– *crack* against his naked back. They never cry with the first blow, Abbé, the wind's smashed out of their lungs. 'One,' said Sury. Twenty-three more to go.

André was in trouble after four, I saw him look away. No, I didn't yell at him, the first flogging's bad for anyone, especially when it's someone you know. Bonnier was looking wide too, he won't have seen more than the executioner's arm. Poor Michaud was trying to set an example, but his freckled face was pale and at the next crack I saw him bite his lip.

'Six,' said Sury. That's a bad stage, the welts start to swell up scarlet, the whip's coming down on raw flesh. Grimauld was a wiry build, strong muscular back, but the skin was beading blood and the eighth blow set it flowing. His feet shifted, he was feeling it hard. André flinched with the ninth cut and closed his fists tighter.

'Dozen,' said Sury. I saw him shift his tobacco from one cheek to the other.

The whip came back for the thirteenth and a tiny spray of blood flew out from its tails. André squeezed his eyes tight shut, but I doubt it helped, we could still hear it. The lashing sounded duller now, heavier and wetter. The man's back was a mess.

'Fifteen,' said Sury.

The seventeenth must have caught just wrong, we all heard the sucking in of breath. André's eyes snapped open, but he didn't move out of line, just stared at Grimauld, willing him to keep going and not cry. It was a close thing now. Grimauld's shoulders twitched with the eighteenth, and there was another sob of breath before he settled.

'Nineteen,' said Sury.

It was bad by then, blood oozing down on to the grass. André's face was white.

'You do not attend, Ravel,' said Fauvel.

Flat-faced bastard. I turned away from André and prayed he'd stay sensible one minute longer.

'Twenty-one,' said Sury. We were on the last stretch, the man wouldn't break now. There was a perceptible shift in the ranks, a relaxation of tension. Michaud lifted his head and made a dismal attempt to look more like an officer. There was no sound at all from André, and I'd have given a lot to look round.

'Twenty-three,' said Sury, the relief clear in his voice. He didn't like brutality, never had. One last crack, a smacking loud one, and he turned to Fauvel while the sound was still heavy in the air. 'Two dozen, M'sieur.'

Fauvel signalled Charpentier to cut the man down. He folded at the knees, of course, it's the relief as much as the pain, and I'll admit to feeling much the same myself. The miracle had happened, André had behaved himself, and the danger was over.

I said 'Parade dismissed.' There were the usual murmurs of 'Well done' and 'Sod the bastards' and some even applauded as Grimauld was helped to his little nurse.

Fauvel snapped 'Silence in the ranks!'

I don't know, maybe relief made me careless. I said 'Come on, M'sieur, have a heart for once. The man's taken punishment without a sound.'

He reddened shockingly, but then an unpleasant gleam flared in those flat lizard's eyes. 'I suppose that would seem impressive to *you*. I heard how your brother behaved in the gauntlet.'

I think the men were still clapping and calling out round us, but I only heard this filthy bastard insulting my dead brother. 'What did you say?'

His mouth stretched into a smile. 'Begging and screaming, isn't that right, Sury? Even the men in the line were ashamed.'

Bernadette Fournier

The sudden silence made me look up. M. Ravel stood still and expressionless, then his fist shot out and landed a great punch on the lieutenant's jaw.

The archers ran at once to restrain him, but M. Fauvel was already skittering backwards, landing on the grass in a heap of fine breeches and polished boots. It was chaos, Monsieur, men crowding and blocking my view, but through their legs I saw distant movement not of men but of horses. Riders were approaching down the rows of tents, and the company quietened as they saw one was our own Capitaine Desmoulins.

M. Fauvel furiously brushed down his clothing as M. Sury bellowed the parade back to order. The men hastened to reform the ranks, for these were senior capitaines of our regiment and with them Colonel Aubéry himself. There was also a tall man I had heard called the Marquis de Praslin, but he held himself apart from the rest as if they had quarrelled.

Desmoulins said 'What the devil's going on, cousin, are we now to fight each other?'

I kept my head very low. The Chevalier had met him only twice and was anyway changed beyond recognition, but I was a different matter.

M. Fauvel's voice was rough as he answered, and I saw blood on his chin. 'This animal struck me, M'sieur, and I demand he answer for it.'

Desmoulins said 'Dear, dear,' then looked towards the other sergeant. 'Was there no provocation, Sury?'

M. Sury said 'None, M'sieur. Ravel just went for him.'

There was a murmur of surprise among our soldiers, while M. Ravel strained in the arms of the men who held him and yelled 'You lying bastard!'

Desmoulins gave a fastidious grimace. 'Then you'd better have him taken to the provost, hadn't you? We'll have his hand cut off before he's shot.'

The Marquis turned to our colonel. 'Very bad for morale, Aubéry. We could be asking these men to give battle tomorrow. Was there really no excuse?'

The colonel nodded at Desmoulins, who at once addressed the parade. 'Well? Does anyone wish to contradict my officers? Michaud?'

The poor ensign could only mumble that he did not know, he had not heard the argument. It may even have been true, for he was a long way back.

'Charpentier?' said Desmoulins, hardly bothering to suppress a yawn.

The caporal was quick to confirm what Sury had said, oh, very quick, for there was bad feeling between himself and M. Ravel as we all knew.

Desmoulins bowed to the Marquis. 'A tragedy, Monseigneur, but since no one has anything to add –'

A voice said 'I do.'

All eyes turned back to the parade as a single man stepped from the ranks. I knew who it would be, and so did Grimauld, for he was struggling to his knees, muttering 'No, laddie, Christ, no.'

Desmoulins looked only irritated. 'And what can you add, fellow?'

He did not hesitate. 'M. Ravel was deliberately provoked, and if he's executed then it's nothing short of murder.'

Everything was quiet. I remember the evening breeze riffling the long grass by the hedges, and the soft ripple of the river. When the Marquis bent forward in his saddle the creak of leather seemed very loud.

'You have heard your officer say there was no provocation?'

'I have, Monseigneur,' said André, still in the rough voice of Thibault. 'And I say Lieutenant Fauvel is a liar.'

Albert Grimauld

Ah, Christ in a cannonball, you'd of thought he actually wanted to be killed.

Fauvel can't believe it neither. He turns red as a pan of lobsters and screams 'Who the hell do you think you're talking to?'

André brushes his hand across his collar like to wipe away Fauvel's spit. 'I think I've already made that clear.'

The officers giggle like children at that one, and Fauvel goes flat mad, he's out with his hand and *whack* across the laddie's face.

André rocks on his heels, but it's only his head cracks round a second then turns straight back. His cheek's stinging red, but he looks at Fauvel and smiles. That's a touch of the old aristocrat, and maybe not so clever with Desmoulins close as he is, but like the rest of them he's only got eyes for Fauvel.

'You forget yourself, Lieutenant,' says he, very stern. 'You can't strike an enlisted man.'

Fauvel looks bewildered. 'Monsieur, you all heard it, the man impugned my honour.'

'Then take it back,' says André, sounding more common nor what I do myself. 'Take back your lies and let M. Ravel go.'

'The démenti, by God!' says Aubéry. 'Who says there's no honour in our army?' He chuckles, bends down to the laddie and says 'Will you fight him for it, soldier?'

André says 'Yes, Sieur, I will.'

Them officers are all but pissing themselves now. Our men ain't laughing though, and neither's Ravel. He's staring at André and looking tense as a bowstring.

The Marquis looks at the laddie thoughtful, then says 'There's precedent, you know, Aubéry, if your man's up to it.'

Fauvel says thickly 'Oh, I'm up to it, Monseigneur. Just give me the word.'

'That is for your capitaine,' says the Marquis coldly. 'What do you say, Desmoulins? Your officer wins, he proves his honour and punishes the soldier as he sees fit. The soldier wins, he proves the lie, and you spare the sergeant's life.'

Desmoulins considers Fauvel, and I know the rumours are right, he'd be happy to see his own cousin dead. 'Very well, lieutenant, you may waive your rank for the occasion.'

Another officer says 'God, yes, Desmoulins, I'll put up twenty pistoles to see it. Who'll give me ten on the boy?'

Ah, they're so clever and funny, these gentlemen, betting their money on my laddie's life. The Marquis ignores them and says 'Just to first blood, of course.'

'Of course, Monseigneur,' says Fauvel proudly. 'All by the rules.'

He bows, stands back, and snaps his fingers for Michaud and Sury to come and squire him. André's got no one a-course, everyone standing back like he's a leper, and I have to keep tight hold of Bernadette to stop her rushing out to help him right under Desmoulins' nose. It's hard though, watching the laddie standing all by himself with nowhere to put his things but the wet grass. Ravel thinks so too, he's back struggling with the archers, saying 'Oh, fuck off, I'm only going to hold his bloody coat.'

The colonel chuckles again and orders them to release him. 'Rather fitting, don't you think?' he says to Desmoulins. 'He is the prize, after all.'

Stefan Ravel

Don't ask. I was so torn up by that time I don't know what I felt myself.

André didn't seem comfortable either. He passed me the sword without meeting my eye and bent his neck to work the bandolier over his head.

'You bloody little fool,' I said under my breath. 'When are you going to learn to keep your mouth shut?'

He passed me the bandolier. 'Maybe when you learn to keep your hands to yourself.'

'I'm not the one meant to be acting inconspicuous.'

'It'll be all right,' he said, undoing his coat. 'I won't fight like a gentleman.'

I lifted his hair to unravel his stock. 'I don't give a fuck as long as you win.'

'Worried?'

I kept on unwinding. 'Should I be?'

He unbuttoned along his sleeves. 'I'm a bit rusty actually. Our bastard sergeant never gave us any sword drill.'

'Ready!' called Sury impatiently.

I gave him a nice look, just to make sure he understood what he'd got coming if I survived. 'One minute!'

André stripped off his coat, rolled up his shirtsleeves and reached for the sword. It was standard infantry issue, hardly what André de Roland was used to, but I gave it him anyway then stood back. His cheek was still red where Fauvel had slapped him.

He said 'Stefan . . .'

I said 'Beat the bastard for me, will you?'

He hesitated, gave me a nod, then walked past to face Fauvel.

He looked fresh from the salles, our noble lieutenant, immaculate linen, polished little shoes pointed in a perfect fencing-school square. André shambled up to take position opposite, feet stuck any old how, sword brandished in his fist as if he'd never used one in his life. I smiled to myself and went to stand by Michaud and Sury. My old friend wisely backed out of reach, but Michaud looked up at me with distress and whispered 'I'm sorry, Ravel.'

'What for?' They were going through the opening moves now, Fauvel with stiff precision, André in clumsy imitation.

'I lied,' said Michaud. 'I did hear the argument, I lied.'

Fifteen years old, and on his first commission. 'Shocking,' I said. 'You'll never make lieutenant that way.'

He risked a little grin, but his eyes stayed sad. 'Thibault didn't lie.'

I looked back at the travesty of a duel. 'Thibault,' I said, 'is the biggest liar on this field.'

Albert Grimauld

You'd of thought the laddie had no idea of it. He'd his sword stuck out like a pin looking for a cushion, watching Fauvel weave about like he'd never seen such a thing in his life. But I knew better. He was watching and waiting, luring Fauvel into doing it clever, and all the time he was learning what he'd got to beat.

Fauvel tires of it, he feints at the throat then drops sharp to the chest, and André just goes wallop and bashes him out of it. Fauvel shakes his wrist like to clear the jar out of it, but he can't be beat by nothing so simple, he's in again sliding and teasing like a snake, try-ing to draw out the laddie's blade, and then whoosh André's in, straight under and clean thrust at the body. Fauvel can't do nothing but hit out himself, slash, slash, crash, and that's torn it to buggery and back, his tempered steel's gone smashing into the laddie's sword, and broke the brittle blade clear in two.

The officers shout in protest, and Fauvel's forced to step back. André drops his hilt and looks round hopelessly, but the Marquis draws his own sword, calls 'Try this one,' and chucks it in the air.

And André catches it. Sharp-edged steel whizzing towards him, but he times it perfect, hand up and neat through the guard as it falls. There's a murmur among the gentlemen, and I'm thinking 'Whoa, that's a mistake,' but the Marquis turns to Aubéry and says 'I think this could be interesting.'

Fauvel scowls. I hear him say 'Takes more than a fine sword to make a swordsman, Thibault,' and André smiles at him loving and says 'Oh, I believe you.'

Then they're in. Ding-dong, bang-smash, steel against steel, the sparks are flying blue. André's playing it canny, beating the man's tricks the simplest way he knows how, but that's a game he can't play long and live. Fauvel's coming in fast now, left hand flung out for balance, stamp and thrust, stamp and thrust, and now André's got no choice, he sends the man back once, *ting,* then again, *clang,* then a third time, sliding his blade along Fauvel's, hooking it out from under, forcing it up, up, up, then in like a white flash with his point, jumping back, lowering his blade, game finished, all done.

'Fight, man!' says one of they capitaines. 'I've got money on you, go in and fight!'

André bows. 'If Monsieur will ask the lieutenant to open his hand.'

They stare at Fauvel, who's still waving his sword like to say 'Come on, come on, I'm ready for you.'

'Show your hand, Fauvel,' says Desmoulins, so bored it's a won-der he ain't asleep.

Fauvel looks at him like a man betrayed, then slowly, reluctantly, he brings forward his left hand and opens the fist. And there it is, a thin line of scarlet scored down the palm.

'First blood, by God!' cries Aubéry, and the gentlemen give a great shout of laughter. Our own men laugh too, and in the middle of it all Fauvel stares stupidly at his own hand and flushes red to his ears. He looks up and stares first at André, who's turning away to collect his coat, then at Ravel, who's watching him with that sardonic look on his face, but then Ravel's arms are dropping, his mouth's opening, Bernadette's crying out next to me and –

Bernadette Fournier

– M. Fauvel simply charged, Monsieur, he threw himself with a scream of rage straight at the Chevalier's back. Perhaps it was M. Ravel he was after, I could not say, only that André ducked and spun round on his heel, his sword coming up so fast I did not see it, but heard only the crash as the blades met.

But M. Fauvel was like a man possessed of a devil, or perhaps one driven mad with shame, and André now needed all his skill to fight for his very life. There was no more laughter from the watchers, no sound at all but the clash of blades and the scraping of steel, the panting of their breath and stamp of their feet on the damp turf. No one called out, no one tried to stop them, for this was two men fighting to the death and that is something in which no one interferes. The Marquis dismounted indeed, but only to stand empty-handed by his horse and watch the contest with sad eyes.

It was not pretty, Monsieur. They were hacking at one another, I saw M. Fauvel's sword slash down the Chevalier's arm so that the blood ran, I saw André punch forward with his guard so that M. Fauvel staggered backwards with his ear bloodied. Time and again I saw M. Fauvel plunge forward with his blade, and almost I saw André spitted and dead, impaled on the driven sword.

'Easy, my poppet,' said Grimauld, as I wound another bandage hard about him. 'I ain't the ruddy enemy.'

M. Ravel was quite as distraught as I, half-stepping forward, stepping back, shaking his head, desperate with need to help a man who would not be helped. Then his face changed, and he started forward abruptly as –

– the bastard tripped him, then thrust in hard with his sword. It was aimed at his face, but André twisted even as he stumbled, sword up to swat the blow aside and in straight at the guts, which were all he could reach as he went down. Fauvel screamed in agony as the blade sheered clear, then collapsed to his knees, pressing his hands against his belly. André straightened and lowered his sword, and Sury yelled for a surgeon.

Everyone moved at once, and even our gentlemanly audience finally peeled their arses off their horses. The two capitaines were busily settling their gambling debts with Aubéry, but Praslin came straight over and stooped to examine Fauvel. Bonnier had already ripped off his stock and was furiously wadding it to stem the bleeding, but it didn't look good to me. Fauvel's face was ashy grey.

Praslin stood and put a hand on André's shoulder. 'Not your fault, soldier. A fair fight, we all saw it.'

'Indeed we did,' said a voice, and there was Desmoulins himself, ignoring his wounded cousin and strolling straight up to André. 'A very fine display.'

André ducked his head, but it was no good, Abbé, I already knew it from the smile on Desmoulins' face. He reached out a languid hand, cupped André's chin and forced the kid to face him. 'But then we should expect no less of the Chevalier de Roland.'

Maybe it wasn't really that quiet around us, but it suddenly felt it. There's no silence in the world like the one that tells you you're utterly fucked.

Bernadette Fournier

'Run,' said Grimauld, rising shakily to his feet. 'They're on to the laddie, you're next. Francine'll hide you, now run.'

It was too late, Monsieur, for faces were already turning towards me, and Mme Messant said 'Then who the hell is that?' Others echoed her, and fat Mme Becquet declared in outrage that they had a whore among them, at which the eyes of the nearest soldiers gleamed with anticipation. They knew as well as I that such women are thrown to the men and followers before being driven from the camp.

Grimauld's hand closed round my wrist. 'Bugger off out of it, the lot of you. She's a friend of the Chevalier de Roland, that's who *she* is, now clear the bleeding road.' His legs were tottery, but he clutched my hand and led me firmly towards André, who was now indeed my only hope of safety. He might be a fugitive but he was also a nobleman, and he and the Marquis were already exchanging respectful bows.

There was no such look on Desmoulins' face when he recognized me. He said 'Ah, our little Bernadette, what a pleasant surprise,' but his eyes were like dark flint.

André reached out quickly to draw me before the Marquis. 'Mlle Fournier is an important witness in my defence, Monseigneur, and I beg you to take her under your charge.'

The Marquis was a very great gentleman, and he did not hesitate. 'Of course, Chevalier, she shall go with you to Paris as soon as I can arrange an escort. I regret I have no women in my entourage, but she can remain here under my protection.'

Desmoulins' face was taut with anger as he saw his prey disappearing under the mantle of the Marquis. Nor was I the only one, for the Chevalier now reminded us of the promise that M. Ravel's life should be spared, and Colonel Aubéry himself conceded it. Why this should matter to Desmoulins I did not know, but he gave M. Ravel a most savage glare and M. Ravel returned him an ironical bow.

Then Sergeant Sury spoke. 'Just a minute. What about Ravel's other crime?'

The Marquis regarded him in puzzlement. 'Other crime?'

Sury pitched his voice that the whole parade might hear. 'Ravel served in the Saillie, he must have recognized de Roland from the start. He's been deliberately hiding a fugitive.'

Oh, but it was true, Monsieur, and André understood its implications all too well. He had saved his friend from one death only to commit him by his own actions to another.

He turned in desperate appeal to the Marquis. 'You cannot punish loyalty, Monseigneur. Ravel knows I'm innocent, he's served the King as well as I.'

The Marquis shook his head sadly. 'That is for a Paris court to say. He may share your captivity, he will be treated well, but I'm sorry, Chevalier, the rest is out of my hands.'

There was nothing to be done. André looked at his friend in helpless apology, but M. Ravel gave him only a little shrug as if it did not greatly trouble him. They walked side by side as they were led away together, their heads held high as if they regretted nothing.

Yet perhaps not quite, for I saw André give a brief look back at the men and the tents and everything that had been his home these weeks past, as if sad this should be his very last time. And in that he was foolish, Monsieur, as you know very well. This was the last night at that camp for any of us, and as they walked away it was already growing dark.

Fifteen

Jacques de Roland

I didn't even know. We were in the village celebrating Raoul's fête day and by the time we got back the camp was in total upheaval. Orders had come for an urgent move, and everyone was packing in the pouring rain.

Crespin had friends on Châtillon's staff so we sent him to find out what was going on. We weren't really worried, there'd been loads of moves already and they only meant swapping one muddy field for another, but Charlot said this one was sudden, the gallopers only brought the news in the last ten minutes. He was quite unruffled himself, of course, he wouldn't even let Philibert pack the pans till he'd made my evening chocolate.

Then Crespin came back, his face pale and his eyes wide and shiny. He said 'It's the whole army, chaps. Heavy baggage off tonight, the rest of us at daybreak. Châtillon's listening to Fabert at last.'

'But why now, my child?' said Gaspard. 'Has something happened?'

Crespin gave a little twitch of his head. 'Some of the chaps think the enemy's moving. Châtillon saw them himself, heading to Bazeilles. If they cross the river in the morning there's talk of them taking the high ground first.'

No one said anything after that, we just got our heads down and went on packing.

Everyone round us was doing the same, moving faster and clumsier in the driving wind and rain. No one could keep the fires going in a downpour, and the only light was what spilled from the field ovens, glowing red in the night like a dozen devils' eyes. People were hurrying everywhere, cursing and yelling and bumping into each other, all the order suddenly gone. Men scrambled up the fodder carts to hurl covers over the top, wet ropes flying about like thick whips. I remember the chaos of it, horses snorting and stamping, gallopers plunging about shouting orders, tents flapping wildly, canvas cracking to the wind like musket shots, rain on my hands and in my eyes and running down my face like tears.

That's what it was like, that last night in camp. That's how I remember Friday the 5th of July 1641, the night before the Battle of La Marfée.

Carlos Corvacho

Oh, bless you, Señor, a little rain didn't bother us, you don't catch veterans of the army of Flanders hanging on for a bit of sunshine. We were only waiting for the report from our men in the royal army, which came in prompt at midnight.

Well, you know all about it, I expect, you know what we learned. The best part was where the Aubéry were to be placed, really almost a gift, as you might say. The Duc arranged for his equerry to stay at the highest point during the battle and give the signal when it was time to make the turn.

But you'll know what interested my Capitán most, Señor, and that was the little story this Desmoulins added at the end. Say what you will about your Chevalier, he had the kind of audacity we like in Spain, and the idea of him hiding in the ranks of France's own army was enough to tickle anyone. The Comte de Soissons says 'That's a man France should be proud of, that's a man I'd like to meet.'

My Capitán smiles and says 'I'm not sure you would, Monseigneur.'

Now that's maybe not the right thing to say to the Comte, given the conscience he's got on him. Three times that day he's been confessed already, the Duc his own self caught him at it in the bushes. Now he says 'You think de Roland would not approve of me, d'Estrada?'

My Capitán sees the danger. 'Not approve of the man who did so much to defend Picardie in the year of Corbie? I meant only that this is one man I would rather have with us than against us.'

Bouillon's quick to agree. 'Quite right,' he says. 'We should just be grateful he's been caught. He'll spend the battle in irons, poor fellow, and what harm can he do us like that?'

Stefan Ravel

It raged all night, that storm. Not that I gave a stuff, I was sat in a tent with a double-canopied roof sipping a goblet of rather good wine. If you're ever going to be captured, Abbé, make sure you do it with a nobleman.

The Marquis himself was dashing about organizing his squadron for the move, but he left us in the care of a charming aide called Lapotaire, who cleared the tent of servants, fetched a nurse to bandage André's arm, stuck a couple of footmen outside as sentries, and left us well alone. It was all very discreetly done, since the Marquis seemed reluctant for anyone else to learn who André was. He didn't want to make the malcontents a present of the best figurehead a popular rebellion could possibly have.

I wasn't sure we wanted to make the King a present of him either, but André was confident it wouldn't come to it. He said 'We'll be travelling together, won't we? We can escape on the way.'

I watched him prowling round the tent tapping his hand against his belt, and knew he missed the feel of a sword. 'Why not now?'

He paused to stare at me. 'And leave Bernadette?'

Little things like life obviously didn't mean much when it came to chivalry. 'All right, we'll take her with us. We knock out the sentries, sneak back to camp, and –'

He was shaking his head before I even finished. 'We can't, it would be abusing the Marquis' kindness.'

I sighed and continued to abuse his wine. 'Well, get us out before Paris, won't you, I don't fancy the block.'

He stopped again and looked subdued. 'I'm sorry. I got you into this, didn't I?'

'Naturally,' I said, refilling his goblet. 'But if I'd stayed in the camp I'd be dead anyway. Sury thinks I'm going to blab on him.'

He took the wine. 'Why?'

I told him. It amounted to bugger all, but I told him and he didn't seem surprised. He said 'At least it proves we're not imagining things. I'd better tell Praslin.'

But he didn't come, Abbé, the man was just a little busy. A fumbling at the canvas announced only the return of a soggy Lapotaire, announcing apologetically that the Marquis thought there might be a bit of bother in the morning and there wouldn't be an escort free to take us to Paris. We'd stay in his care, of course, we'd travel in a nice dry baggage wagon, but since we couldn't be guarded on the road he was afraid we'd need to be put in irons for the journey. Unless, of course, the Chevalier was prepared to give his word not to escape . . . ?

André looked at him.

'No,' said Lapotaire, flustered. 'Of course not. It'll have to be irons then, but I'll have them struck off the moment we arrive.'

'Thank you,' said André. 'But might we speak to the Marquis before we leave?'

Poor Lapotaire. A move and probably a battle on the way, and now a prisoner wanting his officer's attention. He said 'I'll ask, Chevalier, I promise. The very first chance I get.'

I knew what that meant, and our next visitor was a friendly blacksmith who stuck the pair of us in manacles. Ten minutes later we were loaded into a wagon full of Praslin's furniture and trundled off with the rest of the baggage into the black night.

Bernadette Fournier

I too was with the baggage. I travelled with the wounded, for Desmoulins would take no chance of my telling the other women what I knew. Mme Bonnier was permitted to fetch me our own luggage, but other than that my only contact was a friendly wave from Francine, who accompanied us in her own cart.

At least I had Grimauld for company, for the doctor said he should rest while he was still pissing blood. The only other patient was M. Fauvel, who refused to stay in the village with the sickest men and was of too senior a rank for the doctor to deny. He was a strange man, Monsieur. Yesterday I could have killed him with fury at his injustice, but today he lay with his insides cut to pieces and was as bewildered and grateful for my attentions as a sick child. Once he clenched my hand and said I was a good, kind girl, then screwed up his eyes while tears crept out from under the lids.

Yes, I knew he was dying, Monsieur, he knew it himself, but then time was running out for us all.

Jacques de Roland

We were all up at dawn, sitting on horseback waiting for an order that didn't come. The sun rose higher behind the rain, senior officers said 'Sod this' and went to look for breakfast, and still we sat there while Châtillon looked at the weather and went 'Oh dear.' I don't think we moved till gone nine.

At least we went fast. The infantry had mostly gone ahead after the baggage, it was only us cavalry pounding down the broken roads to catch up and get in the nice neat order of battle that came round the last dispatch but six. We were in the first line with the Sieur de Puységur, and had to absolutely thunder down the slow-moving baggage to our proper place at the front. As we passed Chaumont we saw the heights of Frénois looming ahead of us, and I thought 'It's all right, we've beaten the bastards, we're still in time.'

We started to climb by the village of Noyers-Pont-Maugis. The rain had slowed to a soft drizzle, but it was pouring down the ruts and crevices like little waterfalls, the ground was sloshing with it and even the infantry were slipping. It didn't matter, every inch gained was an advantage over the enemy, so we just toiled on, giving the wagons and cannon a shove when they got stuck, getting higher and higher all the time.

Then we saw horses coming down to meet us, the scouting party back to report. Praslin was leading, his horse stumbling and slithering as he urged it faster over the boggy terrain. Then I saw his face and understood. We all did. Behind us I felt the whole army rippling to a stop, as eleven thousand men waited in silence to be told what they already knew.

The enemy had got there first.

Albert Grimaud

We were jolted off the road to form baggage lines, and it was there all round us, that little edge to one man's voice, a high-pitched note to another, people suddenly doing familiar jobs clumsy, others shouting when there ain't no need. Fear, boy, it's as catching as plague.

I knows why too. Coming off the road that hasty ain't what the Maréchal would have planned. We was reacting to something the enemy's done, and that's what you don't want, see, that's them in charge instead of you.

I checked my bundle. I'd got my piece and a full bandolier, but it didn't seem much the way things was looking. I said to Bernadette 'You get out your wheel-lock, I'll find us ammunition,' but I'm just climbing over the side when the lieutenant says 'And me, soldier. Get me a musket too.'

Ah, he was a dead man, sewn up pretty on the outside, ripped to Rocroi on the inside, but he'd a hard-set look on his face and hands fit to hold a gun, and them were things we needed. I said 'Yes, M'sieur,' and dropped down.

It was our own regiment guarding us. There's a company from the Uxelles round the war chest and another by the bread charrettes but otherwise it's all red coats of the Aubéry. Our own company's by the officers' wagons, Desmoulins seeing to the ordering and Michaud tagging after him as acting lieutenant. Our wives are hud-dling up with them of other regiments, and women with babies begging places in the wagons with prostitutes and sutlers, people they wouldn't normally give so much as good morning. They're out in the open with a battle coming, see, them things don't seem so important no more.

I knew the guards on one of the armoury wagons, they'd camped near us at Douzy, and they handed me guns and powder easy when I said they was for the wounded. The younger one give me chaff for it, he said 'What's the matter, dad, think we're that desperate?' The older one behind him, his eyes said 'Yes.'

Stefan Ravel

I didn't usually spend my battles in baggage lines, but it didn't look a very conventional ordering to me. Aubéry had us packed in to form lines two wagons deep, the whole lot making a square with one side missing, like a box without a lid. It seemed reasonable, any enemy would have to attack through that one open side, and we'd a whole regiment to defend it. I can't say I was worried.

André was. He was thrashing up and down between Praslin's stacked chairs saying 'This is it, Stefan, the big battle, we can't be sitting here with the bloody women.' It's difficult for a man to look martial and heroic with his hands manacled together, but he was stamping about enough to shake the wagon.

Our driver brought us neatly to a halt, then called over his shoulder 'We're all in, I'll wait with you till M. Lapotaire sends us a sentry.'

André was up with him at once. 'Could we have our irons off, do you think? M. Ravel's wrists are chafing him.'

It seemed to me M. de Roland was chafing too, but I said nothing, only held out my raw limbs for inspection.

The driver hesitated. He had a country look to me, ruddy skin, puzzled eyes, he was probably straight off one of the Marquis' village estates. 'I'll ask M. Lapotaire, M'sieur, just the very minute he comes back.'

André said carefully 'M. le Marquis will need his aide on the battlefield, he won't have time to return here.'

The driver climbed down to the horses, as if he felt safer when he couldn't actually see us. 'Oh, he'll come, M'sieur, there's always a lot of hanging around before a battle.'

I wasn't so sure. I looked round at the fodder carts without their covers properly secured, the wagon of travelling players backing hastily out of the line and bumping away over the fields, the munitions guard giving muskets to a bandaged figure I recognized as Grimauld. It seemed to me the time for hanging about was over, and I only hoped we hadn't realized it too late.

Jacques de Roland

We clawed our way up to the plateau between Chaumont and Noyers and there they were on the higher ground with the forest at their back. There was no surprise, no ambush, just us scurrying into position at one end of the plain and them lined up at the other actually waiting.

I concentrated on taking my place in the cavalry right wing. I was a bit flustered, actually, I couldn't think what I was doing. My cuirass was digging in under my armpits, I'd never worn one before and wished I wasn't now, hardly anyone else in the light cavalry had bothered. I got my hand to my sword, but Charlot gave a tiny shake of the head because of course it was pistol first. I went for the right holster, then remembered it was better to start with the left, because the right's easier to grab in the chaos of battle. I took out the gun and looked at it blankly.

'It's loaded, M'sieur,' said Philibert helpfully, leaning forward from behind. 'I did them both this morning.'

I pulled back the dog into the firing position, looked up to see if anyone was doing the same, then froze as I got my first proper view of the enemy. They were actually about the same number as us, but somehow looked a lot more. The ranks of pike looked like forests by themselves, with little white flashes where the sun caught the blades. There were musketeers each side of them, sleeves of shot, and I'd never seen so many guns at once, all on rests and levelled at us. In the middle were cannon.

There must have been cavalry on the wing opposite, but the ground dipped in front of us, and I couldn't see. There were certainly cavalry over the far side like an image in a mirror of ourselves. They even looked like us, they were French or Sedanaise not Imperial troops, and there was something familiar about them I couldn't explain.

'The white sashes,' said Crespin from my other side. 'That's really wrong, Jacquot, they're trying to pretend they're in the service of the King. How can our chaps fight them when they're dressed like that?'

I was beginning to feel we couldn't fight them at all. There were banners flying above some of the ranks and I recognized most of them: Soissons, Bouillon, Guise, names of some of the greatest princes in France. We'd got nothing like that to offer, only the poor old Duc de Châtillon who no one rated much anyway. Even having André would have helped, he was someone the men had heard of and cared about. Then I remembered it was these bastards who'd killed him, and gripped my pistol so hard it hurt.

The ground vibrated as cannon fired from our centre. I'd heard them before, we'd used them on the forts, but that was against walls, this was against men. I even looked where the balls went like I expected to see clouds of dusty powder and chips of stone, but there were people, actual people flying out of the yellow smoke like they'd been thrown, and a fine red mist colouring the air with blood.

'Christ,' said Raoul's voice behind me. 'Oh, Jacquot. Oh, Christ.'

Orange balls flared in front of us like giant muskets, a great boom, then off to the left of us screams and yells as the enemy's cannon hit.

'This is not civilized,' said Gaspard thoughtfully.

My hand jerked on Guinevere's bridle but drums were starting next to us, beating the advance. We were going in.

The poor *enfants perdus* of infantry went in front to take the shot and save the lives of those of us who rode behind. It was mainly the Piémont, those grand black-and-white colours waving bravely against the greyness of the sky, but we'd got another regiment even closer, their dark green flag diagonally crossed like a Spaniard's, and an extraordinary noise coming from their ranks like pipes being strangled. They were foreign, of course, people called them the Douglas, but they marched sort of gruffly and gave me a solid feeling I really needed.

The horses in front were moving, and we were off. We went slowly at first, no more than trotting as we got clear of the lines, on to the plain and down into the dip. Charlot said 'Remember, Monsieur, when they fire you must make your horse rear,' and I nodded but didn't think I could really do it, not use Guinevere to take a ball meant for me.

We were outpacing the drummer boys, the beat was behind us, but still the enemy didn't fire. I looked at the backs of the men bobbing up and down in front of me, Gaspard's stupid cape and Raoul's beautiful grey doublet, then between them glimpses of the enemy muskets getting closer and closer. I wanted to gallop, it must be time, maybe if we galloped they'd never fire at all, and then the muskets were flaming orange stars, the crash of gunfire throbbing in my ears, then another as our own musketeers fired back. Our front rank was stumbling, Raoul struggling to control his mount, and I knew ahead of him men were down. Horses neighed in terror and smoke drifted towards us across the plain, floating away to reveal piles of bodies, easily a hundred of our men sprawling in front of us, but the others keeping going, those Scotsmen marching doggedly on.

Little cracks of sound ahead of me, our first rank discharging their pistols. We were spreading out, I'd got a clear view ahead and my brain was clearing too, the gunfire had blown out all the muddle. I raised the pistol, remembered to turn it sideways so the powder fell right against the vent, saw an enemy musketeer levelling at me, fired and dropped him. Someone shouted, swords rasped out of scabbards all round, I dropped the pistol in its holster, clutched the mane, and drew my own.

Guinevere leapt forward, we were galloping, galloping, that same wonderful thunder of hooves across grass, but there was no shouting, none of the exhilaration I remembered by the river, and a ginger-haired man ahead of me was muttering 'My God, my God' till it became all like one word, 'MyGodmyGodmyGod.' Another blast of gunfire swept across our ranks, Gaspard swerved violently and Raoul's back jerked and spat out red, a bright splash against the grey. He flopped and fell, Raoul was down, and I was still galloping forward, leaping over his body and charging on, Raoul de Verville, dead at twenty-two.

They fired again, I felt something whizz past my face, put my head down and galloped on. Pike were coming up to our right, I heard the order then the great thud as they slammed their butts into the ground, thrusting the pike forward at an angle, horse-breast high and the full strength of the earth to take the impact. I thought 'Sod that, I'm not charging that,' and kept right on at the musketeers. They were countermarching, another volley already, but we were up to them, they were breaking in panic, and I smashed down my sword across the neck of the first I could reach.

Then we were crashing through them, all of us, Charlot's great form stooping in his saddle as he slashed at the men on the ground. Pike thrust at us from the side, stabbing at the flanks and breasts of the horses, I swerved a panicking Guinevere back and sideways, but Crespin's horse was screaming, his back was weak and he couldn't hold on, he slid down over her neck, hat off, blond curls spilling over his face. He rolled clear as the horse fell, but he was on the ground with a dozen pike round him, face blank in terror. I thrust Guinevere sideways against the pike, getting closer, close where the blades can't reach, slash down with the sword, hack down at the faces, but a pike stabs in from further away, then a sharp bang and it falls away backwards and disappears. Gaspard lowers his pistol, and I see Charlot hauling Crespin up on to the back of a riderless horse.

Others are driving on behind us and now we're swept along with them, infantry scattering before us, their lines broken in disorder. We're through, we've done the hard bit, we're behind the cannon, we must be, we're ready to turn and take them from the rear. I wrench at the reins to bring the mare round, then stop as I see what's behind.

Our second line aren't following. I'm looking back at a mass of Imperial infantry but beyond them our own men are under attack from a great wing of cavalry, they can't fight through to support us and are falling back into the Piémont. Shots off to our right, bullets whining among us, they've got musketeers in the forest as well. We can't stay here, we can't go back, our only hope is to charge forward.

But the other cavalry aren't coming. Our squad's all there, so's the Queen's, but the rest are breaking up and turning to get the hell out. The officers are screaming at them, I hear Puységur's own voice yelling, but the men shout back 'To hell with this,' and one dragoon rises in the stirrups, yells 'That's what you get for your fifty écus!' and wheels away.

The stupidity of it was blinding. We'd been up against fellow

Frenchmen and hadn't bothered to look after our own, we'd done nothing to win their morale or loyalty and the dragoon was right, this is what you get for it, bloody this. But it was too late now, too late for anything, we were stuck in the middle of a raging battle and we were on our own.

Stefan Ravel

We heard gunfire echoing through the hills. At the next crash André swerved in the middle of his pacing, went to the front of the wagon and jumped straight down. I followed him.

The driver didn't turn. He was chewing a piece of grass and staring nervously towards the open side of our enclosure, and when we looked round we saw why. The guards were leaving us. It wasn't desertion, it was orders, Aubéry was there himself directing his capitaines as they pulled the men off guard duty and led them away.

'I knew it,' said André in an anguish of frustration. 'We should be there, they're calling for reserves.'

'Are they fuck,' I said. Desmoulins was personally ordering the men by the war chest, and Sury directing others away as if he knew exactly what he was meant to do. 'They're leaving the whole baggage train to the enemy.'

Albert Grimauld

An army never leaves its baggage unattended, this was poxy traitorism going on right in front of us. I notice something else too, that it's all the Aubéry capitaines taking their men like lambs, the Uxelles ain't having it. Aubéry's yelling the order's from the Maréchal himself, but the capitaine by the bread train stands arguing the toss right back, and the one by Châtillon's wagons says outright he won't leave the war chest.

Then above it all comes another voice, a young man shouting loud and strong 'Hold fast, all of you. Your officers are working for the enemy, you must stand your ground.'

André a-course, standing in the open with his hands chained together but authority like a ruddy general. The men hear it all right, hardly a one but stops and looks, but they don't see nothing but a tattered prisoner in chains, they go right on hurrying out the enclosure after Aubéry. Our own company know who he is, they're stopping in confusion, but they ain't sure nor nothing like it.

But Fauvel sees it, and there's maybe a lot of things suddenly making sense to him now. He drags himself to the side of our wagon and yells hoarsely 'No, men, he's right, it's treachery. Stand to your posts!'

Our company stop. The Uxelles waver too, they see something's up, but the other Aubéry have got their own capitaines telling them it's all right, they ain't taking notice of Fauvel, no, nor André neither, and him all but screaming at them 'For God's sake, listen!'

I'm flop down off the wagon and running at them, yelling 'That's the Chevalier de Roland, boys, now do what he fucking says.' Ravel's at it too, bellowing alongside in that big fuck-off sergeant's voice of his. That's four of us, now, four and the name of 'de Roland', the Uxelles make up their minds and stop where they are. Most of the Aubéry are already gone, but there's even a few of them ignoring their officers and marching back to their posts.

The rage on Desmoulins' face shows the man he really is. He swings round on the Uxelles, brandishing his pistol and screaming it's mutiny, they're disobeying an order in the face of the enemy. André sees the danger, he's running towards them, but something bangs behind me, and Desmoulins jerks back like someone's punched him, spins on his toes like a dancer, and thuds down flat on the ground. Back on the sick wagon I see Fauvel lowering his musket, and think 'Fuck me to Frankfurt, the man's shot his own cousin.'

Stefan Ravel

There's nothing like shooting your officer to get people's attention. The yelling and arguments stopped with the shock, and the silence was more eloquent than any of it. Fauvel had just proved our desperation, and when I looked at the miserable number of soldiers left I thought he had a point. We had little more than a hundred men to guard a baggage train packed with women and children, and the enemy were obviously on their way.

Someone moved near the crafts' wagons, heads turned all over the enclosure, and there was our friendly blacksmith walking purposefully towards us with his hammer. 'Better get those manacles off, Chevalier,' he said. 'Looks like we'll be needing you.'

He was no one, Abbé, but his words seemed to snap the lot of us out of a trance. The men went back to their posts, their officers headed towards us with determined faces, and followers everywhere climbed out of their wagons.

Only André didn't move. He told the smith to see to me first, then gazed round the whole baggage train with an air of uncertainty I didn't like at all. He looked at a cook's boy perhaps eleven years old, at a clerk with a wooden leg, a bunch of women sitting round a sutler's wagon, another standing with a baby in her arms, and all watching him with the same trusting expectancy. For a second he closed his eyes.

I smacked my wrists down on the wagon step for the smith's hammer. 'What's the matter, little general, forgotten how to fight a battle?'

He muttered 'Fuck off, Stefan,' and shoved past me to meet the officers. There were only three of them, the capitaines of the Uxelles, and poor little Michaud of our own company, looking as if what he really wanted was his mother.

'Orders, Chevalier?' said the first capitaine. That was Valéry, a fine soldier who'd fought beside us at Arras.

André grasped the man's arm in his manacled hands. 'God bless you, M'sieur. The enemy must come through that gap in the enclosure, can you hold it?'

'We can do anything,' said Valéry proudly, 'but it's a big line for forty men.'

'Too big,' said André, and turned to Michaud. 'Enseign, get the company to pull more wagons to narrow that gap, then place them under this officer's orders, can you do that?'

Michaud straightened and the fear evaporated from his face. He said 'Of course, Chevalier,' and ran back to the men, calling out orders as he went.

The second capitaine said doubtfully 'If we all man the line there's no one to guard the war chest. I've taken an oath to protect it.'

I'd have given him an oath or two of my own, but André only nodded. 'All right, but you've a much better chance if we stop the enemy getting in at all. Hold the line, and we'll use another force to stop them breaking in anywhere else.'

The man looked at him blankly. 'What force?'

'This one,' said André. He cupped his hands to his mouth and yelled 'Drivers! Craftsmen, sutlers, everyone! I need men who can fire a musket.'

'Only men, Chevalier?' called Francine. She was sat at her wagon, a pipe in her mouth and an arquebus in her lap. 'You don't want women?'

André looked sternly at her. 'Madame, such a question.'

Francine grinned, took the pipe from her mouth, and clambered down.

She wasn't alone. They were coming from all over: drivers, armourers, smiths, farriers, bakers, cooks, valets, wives, even a prostitute or two, there's a lot of followers in an army who can load and fire a musket. The second capitaine watched them filing to the munitions wagons, said 'All right, better than nothing,' then forced a grin and loped off after Valéry.

The smith got my second pin flattened, yanked it out the cuplock and sprung the cuff open. You won't believe the relief, Abbé, unless you know what it's like to have two pounds of iron clamped like a pig's jaws round your wrist. I yelled at André to take my place.

He was whispering to Grimauld, but turned and joined us in a second. 'I'll need a sword, Stefan, will anyone here have –?'

'Here, Chevalier,' said a girl's voice, and there was his pretty Bernadette, offering him a sword like a squire. 'It's M. Fauvel's, he wants you to have it.'

André looked longingly at the blade, but couldn't get a hand to it. The smith was still working on his first rivet, hammering more and more frantically, but I was hearing something else between the blows, a distant roar from the battlefield, then something getting closer and louder, the rumble of galloping hooves.

I said 'André.'

He was whispering to the smith and didn't hear.

'Chevalier!' called Bonnier, panting towards us with my sword. 'Chevalier, there's . . .'

Cavalry. I could see the shapes pounding through the trees. Christ knows how many, the whole forest was moving. Our men had reduced the gap by four wagons' length, but there was no time for more, they abandoned the next two where they were and spread themselves out to hold the line. A hundred men, and what looked like a thousand charging right at them.

André wrenched his hand out of the first cuff. The smith reached for the second, but André said 'No time, just do what we've talked about,' snatched the sword from Bernadette, and started to run for the gap, the loose manacle swinging heavily from the chain on his left wrist.

I took my own blade from Bonnier and went after him, but he turned, still running, and said 'Lead the civilians, Stefan, show them what to do.'

I said savagely 'What *do* we fucking do?'

'Kill anything that gets through.' He gave what was almost a grin, then turned and ran to the line.

Jacques de Roland

They were Sedanaise cavalry, the Duc de Bouillon's own, they must have ridden right round under cover of the forest and burst out in a mass at some sort of signal. We were still smashing our way blindly across the lines when we saw them hurtle out of the woods ahead of us, crashing into our left flank, jubilant and fresh and cutting them to pieces. Men and horses were screaming, our ranks breaking and scattering as the cavalry drove through them in an unstoppable wedge, slicing through and out the other side.

'The baggage train!' someone shouted. 'My God, the baggage train!'

The cry spread through our lines. The baggage lines are safety, the one bit of home you've got on campaign, our troops had got wives there, children, they were yelling in panic and trying to turn back. Puységur was shouting 'The Aubéry's there, we'll hold them,' but men in red coats were staggering out of the forest, confused and leaderless, and even Crespin was saying 'The Aubéry's gone, the Aubéry's broken,' his lips as pale as his face.

We'd have broken ourselves then, but Praslin was leading the Roquelaure for their own charge and our officers urged us in with them. I didn't need the order, I was dashing to get alongside and be with the man who'd led us at the bridge. But this was heavy cavalry we were driving into now, armoured gendarmes who weren't running from anyone, I was seeing nothing but steel helmets with closed visors, I was fighting nothing human, my sword bounced off plate and a great blade screeched across my own cuirass before Charlot fought to my side to beat the men back.

Praslin was through ahead of us, sword waving high above the carnage, but a cry went up as his blade flailed in the air then vanished as he toppled to the ground unhorsed. I dug in my knees to force Guinevere through the fray, but there were enemy all round and Charlot hauled me back. I heard a man yelling 'Surrender, you fool, cry quarter!' and Praslin's voice saying 'Never, Beauregard, not to Monsieur le Comte.'

I wish that was all I remembered, but the screen of men shifted in front of me, I saw Praslin on the ground and the Sedanaise slashing at him, hacking down long after he was dead. I saw François trying to fight his way through to his brother, but prayed he wouldn't make it, prayed he wouldn't see it or hear the awful baying of men who were suddenly animals. That's what hell sounds like, I'm sure of it. Sometimes I hear it in my dreams.

Other voices were mixing in with it too, rough with desperation. Roquelaure was trying to rally his cavalry, but then he was down and surrounded by the enemy. Fabert's country voice was yelling his men to hold, Sourdis was screaming at our retreating cavalry, de Bauffremont was shouting 'Stand, Piémont, stand!' Uxelles, Andelot, Roussillon, all of them crying the same thing 'Hold the line there, hold them, hold them, *hold . . .*'

I was dancing Guinevere back and whirling round with the sword, man down and on to the next, the next, always the next, and still the voices crying ever more urgently 'Hold them, hold them,' till there wasn't even a 'them' any more, the world was shrinking to nothing but that single word, ranks of men breaking and running and nothing in my ears but that endless hopeless cry to 'Hold!'

Sixteen

Stefan Ravel

There was never any hope. We hadn't enough pike, and all the countermarching in the world wasn't going to turn our two ranks of muskets into the five needed to hold that gap. Valéry's voice was hoarse from yelling, the men loading and firing faster than I'd ever seen it done, but we simply weren't enough.

We held the first charge, the bastards weren't expecting resistance and retreated long enough for us to achieve a full reload, but the second was fiercer and we couldn't maintain the fire. A phalanx of cavalry drove right through one end of our line, scattering and trampling musketeers in their path. I saw Charpentier whirl backwards from a sabre slash, arm across a face suddenly as red as his coat.

I yelled for my first squad to fire. They were ex-soldiers, the best of the civilians, they hit all but one, and I had the last with my pistol. More gunfire at the gap, and Valéry's shouted order as our men retreated a rank on the countermarch. André was turning to yell at me, something about evacuation. 'Make a gap!' he yelled, miming with his hands. 'Pull out wagons, make a gap, get the women out.'

He was right, Abbé, it was their only chance. I said 'We'll take the war chest.'

'No, as far away from it as you can. They'll head for the money, it'll buy us time.' He grinned at me again, eyes bright in the smoke-blackened face, said 'Well, move it, Ravel!' then turned back to the line.

Bernadette Fournier

There was much shouting and jolting as our driver manoeuvred our wagon into position. Grimauld stood below us, bare-chested but for his bandages, waving his arms and bellowing instructions until we lurched to a stop. We now faced into the enclosure, and a second wagon was directed opposite, leaving a clear passage between. Two other wagons were in identical position behind us, so the passage became a tunnel to safety through the gap made in the line.

M. Ravel shouted 'Third squad in these wagons, cover that tunnel while we get the people out.' That was our own squad, Monsieur, and the wagon rocked as other armed women climbed up in frantic haste to line the sides beside M. Fauvel. Below us Grimauld was already urging the unarmed civilians through the passage to flee over the fields. We had above three thousand people to bring out of the enclosure, and our infantry could not hold off the enemy much longer.

'Here,' said M. Ravel, thrusting me up a fistful of slow-matches, 'they're lit, just blow. Good luck, *fifille*.' He turned to run back to his second squad, who lined the wagons further up the enclosure. They were mainly craftsmen and servants, Monsieur, men who could fire a musket but had never been soldiers. One was Colonel Aubéry's own bootboy, and the musket in his hands was taller than his own small body.

I handed round the blackened matches, and watched as the women puffed them into glowing orange life. Mme Bonnier seemed awkward with hers, but would not take my wheel-lock when I offered it, saying 'Bless you, my dear, the matchlock and I are old friends.' She should have fled with the others, Monsieur, for she had still not recovered her health, but it was important to her to fight for her husband, and many of our women felt the same. Even that fat Mme Becquet was with us, who always said her husband was a useless thing she would be happier without.

Grimauld was now almost pushing people through the tunnel, saying 'Move it, move it, there's others beside you.' There were indeed, clustering in front of our wagons in panic, women sobbing and a baby crying. When I looked ahead to our distant line of musketeers I saw how thin it had become, and how many more cavalry broke through with each assault. None had yet reached us, for M. Ravel's first squads were firing at any that got past, yet each time the horsemen came further in before someone shot them down.

Our people knew it, and many dared not wait. A group of

prostitutes were clambering over the bread charrettes to safety, and others crawling under the double line of wagons, wriggling between the wheels to reach the fields on the other side. A woman too pregnant to crawl hunkered down and begged a man who was slithering under to take her baby, but he only kicked out with his heels and continued to propel himself through.

But not all would be saved, not all would even try. Francine yelled at the women who still made no move, but they shrank back into the shelter of their carts, afraid to face the open ground. Some on the outside line manoeuvred their vehicles to drive them away, and that was the worst folly of all, for while our running civilians were not worth chasing, the carts might be valuable and were at once pursued and taken. One viviandiére paid with more than her goods, or so we judged from her screaming, which went on a long time.

In truth it was nothing but screaming and gunfire until I wondered if I should live to hear silence again. The shouts intensified as a horseman rode clear through the fire of both squads and charged for our tunnel with upraised sword. I took him myself, or think I did, for both Mme Bonnier and I fired at the same time. We smiled at each other as he fell, and turned at once to the business of reloading.

The gunfire down the far end ceased, and M. Fauvel's voice said 'The enemy are regrouping, we are falling back.' I heard running feet, and M. Ravel yelling 'Hold your places, civilians. Fire on the order.' I had to look up.

Our troops were pelting towards the tunnel. I thought they must reach us in time to regroup, but cavalry appeared again in the opening, saw it was no longer held against them, and charged straight in, the hooves of their huge horses gobbling up the hard-won yards like inches, gaining on our soldiers with every stride. M. Ravel called to his first squad, and the horses screamed and stumbled in the fire that blasted them from both sides, but it could not stop them all, Monsieur, and the second squad had to fire too.

A bang and shriek from behind made me jump in fear, and something hot bumped against my legs as a musket slid across the wagon floor. There was Mme Bonnier with her poor hand, oh, half off, and at least two fingers gone, she was screaming in pain and shock. It is a hard, hard thing to load a matchlock, for you must keep the match smouldering in one hand while you load with the other, and it takes but a little spark to do what was done now.

'Face front,' said M. Fauvel, as harshly as if I had been a soldier under his command. 'Face front, woman, they're coming.'

The cavalry still came on, our soldiers fleeing before them with the last civilians. The blacksmith was there, Francine's sons leading horses, M. Ravel's first and second squads, all running towards our corner which offered now the only hope of escape. Capitaine Valéry turned our infantry for one last volley at the pursuit, but when the smoke cleared there was M. Valéry face down in the dirt, his men scattering, and the horsemen coming on.

'Third squad!' came M. Ravel's voice from the tumult. 'Third squad, fire!'

I brought my piece to the rim and fired. The world was all smoke and noise, the blackness before my eyes lit only by the ghost of the musket flash still dancing before them. I wished to throw down the gun and curl into a ball and cry, but somewhere in the darkness I heard André's voice crying 'Well done, the women! See that, boys? We're outclassed!'

The shadows were clearing in front of me with the smoke, I saw my own hands reaching out for powder and another ball, then I sat myself straight and began to reload.

Stefan Ravel

Oh yes, the women downed a good twenty, but there were still maybe eight hundred of the buggers, and if they'd kept charging they could have cut us all to pieces.

Greed, Abbé, that's what saved us. They went for the war chest instead, surrounding it in seconds and working at the padlocks to get inside. Other men had their own targets, officers' wagons full of valuables, food, carts of wine barrels, oh trust me, no one was going after a bunch of ragged camp followers when there were money and goods to be had instead. I'm afraid there were women too. Some stupid bints had hidden in their own wagons, and soldiers were dragging them out with yells of triumph. They weren't saving them for later either, some had three on them at once with a queue forming behind.

It wasn't pretty, but it bought us time. Our exit hole was in a corner, so we tipped over wagons to make a barricade with a path in between, then lined it with what was left of our soldiers. There weren't enough for countermarching now, so I just counted them off as they took position, one, two, three, and told them to fire by numbers. It wasn't much, maybe a twelve-shot volley, but André directed one of the giant fodder carts right across our middle to force anyone coming at us to divide in two. He joined the men pushing it himself, eyes screwed shut as if it would stop him hearing the screaming on the other side.

We were driving off the horses when three riders trotted round, saw us waiting with levelled muskets, and turned back out at the double. We didn't shoot, Abbé, I half hoped they'd leave us alone if they saw we weren't bothering them, but less than a minute later we heard someone shouting orders behind the fodder cart. I suppose they'd seen our defences and guessed we'd got something valuable hidden behind.

I yelled down to Grimauld 'How long?'

His voice came back muffled through the crowds. 'Five minutes?'

We'd be lucky to give him two. The cavalry were already streaming round both sides of the fodder cart and I had to shout 'One!' A dozen shots, maybe ten men to fire at, but muskets misfire, Abbé, not to mention the little snag of people sometimes picking the same target. Twelve shots, five men still up, and more coming round the cart to join them. I yelled 'Two!' before the echo had even died away.

I was late even then, two horsemen were already past and charging down the gap in our barricade. I heard the crack of single shots and hoped it was my civilians, but women were screaming down there all the same. No time to look, there were more of the buggers coming already, I hefted my own piece into position, yelled 'Three!' and fired.

It discouraged them. Two more got past, but the stream round the fodder cart stopped, and I guessed the officer was having himself a little think. Behind us came more screaming and the sound of gunfire.

André straightened, and I didn't like the look on his face.

I said 'I've armed civilians all round that tunnel, they can't get more than one or two before they're downed.'

'Too many,' said André. He pressed his hands on to the upturned side of our wagon, and began to hoist himself up.

I said 'You'll make a nice little target up there.'

'I won't,' he said, crouching on the wagon side. 'I won't stand till the last minute.'

I didn't answer. More hooves, they were coming back, you don't waste time talking when you're trying to reload.

This time they meant it. They weren't stopping for anything and were firing right at our musketeers. I yelled 'One!' but had to call 'Two!' seconds later just to hold them, and still two horsemen made it past for the gap. Our threes weren't loaded, we hadn't a shot left to stop them, but André's legs straightened in front of me as he sprang up level with the first horseman. I heard the clash of blades, then the wet punch of a sword sliding home, and the horseman slid to the ground in front of our wagon.

I finished loading while he dealt with the second. It was madness, of course, he'd never keep it up, but I supposed it didn't matter. Even if we got all the civilians out, there was no one to cover our own retreat. I reached for the ramrod and saw Bonnier sprawled on his back beside me, fine ash from the discharge settling on his staring eyes. That didn't matter much either. In another minute we'd all be joining him.

Jacques de Roland

Fabert went on trying. He led us in a charge against the cavalry that downed Praslin, I saw him personally cut down a huge armoured officer on a white horse. People cheered, some even said it was Soissons himself and that we'd turned defeat into victory, but it wasn't and we hadn't, it was just some Sedanaise officer and we were just a knot of cavalry hemmed in on all sides with the enemy moving in for the kill.

It wasn't about fighting a battle after that, just getting out alive. Even Fabert was urging Châtillon and Sourdis off the field, and that was it, it was over, there was nothing but a dull sickness in my belly and a taste like black smoke in my mouth. I said 'We're beaten, aren't we? This is defeat.'

'Defeat?' said Charlot gently. 'Monsieur, this is a rout.'

I learned what that meant as we cut our way through to the woods. I saw it in Crespin's bewildered face, tears running down his cheeks as he slashed out at the enemy like a furious child. It was there in the sight of the great black flag of the Piémont with its single brave white cross flying above the crowd, but tied to a Spanish pike and surrounded by men laughing. I saw it under Guinevere's own hooves, the corpse of a young boy beside a broken drum, its skin gaping like a jagged mouth. Something was rising in my throat in dry little gasps, I remember panicking because I couldn't see Charlot, then hearing his voice saying 'I'm here, Monsieur,' and turning to see we were off the field, the shade of trees closing round us, and for the moment we were safe.

There were only about ten of us together, we'd long got separated from the rest, but my friends were still there, all but Raoul who never would be again. I wanted someone to make a joke, laugh, make things right again, I even said to Philibert 'There's loads of helmets, don't you want one?' but he just said 'No, Monsieur,' and looked down at his bloodied sword with something like shame.

We rode on through the forest in the hope of meeting up with our army, but the sound of sporadic gunfire suggested there wasn't one, just fleeing men being picked off by leisurely musketeers. Sunlight and green flickered ahead and we emerged from the woods on to rough grass, the ground trampled to form a track leading down to fields that looked suddenly familiar. We'd circled the plateau and come out above our own baggage train.

That's where the firing was coming from. The wagons were lined up like a square with Sedanaise cavalry swarming inside, whooping and charging, leaping on to carts and chucking stuff out, galloping horsemen chasing after half-naked women. Bangs and little puffs of smoke came from a tangle of wagons across the far corner, and behind it I saw a stream of people pouring through an opening into the fields, heading for the other side of the forest like a trail of ants. Someone was putting up a defence and getting the people out.

We went faster down the track, seeing more detail as we got closer. The wagons formed a barricade with men firing behind it, I saw little flashes of flame. One galloped past the musket fire, but a man sprang up on top of a wagon and forced him to fight blade to blade. There was something in the man's other hand, a thing on a chain like an old-fashioned mace, I saw him bash out with it and the rider reel back. The man finished him with the sword, wiped his arm across his face, and lifted his head.

Gaspard said levelly 'Who in the name of God . . . ?'

I wasn't even surprised at first. It felt too familiar, André fighting, André in danger, I was already drawing my sword before it hit me that he was meant to be dead and shouldn't be there at all. Then my heels kicked into Guinevere's flanks, my head was down, the ground blurring green in front of me, I was galloping, galloping, because the boy was alive, and maybe, just maybe, I'd got a chance to save him after all.

Stefan Ravel

He'd had it. His footwork was faltering, he was gasping with effort as he fought the next man. He got him, of course, manacle to stun him, sword to cut him down, but he couldn't disguise the tremble in his knee, it was right in front of my face.

I said 'Time to come down.'

'Not till everyone's out.'

Young Michaud called across the path 'It's all right, Chevalier, I'll take over,' and started clambering up on his own wagon.

'No!' shouted André. 'No, ensign, get back down!'

Michaud just waved and stood gingerly upright. The fools at his wagon actually clapped him, and the kid blushed all over his freckled face.

'No!' yelled André. 'Please, Michaud, you can't . . .'

Hooves again, more of the bastards streaming in both sides, yelling to give themselves courage. It was my turn, I shouted 'Three!' and fired, or rather I pulled the trigger, got a flash in the pan, then nothing. Misfire, and the riders weren't half down, I yelled 'One!'

and prayed they were ready. We got off maybe four shots, but there were three riders already past our sightline, pistols blazing as they came. André struck out at the first, beyond him Michaud engaged the next, but the third was loose, belting up to help his colleague with André.

I straddled the side of the wagon and swung my musket like a club. It wasn't my best effort, I got the horse whack across the face, but it discouraged the bastard and gave me time to yell 'Two!' More were coming through, but André had beaten his man's blade and was already thrusting home.

'The pistol!' I yelled, bashing my man back again. 'Get his fucking pistol!'

He leaned precariously forward for the dead man's holster. Behind him the third horseman sent poor Michaud spinning to the ground, then swerved round at André while he was still off balance. The kid swiped wildly at him and chucked me the pistol, but the barrel was warm, the fucking thing was empty and my own man stabbing in like fucking lightning – then his face cracked open in a bang of gunfire right in front of me, blood and bone spraying over his horse's neck. Men were riding in behind us firing pistols and it seemed we'd acquired cavalry of our own.

It wasn't our army, of course, there were only about ten, but there suddenly wasn't a live enemy our side of the cart. I shoved the pistol in my belt, wiped the blood from my cheek, and dragged my leg back over the side of the wagon so I could sit rather than straddle. I was soldier enough to start reloading my musket, but I'll be honest, Abbé, my hands were shaking. André lowered himself beside me, and I doubt he'd the strength to stand another minute.

The newcomers were fanning out, three either side of the fodder cart, while the others were already reloading their pistols. One looked round frantically as he did it, then urged his mount straight at us.

He said 'It's gone quiet now, get out and we'll cover you.'

André swung round. 'Don't you tell me . . .'

He stopped as suddenly as if he'd been shot. I turned to look at the rider.

He was a handsome young bastard, but I didn't see anything to stare at. Nobility, of course, it screamed from the manicured hands and barbered beard, then I saw the bright blue eyes and the scar on the cheek, and suddenly the man before me was unexpectedly familiar. Our erstwhile stable boy, Abbé. Jacques Gilbert.

I said 'And where the fuck have *you* been?'

Jacques de Roland

Sod Stefan, I didn't know what he was doing here and didn't care. I reached for the boy, but he backed away and said 'I can't, the civilians . . .'

We'd saved him with less than a second to spare, I'd found him and got him back and his bloody stupid honour was going to get him killed right in front of me. I said 'They're all out except those in the wagons. We'll hold here, take the musketeers and go.'

'Come on, little general,' said Stefan, actually being helpful for once. 'They'll need us to cover the last retreat.'

That did it. André nodded, squeezed my hand, then turned to the musketeers. I watched him checking the fallen, helping the wounded towards the tunnel, and for a second I felt the old glamour of it, the belief that honour mattered and someone like André could make a difference. The cold steel of the pistol in my hand brought me back to reality. I finished reloading and joined Charlot by the fodder cart.

There seemed to be a lull back in the enclosure, and when I peered round everything looked more controlled than before. Naked women were huddled together but there was no one molesting them now, while a man in magnificent armour was calling on the troops to leave the civilians alone. A foreign-sounding horseman was doing the same, a man with an open helmet who was waving a sword in his left hand, and when he turned his head I recognized d'Estrada.

I slammed back fast. It wouldn't have made any difference if he'd seen me, but you don't hide from someone for four years and react any other way. At least André hadn't seen him, he was leading the last musketeers towards the tunnel and never turned round.

But angry voices were rising in the enclosure, argument and

recrimination. I risked another peep and saw officers gathered round a broken wagon, questioning a bunch of troopers who were shouting and gesturing, then one of them pointed our way. Horses started to turn, an officer drew his pistol and others did the same. They were gathering for another bloody charge.

I yelled a warning to the others, levelled my pistol and waited.

Bernadette Fournier

The last of our unarmed people were through, and we were scrambling down to take our turn. The Chevalier himself ran back from the barricade with the remnants of our soldiers, and oh, Monsieur, out of a hundred men there were left perhaps twenty. They ranged themselves either side of the tunnel for one last stand, while M. Ravel shouted at us to move faster, for our small cavalry were holding the barricade alone.

This was no orderly departure now, Monsieur, women dropped their guns and threw themselves over the sides of the wagons in their haste to be gone. I went to help Mme Bonnier, but she was dead, she and her poor little baby inside her, a ball must have struck her as she lay helpless and wounded. André came himself to lift down M. Fauvel, but the lieutenant struck away his hands and said he would not come. The effort of speech spattered his chin with blood and spit, but his eyes were fierce and he clenched his musket as if it were all that mattered in the world.

'There's time,' said André. 'Everyone's safe, we've time to take you.'

M. Fauvel said hoarsely 'Damn you, leave me this, can't you?'

They stared at each other, then André took M. Fauvel's free hand and said something so softly I could not hear. M. Fauvel pressed his hand in return and I thought his face seemed calmer.

I snatched up our own bundles and André lifted me down, for gunfire was banging again from our barricade. M. Ravel bellowed towards it that all was clear, then smacked his palm between my shoulder blades to propel me down the tunnel between the wagons. I was almost the very last, Monsieur, with me were only the smith and Francine's sons leading the Chevalier's horses, which seemed unusually heavily laden. We hurried together with panicked urgency and stumbled suddenly into the startling openness of the fields outside.

Around me was the clear space of the real world. A sky that was not grey with gunsmoke, pasture with the distant brown shapes of cattle, a village beyond, the spire of a church, and curling all about it a ribbon of white chalk I recognized as the road we had left little more than an hour ago. I remember the scarlet poppies in the grass.

Ahead of me a dwindling line of our people was running towards the safety of the forest, but I remained outside the wagons to wait for the end. First came Grimauld waving his arms and screaming at me to get out of the way, then the ground shook to the impact of hooves as our cavalry hurtled out of the opening. Behind them came one more volley of gunfire as our musketeers discharged their final round to discourage the pursuit.

Grimauld grabbed and pressed me against him as the horses swept by. His bandaged chest was moist with blood and sweat, and his bony arm cold and clammy, but his nearness was a comfort and it steadied me. I said 'Is André there yet, Grimauld? Is André there?'

'Coming now, my poppet,' his voice said above me. 'Any minute now.'

I saw the legs of horses shifting restlessly nearby and knew some of our cavalry were also waiting for the infantry. They were coming, I heard men running, and wrenched my head from Grimauld's chest to see them spilling out on to the field. All but André, I did not see André, but then two more figures appeared between the wagons, and the big one was M. Ravel and the slighter was laughing as he ran.

'Now!' said Grimauld, but I heard hooves, a horseman close behind them, and my heart leapt in terror at the sound of a shot. Yet André did not fall, neither did M. Ravel, and as they emerged into the field I saw behind them a horse bolting with fright, its Sedanaise rider dead on its back. Then I remembered M. Fauvel and thanked God for him, for he was a brave man.

I ran then with Grimauld, for we did not know if the pursuit would follow us even over the fields. Our horsemen seemed to fear

it too, for the largest reached down a great arm and hoisted a protesting André up into the saddle before him, and as he galloped past
I recognized the Comtesse's servant Charlot. Another man rode
hard behind him, and this one I knew even better, for it was Jacques,
Monsieur, Jacques Gilbert himself, shouting and waving a bloodied
sword like the noblest warrior I had ever seen.

Stefan Ravel

No one lifted *me,* Abbé, I ran with all the other scum, but you'll be
glad to know I made it unscathed. I heard a couple of half-hearted
shots fired after us, but no one bothered to follow. A few poor devils
of running infantry weren't worth anyone's powder, and no one
was going to be arsed to hunt us through the woods.

It was just as well as it turned out, since a good hundred of our
civilians had decided to flop on the ground to wait for us rather than
running sensibly for the nearest village. I knew what they were after.
As André slid off his friend's horse and started to wander through
the crowd there wasn't a single face that didn't turn to follow him,
and every one with the same dumb, trusting expression. I'd been
here before, Abbé, I knew the signs. André had just acquired another
hundred hostages to sling round his eighteen-year-old neck.

He didn't see it himself, of course, he was heading for Jacques,
who was already dismounted and coming forward to meet the boy
I now knew was his brother. I dug out my flask, had a good long
suck, and leaned against a tree to watch.

They didn't say anything at first, just gazed at each other in
silence. Then Jacques cleared his throat and said 'That's a fucking
terrible beard.'

André's mouth quivered. 'Better than yours.'

Jacques gave a little smile that was almost shy, and I'd have known
him then, Abbé, I'd have known him anywhere. A blink, no more,
then they were hugging each other fiercely, almost bowling themselves over with the force of it. Jacques was saying something, but I
didn't really catch it, only the words 'bloody, bloody, bloody' over
and over again.

I strolled to the edge of the trees to take stock of our position. The sun was almost directly overhead, and I guessed we were pretty well on midday. An hour ago we'd been sat comfortably in a baggage wagon with eleven thousand King's troops confidently marching to beat back the invaders. Now we were the battered remnants of a beaten army, and the raggedness of the distant gunfire suggested that what was happening around us resembled a hunt more than a battle. I know defeat when I hear it, and the triumphant whoops from the captured baggage train seemed to drift like smoke all over the green Champagne fields, which were maybe Sedanaise now, or Spanish, or Westphalian, or anyone's other than ours.

An hour, Abbé. Sometimes that's all it takes to change the world.

Seventeen

Carlos Corvacho

So he was that close, was he, Señor? Bless me, that would have amused my Capitán, he said so all along. We'd guessed the prisoners would be in the baggage train, and as soon as he saw the organized way someone was getting the civilians out he said 'Carlos, I'll lay you fifty pistoles that's the Chevalier.'

He was even more sure when we saw the *voiture* broken into and half the money gone. He said 'Looting troops would just take the *caisse* and run. Who but de Roland would go to the trouble of shutting it up and putting the padlocks back on to delay us?' But there was nothing to be done about it now, Señor. We weren't going to chase after harmless women and children, not when they'd have got the money out first and halfway to Mézières by now.

So we set off to report to Monsieur le Comte, but my Capitán was confident he'd still back our campaign. He said 'There's nothing like victory to ease a man's conscience, Carlos, and I've never seen one more complete than this.'

Well, I couldn't say he wasn't right. As we rode back to the battlefield we saw Frenchmen running all over the woods, abandoning their guns and plain running for their lives. That was the end of Châtillon's army, Señor, and there wasn't another between us and Paris. The road was open all the way.

Jacques de Roland

I remember those poor ragged women crowding round us to ask about their husbands. They were touching my sleeve and making timid little curtseys, 'The Roussillon, Sieur, please, did you see them?' 'Please, Sieur, the Bussy-Rabutin?' Charlot said 'The Maréchal ordered a withdrawal, we'll meet up with them soon,' but the doubts stayed unanswered in their eyes.

Their fear made me feel almost guilty for my own miracle, my brother alive and next to me. He was insisting he'd written and I'd find the letter when I got home, but I was just taking in that it was really him. His voice was rougher than I remembered, he'd lost all the polish Charlot had rubbed into him, he even looked different. He was lean and hard, ragged and battle-stained, but he walked upright and confident, the red coat vivid against his black hair, and I realized with a jolt he was at least as tall as me. The manacle dangling off his wrist felt degrading and wrong.

He shrugged dismissively. 'I got caught, that's all. Look, here's someone else you'll be glad to see.' He gave me a little push then turned back to the crowd.

I was looking at two horses tethered to trees, and when the black one tossed his head and turned out to be Tonnerre it felt like everything I'd lost was all turning up at once. It was odd though, he and Héros were stood with two depressed-looking pack mules, all laden with heavy leather bags, and when I went to pat them a brawny civilian with a hammer stepped in front of me, flanked by two lads with muskets.

'He's all right, boys,' said a familiar voice, and there was Grimauld sitting cross-legged on the ground while a girl adjusted bandages round his chest. 'Chevalier's brother, this is.'

The man with the hammer stopped swinging it, the lads with the muskets lowered them, the girl with the bandages turned her head, and I forgot all about the horses because it was Bernadette. My tongue went stiff in my mouth and I sat down beside her with a bump.

She gave me a glorious smile over her shoulder. 'You will dirty your breeches, Monsieur.'

I'd forgotten how beautiful her voice was. 'It's still "Jacques", Bernadette.'

She smiled. 'But no longer Jacques Gilbert.'

Her face was grey with gunsmoke, her dress ripped, her skirts were splattered with blood, and I could hardly bear to look. She shouldn't be here, André should never have allowed it. I said feebly 'Are you all right?'

'As you see.' She continued with the dressing. 'And you, Monsieur, you have been comfortable in Paris?'

I said 'It's not like that,' but couldn't manage any more. She wasn't even looking at me, she was wrapping fresh bandages round bloody Grimauld. He knew I was struggling, he even gave me a commiserating grin, and I thought 'That's it, that's bloody it, how can anyone tell a woman he loves her when there's a man with about four teeth sitting listening to every word?'

I said 'You knew I had to stay, you must have understood.'

'Of course,' she said softly, and tilted her head to indicate over my shoulder. 'But hush now, André is talking.'

I stared at her. I was 'Monsieur', but my brother was 'André'. Then his voice sort of penetrated, and I forced myself to turn round.

He was standing on a tree stump to address the crowd. I think he was trying to get rid of them actually, he said they'd have a much better chance in the villages with nothing to connect them with the army, but they weren't having it, they wanted to find the army and their husbands. One little grey-haired woman was tapping anxiously at his boot, saying 'I have to find my Jean, I've got his baggage, all his things, what'll he do without his things?'

He looked at her, then round at all the expectant faces, and I saw him swallow. 'All right then. M. de Chouy will look after you while I take a party to search for the army.'

'And if you don't find it, M'sieur?' It was a big fat woman speaking, bare arms crossed aggressively against her bulging bosom. I saw Bernadette look at her with dislike.

'Then we'll try the villages together,' said André, smiling at her. 'An army does not simply disappear, Madame. We'll find them.'

They believed him, I saw it in their faces. I wished I could feel the same, I wanted to go back to believing André had all the answers, but I knew better now and couldn't pretend I didn't. It didn't stop me loving him, it's just how he was and why he needed me to look after him, but I hadn't bloody been there, had I, he'd had no one but Grimauld and Stefan. No wonder he'd ended up in such a bloody awful mess.

At least I could go with him this time. Charlot was coming with us, the Comtesse would have killed him if he'd lost us both, but we'd hardly cleared the crowd when Stefan came muscling up and said 'Bugger off, André, you're not going near the army.'

Charlot's face looked like someone had set it in aspic. 'Monsieur, I do not think you realize –'

André patted his arm and turned to Stefan. 'There's no danger. If they've heard I'm around, they still won't know it's me.'

'Apart from the manacle, you mean?' said Stefan. 'Or the fact you might run into Praslin?'

I shut my mind on the memory of a severed head on a pike. 'We won't run into Praslin.'

André looked sharply at me, then softened his voice. 'Well then, it's quite safe. Only the Aubéry officers would know us, and they won't be there, will they?'

Stefan began to check his pistol. 'All right, but we'll keep out of sight all the same. We'll just see where they are, then come back for the others.'

André shook his head impatiently. 'No, we need to bring back an escort for the money.'

We stared at him, but he was tucking his manacle into his cuff and didn't look up.

Stefan rammed the pistol in his belt and said expressionlessly 'What money?'

Albert Grimauld

Ah, I knew. 'Thief' they called me, 'thief' that Ravel said to my face, but André trusted me when it came to it, me and no one else.

Ah yes, he maybe told the smith, but he'd no choice there, see, he needed him to break open the *voiture* and put on new locks. I'd told Francine's boys myself so we could load the horses, but not one other soul. Oh come on, big chunk of money all in gold? *Not* something you want to tell the troops about, no, nor yet no females. They'd have been halfway to Hamburg with it in less time than it'd take you to pass that jug.

It wasn't just our own lot we'd to worry about neither. Our sentries picked up dozens of our men lost and looking for their units, all wanting the comfort of company and finding it with us. 'De Roland,' says our guards, 'we're being looked after by the Chevalier de Roland', and in they come, more and more of them setting down comfortable to wait for André to lead them out of it.

There was a lot of Aubéry there, poor buggers. Their officers had just abandoned them in the forest, left them with nothing but the knowledge they left their posts in a battle. There was one old veteran crying like a baby, twenty years in the army and never done nothing but his duty, and they'd gone and made a traitor of him with their lies. Bernadette tries to cheer them, she's smiling at them nice, saying it's not their fault and André'll put them straight.

But time's going by and after a while I says 'Seems to me they ought to be back by now,' and she looks at me with no smile at all and says 'Yes,' she says. 'Yes, they should.'

Stefan Ravel

We found the battlefield all right, but it didn't get us any nearer the army. Oh, we met a few stragglers, a lot of Aubéry, some German pikemen from the Streiff, a couple of musketeers from the Persan, but they knew even less than we did. We directed them down to our own little camp, which was beginning to look like the closest thing to an army we'd got left. The only other soldiers of our own were sprawled on the ground with bullets in their backs.

We heard desultory fire and shouting as we approached the fringes of the battlefield, so it seemed wise to go the last part under cover. An overgrown gully took us to within ten feet of the open, then we crouched behind the biggest trees we could find and peered round.

You ever seen a field after a battle? No, I don't mean the fucking paintings, all that magnanimous piety of a dignified surrender, there was nothing dignified about La Marfée. We were looking at three thousand dead men on that field, and the grass was soaked red. Horses were down too, some still kicking, poor brutes, but at least the screaming had stopped. There were moans though, feeble little sounds coming from the heaps of men, and here and there maybe an arm or a leg moving. The air smelt of blood, and the flies were already moving in.

'Christ,' whispered André beside me. 'Oh, dear Christ.'

I pressed his head back down. We weren't in the healthiest position just there, Abbé, with Imperial troopers picking through the debris and Sedanaise infantry marching off prisoners into the woods beyond, but what I liked the look of even less was a bunch of officers over the far side talking to men from the cavalry who'd attacked our train. No, of course I didn't recognize them, I'm not a fucking hawk, but I saw they were unhappy about something and had a nasty feeling I knew what. An armoured bastard on a white horse stood in his stirrups and shouted, and next moment the horsemen were wheeling round again, back towards the baggage train and coming our way.

We crawled back down the gully rather quicker than we'd come up it. It was only a couple of feet deep, but the bracken was thick above us and I thought we'd get by. The sound of hooves crossing the field was still distant when I heard something closer, a rustling of leaves, then footsteps and voices. They sounded French, which didn't mean much under the circumstances, so I lifted my head to peer through the fronds. A second later they came into view, glimpses of red flashing intermittently between the trees, men dressed like ourselves. The approaching hooves were growing louder.

'They'll be caught,' said André. He sprang to his feet and was out of the ditch before I could get a hand up to stop him. All right, they were Aubéry, but they weren't running or creeping furtively, they were a sight too confident altogether. I hissed at the others to stay put and leapt out of the gully myself, but André had already reached the men, I heard him say 'Quick, into cover, cavalry coming.'

They whipped round at the sound of his voice, and André stopped dead. His hand shot to his sword, but three of them piled on him, grabbing his hands, arm round his neck, jab in the guts to quiet him, while the fourth pressed a pistol to the side of his head. No, I wasn't surprised, Abbé, not now I saw their faces. Three looked vaguely familiar, NCOs from other companies, but the fourth I'd known for years.

I nudged my coat over my pistol, stepped into the open and said 'Hullo, Sury.'

He was a cool bastard. His eyes turned to me all right, but he kept that gun screwed tight to André's head. 'Ravel,' he said pleasantly. 'Looks like you chose the wrong side.'

'Depends how you look at it.' I moved slightly aside to make sure Jacques saw what we were up against and didn't try anything stupid. 'No harm to come to the men, isn't that what you said?'

'There wouldn't have been, would there?' said Sury. 'You could have all been out of it, if it hadn't been for this one.' He ground the gun against André's temple, sending a little trickle of blood down his face.

Those hoofbeats were getting nearer, there was no time for argument. 'Come on, let him go. What's one more prisoner on a day like this?'

The others were watching the bend for the horsemen, but Sury looked at me and I looked right back. André was only a blur on the side of my vision, but he didn't seem badly hurt, he could bluff if he had to.

I said 'You owe me, Jean.'

The sound of hooves lightened as the first horsemen rounded the bend. Sury muttered to the others 'Let him go,' stepped back and lowered the pistol. André shook himself free, but the horsemen could already see us, and there was nothing to do but stand still as if we were all the best of friends.

We bowed respectfully as the first riders passed. Then another horse's legs came into view, but these were slowing, the bastard animal stopped, and then above my head a familiar voice said 'Good afternoon, Chevalier.'

My favourite don, Abbé. The fucking Don Miguel d'Estrada.

Jacques de Roland

They couldn't let him go now, not in front of an officer. The one called Sury brought his gun back up to André's head, while another pulled his sword from his belt and chucked it away. Frustration banged in my head. There were six now, we should have rushed them when they were only four, I'd just lain and let it happen and now the boy was disarmed with a gun to his head, and more riders already appearing round the bend.

D'Estrada glanced back at them, then leaned forward in his saddle. 'Oh, Chevalier, what *have* you been up to?'

André actually smiled. 'I think the Señor already knows.'

D'Estrada smiled back. 'I think he does too. Will you tell me where it is?'

The money, of course, the bloody stupid money, we should have just left it. André had insisted the guard had sworn oaths to protect it, he'd said he was bound to honour them, but it was all bollocks, he should have just left it and run.

He said 'I'm afraid it's out of the Señor's reach.'

D'Estrada shrugged gracefully. 'I regret it is also out of my hands. These gentlemen have a greater concern in it than I.'

The last horsemen had caught up now, four more. One was that treacherous git Aubéry, two were Sedanaise officers, but the one on the white horse was in full gold-inlaid armour. He was obviously someone very grand, the infantry all sort of grovelled and even Sury swept off his hat, though he made good and sure to keep his gun on André.

Charlot was fidgeting beside me. 'That's . . . But Monsieur, that's . . .'

I stopped listening. Stefan had edged to the back with his head well down, but I saw his hand sliding under his coat and suddenly remembered he had a pistol.

Hope and panic clamoured together inside me. Only one shot, and it had got to be Sury. André was unarmed and helpless, if Stefan shot anyone else he was dead. I was willing him in my head, Sury, shoot Sury, do it *now*.

Stefan Ravel

I couldn't shoot Sury, there were three men between us. Considering the last time I'd seen d'Estrada he'd cut a slice out of my face in revenge for his own little scar, I rather thought the best place for me was at the back.

But there was something else Jacques had missed. André had a weapon no one had even thought of, it was there right in front of them, dangling from his left wrist. I missed it myself until I saw his hand curl round to grasp the chain into his fist. He was going to go for it, Abbé, one against ten and with a gun to his head, he was going to fucking go for it.

He needed a distraction, and I knew what. My pistol was dog-back and ready, I'd a clear sightline to the front horsemen and only needed to choose which. I'd have gone for the armoured one, anyone encased in that much steel was obviously important, but it was the expensive kind and I wasn't sure a pistol could pierce it. Corvacho wasn't worth the waste of the ball. It had to be d'Estrada, and if you think I was sorry about it you'd be wrong.

Then the armoured man leaned right across my line of fire to speak to André. Sury stepped back a little in respect, the man raised his own pistol to lever up the visor of his helmet, and there was his face right in front of me.

Well, what do you think I did? I fired.

Jacques de Roland

I didn't understand at first, no one did, I thought he'd shot himself with his own pistol.

Everything froze like a tableau in a play, then the armoured man slumped sideways and everyone cried in shock. His officers pressed forward to support him, Aubéry backed away in a kind of terror, the men on the ground looked wildly about them, Sury lowered his pistol – and André moved. He bent his knees and swivelled, left fist smashing upwards and driving that heavy manacle crack into Sury's skull. I didn't see any more, I was out of the ditch and running, Charlot hard after me, and I was yelling as I ran. Someone else was shouting, Stefan had his sword out and was attacking the infantry from behind, we'd got them from both sides.

D'Estrada reacted first. He was already sliding off his horse, sword whistling out of the scabbard, but André dived sideways and whirled the manacle crash against his helmet. D'Estrada reeled back against his horse, then I was at the infantry and lunging straight for the man nearest André. Stefan had another in the back, and the third just turned and ran.

The riders were panicking. Their leader was dead, they were being ambushed and didn't know by how many. One officer wrenched his horse round and galloped back up the track, but the other was pinned in his saddle by the weight of the armoured man's body, and sat screaming like a woman. Corvacho's horse was trying to bolt from the noise, it was all he could do to control it. Aubéry was the best of them, he'd got out his pistol and was tracking for André, but Charlot simply lunged from ground level and took him clean through the side. The pistol thudded to the ground and Aubéry sagged in his seat, the stupid nut-brown wig slipped ridiculously skew on his grey head.

André was searching the ground for his sword, but I heard more horses, what sounded like the whole rebel army on its way. Charlot shouted 'Run!' but André whirled the other way and I saw d'Estrada was still up. He was dazed and off balance, clutching at his horse while he shook his head to clear it, but Stefan was straight in with raised sword.

André threw himself forward, grabbed Stefan's sword arm and screamed 'No!' Stefan wrenched free, but Charlot was still yelling and the first horses already charging round the bend. Stefan gave d'Estrada one brief regretful glance, said 'Fuck it,' and turned to run, dragging André with him. Charlot and I belted after them.

The horsemen stopped as they caught up with their dead leader, but we just kept our heads down and kept going. Men shouted behind us, a loud bang and a tree in front of me splintered into clean white wood. A fragment whizzed back into my cheek, a sharp sting and sudden wetness of blood, I screwed my eyes shut and swerved blindly into Charlot. His hand struck me hard between the shoulders, I opened my eyes and ran on.

We were running for our lives. No talking, no thinking, just legs pumping, boots hammering the ground till our feet burned. Stefan veered into the trees and we raced after him, anything to get off that track before a hundred vengeful horsemen came thundering down it. We zig-zagged through trees, I bashed my shoulder into one, squashed down the sick feeling and ran on. André was alongside now, Charlot behind us panting 'Faster, Messieurs, faster.' I kept my eyes on Stefan and ran.

My chest was hurting, my throat tight, odd little black specks came and went on the back of Stefan's coat. A large branch appeared in front of my face, I whacked it away, ignored the pain and stumbled on. We were slowing, wading up to our thighs in bracken, the green blurring into a kind of sea, I heard André gasping for breath and knew we'd have to stop, then I banged into Stefan in front of me and realized we actually had.

'Steady now,' said Stefan's voice. 'Steady.'

His hands were firm on my shoulders as he pushed me down into the bracken. André flopped beside me, then Charlot flattening the stalks as he collapsed on top of them. Stefan sat leisurely beside us, stretching out his legs into the green fronds. No one spoke, I don't think I could have, my throat burned like I was breathing smoke. We were listening desperately for sounds of pursuit, but all I heard was the panting of our own breath and an odd kind of roaring in my ears.

Stefan Ravel

La Marfée's a big forest, Abbé, we'd gone fast enough to get out of sight and they hadn't a chance of tracking us. I relaxed and took out my flask.

Jacques was still struggling to get his breath. The big valet was suffering too, I'd never seen quite that shade of red on a man's face before, but he hadn't done badly for someone over fifty. André was quiet and exhausted, but his eyes were open and I knew his mind was with us. I shoved the flask at him and said 'Here you go, soldier, get that down you.'

The valet's face became even redder. 'Monsieur, I *beg* you not to use this form of address –'

'It's all right, Charlot,' said André. 'Stefan's my superior officer.' He took a sip of the brandy, looked at it in surprise and took another before handing it back. Oh, it was good stuff, Abbé, I'd swiped it from Praslin's supplies when André wasn't looking.

Charlot didn't seem reassured. 'Chevalier, Madame would –'

'Madame would have a fit,' said André. 'But she isn't bloody here, and you're not going to tell her.'

I thought the poor bugger was going to choke. I offered him the brandy, but he refused with a slow shake of his head and a distinctly cool look in his eyes, so I chucked the flask to Jacques and turned to reloading my pistol.

Everything seemed suddenly rather quiet, and when I looked up both André and Charlot had their eyes riveted on my hands. I said 'What?'

André swallowed. 'Stefan. That shot back there – was that you?'

I turned the spanner and listened for the click to lock the wheel. 'We needed a distraction, didn't we?'

The silence was even deeper as I primed the pan. As I shut the cover I heard Charlot saying 'Soissons. Monsieur le Comte de Soissons,' and he made it sound like a prayer.

André said 'Stefan, do you realize . . .?' He stopped and tried again. 'You're saying you shot a prince of the blood as a *distraction*?'

'Oh, did I?' I said, and blew away the loose powder. 'Oops.'

Eighteen

Stefan Ravel

Look, the man was an enemy soldier, he was in the fucking way and I shot him, all right? But you'd never believe the fuss they made about it, they were yapping all the way back.

'The rebellion will have to fold now, won't it?' said André cheerfully, ignoring the fact the woods were full of Imperials just listening for our voices. 'It's nothing without the figurehead. We must tell the Maréchal at once.'

Charlot demurred. 'We must tell no one, Chevalier. This was a prince of the blood, and assassination rather than death in battle. You know the penalty for *lèse-majesté*.'

I did, as it happened, they have you torn in quarters between four horses and doubtless do something unpleasant to the pieces afterwards. I suggested we keep our mouths firmly shut, starting right now, and concentrate on making our way back to the others.

We found them all right. De Chouy had had the sense to move them away from the track, but he'd left sentries to watch for us and they pointed the way. A baby was crying as we got nearer, a thin, unhappy sound, but strangely clean and familiar just then, and we followed it like a lantern to guide us home.

They were waiting for us, men, women and children huddled under the wet trees, their hopeful faces lifting as we strolled into their midst. There seemed to be twice as many as when we'd left, and all with a tired and edgy look that sank into outright gloom when they saw we'd returned alone. Even young de Chouy had a listless feel to him, which was nothing like the man I remembered from the old days.

André got them moving. He sluiced the blood from his face with rainwater, Bernadette dug out his rapier to replace Fauvel's sword, then he told the crowd casually that our army had already made its way to safety in the villages and we'd better go and join them.

I doubt they were really fooled, Abbé, but he strutted about as if he'd won the bloody battle and they smiled at his youthful arrogance and followed him.

We returned to the road at Noyers-Pont-Maugis, a train of refugees straggling wearily along while peasants watched sullenly from the fields. When we asked if they'd seen the army the most we got were shrugs and sometimes a silent finger pointing south towards the Bar. At least there was no sign of the enemy.

We picked up a few more stragglers in Bulson, but the army wasn't there. It wasn't in Chémery either, but some wounded gendarmes said Châtillon had crossed by the ferry, heading for Rethel. The cavalry could make that by nightfall, but the women and children would be lucky to do it in a whole day. They stood waiting patiently on André's decision, but were already shifting from one foot to the other with weariness.

'Leave them,' said Jacques, with the superiority of a man who's done his marching on horseback. 'They're quite safe here, and we can't afford to wait.'

There was something new in the way André looked at him, something very different from the devotion I'd got depressingly used to in the past. 'We can at least get them nearer, Chagny or somewhere like that. But they've got to rest first or they won't move at all.' He went to one of the pack mules, dug in a bag and drew out a handful of gold coins.

'You look more respectable than me. Will you get them food? Bread, meat if you can get it, wine, anything you can find. We'll stop a bit to get their strength back.'

Jacques looked doubtful. 'It's the army's money.'

'We are the fucking army,' said André, and for the first time I heard an edge of temper in his voice. 'Please, Jacques, just do it.'

Jacques bit his lip, stuck out his hand for the money, and went off without a word.

Bernadette Fournier

My poor Jacques. It was hard for him, Monsieur, to be told what to do by his little brother. But it was the Chevalier we followed, the

Chevalier who had saved us, and what is more it was the Chevalier who was right.

But yes, I know what I say. To you perhaps it seems foolish, for we were refugees on roads that might be overrun by the enemy, yet those two little hours in the fields made all the difference to who we were and how we felt. We were tired and unhappy, we had friends to mourn and no future to speak of, but the food helped, and the wine more, and the fires and company made it for a little while like our own camp again. Someone brought out a flute, someone else a fiddle, and we had music all over the field.

To me too these things made a difference. I did not dance as some did, but sat on the grass and waited until Jacques came to sit beside me as I had known he would. I would have liked it better had he kissed me, but he was a gentleman now, he could not do such a thing in front of these others.

He said 'It's all my fault you've had such a wretched time, I should never have let you go with André. But it's all right now, Charlot and I have been discussing what to do with him.'

I began a daisy chain to occupy my hands. 'Do with him?'

'Yes,' he said importantly. 'We've got to get him out of France. But there's no need for you to go with him now, we'll find you somewhere safe I can visit.'

I was watching André. He was tired and in pain, but he was taking the hand of a little domestic from the retinue of M. de Chalancé and leading her into the dance. I said 'Thank you, Jacques, but I will stay with the Chevalier.'

He rolled over to look at me, and oh, just the movement of his body on the grass stirred me with memory. I could have torn the boots and breeches off him until he was Jacques again and mine.

He said 'But it's not safe, *mignonette*. André can't look after you, he ought never to have let you near the army.'

I stabbed my nail through the next stem. 'Was I not able to choose for myself?'

His eyes clouded with perplexity. 'Well, he shouldn't have let you. It's not just the battle, how could you possibly be safe with all these men?'

'They would not have touched me,' I said. 'They had too much respect for my husband.'

He sat upright with such speed I wished to laugh. 'But you're not . . .'

I smiled. 'It was only pretence.'

'But you'll have had to do stuff. You'll have had to sleep in the same bed.'

His mistrust enraged me. I had never betrayed him in my heart, and if I had offered my body that was something he could not have known and should not have imagined. You will call that hypocrisy, but I knew myself guiltless of what he really meant, and said boldly 'What right have you to question what I do?'

There was a little silence. I looked up from my chain, and there was my poor Jacques, his face creased with the hurt I had inflicted myself. He said 'None, I suppose. I wouldn't blame you if you chose André. Everyone else bloody does, whether he's right or not. But I love you, Bernadette, doesn't that give me any right at all?'

Oh, Monsieur! We were not in bed, we were not so much as touching, and still he said he loved me! I dropped my foolish chain and said 'I have not given myself to André, nor do I wish to, because it is his brother I love.'

There was no lie in it, nothing but the light in his eyes and the joy in my heart. So I kissed him, I leaned forward and kissed his mouth and he did not pull away.

'Darling Bernadette,' he said. 'Please don't frighten me like that.'

I kissed his nose, and over his shoulder saw André advancing with the smith. I said 'Your brother will need tending, he is to take off his manacle and his wrist will be sore.'

He stroked my cheek. 'All right. But you mustn't think of him more than that, I can't bear it.'

'But I will stay with him, Jacques,' I said gently. 'He needs me, and perhaps I need him too, for he keeps me safe.'

His hand left my face. 'He can't. He means so well, but he's only a boy.'

I said 'He is a man, Jacques, you must let him go his own way.'

'Must I?' he said, and it might almost have been André himself who spoke, for the voice and narrowing of the eyes were just the same. 'Why?'

No, Abbé, I didn't fucking dance. We were on the run from an invading army, so I did what soldiers do and kept watch.

A few battered remnants of our own army went by, but they didn't know anything and were only too glad to join us. One exhausted arquebusier was leading another with bandaged eyes, and André fetched them on to the field himself. The wounded one sat turning his blinded head from side to side in confusion at the music, then bit into a roasted chicken leg with a kind of incredulous wonder. Poor sod, he probably thought he'd died.

But next came a pair of well-dressed horsemen, our first sight of officers, and of course they headed straight for the women. I strolled over to make sure they behaved, but the girls seemed happy enough, they were passing the wine and giggling like fools.

'Stay and eat with us, Messieurs,' said the youngest girl. 'Everyone is welcome.'

'We'd love to, my pretty one,' said an officer patronizingly, reaching down to chuck her chin. 'But the enemy's moving on Donchery, and we must warn the Maréchal at Rethel.'

'Donchery?' I said. 'They're not coming this way?'

He flicked his eyes briefly in my direction, but since I had neither tits nor a title I was clearly invisible. 'Tell me, child, who's your officer?'

The girl laughed. 'We have none, we're led by the Chevalier de Roland himself.'

I should have seen that coming, but it was too late now. The officers were already heads up and scouring the field.

'There, Monsieur,' said the girl and only went and pointed. 'There.'

They couldn't fucking miss him. André was actually resting his arm on a barrel while the smith struck off that second manacle.

'Thank you, little one,' said the officer quickly. 'Perhaps we'll meet again at Rethel.'

They turned their beasts and were off in a second, hooves splashing up water from the puddles in an aggressive spray.

I'd told him it was stupid, I'd said we shouldn't stop, but he wouldn't listen, he never bloody did. When Stefan told us he only said 'That's a bugger, I can't come to Rethel.'

I said 'Where will you bloody go then? You can't sleep rough in this damp.'

He was stretching and flexing his wrist, and Bernadette was right, it did look painful. 'We'll stay with you till Chagny, then strike off for the Saillie in the morning. Can you let us have money for the journey?'

I suddenly felt like shit. 'Give me your arm, that needs dressing.'

Bernadette reached for it. 'Let me, Chevalier.'

'No,' he said, smiling at her. 'Let my brother do it. You and Stefan had better eat something, we'll have to move in a minute.'

She dropped a funny little curtsey that made me want to curl up with loving her and walked obediently away.

I sat the boy down and spat on my handkerchief to clean his wrist. 'Look at the bloody state of you, I can't leave you alone for a minute, can I?'

He turned away. 'Couldn't be helped.'

The side of his cheek was all bruised. Someone had hit him, and I didn't know who. As I lifted his arm I felt the thickness of a bandage under the coat, another wound I hadn't even known about. I wondered what else there'd been.

I said 'You can't go on like this, André.'

'No,' he said. 'I know.'

'All right then,' I said. 'You can go to the Saillie till we get organized, but you can't stay there, it'll be watched. Charlot and I have agreed we'd better get you to England.'

'Have you?'

I knew that tone. 'It's all right. I've been legitimated, the estate's safe, there's nothing for you to stay for. The Comte says we should have done this from the start.' I folded my handkerchief to make a dressing.

He said 'I'm not going to England.'

'Well, Rome then,' I said, tying the handkerchief in place. 'It doesn't matter, just somewhere we can keep you hidden.'

'I've tried hiding,' he said. 'That's what's been wrong, don't you see? I've been running and hiding while they've done what they like, and we've got to start fighting back.'

He never understood that there are things you can't fight. 'It's not like that, this is politics.'

'Is it?' he said. 'You want to tell these women that?'

I ran my hands through my hair in frustration. 'But there's nothing we can do.'

'We killed Soissons, didn't we?'

'So?' I said. 'They'll find another figurehead, there's still Orléans and Cinq-Mars. And Spain won't give up, not now they've come this far.'

'They'll never give up,' he said. 'All we ever do is push them back a bit and think we've won a victory, but it's not enough. We've got to stop thinking about just surviving, we've got to go out and fucking beat them.'

I thought back to the battlefield, seasoned Imperials smashing into our demoralized troops. 'It can't be done. I saw our men facing them, I saw them break and *run*.'

'They won't always.' He put his hands on my shoulders and looked in my face. 'One day we're going to stand side by side, you and I, and see the Spaniards run the way they made us run today.'

He was so young, you've got to understand that, he was so bloody young. I said 'André, stop minding so much. Let them eat each other up, let them bloody have it.'

'Give up?' he said. He seized my hand and pressed it down on the rough grass. 'Champagne, feel it? Our neighbours. A few miles west is Picardie and all our friends. South is Paris and our grandmother. How in honour can we possibly –?'

'Oh, stuff your honour!' I cried. 'There's more to life than that!'

For a dreadful second I thought he was going to hit me. Then his face went sort of blank, he stood very slowly and looked down.

'So I just leave it? They have me hounded out of Paris, they open our whole country to the enemy and I just hide and do nothing?'

I had to stand too, I'd got to make him see. 'What else is there to do?'

His eyes moved over my face, like he was taking in what I looked like. He said 'If you don't know, then it's not a bit of good me telling you,' and turned to go.

I wasn't having it. I grabbed his arm and swung him round to face me, I shouted in his face 'You're wrong!'

He shouted back at me *'So what?'*

For a second we stared at each other, faces inches apart but the whole world between us, then he wrenched himself free and walked away.

Stefan Ravel

The last part of the march was a piece of piss. The cavalry didn't ride aloofly at the rear any more, they marched like the rest of us and gave the women and children turns on the horses. Charlot even perched a little boy on his shoulders for a ride, the kid waving and saying shrilly 'I'm a giant, look at me, I'm a giant!' The pikemen round the war chest started singing marching songs, and soon they were all at it, the whole damn train.

The only sour note was Jacques, who was stomping along in a black sulk that kept its own space around him. André started in a temper too, but it seemed to cool as we marched, and more than once I saw him look round regretfully at his brother. Oh, yes, Abbé, I'd seen that split coming two years ago now, but I found it rather sad all the same.

It was falling dark when we reached Chagny. The gate was shut but the flags looked right, so de Chouy trotted up to parley with the men on the wall. I watched warily, which is how one survives in this world, but de Chouy knew the officer personally. Chagny was in French hands and we were home. Women lifted tired children down off the horses, André got the pikemen to transfer the money bags from his own beasts, and the gate began to open.

The man who rode out was a King's Musketeer, but he wasn't alone. A dozen more came filing out after him, while militia cantered up the sides of the column like Beauceron dogs guarding sheep.

I said 'Forget tomorrow, André, go now.'

He took one glance and turned away from the gate. 'Grimauld,' he muttered. 'Bernadette.'

'Come back in an hour,' I said. 'I'll bring them out, now go.'

He nodded and disappeared into the crowd.

Jacques was staring at the Musketeers. 'Rethel, those horsemen said. Rethel . . .'

But Chagny was on the way and I should have bloody seen it. News like that wasn't going to wait for fucking Rethel, they'd have tossed it about in every town they passed.

There was still time if he ran. It was dark, there were two hundred bodies around him, but the crowd realized he was leaving and hemmed him in as he struggled through, women thanking him, clutching at his arm and holding him up.

'The column will stand!' called the lead Musketeer. 'No one is to move!' Horsemen were crowding us on all sides now, and the air suddenly filled with their shouted orders. 'Stay where you are! No one to move! Everyone stand still!'

The civilians milled in sudden panic, but André's purposeful movement stood out in the chaos and two different horsemen yelled 'Stop and turn!' at once. I hoped he could still bluff it out, the manacle was off, the coat was ordinary Aubéry, but when he turned to face the Musketeers I saw the one little anomaly I'd missed. The unkempt appearance and soldier's coat were all right, but there on his hip hung the unmistakable length and elegance of a gentleman's rapier.

The crowd hushed as the Musketeer picked his way delicately through them and reined up before André. 'Have I the honour of addressing M. de Roland?'

There was no way out and the kid knew it. 'I'm the Chevalier de Roland. What do you want with me?'

The Musketeer doffed his hat. 'Monsieur, there is a royal warrant out against you, and I must ask you to accompany me to my officer.'

De Chouy bobbed angrily in front of him. 'Oh come on, d'Espernay, this is ridiculous. He saved a great part of the baggage train, the Chevalier should be thanked, not arrested.'

The Musketeer hardly glanced at him. 'That's not for me to judge.'

'Then what about this?' said Jacques. 'The Chevalier's saved part of the *caisse* from the enemy, he's bringing it back to the army.'

He flapped a frantic hand at the pikemen, who obediently trundled the mules and baggage horses forward to be examined. The horsemen murmured, though not as much as our civilians, who were probably cursing themselves silly at missing the opportunity to nick it.

But the Musketeer was one of those dutiful bastards who won't fart without his Colonel's leave. He waved a dismissive hand and said 'That cannot affect my orders. This is France, Monsieur, you surely don't imagine justice is to be bought with money?'

I knew damn well it was, and this was the first time in my whole principled life I'd have welcomed a little venality. But we'd got the real thing here, Abbé, idealism, duty and hypocrisy down to the last thread of his silk hose. He leaned down to André and said 'Your pardon, but these are my orders.'

André bowed. 'I understand.'

'Well, I bloody don't,' shouted a voice. It was Becquet's wife, a great carthorse of a woman, she elbowed her way right in front of André and glared up at the Musketeer. 'This man saved our lives, so you can turn your arse round where it came from and fuck right off.'

The Musketeer blinked. 'Madame –'

That was as far as he got. There were shouts of 'Fuck off!' ringing all through the column, and a great crush round us as people surged forward, streaming between André and the militia, pushing him back towards the rear. Messant's wife was screaming 'Where were you when we needed you?' and people took that up too. 'Where were you?' 'Where were fucking you?' The smith got to the front, hammer in hand, bawling 'You get your hands off him, you oughter be ashamed.' The soldiers who'd joined us in the fields were there too, the blinded one shouting 'God bless you, Chevalier, we're all right, get away!' Oh, yes, highly blasphemous no doubt, the poor sod wasn't even facing the right way, but it's his voice I remember most, Abbé, his 'God bless you, get away!'

Oh, André knew what they were doing all right, I saw the wetness in his eyes. He waved gratefully back at the crowd as they swept him away towards the darkness and safety of the open road at the rear.

Then the shot. A bang, a spray of cloudy sparks somewhere to my left, voices shrilled in alarm then abruptly stopped.

The Musketeer lowered his smoking pistol. 'That was in the air, de Roland. The next is in the crowd.'

Jacques de Roland

The horsemen all levelled their pistols and I heard heavy metallic clicks as they cocked them to fire. The crowd shrunk in on itself, getting closer together and further from the guns, but they didn't open to leave André exposed, they were tightening round him to form a fence.

The Musketeer stood in his stirrups. 'We'll shoot if we have to, Chevalier. My orders are to take you at all costs.'

Those women, those frightened children. André was close to the edge now, he could have just run, but I saw the rippling movement in the crowd and knew he was coming back. His voice called 'Don't shoot. I'm coming.'

I shoved frantically into the crowd towards him, I spread out my arms and said 'They won't shoot, just run.'

He said 'Look after them, won't you?' then pushed past me for the open. I grabbed for his arm, but people were moving between us and I couldn't reach him. He cleared the crowd, the lead Musketeer dismounted, and the horsemen closed all round him.

I struggled to the front. I couldn't see the boy, he was lost in all the horsemen, then he seemed to rise above the crowd as they mounted him on a horse so he could ride into captivity like a gentleman. I cried just 'André!'

He turned his head to find me and our eyes met. Then he drew his sword.

The crowd gasped. The militia drew their own blades together with one great *zing* of sound, but he never even looked at them, he raised the sword and kissed it in salute to the crowd. A few cheered, I think all the children did, but most of us were silent, and I heard a woman saying to her boy 'Remember this, Dédier. That is the Chevalier de Roland. Remember this.'

And I did, I did remember. When he bent his elbow I knew exactly what he was going to do and was willing him to do it. So were the crowd, I heard someone say 'Throw it, Chevalier!' and knew that was another story that had gone ahead of us. We stared at his hand, waiting to look upwards, but he hefted the sword round, then threw it, not upwards but down. He threw it to me.

It looked so easy when André did it, but the swept hilt was all steel swirls that bashed against my knuckles, I had to snatch at it twice before I caught it. I heard a faint sigh of disappointment from those around me, but I was just gazing stupidly at the rapier in my hand.

They were leading him away, the horsemen ushering him through the gate towards the horror I know now was awaiting him on the other side. It wasn't my fault, there wasn't a thing I could do to stop it, but I stood there watching with my father's own sword in my hand, and all I remember is the coldness of the metal in my palm and a chill in my heart I knew was shame.

Nineteen

Carlos Corvacho

Well naturally it was a blow, Señor, our leader dropping dead at the moment of victory. Lamboy had orders to pull out, the Duc de Bouillon had lunch with Puységur, why, the whole thing was over in a week.

And all because of your Chevalier. My Capitán was brooding on it all the way home, and one night he says to me 'Do you think I was wrong not to kill that young man when I had the chance?'

I said I understood it, that was all.

'Do you?' he said, rubbing his palm thoughtfully down the side of his face. 'Then tell me why I did it.'

'That's easy, Señor,' I said. 'You wanted to fight him again.'

He stopped rubbing and stared at me, then back went his head and he burst out laughing. 'Well, perhaps. But next time there'll be no mercy from either of us.'

I hoped so, Señor, I did really, but can't say I was sure. He'd had another chance to kill him in the forest, he could have pulled his pistol without so much as jumping off his horse, but he didn't do it, now did he? Oh now yes, I won't deny your Chevalier spared him too, but that was only right and proper, seeing as my Capitán was wounded and that filthy tanner looking to take advantage. Yes, we recognized him, and M. Ravel was someone else my Capitán couldn't wait to fight again, don't you doubt it.

But there was worse on its way, and come the winter we hear they're going to give your Chevalier a trial. It mightn't have mattered in the summer, Señor, there was an amnesty for the Soissons rebellion and no harm done, but it was nothing less than fatal now we were trying again.

Now naturally we were, Señor, but there's no denying the Chevalier's an even bigger problem than before. Last time we'd mostly dealt with your M. Gondi, but this year Fontrailles was the main go-between, he was coming to Madrid himself with a treaty for our King. Last time Cinq-Mars had been a sop to keep the court quiet, but this time he was our principal his own self, him and Orléans and Bouillon as before. We couldn't have your Chevalier exposing them in court, Señor, he had to be silenced at all costs.

We met up with our Paris contacts on the border to discuss it. A low breed they were, in my opinion, especially this Bouchard we were to call Duc de Montmorency. Everything had to be handed him on a tray as if my hands were dirty, and even then he'd sit polishing it in case I'd touched it in the kitchen. As for the way he talked about your Chevalier, well it's not what I was used to from a gentleman. My Capitán looked at him very doubtful indeed.

'Quite, Monseigneur,' he says. 'But will he be a problem at this trial?'

Bouchard snorts. Snorts, Señor, like a bull. He says 'God no, that's only Fontrailles panicking again. It's going to be held in camera, no one who matters will hear it.'

My gentleman raises his eyebrows. 'But surely His Eminence, the Cardinal –'

'Richelieu doesn't matter,' says Bouchard rudely. 'The King won't take his word against his dear Cinq-Mars. Why, Fontrailles has seen the boy carried to the King's bed slathered in oil of jasmine and dressed as a bride!'

That's no laughing matter, Señor, that's filth and perversion as you know yourself, and not something a man wants to think about before food. My gentleman turns the subject quick and says 'But if the verdict goes against you, Monseigneur. Surely His Majesty will pay attention then?'

'It won't,' says Bouchard, a smile slinking over his face that makes me want to reach for a crucifix. 'I've personally taken steps to ensure it. Poor de Roland is going to be very, very sorry he's put me to the trouble.'

He didn't tell us what he had in mind.

That night my Capitán stood a long time at the window watching the snow fall. Very pretty it was, we don't get it so much in Spain outside of the mountains, but I'm not sure my gentleman even saw it.

'You were right, Carlos,' says he. 'I should have killed de Roland back in 1640.'

'You weren't to know, Señor,' says I. 'Who could have seen a boy like that growing up to give us all this trouble?'

'Perhaps,' he says. 'But that's not what I meant.'

Jacques de Roland

It was so bloody unfair. All these people who'd been traitors got away with a ticking-off but André was locked up in the Château de Vincennes with that death sentence over his head. I'd hoped giving back the money would save him, but Bouillon handed over the rest when peace was signed so we hadn't really made much difference at all. It helped me and Stefan, I suppose, Châtillon was grateful enough not to charge us for harbouring André, but that only made me feel worse. The boy had fought so hard and done so much, and the only person he hadn't saved was himself.

I thought of him all that autumn, André in prison, pacing up and down in a room maybe six feet square, kicking the door, punching the walls, and maybe to be left like that for ever. I was almost relieved when we heard they were going to give him a trial. We didn't stand much chance really, but I'd hidden Bernadette, Stefan and Grimauld at the Porchier farm, and the Comtesse was confident Richelieu would help.

We went with the Comte to see him at Fontainebleau. It was the beginning of February and my uncle was swathed in blankets, but I could still feel him shivering through the seat. The fields we passed were all silvery with frost.

I think it was even colder when we got there. Fontainebleau's the size of Dax, and the cour d'honneur wasn't the usual square with stables and servants' quarters round the sides, it was a whole bloody crossroads and the wind blowing right through. Inside was just terrifying. Servants led us through grand chambers and long corridors with tall doors flanked by bored-looking halberdiers, and I was feeling really insignificant when a tall officer in a curly black wig stopped and exclaimed at the sight of the Comte.

'Vallon!' he said, seizing my uncle's hands, and if he minded the gloves he didn't show it. 'This is splendid. What brings you here?'

'Hullo, Gassion,' said the Comte, and his voice was suddenly stronger and younger. 'Nothing good, I'm for His Eminence.'

Gassion made a face. 'Sooner you than me.' He glanced at our footman and lowered his voice. 'Something's up there, Hugo. He was in with the King last night, and everyone heard Louis shouting. At Richelieu – imagine! I passed him in the corridor afterwards, and I'll swear he was shaking. People say –'

He broke off abruptly as a group of gentlemen strode down the long salon, talking and laughing like women at a soirée. The one in front was dressed all in gold, seeming almost to shimmer in the grey daylight, and his shoes had the biggest silk bows I'd ever seen. His face had the same petulant prettiness I'd noticed on the road outside Amiens.

Cinq-Mars.

He drifted past in a waft of jasmine. His friends came simpering behind, but last in the procession was Bouchard. He smiled at me, the bastard, he actually went and smiled, and I felt my nails digging into the palms of my hands. Then they were by, with more chattering and laughter, someone saying the word 'Vallon' and them all giggling like girls. My uncle didn't move, but his cheek where the mask ended flushed a dusky red.

Gassion went on his way with an eloquent gesture, and the servant led us to Richelieu's apartments. I'd expected something spectacular, but it was a bit dingy, actually, with lots of secretaries packing stuff into trunks for a journey. He himself was in a little dark room behind a desk covered with papers, and when he looked up I felt something drop inside me like a stone. His skin was all mottled and his eyes bloodshot, it was hard to believe he was the man who'd got André out of Paris.

He lifted a pale blue-veined hand and said at once 'I cannot help.'

The Comtesse didn't blink. 'Your Eminence will forgive me if I find that difficult to believe.'

He gave a pale smile. 'So do I. But only the Chevalier can save himself now. He could stop the trial at once if he accepted the verdict of the first.'

'And if he did?' said my uncle.

The Cardinal picked up a quill from his desk. 'Then he would be on the mercy of the court and I might assist him. But he will not be helped. He is determined to make a full statement and justify everything he has done.'

He would, of course, he'd go on being honourable right till the end. I thought of the executioner holding André's head in his hands and nearly vomited.

'You've seen him?' said the Comtesse. 'How was he, Monseigneur?'

He rippled his finger along the feather's edge. 'As you would expect. They have given him a foil and I found him practising fence.'

That sounded right. André fighting the empty air.

'I would like to help him,' said the Cardinal, brushing the feather backwards and forwards over his papers. 'I have tried. I spoke to His Majesty last night about the Marquis de Cinq-Mars, but we are not of one mind.'

I remembered what Gassion had said and guessed that that was an understatement.

He went on brushing. 'I have, I think, secured an honest president for the judges. I have obtained a pass for the Comte de Vallon to watch the proceedings, but I can do no more.'

'And us?' said the Comtesse. 'What must we do?'

He tossed the quill aside. 'Change his mind, Madame. That is all.'

She lifted her chin. 'Order my grandson to confess to a murder he has not committed?'

Richelieu looked up. The gleam I remembered was back in his eyes, only harder and hungrier than before. 'Then find me evidence. Give me that and I will save more than just your grandson.' His thin hand clenched and gave the desk a single, desperate thump. 'For the love of God, Madame, give me a weapon *I can use.*'

Anne du Pré

Extract from her diary, dated 3 February 1642

Bouchard arrived back from Fontainebleau in high spirits, announcing that my father is to become a marquis after the coup, Florian will be chevalier, and d'Arsy will become a baron.

'If we can trust Cinq-Mars,' said d'Arsy ungraciously. 'There's nothing about it in Fontrailles' treaty, is there?'

'It doesn't matter,' said Bouchard, spreading himself in front of the fire so the rest of us were excluded from its warmth. 'He's agreed I can draw up a separate agreement and get d'Estrada to endorse it. He can't renege if Spain's involved.'

D'Arsy said 'How the hell did you . . . ?' then swiftly turned to me. 'I beg your pardon, Mademoiselle, I do apologize.'

I thought how strange it was that they should think it wrong for me to hear the word 'hell'.

'Cinq-Mars thinks it's for his sake,' said Bouchard, massaging his neck with abominable complacency. 'I told him we could guarantee the decision of the judges.'

'Can we?' said d'Arsy.

Bouchard smiled lazily. 'What do you think?' He pulled a sheet of paper from his coat and passed it to Florian. 'Here. Would you like to see a carte blanche?'

I looked over Florian's shoulder and saw the paper was not blank at all. At the bottom was the signature of Anne of Austria, the Queen herself.

'That'll fetch de Fresnoy,' said Bouchard. 'He'll bring in any judgement we want, and think he's serving his country too.'

'What about the other judges?' said d'Arsy. 'Have you got any more?'

'No need,' said Bouchard. 'Two are our friends, and du Pré's esteemed father has given us the money for the others. Trust me, d'Arsy, it's dealt with.'

D'Arsy grunted and stared down into his glass. Florian too had the decency to look uncomfortable, but neither stood up and said 'This is an innocent man, this is wrong.' I am in a world where such things no longer matter.

Jeanette says I should be pleased they speak openly in front of me, but in truth I feel stained by their trust. I have now been playing this terrible charade for *a whole year*, and it is as if I have truly become one of them.

They believe it themselves. Last night Father asked again if I would consider a betrothal with Bouchard, and it horrifies me that he could even imagine it. He will not insist, he says Bouchard will only take me if I am willing, but I do not understand why the man even wants me. He may believe me loyal, but he must know he disgusts me personally, he *must*. Sometimes I think I am going mad.

And what use is it anyway, what I have discovered? I could write to the Comtesse, but she will not believe me, nor would it help her if she did. I had thought to somehow escape and give a statement myself, but if the judges are corrupted then nothing I say will ever be heard. They are going to destroy André and there is nothing I can do to stop it.

Jacques de Roland

The trial started the day after we got back. They'd made some concessions to nobility, it was in the Hôtel de Ville rather than the Palais de Justice and at least he'd got a chair rather than the *selette*, but it was still vile and got viler. André gave a full statement, he told them everything that had happened except about us telling Richelieu, but the Comte said the judges never even blinked. He said 'They knew it already, Jacques. They've been bought somehow, every last man of them, even de Fresnoy.'

I'd still got to go. There was a *monitoire* out, anyone with information had to give their statement or get excommunicated, so I'd given my name and got called the next day. André wasn't there, of course, it was just me and the judges and scribes with a few nobles watching from the gallery. Crespin and Gaspard couldn't get in, it was only friends of Cinq-Mars who seemed to be allowed past the guards. My uncle leaned over the rail in a corner all by himself.

It was a waste of time anyway. They got me to admit I hadn't seen the start of the fight, I hadn't seen the face of the monk, I'd never heard anyone mention Cinq-Mars, they made me confess I knew bugger all and by the end I almost agreed. I did say Dubosc went for André first, but they just said 'Ah yes, you're his brother, aren't you?' and that was the end of that.

That night Charlot fetched our witnesses from the Porchiers'. I watched them climbing out of the carriage like refugees in the dark, and it was hard to feel confident. Stefan and Grimauld were far too rough to impress the judges, and Bernadette looked so small and fragile under a big travel cloak that I just wanted to pick her up and run. She wasn't, though, she ran across the courtyard, hugged me savagely and said 'We will save him, Jacques. Do you hear me? We're going to get him out.' The Comtesse was watching, but she didn't look disapproving, I saw her give a quiet little nod.

Stefan was called first. He could testify to what had happened at the baggage train, his story would prove Desmoulins was a traitor and a liar, it should tell anyone what had really been going on at Le Pomme d'Or. We hoped it would nail the whole thing.

The judges said it was irrelevant. They claimed anything at La Marfée came under the general amnesty and Desmoulins' being a traitor didn't prove a conspiracy against André back in 1640. They said 'And do you suggest that the Duc de Bouillon was also plotting to murder the Chevalier de Roland? Or the Comte de Soissons?' Stefan looked them in the eye, said 'How the fuck do I know?' and was put out straight away. My uncle didn't say anything when he brought him back. He just looked out of the carriage window and shook his head.

But next day they summoned Grimauld, and he held his ground like a leech. He said over and over again that he saw Dubosc go for André first, nothing they said could shake him. They asked sneerily 'And what do you know about swordsmanship?' and he said 'No more than you do about fireworks, Messieurs, but you'd know if one went off in your face.' My uncle said he had the nobles in the gallery laughing, the judges couldn't do a thing to stop it.

That's when I knew we'd got a chance. The judges couldn't go against written evidence and the records showed Grimauld had beaten them. He was strutting about next day acting out his testimony in front of the servants, but nobody grudged it him, even my grandmother laughed. Only Bernadette sniffed and said 'There is still my evidence to come, Jacques, and that will be even better.' She was so fierce about it all, Bernadette. That night she pinned me down on the bed, clamped her hands on my wrists and said 'Now, Monsieur, tell me you think I will break before your old men.'

Monday morning I was woken by shouting outside my window.

There were guards in the courtyard, maybe a dozen, and more clustered by the kitchens. I hurled on my breeches and slung on my coat as I ran, but by the time I got down Grimauld was already being dragged from the servants' quarters, digging in his heels and shouting at them to get their hands off. Charlot was standing imposingly in the centre of the courtyard saying 'Not without permission from Madame la Comtesse,' but they streamed round him like waves breaking over a rock. Then a calm little voice said 'And will someone tell me the meaning of this?' and there was my grandmother in her nightdress with nothing over it but a shawl, but her hair was immaculate, her control was absolute, and everyone went dead quiet.

The lead guard held out a paper. 'I have an order from the justices to remove the person of Albert Grimauld to give further testimony.'

My grandmother read the paper and lifted her head. 'To put him to the question?'

The guard looked embarrassed. 'He has been declared a suspected accomplice.'

Torture. That's what they meant, they were going to bloody torture him till he said what they wanted. I looked at the Comtesse, but she was hesitating, and I realized with sudden shock that she didn't know what to do.

'It's all right, Madame,' said Grimauld. He jerked himself out of the guards' hands, yanked his breeches up higher and wriggled his shoulders in a manly, independent sort of way. 'Don't fret yourself. I've told no lies and nothing to fear.' He looked up at the lead guard, said 'Right you are then, let's get it over with,' then swaggered after them to the gate.

It felt unbelievably wrong to let him go. André would have tried to fight them, but we couldn't, these were our own people and our own laws. Stefan stared accusingly, Bernadette looked ready to cry, and all I could do was say 'But they can't, can they, they can't do that.'

'They can, Monsieur,' said Charlot. 'He has not the Chevalier's protection of rank.'

'No rank,' echoed my grandmother. She dragged the wig off her head, and underneath was her own silver hair, dishevelled and tangled from sleep like an ordinary person's. 'No rank, but a man for all that.'

Nothing heroic about it, was there, just no bleeding choice. It's the law, ain't it, and nothing else to it. It's the law.

All very polite and proper they was about it too. They shoosh me in the Hôtel de Ville through a side door, down a corridor to a room with a priest and clerk at a table, and there's one of they judges saying 'Now you understand why this is, fellow, we're not totally satisfied with your answers.' I says 'Well, I'm not totally satisfied with your questions,' but that don't go down so well, that don't, the judge nips up his mouth very thin and reads me a lot of rigmarole about the decision to have me interrogated, then the clerk shows me where to put my mark to say I agree. There don't seem to be a space to say 'Fuck off out of it', so I signs, then a skinny little doctor tells me to get my shirt off so he can see I'm fit to be tortured.

It seems to me there's a slide-by in this, so I gets up wheezing and coughing while the doctor pokes me up and down, then he turns to the judge and gives it his opinion it's not safe for me to take the *estrapade* as I might end up dead, which ain't allowed at all. The judge says 'Then we're authorized for the *question extraordinaire,*' but the doctor says no, the water torture's even worse for the lungs than having your arms yanked up behind your back to pull your shoulders half out your body.

The judge glares, but the clerk's writing it all down word for gospel, so he sweeps out to talk to someone in the corridor, then comes back and says they'll use the brodequins. That's the laced boot they normally use on females, see, but the little doctor still don't look happy, and reminds them on his way out they can't do no more than half an hour. Ah, he was a decent chap, that doctor, for all he looked like a fishbone with clothes on. The priest's more of a slipperer, he asks wheedling if I'd like to give a statement to himself instead, and I say 'No, I'll take my chance with the court,' and he don't say another word.

So we waits a while, me standing on parade and the priest slumbering on a chair with dribble coming out his mouth and crumbs from his breakfast down his front, then it's in with the guards again and off to the torture chamber itself. There's the judges on raised chairs, there's the clerk at his table, and there's the executioner with the planks propped against the stool, and a little pile of rods right by them.

I weren't sure, not even then. They play games sometimes, see, they'll show a man the instruments to scare the skin off him, and if he holds out fair they take them all away and let him go. So I stick it out, I swears the oath to tell the truth under torture, and the executioner swears to keep his gob shut, then the guards strip off my breeches and hose and slap me down on the stool, and I know they're going to do it for real.

The clerk glances at the clock and makes a note, and I think of that doctor and get a good squint myself. It's five past ten and only half an hour to last.

It's a cold business in more ways than the one. The executioner sticks the planks round my legs and ties them at knees and ankles and says to me 'Comfortable?' like he means it, and I say 'Yes,' because I've got skinny shanks, see, it don't hurt much at all. Then it's in with the first rod, out with the hammer, and down it goes, bang, bang, bang, scraping against my shin, the wood sides drawing tight so they're squeezing my ankles, my legs pressing inwards on themselves, the skin scrunching itself up till I'd swear the wood's scraping right on the bone.

It's the shock, see, it wipes out your mind so there's nothing but your own voice saying 'That's enough now,' like this is a civilized situation we're all in. But the hammering goes on till it's all the way in, and the sweat's sprung out in beads on your face and your mouth's breaking back from your teeth till you're grinning like a skull, and you look up at the judges and they're leaning forward to see better, then the lead one starts again with the questions.

You know what goes first under torture? The 's'. A man tries to say 'yes' like he's done since a babe, but it comes out bleeding 'yесsss'. You need it a lot too, the questions are all simple as a catechism. Is this his name? Did he work as engineer of fireworks in the gardens of the Luxembourg? Was he present when the Musketeer Dubosc was killed? And it's 'Yesssss, yessss, yessss,' then in like a knife with 'And will he confirm the Chevalier de Roland stabbed the

Musketeer before he was offered any violence?' By then you've said so many yeses your mouth's almost stuck, it takes everything in your brain to change and say 'No,' loud as you bleeding can, 'No!' and let them write *that* down wrong if they can.

The judge nods, then in comes the second shiv, bang-bang-bang, quicker this time and your shin going to snap like a rotten branch, you see it in your head, the leg, the bone, the snap, your head's going to blow like a rocket with the pain. You don't even hear the questions start again, all that's out there like it might be bloody Belgium, there's only the pain and your mind screaming at you to make it stop. Your kneecaps are being squeezed with it, dug out and it feels like peeled off, and now there's something else steering your body, trying to make you run away from your own leg. You're half off the stool, but there's hands pushing you back like there's no escape, and you're shaking and whimpering like a little girl.

But you're still a man and a part of you knows it. The next question comes like a rope to pull you out of it, but you know the answer, you looks right at them and says it, 'No,' then you slew your eyes to the clock and think 'Not much longer,' and the hands say just before ten past the hour, and you know you've had four minutes and the rest still to come.

Jacques de Roland

I dressed myself so fast I did half the buttons wrong. I gashed my hand on my belt buckle, swore like Stefan, and threw it against the wall.

'I can save him,' said Bernadette. She walked calmly in, picked up the belt and began to put it round me like a valet.

I said feebly 'Where's Philibert?'

'I hit him,' she said, fastening the buckle and giving it a little pat. 'I said today it was my job to dress you, and he disagreed, so what would you?' She pushed me down on the bed and reached for my shoes.

I said 'You can't save him, no one can.'

'Not poor Grimauld,' she said, working a shoe over my heel. 'But

I can save the Chevalier. There is still my evidence, never forget that.'

I had, and it came roaring back in a wave of terror. 'You can't, they'll torture you too.'

'Then they do,' she said. 'But I will not break, and then they will let the Chevalier go. We owe him that, you and I.'

She knelt up to adjust the lace collar over my doublet. Her face was serious in concentration, a tip of pink tongue showing between her lips, her hands were soft and smelt of Marseilles soap. It was impossible to believe that anyone would want to hurt her, but she could say far worse stuff than Grimauld, and they were going to rip her in bits till she took it back.

I caught her waist between my hands. 'It won't come to that, Grimauld won't break.'

'Will he not?' she said.

Albert Grimauld

Ah, I don't know, you lose count. You ain't wondering 'Is that five they've put in now or six?' Your mind's not doing much of anything by then, there's only your mouth saying 'Oh Christ, Holy Mary, I'm telling you, ain't I? It's the truth, Christ help me, oh God, God, God,' and the rush in your ears dies a little, and you hear the clerk murmuring as he writes, 'Christ help me, oh God, God, God.'

Nothing touches them. You've heard tears are a sign of innocence, you try all you know to squeeze out a few drops, but everything's dry, your mouth, your skin, your eyeballs, even your blood's buggered off somewhere and left you to face it alone. You close your eyes and slump, you think 'Maybe they'll stop if I faint,' but no such a thing, there's hands dragging your head up, then a voice speaks behind you and you know they've seen the ears.

The questions stop a moment and there's murmuring instead. Then another question, 'And is he a convicted felon?' and I know it's hopeless, there ain't anyone going to take a word out my mouth now they knows. I say 'Yes,' and wait for them to stop.

But they don't. Now it's 'Did he see the Chevalier strike first? Is he sure? Is he sure? *Is he sure?*' and then I gets it, late but I gets it, they're giving me a get-out, a chance to cop to a mistake. The judge says 'It was dark, wasn't it? You were overwrought,' and I say 'Yes,' and 'Yes,' and then it's 'Will he confirm he could have been mistaken and the Chevalier could have struck first?' I can't work out if that's a yes or no or even why it matters, I'm discredited anyway. The voice says soft 'He could have been mistaken?' and I say 'Yes.'

Silence and a pen scratching. Then a voice saying 'Time,' and I can't bear another second, I'm begging them to get the thing off of me. The executioner cuts the ropes and the planks clatter apart like four quarters of a nut, and there's my legs crushed and blue-white, jagged red down the shin, one ankle sticking out odd, the other pushed back into the heel. The pain's suddenly the worst it's been yet.

The judges go while I dress, but I still can't leave, the guard says I've got to go back and say it all again in a room where I can't so much as see the brodequins, it's all got to be done fair. Yes, that's what he said. Fair.

So it's back into the big room of last week, with the judges in place like they never moved, and others of parlement and the like perched up in the gallery like crows. I know one of them, that blue mask draws the eye in a second, that's the Comte de Vallon himself, and I'm face to the ground and not looking up for no one.

So they ask the questions and I give the answers, yes, I could of been mistaken, yes, the Chevalier could of struck without provoca-tion, yes, just let me get out of here and find a hole to die in, yes, bleeding yes. Then it's done, and the guard helping me up again, but the president says 'Now you have heard this man's testimony, Che-valier, perhaps you would like to reconsider your own statement?'

Ah, Christ. My head's turning round and there's André himself sat bareheaded like a criminal, they've brought him in special to hear me sell him for a heap of nothing and legs that are fucked any-way. He's blazing with fury, but he looks steady at the judge and says in a voice that shakes 'I believe I should like to consult my uncle.'

The judge says 'An excellent idea,' in a voice purry as a cat's, and I know they've beat him and it's me that's done it, me he called his friend. I'm trying to say I'm sorry, but the guards are already hauling me off, and *now* the tears come, now when they're no use to no one, now when they drag and chuck me out like nightsoil on the Place de Grève, with the tears down my face like a child.

Jacques de Roland

The great long front of the Hôtel de Ville blocked out the whole of one end of the Place, pale grey and formidable. Grimauld looked like an insect when they chucked him out of it, a crippled beetle trying to crawl away and hide itself in the vast empty space.

I jumped from the carriage and ran, but he saw me coming and flailed out with his arm to drive me away. I banged down on my knees beside him and said 'Did you break, what did you say, did you break?'

He screwed his neck to avoid looking at me. 'Yes, I broke, I bloody broke, now fuck off and leave me alone.'

For a second the fear and anger blotted out everything else, I could have kicked him smash against the wall, but then I thought of André who loved him and the anger sort of drizzled away into hopelessness instead.

I said 'Don't be silly, we're here to take you home.'

He looked at me then, a face smeared with tears and snot, a mouth of missing teeth, he was disgusting and horrible and he made my heart ache. He said 'I'm sorry, laddie, I'm so . . .'

His hands reached out blindly, tentative, ragged claws. Something broke inside me, then I was leaning forward and holding him, my arms round his scrawny back and his face in my coat, I was hugging him and saying 'It's all right, it's all right, I'm going to take you home.'

Stefan Ravel

The first time, Abbé. The first time I ever looked at Jacques Gilbert and thought he really might be André's brother.

We carried the poor wretch to the carriage and wrapped the

Comte's own blanket round him, but he wasn't going anywhere till he knew what was happening to André.

We didn't have to wait long. The Comte came out, walked straight up to Jacques and said 'I need you. Richelieu's offer still stands, and you've got to persuade André to take it.'

The Comtesse drew herself up. 'The case is not lost. We still have the serving girl.'

'No we don't,' said the Comte. 'The Chevalier says we're to get her out of Paris and hide her. He won't have a woman tortured for him, he'll die first.'

That was André. I'd seen that coming a week ago, that was André.

'And will he?' said the Comtesse. 'Will they execute him?'

He shook his head. 'It's been done in effigy, Richelieu's said he won't let them do it twice. It'll just be banishment and confiscation as before. Except . . .' He hesitated, and behind the mask I saw his eyes shift.

'Except?' she said.

He cleared his throat. 'That statement of his. Accepting the verdict now means that was slander. They have no choice but to impose the *amende honorable*.'

She made a hissing noise through her teeth. 'Dear God, Hugo.'

Jacques had gone very pale. 'He can't make a public apology for something he hasn't done.'

'He must,' said the Comte. 'Don't you realize how far they'll go? It's not just his own life. They'll torture the girl till she breaks, then execute her for perjury when she's done it.'

Jacques shook his head violently. 'André said to hide her –'

'And take away his last chance?' said the Comte.

Jacques closed his eyes and gave a curious jerk of his head. It's not often I felt sorry for him, Abbé, but I did right then.

The Comte laid a gloved hand on his arm. 'They're both dead, Jacques. Unless you can go in there right now and persuade him to change his mind.'

Twenty

Jacques de Roland

We walked to a cell at the back of the building, with four guards outside who searched us and took away our swords. They unlocked it to let us in, and there was a little grey windowless room with a single wooden chair and my brother standing with his hands in his pockets glaring defiantly at the door.

His face changed when he saw me, and we couldn't either of us speak. I just grabbed and hugged him, and for a moment I felt he was safe and home, that if I just hung on tight enough they couldn't take him away. But of course that was stupid, and after a minute we pulled ourselves together and stepped back. He was pale from being kept indoors and his beard was gone, it was the boy I remembered from the old days.

He rubbed his hand over his face and smiled. 'I've been shaving. It gives me something to do.'

The Comte said 'You have to be alive to shave, André.'

The boy looked at him, and the anger was back on his face. 'I'm sure Grimauld will take great comfort in that. Have they crippled him?'

I said 'He's all right, we're taking him home.' I tried not to remember what Grimauld's legs had looked like when we put him in the carriage.

André squeezed my hands. 'I can rely on you, can't I? You'll see he's looked after.'

I avoided his eyes. 'You'll see it yourself. You could take him with you to England.'

His hands slowly slid out of mine, and I felt him looking at me. He said 'Uncle, would you mind if I spoke to Jacques alone for a moment?'

'Not at all,' said the Comte. 'But I hope you listen to him for all our sakes.'

He knocked on the door, and a moment later it opened and closed behind him.

André stepped away from me and let out a long breath. 'It's all right, you can say what you like now. Have you got somewhere safe to take Bernadette?'

I said 'They know where she is, they won't let us take her anywhere.'

'So?' he said. 'Dress her up, smuggle her out, you can do it.'

He always thought anything was possible. 'She won't go.'

'Make her,' he said. His lip was stuck out and his eyes hard, he looked like a little boy in a temper. 'You don't want her tortured, do you?'

I pictured Bernadette mangled and sobbing like Grimauld and my mind screwed itself shut. 'No!'

'Then save her,' he said, gesturing so vigorously his hand struck the wall. 'Get her out.'

The lump in my throat was almost choking me. 'No, *you* save her. Do what they want, say what they want, then no one gets hurt and you're free.'

He went very still. 'Dishonour myself? Shame myself and my whole family for ever and in public? Is that what you want?'

I gripped his arms. 'It's just words. Get it over with, then you're free.'

'No,' he said, and I felt him trembling under my hands. 'No, you can't make me.'

'They'll execute you if you don't.'

'Good,' he said, and gave a little jerk of his head. 'Good.'

'It's not,' I said. 'I saw it done in effigy, remember? How am I going to feel if it's really you, how the fuck am I . . .?'

'Don't,' he said. 'Dear Jacques, don't. It'll be all right, you know it's what I want.'

I stared over his shoulder at the wall, grey, cracked plaster with odd red smears like someone had tried to write on it in blood. 'They'll still make you do it. The *amende honourable*. You'll have to do it on the way to the scaffold.'

His mouth tightened. 'They can't force me.'

'They'll torture you.'

For a moment he almost smiled. 'And you think that would work, do you?'

I pushed him away in frustration. 'All right, do it your way, let them make you an example. They'll break you on the wheel, you'll take days to die, they'll display the body, you think that won't shame the family?'

He made a sort of muffled noise and turned away, but I couldn't stop. 'You're not thinking about any of us. You'll let Bernadette be tortured . . .'

'I won't,' he said to the wall. 'I've told you, get her away.'

I came up behind him. 'Suppose we do, suppose I break her heart and get her out. What'll they do to us then? What'll they do to your grandmother?'

'Nothing,' he said obstinately. 'She'll say she didn't know.'

'And me?' I said. 'We'll all lie our faces off because you're too proud to do it yourself?'

He swung round, face stark with anger. 'That's enough.'

I ignored him. 'Can't you see what it's going to mean? The servants dragged off and questioned, your grandmother interrogated, Bernadette caught after all, her being tortured and killed, me having to watch it, all of us broken in bits just to save your bloody honour?'

There was only the slightest twitch in his shoulder to warn me, but I'd fenced him nearly seven years, my hand was up and smack round his wrist before his fist reached my jaw. His eyes widened in sudden disbelief, and my brain caught up in shock. He'd tried to hit me. My hand opened by itself, he snatched back his arm, and we stared at each other, wide-eyed.

'I'm sorry,' he said. 'I'm . . .' He looked at me helplessly, then slumped on the chair and put his head in his hands.

Outside the door the guards were talking and laughing and I wondered how long they'd been doing it.

André spoke through his hands. 'If you could get me something. They wouldn't hurt anyone else then, it'd be over. I know you're searched, but –'

I said 'André, you can't.'

He still didn't look at me. 'You suggested it yourself once.'

'That was for other people.'

'So's this.'

'Not if there's another way.'

His hands slid down off his face and I saw the hopeless misery in his eyes. 'I don't want to go to hell.'

I said 'No.'

His head moved from side to side. I followed his gaze: wall, wall, floor, ceiling, door with armed guards behind it, wall. He said 'There's no escape from the château either, not without killing someone.'

I said 'This is the only way. Please, André, you've simply got to.'

He rubbed his hands over his face, then sat staring at them.

I waited. Even the guards outside were quiet.

'All right,' he said at last. 'I'll do it. Tell the Comte he wins.'

I looked at him doubtfully.

He stood up. 'No, I'll do it. You can have my word if you like.'

'It's not that –'

'Good,' he said. 'Then go and tell them, will you? I'll see you tomorrow.' He forced a smile, thrust his hands in his pockets, and went back to glaring at the wall.

Anne du Pré

Extract from her diary, dated 10 February 1642

Florian said nothing on his return from the trial, but went straight to his room to wait for Pére Ignace. I was terribly afraid I knew why.

He was still there when Bouchard himself strolled into the salon. I told him my brother was indisposed, but he said it was me he wished to see, and actually ordered wine.

He dismissed Clement as soon as it was poured, then sprawled into a chair, propped his elbow against the arm and regarded me with malicious amusement. 'I'd like you to come out with us tomorrow, Mademoiselle.'

I said 'Monseigneur is very kind. Is it to be the theatre?'

He smiled. 'Almost. We're going to see André de Roland perform the *amende honorable*.'

His face blurred and I had to grip the arms of my chair. 'I don't believe it.'

He laughed delightedly. 'You do still care about him, don't you? I've often thought so.'

I could hardly think sufficiently to answer. 'I've never pretended otherwise, Monseigneur, I owe him a great debt of gratitude. Even if our allegiances are now different that cannot change the obligation.'

'Obligation,' he said, polishing the rim of his glass. 'And that's all, is it?'

I pulled myself together. 'Monseigneur does not doubt my loyalty?'

'Oh, no,' he said dismissively. 'You wanted a title and the tabouret, that's perfectly natural. But I've wondered sometimes if there wasn't something else. What you wrote in your charming little journal, for instance.'

I stared at the floor and tried to will away the burning of my cheeks.

'Ah well,' he said kindly. 'Perhaps that's natural too. But there was more to it for de Roland, wasn't there? He could have had far better than a tradesman's daughter.' He sipped his wine and looked at me with an air of calculation. 'So why you?'

I could not stop myself saying 'I might ask you the same question.'

He waved that away. 'Oh, that's different. I need the money, and you're an obedient little thing now you've learned proper manners. But do you know, I think de Roland actually has a passion for you. I really do.'

Then I understood him. I said 'M. de Roland did no more than honour a childhood agreement. I was never very much to him.'

'Really?' he said. He drained his wine, slammed down the glass and stood up. 'Well I don't agree. So you'll come with me tomorrow, and I'm sure he'll be glad to see you.'

I rose hastily. 'I beg you to excuse me, it would not be right.'

He smiled even more. 'I'm afraid I'm insisting.'

I said 'My brother shares the obligation, and would never force me.'

'He might,' he said, and took a step closer. 'If I told him you'd insulted me I'm sure he would.'

I had to fight the urge to step back. 'I haven't insulted you.'

'Of course you haven't,' he said, laying his hand soothingly on my sleeve. 'But that needn't stop me saying you have, need it?'

He is sick in his mind, he must be. 'Please, I beg you.'

There was a tickling sensation on my arm and I saw his fingers playing with my sleeve ribbon. He said 'But I really do want this, Mademoiselle. Would you like me to suggest your brother has you confined to your room again? You know I could.'

I felt a heavy softness on my arm as the ribbon gave way to his prying fingers and the gathered folds of sleeve fell loose. My mouth was suddenly dry.

'Decide in the morning,' he said, and turned away. He paused at the door and held out a loop of yellow silk. 'My apologies, Mademoiselle. Your ribbon.'

I could not make my legs move towards him, I could not so much as reach out my hand.

'As you wish.' He opened his fingers and let the ribbon flutter to the floor. 'But it's a pretty gown, Mademoiselle. I'm sure de Roland would like to see you wear it tomorrow.'

Stefan Ravel

I couldn't see what the fuss was about. I'd have told him to cross his fingers behind his back, say what they wanted, and then kill the bastards afterwards.

But it was a serious business at the Hôtel de Roland. The Comtesse shut herself in the chapel, the servants went round weeping, and the shutters were closed as if someone had died. They didn't dare tell Bernadette. Jacques gave her some balls about André just being banished for a while, then packed her off with Grimauld to the Porchier farm to wait for him. He wanted me to go too, in case André backed out and the judges decided to torture all the witnesses, but I somehow didn't think that was likely. André had given his word, so I stayed right where I was and sharpened my sword.

There was a light snow that morning, and the syphilitic Comte wore furs when he went to hear the sentence. I suspect the judges knew they were pushing it and only banished him for seven years, but the *amende honorable* was pretty vindictive. It wasn't the *simple* version that he could do quietly before the judges, but the full *in figuris* to be done in public. He didn't have to say he'd murdered anyone, which was possibly just as well, but he had to say sorry to the lot of them, name by bastard name, and ending with the one they called Bouchard. I made a little point of remembering that name, Abbé. Bouchard.

They delayed till after noon to attract a nice crowd. The Comte and his mother said André would hate them to watch, but Jacques was going, he said he wanted his brother to have at least one friend in the crowd. I thought 'Sod it, we'll make it two.'

I watched Jacques ride off with Charlot, then strolled down to the Place de Grève, mingled with the scum who'd braved the sleet and slush to see a nobleman on his knees, and elbowed myself to a nice little place at the front. Not that I could see a great deal, there were soldiers all round the square with bayonets facing outward, and I guessed they were expecting a demonstration. The one in front of me was a sunburnt, grizzled trooper I rather liked the look of, so I said 'Listen, soldier, the man they're about to humiliate saved my life in battle, I'd like him to see I'm here.' He looked me over, seemed to approve, and moved aside to give me a clear view.

Empty space, that was all. Empty space and a square blue cloth arranged with a row of chairs for the people André had maligned. Some had only drapes over them indicating the crests of the families, but two were occupied, one by a dark man in the crimson and gold of the Cardinal's Guard, and the other by a stocky blond with a thick neck who sat with his arms folded and legs splayed arrogantly apart.

'Bouchard,' said the trooper, with a contemptuous jerk of his head. 'Calls himself other things these days, but everyone knows he's just a bastard called Bouchard.'

More vultures were gathering behind the blue square, all huddled in thick cloaks while a pack of liveried servants laid out stools for their pampered bottoms. I guessed them for friends of those named in the petition, but a girl sitting quiet at the front looked faintly familiar and so did the fidgety young man next to her. Then Bouchard swung round to say something, the girl lowered her hood as if in obedience to his wish, and the mass of red-gold hair that tumbled out was all the reminder I needed.

I'd liked that girl, Abbé. I hadn't wanted to believe she'd become as treacherous as Jacques said, but there she was in the ranks of the enemy, Anne du Pré herself.

Anne du Pré

Extract from her diary, dated 11 February 1642

I had no choice, for today was the one day I must not be locked up. Today André would at last be freed from prison, and my plan was to escape and find him.

I would do it from the Couvent de la Visitation. Father loves me to visit there, since it is frequented by so many fashionable ladies, so when I asked if I might spend tonight with the sisters he agreed with alacrity. From there I knew I could easily escape to the Hôtel de Roland, where the Comtesse would now have no reason to conceal her grandson's whereabouts and would surely direct me to André.

But first he had this ordeal to survive, and I knew how hard Bouchard would make it. He was well aware what vengeance André would seek if he survived the day, and I was certain he hoped to break him and secure his execution after all. I told myself he would fail, but even I was finding the prospect unbearable and what it would be for André I could not think.

'I can't see your dress,' said Bouchard petulantly over his shoulder. 'Can't you take off the cloak?'

For once Florian protested. 'It's very cold, Monseigneur.'

It really was. The sleet had stopped, but the muddy slush on the ground was icy and my shoes already soaked through.

Bouchard shrugged. 'Well, I wouldn't want you to be uncomfortable.'

He turned back to face front, but a moment later spoke again. 'Oh, look,' he said. 'A friend of yours, Mademoiselle, how nice.' He lifted his hand and gave a little wave.

Jacques de Roland

Crespin grabbed my arm, babbling 'No, Jacquot, no!' I shook him off but Charlot moved smoothly in front of me and said 'Tomorrow will do for him, Monsieur, today we are here for the Chevalier.' He spread his arms wide, blocking the sight of that filthy grinning face, and the rage sank to a slow, dull thumping in my chest.

'Charlot is right, my friend,' said Gaspard, but his aristocratic face was hard and set. 'There will be other ways, and we shall take much pleasure in thinking of them tonight.'

Tonight felt like a sort of haven to be reached when this was over. Tonight we'd be at the Porchiers' and the boy safe. He'd got a week's grace to leave the country, so we'd sit in front of that blazing fire and have time to be warm and comfortable together before he set off for the coast. Tonight.

A drum rolled, and people hushed to expectant quiet. My heart seemed to be beating in the top of my throat. A crier read out the verdict and sentence, then moved aside to show half a dozen pikemen standing either side of a wooden door. It had all carved panels on it, like pictures in thick frames hung on top of each other on a wall, then the whole lot jolted forward as the door began to open.

The judges processed out first, long robes swishing the ground. The priest was next, but he stepped to one side to let the pikemen shuffle themselves into two ranks like a tunnel. Glimpses of white showed moving through the dark bodies, then André was walking out between them, the executioner on his heels to urge him on. The pikemen moved forward with them like walls, but were careful to fan out at the front to make sure everyone got a good look at the man inside. A sigh like a groan went up, as if everyone had breathed out at once.

I'd known how he'd look, but I still wasn't ready for the sight of him. His bare head seemed even more degrading between the floppy-hatted pikemen. His hair was dressed and the white shirt a good one of his own, but that made the shock even more brutal when it ended there, no breeches, no hose, nothing but bare legs and feet, as ridiculous as if a gentleman had gone out in the morning and forgotten to dress. Children near us pointed and laughed.

'Steady, Monsieur,' said Charlot.

The candle was a big one, I think they'd said four pounds, and the flame flickered as he adjusted the weight in his hands. I looked at the whiteness of his bare legs and shivered in the warmth of my woollen cloak. I thought of the roughness of the stones under his feet, and saw the brown line on his soles left by the snow-puddled mud. The wind gusted at his shirt and he pressed the candle hard into his body to hold it back down. His face was scarlet with humiliation, but when he lowered it the executioner said something sharp and he had to lift it again so people could see.

And they did see, everyone was staring, he must have felt their eyes like so many stones. A bunch of well-dressed merchants were grinning and murmuring, a lady leaned out of a carriage to get a better view. A red-nosed pedlar chuckled to himself, took a slurp from a bottle, and wiped his mouth with the back of his hand. A hard-faced old woman stared with dull eyes like she'd seen it all before, she'd seen people hanged and tortured, this was nothing. A little boy said 'Why's that man got no breeches on?' and I wanted to close my eyes with misery, but a woman's voice said 'Hush, little one, that is a very brave man.'

Something sparked inside me. I looked again at the crowd and saw that lots weren't jeering at all, some even looked angry. A woman's voice called 'God bless you, Chevalier!' and I remembered the people at Chagny, the way they'd tried to save him. Another shouted 'We know you didn't do it!' Then a man yelled 'Fuck the bastards!' and I felt a sudden rush of hope as people surged forward. But the troopers were ready, someone shouted an order and the muskets came up levelled at the crowd, jagged knives plugged into the barrels to make bayonets. The yelling lapsed into mutters, and the little resistance faded and died.

I think a bit of me died with it. I saw it then, I saw what I'd missed. It wasn't just André being spat on, it was everything he stood for and people believed in, and at last I understood what that was. I should have died before I let him do it, I should have done anything to save him from this. Honour? *This* was honour, a man stripping himself of all self-respect to save the people he loved, *this* was honour, and the only shame in any of it was ours for watching it and mine for making him do it.

Stefan Ravel

Yes, yes, I know, Abbé, I'd thought it was only a lie, but I saw and heard it all, remember, and the reality was something else.

André reached his position and the executioner prodded him to a stop. Then Bouchard looked at him. He leaned back in his chair, legs wide apart, and looked at him. Muddy feet, bare legs, flimsy shirt, and that flushed, humiliated face, he studied the kid as if he were a work of art. Then he said to the executioner 'All right, let's see him kneel.'

Oh, it was deliberate, Abbé, he was goading him into doing something stupid. He wasn't far off it either, André stiffened as if someone had stuck a rod up his back, and I knew he was within a heartbeat of smashing the candle over the bastard's head and damning their whole stupid pageant to hell. If he did it he was dead, and that's just what Bouchard was playing for.

But André had given his word. I saw his shoulders heave as he took a deep, deep breath, and slowly, carefully knelt on the stones. The crowd sighed.

'Close,' said the trooper in front of me, chewing on his tobacco. 'He's good, that Bouchard. You want to put money on it?'

Possibly my expression answered for me. He shrugged, said 'Suit yourself,' and spat a stream of brown juice on the stones.

André lowered the candle, and the executioner thrust the paper in front of him.

Bouchard said loudly 'I can't see his face.'

André wasn't lifting it either, his only hope was if he didn't have to meet that vicious bastard's eyes, but the executioner said 'You must look up, Chevalier,' and when the kid didn't react immediately he grasped a handful of his hair and jerked up his head, forcing him to look right at Bouchard.

I watched Bouchard's squint-eyes on André's face, I heard his soft little chuckle of enjoyment, and something curled inside my belly like a snake. This wasn't punishment, it wasn't even politics, this was fucking rape. I stopped wanting André to stick it out to save himself, I wanted to see him get up and smack that yellow-haired monster back into the mud where he belonged. I like my skin where it is, Abbé, but my hand was on my hilt, I was edging nearer the trooper, and God in his bloody heaven I was ready to fight.

Bouchard knew André needed only one little push to send him over the brink. He said over his shoulder 'Can you see all right, Mademoiselle?'

Anne du Pré

The shock on his face was like a blow to my own. I was gripped with the terror of what it would drive him to, but then his horror changed to a dreadful contempt and he looked away.

I tried to speak, but my throat was swelling with the hardness of tears. I had no sword, nothing but my own wretched self and a desperation to do something, anything to save him, anything at all.

Stefan Ravel

The executioner shook the paper. 'The words, Chevalier, you must say them.'

Bouchard leaned forward. His voice was low but I heard it, me and maybe half a dozen others at the front. 'You've never had her, have you, Chevalier? But I'm going to marry her and have her whenever I like.'

André's hand batted away the paper. His knee was off the ground, foot bracing to stand, but a loud clatter broke the silence, his head jerked towards it, and there was Anne on her feet, her stool rolling loose on the stones.

She was just standing helplessly with tears running down her face, but it was enough to stop him dead. He stared at her in bewilderment, and I felt a wild return of hope.

The crowd were murmuring, I heard the name 'Mlle Celeste', but she kept looking at André, no one else. Her bloody brother was cringing with embarrassment and reaching out to pull her back down, but she brushed him aside, took a step forward, then slowly and deliberately knelt on the muddy stones.

The crowd gasped, then erupted into a great roar. Even those foul merchants stared and clapped. Bouchard's face screwed up with rage, but André was just gazing at Anne, the bewilderment gone and understanding growing there instead. She loved him. No one in the Place could have doubted it now, and the knowledge made him almost shine.

'Magnificent,' said Gaspard in sudden passion. 'Ah God, she is magnificent!'

The brown slush was seeping up her dress, the hard ground must have been agony on her legs, but she knelt upright as André and never flinched. Her brother tugged feebly at her arm but she resisted and he only succeeded in dragging her sideways on the flags. The crowd hissed with annoyance and he backed off fast, but Anne just knelt back up and pushed her hair out of her eyes, leaving a little smear of mud on her cheek. Gaspard was right, she was brilliant, and the crowd watched her in something close to awe.

Anne du Pré

I felt I could stay like that for ever, just the two of us with our heads on the same level and André looking at me with that new softness in his eyes.

But his punishment was not yet over and the executioner again thrust forward his hateful paper. André looked at me in anguish, and I said 'You don't have to, it's all lies.' He blinked in surprise, but how could I say anything else? It was his own life, how could I wish him to do anything with it but what he wanted?

The executioner said 'Do you refuse, Chevalier?'

André tore his eyes away from me, cleared his throat and said 'No.'

I did not understand, only that he felt he had to, and it was therefore my job to help him. He lifted his head and began to speak, and the crowd became hushed as a church.

He did not read from the paper, the words were clearly already burned into his soul, he kept his eyes on me and began to say them. He confessed his wickedness in offending God, the King and Justice, and begged forgiveness of all of them. He faltered a little and I knew the worst was now coming, but I kept my eyes on his face, listened to the start of each word and said it aloud with him. If he had to be shamed then I would be too.

We said we had wronged the dead Musketeer Dubosc, we had wronged MM. Fontrailles, d'Arsy, Desmoulins and Lavigne, we begged their pardon and declared them all worthy men. Last of all we begged pardon of Bouchard and said he too was a worthy man, but André's mouth twisted and the words came out in more spit than breath. The executioner removed the paper, then André lifted his head, closed his eyes, and said 'And may God forgive me if I lie.'

Bouchard said 'Those aren't the words, he can't say that, make him do it again,' and the judges murmured together and looked grave. I almost choked with rage, but the priest demanded 'How can it ever be a crime to ask forgiveness of God?' and they lapsed at once into silence. They were right to be ashamed, I wish they would *die* of it. They have forced an innocent man to shame himself in front of all Paris for something he has never done.

Jacques de Roland

It was over. The pikemen marched him to the carriage, a horrid, manky thing for smuggling out people whose names were like swearing. The crowd was thronging round it, but Crespin called out 'The Chevalier's brother, please let him through,' and people parted for us in silence. Their scorn burned my skin like hot wax.

Then I was through to the carriage and there was André sitting on the step to put on his breeches. I ripped off my cloak to wrap round him, needing to cover him, hide him, keep him warm.

He ducked away and stood to pull up his breeches. 'They've seen it now, they can't unsee it, can they?'

Neither can I. Not even now I can't, my brother stripped and humiliated and me standing by and letting it happen.

'Anne,' he said, fumbling with his belt. 'She might be in trouble after today, you'll look out for her, won't you?'

I glanced back at the Place. Bouchard was certainly giving her a nasty look, but her brother was escorting her back to her carriage and she was obviously safe with him. The crowd was dispersing noisily beyond them, but one figure stood still in the midst of it, a tall, rough-looking man in a brown coat who was watching Bouchard with an intensity that meant business. His hat was tipped low over his eyes, but I knew it was Stefan.

'Come on, M'sieur, move it, will you?' said one of the pikemen. 'Ain't you got a home to go to?' His mates guffawed.

For a second there was a flash of anger back in André's eyes, but then it faded and he turned silently back to the carriage.

I said 'I'll see you tonight, we'll find a way to put it right.'

'If you say so.' His voice was as dead as his eyes.

I couldn't stand it, I'd got to reach him somehow, then in sudden inspiration I scrabbled out my sword. The pikeman backed off in alarm, but I shook my head impatiently and pressed the guard into André's hand.

'Your rapier,' I said. 'It's time to take it back.'

He backed away, banging into the carriage step. 'No.'

'You must,' I said, forcing it into his hand. 'It's yours.'

'Is it?' he said. His voice was louder again, there was something almost wild in his eyes. 'Is it, Jacques?' He took the faible in his other hand, then smashed the blade across his knee.

I stared in disbelief. His father's rapier. His father's dress sword that M. Gauthier had brought out of the ruins of his home.

'It's a gentleman's sword,' said André. 'What's it got to do with me?' He dropped the pieces to the ground, climbed into the carriage and slammed the door.

I stooped to pick up the bits. They were useless, of course, you can't reforge a rapier, but it had been our father's sword, my father had worn it, I'd seen him with it a hundred times. The carriage jolted forward.

'Come on,' said Crespin. He was already mounted, so was Gaspard, and Charlot was leading up Tonnerre. 'Aren't you going with him? Come on.'

As the carriage rumbled past I saw the spectators on the other side, faces and faces of condemnation staring back at me. It was like looking in a bloody mirror.

'No,' I said, and grabbed Tonnerre's reins. 'You go, Charlot will show you the place. There's something I've got to do first.'

Most of the crowd were running whooping after the carriage down the Rue de la Vannerie, so I was home in two minutes. I leapt off Tonnerre, flung the reins to Guillot, said 'Get Philibert, I need my things packed in ten minutes,' then strode indoors, took the stairs two at a time and was on the gallery in a moment. Robert was outside the salon, I heard him say 'But Madame is with –' and batted him out of the way with the back of my hand. I said 'Madame is with *me*,' pushed open the door and went in.

There was a man inside with his back to the door, but he turned as it crashed open and I stopped as abruptly as if it had been the Cardinal.

That face. I'd known there was no nose, I was prepared for a kind of hole, but there was this great red spongy thing growing there instead like it had squashed the nose out the way and was starting to eat the rest. I flinched and had to look away.

'Don't fret, Jacques,' said the Comte. From the corner of my eye I saw him move to the table and pick up his mask. 'This hurts a little if you wear it all day, surely you understand that?'

I understood a lot of things. Those cosy little chats I'd had with him, happy to let him say honour was rubbish, everything was rubbish but us and our survival. I'd listened to his wisdom as he spoke in my father's voice, and all the time what was behind the mask was this.

'All right, Monsieur,' said my grandmother soothingly. 'We understand how hard today has been. Will you tell us?'

It was nothing that could be understood in this beautifully decorated room. I took the pieces of sword, flung them on the floor, and said 'There you are, that's what we've done. We've been wrong about everything. The only person who wasn't shamed today was André, and the only one who didn't let him down was Anne.'

My uncle stooped to pick up the pieces, then turned them over slowly in his hands.

I said 'Disinherit me if you want, I won't be here anyway. I'm going with André and not coming back till I can bring him with me.' I looked at my grandmother, said 'I'm sorry,' then turned and walked out.

I went straight to André's room. It was quiet in there, the air heavy and muffled with dust. It was cold too, there hadn't been a fire for more than a year, and the bed curtains were damp to the brush of my hand. The presses were all open and his clothes gone, Charlot had had them packed to send to the Porchier farm, but I knew what he'd have missed.

There was a great oak chest by the far wall. When I lifted the lid a tiny breath of warmth wafted out, like a memory of a summer day in 1640. We'd packed all his old stuff in here, the things he wasn't going to be needing for a while, and right at the top was the sword.

I unwrapped it and held it to the window. This was a real battle sword, the one André had taken from his father's own hand, the one he'd fought with all through the Occupation and used in the last stand at the Gate. He was right, he didn't need a gentleman's dress sword any more, the time for posing and duelling was over. He needed a weapon for war.

'Antoine's sword,' said my grandmother's voice. She was standing behind me, looking smaller than ever next to the great swathes of the bed curtains. 'May I?'

I felt oddly reluctant to give it to her, but she grasped it quite naturally and seemed quite prepared for the weight.

'We gave it to him for La Rochelle,' she said, checking down its length. 'He was riding the Général with his father's gold saddle-cloth. He looked very fine as he rode away.'

I said 'I'm sorry, I can't live up to all this. You were wrong to try and make me.'

'I was right,' she said calmly, and reversed the sword to offer me the hilt. 'I said you were a Roland, and now you are proving it. Go and find André, do what you have to do to restore our honour. I only wish I could go with you.'

I took the sword, laid it on the chest and hugged her. For a moment she clutched me fiercely, then she patted my shoulders and reached up to kiss me correctly on both cheeks.

'Take care of yourself, my dear. Remember I have two grand-sons now.'

I stroked her hair, and found it was actually soft. 'I'm sorry, I know it leaves you in a mess. If my uncle dies –'

'He will not die,' she said firmly, stepping back and patting her hair back into place. 'He will not *dare* die until I am ready. Now go quickly before I change my mind.'

I found Philibert in the courtyard with my things piled on Tonnerre, but he was holding another horse and there were bags on that too. I said 'It's all right, you don't need to come,' but he looked at me with eyes bright with hurt and said 'I go where you go, Monsieur, unless you don't want me.' I nearly hugged him too, but he'd probably have hated it.

Guillot bowed low as we swept through the gate. The Rue du Roi de Sicile was half empty, so I looked over at Philibert then the two of us dug in our heels.

Tonnerre was at the gallop in seconds. The wind blew off my hat but I didn't care, the speed was uplifting, the clatter of the hooves stirring me like drums before a battle. I wasn't noticing how grand and impressive the great street was, I wasn't intimidated by the towering buildings and elegant pedestrians, it was just a road to get me where I needed to be and for the first time since I'd come to Paris I knew where that was. My place was with André and always had been, I was turning my back on everything to follow him, and some-how, between us, we were going to put things right.

PART THREE

The Man

Twenty-One

Stefan Ravel

Paris is a wonderful place for a footpad. Bouchard's carriage was stopped in the traffic down the Rue de la Ténarue, and when I saw it finally inch its way on to the Pont Notre-Dame I knew I had him. He was following the du Prés on to the Île, so I belted down the riverside, nipped up the Pont-au-Change, and got to the Place Dauphine first.

No, I didn't know the house, but you know the layout, Abbé, the houses are built in a triangle to ensure everyone gets the same river for his money. I only had to loiter on the bridge, watch the road in both directions, and wait for the du Prés to show me their home. One house on the Right Bank side seemed particularly busy, with a succession of armed ruffians being admitted through the porte-cochère, and I somehow wasn't surprised when the du Prés' carriage trotted in through the same entrance. It was a splendid property, right opposite the first steps to the river, but it wasn't much more than a den of thieves inside.

It was also a little public for what I had in mind, so I strolled round into the Place itself, waited a few minutes to be sure my target was settled, then knocked at the kitchen door and announced I had a message for M. Bouchard.

Anne du Pré

Escape now seemed impossible. Florian was furious and said that when Father heard what a spectacle I had made of myself he would have me locked up for a month. I was afraid this was all too likely, and knew I must now forget the convent and find some other way of slipping out before Father came home.

317

This, however, proved quite as difficult, for Bouchard was angrier even than Florian and wished me constantly under his eye for the sole purpose of tormenting me. I curtsied to beg his pardon, but he only said 'Don't you think you've spent enough time on your knees for one day?' When I pleaded to be allowed to change my muddy dress he said 'But I like the way you look, Mademoiselle, it becomes you very well.' I was becoming quite frantic. Father was only at the Chambres des Comptes and expected back within the hour.

Then Bouchard's own manservant appeared, saying a man was come on business so private he wished to speak with him outside. Bouchard hushed him quickly and I guessed he had been expecting just such a visitor on some purpose he did not wish us to know.

He said 'Bring him to the courtyard garden, Huon. We can speak there undisturbed.'

Stefan Ravel

It was all one to me, Abbé. All I needed was privacy.

I followed some liveried minion through a vast kitchen and scullery labyrinth, then was finally hustled through a door into a little covered garden. It was the usual kind of thing, clean white gravel, a swirly little green parterre, and a row of depressed-looking orange trees in tubs, but what appealed to me most was the absence of ground-floor windows. I planted myself near the orange trees and waited.

He shot out, banged the door shut behind him, and started speaking before he even reached me. 'What's wrong? Don't dare tell me you've lost him . . .' He saw my face under the hat and stopped abruptly. 'But you're not . . .'

'No,' I agreed, bringing my hands out of my pockets.

He drew himself up in hauteur. 'Then what is your message, fellow?'

'This,' I said, and drove my fist into his gut.

It's a satisfying punch, that one, especially when you've a soft pot belly to work on and enough anger to drive it through his spine. The air grunted out of him in a soggy rush of spit, his eyes bulged white and bloodshot, and his hands clawed at my cloak as he wheezed for breath. I stuck my knife under his chin, and said 'Shout and I'll kill you.'

He wasn't up to so much as a squeak. I shoved him down on his knees and ran my eyes quickly over the upper windows to check we hadn't yet attracted an audience. It was all clear.

'Now then,' I said pleasantly. 'Let's talk about the *amende honorable.*'

His cross-eyes gleamed with porcine understanding. 'De Roland. The little coward's sent –'

I slammed his head on the ground and began to wipe the gravel with his face.

Anne du Pré

'We can't go till Bouchard leaves,' said Jeanette, furiously buttoning me into the green dress. 'Huon never stirs from the kitchen while his master's here, there's no sneaking out that way.'

I glanced down into the courtyard, but the two figures were still bent close together as if in deep conversation. 'The message sounded urgent. Perhaps he may be called away.'

'He'd better be,' she said. 'There's no other way, and that's a fact. Clement's in the hall and Denis by the Place door, there's no end of gallows-faced ruffians hanging about in the cour d'honneur, not a way out anywhere without your brother's say-so.'

I looked again out of the window. Bouchard seemed to be crouching and the other leaning solicitously over him, but then the man's arm made a jabbing movement and Bouchard rocked to one side. The man dragged him back up on his knees, hesitated, then looked up and round at the windows.

I stepped back fast. The face, the rough beard and ragged brown coat were all familiar, and in an instant I was transported back to the night when André brought me out of the château, he and his friend, the big man he called –

'Say it,' I said, and showed him the knife.

He managed to spit out the words 'André de Roland is an honourable man and I . . .'

'And the rest,' I said encouragingly. There was movement at one of the upper windows and it was time I wasn't there. 'Now.'

'And I'm a lying piece of shit.' He gurgled and spat blood.

It didn't make me feel as good as I thought it would. It was just words in the end, it didn't undo anything. For a second I nearly sliced his windpipe anyway, but I'd the oddest feeling that wasn't going to help either.

A distant shout reminded me my position was somewhat precarious, so I whacked my boot into his groin for luck, turned and legged it for the door.

The corridor was still empty. I turned to head back to the kitchens, but a voice behind called 'Stefan, no! Not that way!' and there was Anne herself with Jeanette Truyart at her side. 'Too many servants,' she said. 'Come on.'

Anne du Pré. Different dress from this afternoon, hair wild and undressed, but the same calm voice and steady head from two years before. She'd even remembered my name.

Sod it, I followed her. She led us briskly through a storeroom, a clerks' office, then finally into a little robing room. I heard footsteps and voices in the hall beyond, a man saying 'If he comes this way yell.' The steps hurried off, Anne signalled us to wait, and walked out.

A second later there came quick, light steps in the hall, then her voice panting as if from running. 'Oh Clement, Clement, there's a man –'

'You've seen him, Mademoiselle?' said a man's voice. 'Where . . .?'

'Down there,' she said, and fuck me if she didn't sound scared. 'Oh be careful, Clement, he has a sword.'

'Trust me, Mademoiselle,' said the invisible Clement. More footsteps, then Anne was back at our doorway, beckoning us to follow.

The hall was empty, so I ripped back the bolts on the door, pulled it open, and there was the Right Bank road and beyond it the river.

I've nice manners, Abbé, I turned to thank my guardian angel, but she was already ducking under my arm with Jeanette in tow, and I realized they were coming with me.

It seemed a touch ungracious to shove her back in, but I wasn't sure I wanted a couple of women round my neck when what I needed most was speed. The road was empty, but I didn't see it staying that way long. The pursuit had rushed to the back entrances, they could be out of the Place and round the corner long before we reached the bridge.

But I told you, Abbé, Anne had a head on her. She simply led us across to the river steps and in seconds we were down out of sight of the road. I was a little concerned about the water at the bottom, but she only smiled and said 'Boats cross all the time, Stefan, someone will come when they see us waiting.'

I didn't think so somehow, but what I hadn't appreciated is the power of a dress, especially a grand one that suggests its wearer has money. Three boats headed for us at once, and we were in the first in less than a minute. I kept low in the bottom as we pulled out into the open, and ripped off my coat so as not to present a familiar brown patch to anyone on the road above. Yes, it was cold, but we didn't want a reception committee riding over the bridge to meet us when we landed.

They could have done it twice over at the speed we were going. The current was like pulling through glue, never mind the bloody traffic. There were three wood-laden barges manoeuvring in, a towering hay load wobbling precariously into dock, and Christ knows how many boatmen pausing mid-stream to lean on their poles for a chat with their neighbours. It took us the best part of half an hour to reach the Pont-au-Change.

I didn't think it mattered. No one on the Île had thought to look waterside, and by the time our pursuers had stopped scurrying up and down the houses we were long lost in the muddle of water traffic. I took one last look up at the receding Place Dauphine and saw only one figure there, a man on horseback reining to a stop outside the very house we'd just left. It was too far away to make out the detail, but the distant tan blob suggested a buff tunic like my own, while the gleam at his hip looked rather like a naked sword. I guessed him for an ex-soldier, someone exactly like myself.

He vanished from sight as we slid under the bridge, but my mind stayed right with him. Bouchard had been expecting someone like me and if I'd thought about it I ought to have guessed why. 'Don't dare tell me you've lost him,' he'd said. He didn't have to mean André, but I remembered the assorted street scum I'd seen admitted earlier and felt a jolt in my stomach that had nothing to do with the boat.

The clocks struck six before the boatman dropped us at the Pont Marie, by which time I was more than a little desperate. Oh, I'd only got suspicions and vague ones at that, but I still thought André ought to be warned. I didn't say a word to the women, just herded them fast to the Hôtel de Roland in the hope of getting transport.

I wasn't sure of the reception Anne would get, but the Comtesse had obviously already heard what had happened on the Place de Grève. She came to greet Anne herself, and when I told her I'd beaten the shit out of Bouchard her aristocratic eyes positively gleamed. She ordered a carriage for the ladies and would even have let me travel with them if I hadn't said humbly I'd rather have a horse. Oh, propriety my arse, but a carriage would take ten minutes to harness and God knows how slow it would be through the streets. I took the horse they gave me and was out of the gate in seconds.

Oh yes, yes, no doubt your superior wisdom has already spotted what I'd missed. But I'd other things on my mind, I'm afraid, I galloped like hell for the Faubourg Saint-Martin and never once looked back.

Jacques de Roland

We bought muskets and powder, pistols and shot, everything we'd need for a small war, then rode on for the Faubourg Saint-Martin.

Dusk was falling by the time we got to the Porchier farm. We followed the track through fields of leeks and beetroot and there was the farmhouse just as I'd remembered it, safe in its own little courtyard within grey stone walls. One of the strapping farm lads was hanging a lantern outside, and he smiled and said 'Welcome back, M'sieur,' in a soft Picardie voice that made me think of home.

We couldn't all stay in the house, of course, but they'd opened up the floor of the apple barn as a dormitory and extra stable, and it felt really warm and comfortable. Gaspard was actually dozing, while Crespin was making up beds from the straw we'd sent in the morning and glowing with an enthusiasm he hadn't shown since La Marfée. 'It's just like the Hermitage, isn't it, Jacquot?' he said, attacking a truss so exuberantly the straw flew everywhere. 'Just like the old Hermitage.'

I said 'Where's André?'

'In the house.' He straightened a moment, the straw in the air settling slowly on his head and shoulders like dust. 'He's awfully cold, Jacquot. He's had a hot bath, of course, but . . .' His voice tailed off uncertainly.

'I know,' I said, brushing straw off my cloak. 'I'll bring him out of it, you'll see.'

I took the sword off my baggage and strode back towards the house. Philibert padded warlike beside me, swishing his sword dangerously against the artichokes, and I knew he was as desperate as me for someone to hit.

I dumped him in the kitchen to help Mme Porchier prepare supper, and found Bernadette larding mutton. I thought she'd be angry now she knew I'd lied about the sentence, but she just clutched my coat and said 'The Chevalier, oh Jacques, what have they done?' I kissed her and said everything would be all right, but she said 'You do not understand, he is not André any more, I think they have killed him.' I said 'It would take more than that, my darling,' and hoped it was true.

I went on up to the parlour and found Charlot in the anteroom, pacing up and down like a sentry.

I said 'There's no need for that, he's here perfectly legally.'

Charlot bowed. 'As you say, Monsieur.'

He was really irritating that way, Charlot, he'd sort of agree with you in a way that made you know you were missing something. I said 'What?'

'We were followed, Monsieur, right to the farm.'

I'd seen them, the rabble wanting their entertainment. I patted his arm, said 'He's safe now, you'll see,' and went through into the parlour.

The fire was burning cheerfully, just as it was the day they separated us and everything went wrong. Grimauld sat at the table watching a huddled figure by the hearth it took me a second to recognize as André. He was dressed smartly in a black-and-gold doublet, his hair was neat and someone had shaved him, but André never sat hunched like that, never, he oughtn't to have been sitting at all, he ought to have been pacing up and down kicking things and saying 'Those bloody bastards' and stuff like that.

'Ah, now look here, laddie,' said Grimauld with that false heartiness people use when you're ill. 'Here's Monsieur come to see you.'

André looked round, but his eyes sort of blinked and slid away. Grimauld said 'I'll see about more wine,' and hobbled to the door using two sticks for support.

André watched him go. 'You see what I've done? The surgeon says one leg's so twisted he'll never walk properly again.'

'He'll be all right,' I said. 'We'll have special shoes made, there's stuff we can do.' I sat beside him on the floor, laying the bundled sword carefully by my side.

He lowered his head again. 'That'll make up for it, will it?'

'It'll help,' I said inadequately. I'd been planning a rousing speech on the way here, but it was hard even to talk to him. He was sitting with his arms tight round his knees and his head so low I could hardly see his face.

He made an odd flinching movement with his shoulders. 'Don't look at me, all right? Just – don't look at me.'

I stuck my arm round him. 'Don't you be ashamed. You've done nothing.' I heard my own voice and knew I sounded as hearty as Grimauld.

'It felt like something,' he said. 'It felt like letting a lot of people down.'

'You saved Bernadette.'

His shoulders shifted slightly. 'I put her in danger in the first place. Her and lots of others. I just want to stop people getting hurt.'

'You can't,' I said bluntly. 'You've got to let them choose for themselves. Grimauld did, didn't he?'

'Anne,' he said suddenly, and looked up. 'She's another. She loves me, I'm sure of it, and life's going to be intolerable for both of us because we can't be together.'

'You can,' I said, furtively starting to unwrap the sword. 'You'll be going back to Paris one day, you'll go back in triumph.'

He almost shuddered. 'I'm never going back there. Not unless they ask me. Not unless they bloody *beg*.'

'Then we'll make them. We'll clear your name, expose the lot of them, and they'll grovel for you to come back.'

He laughed, a horrid dry sound like a sob. 'How can you get justice when they own the bloody judges? Even Richelieu couldn't stop them. It's over, Jacques. Spain will come, the country will be run by bastards like Bouchard. You were right, it's time to get the hell out.'

'No. You said it yourself, it's time to fight.' I presented him with the sword.

He recognized it at once. I think I'd hoped he'd grasp it and leap to his feet, but after a moment he just reached out and tentatively stroked the guard. Outside I heard the distant sound of hooves.

He said 'It was a good sword, wasn't it? I did it proud once.'

'You will again,' I said, hauling him to his feet. 'Just let me get this on you . . .'

'No,' he said. 'I'd dishonour it now.'

I said 'Don't be so bloody silly,' and worked the scabbard into the frogs of his belt. 'You've got to wear a sword, you know that. But don't go breaking this one, you'd never forgive yourself.'

He watched me harness him in. 'I shouldn't have broken the other, it was yours.'

I tried to sound dismissive. 'That was just a dress sword.'

'So's this,' he said. 'You only want it on me so I'll look right.'

I said 'You'll use it one day. Walk with it a bit, try handling it –'

'No,' he said. 'Can't you understand? My father put this into my hand himself so I could fight and be a hero, not be a liar and a coward and shame our family in front of the whole of Paris. I shouldn't even be wearing it, it's wrong.'

He was trying to take it off, I had to grab his hands to stop him. 'You can wipe it out, you'll show them, we'll fight it together . . .'

'How?' he said, his voice rising. 'What is there to fight? Whispers?

People laughing? Those judges today, should I have drawn sword and gone after them? Tell me, Jacques, what is there I can fight?'

Stefan Ravel

There were ten of them. Ten to kill one man.

They caught up with me as I reached the Porte Saint-Martin, and I hadn't the slightest doubt who they were. Oh, you can pick up a couple in most cabarets these days, there are men who'll do it for twenty écus and a pint of wine.

This lot were in a hurry, probably afraid André would move on before they reached him. I could outride them a little while, but they were going to spot me belting just ahead of them and I didn't think that would be healthy. I was still puzzling what to do when they swept me through the gate with them and the nearest man nodded and gave a half-smile.

They didn't know each other. Why should they? Hired at different places, theirs wasn't the kind of profession in which you make friends. I grinned at the man, dropped back through the ranks to get further from the leader, then adjusted my pace to my neighbours' and rode right along with them. As we came out into the Faubourg Saint-Martin there wasn't one of them who noticed they'd suddenly become eleven.

We rode on into the open country. The men closed up tighter together, scared of the air and the land and a world outside their own sewers, and I took the chance to observe as many as I dared. It was mostly swords we'd be up against, cheap infantry jobs like my own, but one had a musket strapped by his saddle and the man in front had a pistol.

'All right, lads,' he said. 'Here it is, make it quiet now.'

We followed the track till it curved round between two high buildings, orangeries with slated roofs to keep out the chill. The leader turned his beast to face us, and began to load his pistol. I thought 'That's a good idea,' and promptly did the same. Unfortunately I spotted another man at it, which was one more than I'd thought. Three guns to beat.

'You know what he looks like,' said the leader. 'Black hair and clean shaven, though he'll probably be dressed a little different from this afternoon.'

My neighbour sniggered. I went on loading and mentally promised him my sword through his neck.

'Don't worry about the others,' said the leader. 'Go straight for de Roland, and don't forget he can use a blade.'

'Witnesses?' said a man near the front.

'Doesn't matter,' said the leader. 'He's had the *mort-civile,* he doesn't exist, we can do what we want. If someone's in your way then deal with it, but keep your mind on de Roland.'

He finished loading and looked up. I kept my head well down.

'Right. Leave the horses here, round the bend one at a time, find your cover, then wait for me. If the door's bolted I'll knock, be ready to rush whoever comes.'

There's not a lot of cover in vegetables, Abbé, a man my size can't hide behind a leek. The obvious places were already taken when I got round the bend, shapes lurking behind a loaded wagon, one behind a water butt, and one enterprisingly crouched behind the wall of the farmyard itself. In the end I just pressed myself against the manure-warmed orangery and let the slope of the roof cover me in shadow. The house looked quiet and peaceful, there wasn't a hint of anyone on watch.

Oh, I knew what I'd got to do, the trick was going to be surviving it afterwards. I watched the last men hunker down among the leeks, then here came our noble leader striding confidently up to the farm-yard, opening the gate and heading for the door. I'd intended to fire into the air, but fuck it, why waste a good ball? I lowered my pistol and shot him in the back.

Jacques de Roland

Charlot yelled 'Stay where you are, Chevalier!' and his footsteps thundered down the stairs.

André leapt for the door, but I thrust myself in front of him. 'No, stay out of sight!'

Someone shouted outside, Stefan yelling 'Ambush!' André pulled open the door so fiercely it bashed me in the back, and was through into the anteroom before I could stop him.

I skidded out after him, trying to untangle my sword from my cloak, but he just stuck his hand on the rail and vaulted over, down the stairs and out of reach. I heard him yell at someone 'Go back, all of you, get back, I'm going out!'

I went thudding down the wooden stairs, my body jolting at every step, but he was already at the door and opening it. I screamed 'They'll kill you!'

He turned in the doorway, and I'll never, ever forget the look on his face. Then he swung back round and was gone.

Stefan Ravel

I drew my sword and belted for the house. Figures were rising confusedly from the field, but no one went for me, they probably thought I was going in heroic support of our leader. The man hiding by the wall actually held the gate open, poor sod, I felt almost bad about sticking him in the guts.

That rather gave me away, I'm afraid. Men dashed from cover, and I'd nothing at my back but a silent house with a closed door. I yelled 'Ambush!' and turned to slam the gate behind me, but one was already through, sword slicing down, open mouth and a yell like a fucking Saracen. I felt the shock of steel scything down my left arm, and whirled my own sword to drive him back, but he dodged and came back, the others behind him already at the wall. At least the door was opening, I saw the shadow crossing the lantern light and shouted 'Give us a hand for fuck's sake!'

It was Charlot, and for the first time ever I was pleased to see him. He charged out like a bull, sword in one hand, dagger in the other, and stuck my man neck and thigh. I forced myself back to the wall, slashing out at the shapes behind it, but a crocked left arm does nothing for your balance, Abbé, I was hitting nothing but darkness and buying us nothing but seconds. Charlot stood to the gate, and just the sight of him made them back off, but there was movement by the wagon, I remembered we'd still two guns against us and swore aloud.

Then shouting behind, someone coming through the door, I looked and it was André, bloody André, not even a sword in his hand, standing in the light like a target at a fair.

I yelled 'Get down!'

Jacques de Roland

I hurled myself out after him, but heard a yell of 'De Roland!' and knew I was too late. Stefan tried to grab him, but there was something wrong with his arm, André brushed him off like straw and got his hand on the gate.

Yellow light cracked in the darkness, but a huge mass blotted it out as Charlot sprang forward, knocking André down on the stones. I saw the gun now, a long-barrelled pistol glinting briefly in the lantern light as the man ducked below the wall to reload. I bloody charged him, I leapt and got my knee on the wall, slashing down at the crouching shape beneath, I remember swiping once, then back, and the crunch of bone at the end of the slash. Another blade whipped in from somewhere, I didn't know where, it was just blades and bullets in the dark and the boy behind me probably dead, I swung my sword two-handed to smash it back.

More shadows loomed at me, but I was off balance from the swing, my knee sliding off the wall and my elbow crunching sickeningly on the parapet as I went down. I was dizzy and useless and another sword striking at me from above, but someone else drove it back, and there was Philibert dancing beside me, jabbing at the dark shapes and saying 'Don't you try it, Messieurs, don't you even try it.'

I don't think they'd expected so many of us. They moved back uneasily, I had a moment to turn, and there was André kneeling up like a miracle, but Charlot was huddled in an untidy heap beside him, a gleaming wetness spreading down his side. I heard him whisper 'Please, Chevalier,' and saw him reach for the boy's hand. André said 'Yes, all right, yes,' and his face was desolate.

But he was staying down, and the enemy backing off, I thought we'd got a chance. Stefan glanced at André, said 'They've still got a musket, stay where you are,' then strode to the gate and shouted into the darkness. 'Give it up, why don't you? We're armed and ready, de Roland's not coming out, you'll never get your money so why fucking die for it?'

I heard murmuring and shuffling all round. At least they didn't shoot him, but then I suppose there was no price tag on Stefan.

'Go home,' said Stefan. His hand was clasped tight round his wounded arm, but he still managed to sound matey and reasonable. 'There's easier ways to make a living. Go home.'

More movement and muttering, then someone made a hushing noise and I heard something else. Horses. Horses and wheels. A carriage was coming up the track.

Stefan Ravel

Yes, yes, all right, *mea culpa*, I should have told the women. What you might remember is that I hadn't expected an army of the bastards, I'd hoped to get here before them, and I certainly couldn't have foreseen Anne clip-clopping herself into the middle of a fucking battle.

I yelled 'See, there's more of us, now give it up and go!' but I'm not sure that helped. The carriage rattled briskly past the orangeries, then the assassins just leapt at it, two grabbing the horses, one springing up by the driver, another wrenching open the door.

A woman screamed. André's head came up like a dog at a hunt, but the yard was our fort, if we left it we were mincemeat. I dived back for the door and groped over the dead leader for his pistol, but the lackeys were dragging out a girl in a grey cloak, and André had already seen her.

'Anne,' he said, coming up off his knees like a man in a trance. Charlot gripped his breeches, Jacques jumped back from the wall to block him, but André just straightened and yelled 'Anne!'

Mistake. They didn't want the women, they'd have simply let them run, but André's yell told them the value of what they'd got.

'Come out, Chevalier!' called a taunting voice, and another of the bastards picked it up. 'Come on, Chevalier, come out and get her!'

André drew his sword.

Jacques de Roland

He didn't even look, his hand just went there like it always had and came out smooth with the sword, the blade flashing white in the glow of the lantern. Then he was moving, no scrabbling on the wall like I'd done, he simply leapt on the body of the dead man, jumped to get one foot on to the parapet, then sprang over into the darkness.

I hurtled after him, the shock jolting bang up my knees as my feet slammed to the ground. I jerked up my head to see them waiting for us, one on the carriage box to stop the driver jumping down, one holding Anne, but three with swords out and levelled, a wall of spikes André was charging straight into. They weren't moving, there wasn't an opening, he'd have to drop his guard to strike.

He didn't. He veered at the last second, reached up to the man on the box, grabbed his belt and hurled him down into the others, knocking one sprawling on his back. The other two dodged and darted forward, but André was balanced and ready, he smashed the first blade aside, twisted for the back-handed parry against the second, then struck up at the first's chest, a straight thrust in *tierce*, the point shooting out the other side. The other was recovering and at him again, but André sidestepped without stopping, and charged the one at the back who was holding Anne. The whole thing took about five seconds.

But the two on the ground were scrambling up already and the one he'd dodged was coming straight after him. He was the closest and most dangerous, I threw myself at him, sliding my blade under his own to drag him round to face me. He was stronger than he looked, wrenching his sword free and walloping mine so savagely I nearly dropped it, but I adjusted my grip and bashed back, I'd got to buy André the time to get Anne.

He couldn't reach her. The man was holding her in front of him, jabbing out with his blade to keep the boy away, shifting to get the carriage at his back. Jeanette tried to climb out to help, but he slashed round at her, driving her back inside, then planted his back against the door. Anne was twisting and struggling, André was frantic but couldn't get his sword in, and even as he hesitated the other two were coming from behind.

I yelled the warning but couldn't get to him, my man was blocking everywhere I lunged. Philibert was panting up to us, the unarmed coachman was leaping down off the box, but we were all too late and by the time André turned both men were lunging at once.

All they got was air. André twisted into a crouch, whirled back on himself to skewer the man holding Anne through the foot, then spun round to lunge smack in the groin of the man who'd been on the box. The other backed off and Philibert caught up with him screaming with Gascon fury, but the one with the stabbed foot bellowed in rage and threw Anne slam into the side of the carriage so he could go after André himself.

Anne gasped with pain, and that was it, André stopped even being human. He leapt screaming at the man who'd hurt her, sword flashing high in the air then smashing down on the joint of neck and shoulder, ripping through bone and muscle halfway to the navel. I'd never seen a slash like that, never, I think there was a second we all stopped and stared while the man spouted blood like a fountain then toppled heavily to the ground. In the silence I saw the coachman shove Anne back into the carriage and pick up a fallen sword to guard the door.

A clash of blades behind me, then Philibert gave a cry and dropped on one knee. André spun round to take on his opponent and I threw myself back at my own. He was still good, still blocking me, but I didn't give a stuff. His eyes were dead, he was looking at me as just one more to kill, but something inside me was singing like the swords because I knew he was wrong. That hard, grizzled face was probably the last thing dozens of innocent people had seen before they died, but it was ending here tonight, they were every one of them going to be avenged, because André was back and nothing in the world could beat us now.

Oh, fuck all that, Abbé, I was looking for the musket. I'd been count-ing, I knew we'd a man unaccounted for somewhere. He wasn't behind the water butt, the barrel would have stuck out. I kept the pistol steady and let my eyes flick between the only two possible places, field, wagon, field, wagon. Not a thing.

He was there all right, he simply hadn't had a chance at his shot while his target was surrounded by his own people. But there were fewer of them now. The ground round the carriage was piling up with bodies, and there was nothing to see but André and Jacques working themselves back to back as they fought the last two men up. Then it was only one, as André's man went down. He still hadn't had enough, he was swivelling as soon as his blade was out and I knew he wanted Jacques' too – and Jacques, like a gentlemanly fool, stepped aside. André's back was exposed, the gold on that bloody doublet gleaming in the dark.

Something moved. A glow from the lantern was shining through the wagon on to the orangery wall, and in it was a hunched black shape and a barrel already levelling. I fired.

And missed. The barrel wobbled, but the movement drew my eye back to the wagon, and there he was, kneeling and ready, I'd shot at his fucking shadow. I yelled to distract him and grabbed for the gate, but the shot cracked out before I could take another step.

A thump and clatter by the wagon, and there was the musketeer sprawled on his belly, the gun lying harmlessly beside him. I looked round in confusion, and saw two figures on the track to the barns I'm sure hadn't been there before. One was de Chouy with a sword in his hand, but the other was his Spanish-looking friend Lelièvre, standing elegantly still, the pistol levelled perfectly across his arm.

I'm not sure André even noticed. He was dancing about to lure his man into engaging properly, but this was a dour bugger, he was just blocking, blocking, never leaving an opening in his guard. Then I walked through the gate, André turned his head to the movement, and the man was in like a snake.

But André'd expected it, I'd guess he even planned it, he was already twisting aside, sword thrusting straight through the broken guard into the heart. He pulled out and skipped back, bloodied blade swinging as he looked for the next opponent, but there was nothing but us and a silence in which I could hear him breathe.

Anne du Pré

I watched the realization slowly illuminate his face. He gazed wonderingly at his sword as if he had almost forgotten he was holding it, then looked up again at Jacques, and I saw them exchange a smile. Then he looked at me.

I felt quite shy suddenly, but our driver was offering me his arm and I had no choice but to climb down. I could move no further and stood like a fool while André approached me over the grass.

'Anne,' he said. His hand crept out to rest on my sleeve, the first time he had touched me since the night of the maze. 'Anne, what on earth are you . . .?'

I looked up, and it was just André, looking at me almost humbly and with not a trace of blame. I said 'I know I'm late, but if you still want me to come with you . . .'

His fingers tightened with the intake of his breath. 'If I . . .'

I gave a tiny nod, I could not speak again.

I heard a faint thump as his sword fell to the grass. Then his hands slid to my shoulders, he gathered me up against him, then he was kissing me so hard my breath was lost. His hands were bloody, he was sweaty and trembling, everyone was looking, but I kissed him back as if I could never let him go.

Twenty-Two

Stefan Ravel

Oh, Christ knows, Abbé. Jacques said it was the sword, I thought it was the woman, but something had certainly lit a fire in André. When he came out of that farmhouse I'd seen a dead man looking for a bullet, but we'd got something like the old André now.

But perhaps a rather harder and darker version. We'd got ten dead Frenchmen at our feet, but there was none of the sentimental moping I expected, he just ordered us to pile them in the Vallon carriage and dump them in the nearest woods. He sent a bunch of farmhands to abandon the assassins' horses in a distant churchyard, set another as sentry in case Bouchard sent anyone else, packed de Chouy off to the Faubourg to get a surgeon for me and Charlot, then calmly began to rake up the trampled and bloody leeks to get rid of the evidence. We ate them for supper, and very good they were too.

The Porchiers certainly weren't bothered. Loyal retainers, Abbé, they cleared beds and prepared food like a besieged town looking after its defending heroes. Our own women helped. Bernadette nursed Charlot, while I had my own plebeian arm dressed by Mlle Anne du Pré. I'm still glad she wasn't doing the stitching. She had the besotted look of a girl about to stop being one, and her first attempt at a sling brought my arm right up to my ear.

But no, there wasn't anything wrong in it, Abbé, I'd say there was a lot right. The Porchiers brought us barrels and boards to make tables in the barn, and it was almost like a meeting of the old Occupied Army. Charlot was still resting but the rest of us were there, all ten together for the first time. We had servants next to ladies and none of it mattered a fuck. We'd got a purpose. There was no more talk of taking André to England, we were going to stay in France and fight, and all we had to do was work out how.

Oh yes, I know it was ridiculous, I saw it myself just looking round those boards. Lelièvre was worth having, the man had a level head and steady trigger finger and I'll tolerate even an aristocrat who's got those, but de Chouy was bouncing on his stool like a child playing horses, and the rest of us . . . well. André was a disgraced nobleman, Jacques a jumped-up stable boy, Anne the daughter of a corrupt baron, I was a soldier with a wounded arm, and all we had to support us were a lackey, a ladies' maid, a serving girl, a valet with a wounded shoulder and a thief with a crippled foot. But you know what, Abbe? That night I thought maybe, just maybe, we could change the world.

Jacques de Roland

Anne changed everything. I'd been dashing round fighting and never achieving anything, but Anne had stuck it out where she was and found out everything we needed to know.

Bernadette was doubtful at first. She whispered 'Why do we make this fuss about a lady who has been warm and safe while the Chevalier has been chased for his life?' But as Anne went on talking she ate slower and slower and finally put her knife down altogether. Others were doing the same, till even Grimauld stopped slobbering and the clatter of plates faded to silence as we all went still.

She told us all of it, and I remember an odd kind of stirring in my stomach as I understood what we were really up against. They were all in it together, maybe even the Queen, they wanted rid of Richelieu and didn't care if they had to bring the Spaniards in to do it. But I knew what that really meant, so did Stefan, so did André and Anne, we'd seen it first-hand and never wanted to see it again. We had to beat these people anyway if we wanted to save André, but there was a bit of me started to wake up while Anne was talking, a bit that wanted to save France as well.

'And we will,' said André. 'We only need the evidence so His Eminence can act.'

'Only?' said Gaspard. 'It will need to be quite some evidence to convince His Majesty. I do not think these *canaille* are likely to commit anything to paper.'

Anne said 'But they have, Monsieur, Fontrailles has already set out with a treaty. They are making an addition to be witnessed by Don Miguel d'Estrada himself.'

I was lucky I was still on the soup, I heard horrid whooping noises as Crespin choked on the mutton. André looked like he'd been hit by a hammer.

'They're signing it?' said Stefan. 'When? Where?'

Anne looked contrite. 'I'm sorry, they didn't say.'

He leaned forward over the board. 'Could you find out?'

She hesitated. 'I don't know, I . . .'

André woke up and glared at Stefan. 'Do you want her to go back and ask them?'

Stefan shrugged. 'That's the evidence you need, isn't it?'

There was a little silence.

'No,' said André, laying his hand firmly on Anne's. 'There'll be another way.'

'Like what?' said Stefan.

'We can watch them, can't we?' said André. 'We could get some-one in as a servant, perhaps listen at a door . . .'

'I do not know His Eminence the Cardinal Richelieu,' said Gasp-ard, pouring more wine. 'But I would rather think he has these options covered already.'

André swung round on him. 'We know things he doesn't, we've got –'

'A woman right in the house,' said Stefan. 'She'll know when and where, she –'

'I said *no!*' said André, leaping to his feet. 'She's just escaped. She can't go back now.'

There was a rustling of straw as Anne got to her feet beside him. 'Yes, I can,' she said. 'And I will.'

Stefan Ravel

I'd always said that girl had guts.

Oh come on, Abbé, she was our only hope, and even André saw it in the end. Her charming relatives were hoping to attend the signing themselves, so obviously she was going to hear about it. All right, she'd escaped, but they'd trust her more than ever if she'd had a chance of freedom and deliberately chose to go back. It was perfectly safe, perfectly reasonable, and the only fucking way.

André still insisted that she'd got to be able to communicate with us at all times. Philibert would establish himself as a follower of Jeanette's so he could call every morning, but we'd also have a system of signals at Anne's window which de Chouy was to check three times a day and Lelièvre twice at night. I said 'Are you sure you wouldn't like us all to sleep on the Place Dauphine?' but he just said 'If we have to, yes.' Love, Abbé, there's nothing like it for rotting the sense of humour. He and Anne were hard put to keep their eyes off each other and their minds on the plan, and I'd a suspicion they wouldn't last the night.

So I was rather surprised when I finally went to my truckle bed in the room set aside for wounded heroes and found André there ahead of me, kneeling on the floor by Charlot's side. I watched until the sentimentality got too much for me, then shut the door with my boot.

'Hullo, Stefan,' he said, without turning round. 'How's your arm?'

'Sore,' I said, and laid my lamp on the chest. 'But I'll live, and so will Charlot.'

He'd been lucky, the old man. He'd been sprawling forward when the ball hit so it only scorched its way up his back and out his shoulder, but if he'd been standing it would have been straight in the heart. If he hadn't been there at all, it would have been André's face.

'He took the ball for me,' said André. 'He did it on purpose.'

'Very stupid,' I agreed. 'You want to have a word with him about that when he's better.'

He sat back on his heels, bringing his head into the pool of lamplight. 'Why did they come anyway? What was the point?'

I shoved the lamp along and sat on the chest. 'Put yourself in Bouchard's place. Does he really think you'll take today lying down? I'd bet good money he checked behind his curtains before he went to bed tonight.'

Lamplight's a funny thing when it's above a man, Abbé. It made black shadows of his eyes. He said 'It's not going to save him.'

'That's the spirit,' I said cheerfully. 'Maybe you can have a little duel at the signing.'

He didn't move. 'You think it's funny, don't you? Gentlemen and their pride.'

'Oh, yes,' I said. 'I'm laughing myself sick. I doubt he is, though, unless he's got a bloody good surgeon.'

He turned to look at me. 'I don't . . .'

'Look,' I said, and thrust my grazed hand in front of him. 'Bouchard's teeth, probably. Maybe the gravel when I rubbed his face in it.'

He reached out and touched the scratched knuckles. 'Tell me.'

I made a pretty good tale of it, if I say so myself, and didn't hear so much as a breath out of him while I talked. When I'd finished he sat back and said 'I wish I'd seen it.'

'You will,' I said. 'You'll have him on his knees where he belongs.'

'Oh yes,' he said, with a casual conviction that wouldn't have done much for Bouchard's sleep if he'd heard it. 'Yes, I'll certainly do that.'

We sat in companionable silence a while. Charlot was sleeping peacefully, his face as smooth as a baby's, his breathing soft and steady.

I said 'Go to bed, André. We're all right here.'

Anne du Pré

Extract from her diary, dated 12 February 1642

I cannot sleep. I am sat by the window with a book propped open to mask the candle, and there in the bed is André.

He looks so young in his sleep, his cheek flushed, and his hair sprawled over the pillow. One hand lies on top of the blanket, and my skin tingles with memory where it has touched. My legs are trembly, my face prickly from being rubbed so close against his cheek, and there is a little hollow ache inside me, as if it will always now feel empty when he is not there.

It did hurt, I have to write that, but at last even the pain became only a soft ache with ripples of something so glorious that I pushed and strained for it even as he did, as if the pleasure were not something we chased but something we made together. It was almost frightening to lose myself so utterly I had to cry out with the release, but André was lost with me, so that a moment later I was full and warm and wet, and *that* was so beautiful a feeling it made the ripples come again, only now they were great waves that pounded until there was nothing but my own heart hammering in my aching throat and the tears on my face that were his as well as mine, because we both of us died together.

Yet when at last we faced each other with our breathing calm I felt a sudden foolish embarrassment as if he might respect me less for such a display. I said 'Whatever will Jeanette think of me when I tell her?' but he laughed with such pleasure and rubbed his nose against mine and said 'Sweetheart, I think she already knows.'

Stefan Ravel

Oh, please. The whole of Saint-Martin must have known, it's a wonder any of us slept at all. Even Charlot woke and muttered in panic for his Chevalier until I said 'Relax, granddad, he doesn't need any help with this one.' Another shriek of girlish enthusiasm came bursting through the wall, and Charlot subsided on his pillow with the merest hint of a smile. André was clearly making up for lost time.

Well, I hope he enjoyed it. We were up early in the grey morning getting Charlot in the carriage, all of us a little worse for wear after last night's wine, and there was bloody André strolling round singing. I told him sourly to shut his gob, but he only tipped my hat over my eyes, said 'What's the matter, Stefan? Bad night?' and sauntered off with a swing in his hip like the last cock in the barnyard.

He sobered up fast when Philibert brought out the women and it was time to say goodbye. Anne looked very small swathed in a grey travelling cloak, and I'll admit it, Abbé, I felt a moment's qualm about what we were asking her to do. I heard André murmur 'You don't have to, we can go away and be together, none of it matters,' but she said 'It does to me', and kissed him as chastely as if we didn't every one of us know how she'd spent the night. I handed her into the carriage myself, but she wouldn't let me just shut the door on her, she reached up to my bristly face as she'd done all those years ago and whispered 'You will look after him, won't you, Stefan?' Her fingers were cold.

The carriage wobbled on the rutted track as it swerved away between the orangeries and vanished into the mist. I remember the silence as the rattle of the wheels died away into nothing but the cries of rooks harsh in the morning air.

Anne du Pré

We drove straight to the Hôtel de Roland to deliver Charlot to the Comtesse's care, then continued on foot to the convent on the Rue Saint-Antoine. I spent an hour with my friends among the sisters and learned that Father had already enquired after me, but André and I had given this much thought and I had my story ready.

The walk home was chilly, but Philibert's enjoyment coloured the journey for us all. For him it was an adventure, escorting two fine ladies through the streets, and he insisted on paying for hot sweet chestnuts from a vendor with a brazier outside the Galeries. We ate them in our fingers like ordinary people, we cooled our burnt throats at the Samaritaine like anyone else, we chatted and laughed at Philibert's stories, then we entered the Place Dauphine and fell silent.

Clement himself opened to us, and his relief at seeing me was so overwhelming I felt ashamed to have worried him. It was hateful to have to lie to him again, but Jeanette was so wonderfully vociferous I had hardly to say a word. She gave a most spirited account of Philibert's gallantry in saving us from a cutpurse on our way home from the convent, and Clement clearly never doubted her. He led them away to take wine in the warmth of the kitchens, but I had now my family to face, and turned with dread for the salon.

But the knowledge that I am no longer alone made an extraordinary difference. Father and Florian confronted me with shocked disapproval, but I seemed to see for the first time how small a man my father is, how ridiculous Florian's pretence of dignity, and how foolish I have been ever to fear them. The father I respected does not exist, the brother I loved is lost for ever, and my only loyalty is to the man who before God has become my husband.

The thought of André dispelled any lingering guilt, and I told them where I had been with as much hauteur as the Princesse de Condé herself. I said truthfully 'The sisters do not disapprove of my actions yesterday, they quite understood I was repaying a childhood obligation to André and say all Paris respects us for it.'

Father's face brightened at the word 'respect' then clouded again into confusion. 'But I sent to the Couvent, Mademoiselle, they said they hadn't seen you.'

I didn't flinch. 'Naturally they did, since you refused me permission to seek spiritual guidance within their walls. I had to persuade them not to complain of you to the King.'

Father's fingers crept up to his beard, and for a moment he looked just like Florian. 'But you didn't wait to ask me, you simply ran away.'

I said 'Can you wonder at it? When the courtyard was full of armed ruffians, and our home invaded by a bandit with drawn sword? Ours is hardly a respectable household at present, and you should be glad I did not tell the sisters so.'

His little eyes blinked twice in consternation. 'Yes. Yes, you are right. We must speak to Monseigneur. He must be made more cognizant of our position.'

'I'm very aware of your position,' said a cold voice from the doorway, and there was Bouchard himself, waving away a cringing Denis behind him. 'Have you perhaps forgotten mine?'

He made a ludicrous figure, for there was a dressing over his nose and abrasions about his mouth while his body was clearly bulked by bandaging under his doublet, yet his eyes seemed shallow and hard, and when their crooked gaze slid on to me I wanted to shiver at their expression.

'Back already, Mademoiselle?' he said. 'Didn't he want you after all?'

Father exclaimed 'Monseigneur!' and Florian made a high-pitched noise like a bleat, but Bouchard only smiled with such insolence I felt my cheeks sting red. 'Let her answer, du Pré. I should like to hear.'

He could not know. He could not *possibly* know, for the men who followed André are all dead. I said 'You are mistaken,' and felt warmed inside to know it was true.

Father explained nervously where I had been and why I had fled, but Bouchard regarded me with such detachment I felt a spider walked over my skin. At length he said 'No more guts than that, Mademoiselle?' and turned dismissively away.

Even Florian flushed. 'Monseigneur, I beg you not to insult my sister.'

Bouchard swung back round. 'After her behaviour at the *amende honorable?*'

Florian's face was all eyes. 'It has done us no harm, Monseigneur.'

'Harm!' said Bouchard. 'You let this woman back into your house and your friendship, then that's your choice. But you can forget your titles, both of you, because from now on I go my own way.'

He turned for the door, he was going out of our lives as I had always prayed he would, but not now when we need his information to save André. I stepped in front of him and said 'Please, Monseigneur, don't abandon my family. If I've offended you that's my own fault, but don't punish my father and brother.'

His detachment seemed to quiver and break up as he looked at me. 'Offended?' he said. 'Do you have the smallest idea what you've done?'

I think I did then. All this time I have seen his malice and even his sickness, but today I saw also his pain and it struck me like a fist. I was in my own home, my feet on solid floor, yet felt I spoke directly with a man in hell.

'This is what you did,' he said, and his tone was almost conversational. 'That man, de Roland, he with his inferior birth that is recognized only because his mother had the sense to marry his father. He made me look *a fool*. I dealt with it, I had him brought to his knees in public and made to admit I was the better man. It was my moment.'

He nodded at me, easy, polite, but I heard the air whistle as he drew in breath to continue. 'And you destroyed it. You gave him face to get through it and played to that crowd like a whore in a play. You know what they're saying in the streets today? "That poor Mlle Celeste. That evil man for doing this thing." Me, Mademoiselle. They mean *me*.'

He turned away abruptly and began to examine the ornaments on the escritoire. 'It was my moment,' he said again. 'And you took it away.'

The salon clock ticked. Florian's face, white as porcelain. Father's, red and confused. The bell on the table, I had only to ring for Clement and Bouchard would go away for ever. A terrible pity was growing in me, and I tried to quell it with thought of another man I know, one also born a bastard but who is as honourable and true as any man in the world. Yet even Jacques had an André to care for him, and Bouchard has had no one at all.

The clock ticked. It is so pretty, the sun in gold and the moon in silver, the whole world in a single dial. The scales at the top, heaven and hell in an easy little painting. Bouchard, Jacques and André, André who cared nothing for reputation if he could only save his friends.

I said 'Tell me what you wish, and I will do it.'

He took the little statue of Niobe and weighed it in his hands. 'You rely a lot on words, don't you?'

I said 'I will give them actions. I know this alliance is important for my family.'

He turned. 'Then cement it. Prove your commitment and become my wife.'

His face blurred in front of me, I saw only the whiteness of his dressing and the thickness of his swollen lips. My father was speaking, I heard him exclaim on the magnanimity of Monseigneur, but his voice seemed to come to me from a great distance.

Bouchard didn't even look at him. 'Well, Mademoiselle? Let's see the worth of those words. Do you accept?'

I had an alternative. I could leave the house that moment, go back to André, travel to England, and marry him there. Yet he would always be disgraced, always an exile, and to save him I had only to tell one more little lie.

I said 'Yes, Monseigneur. I accept.'

Philibert reported that she was home safe, but he also brought a note. André shot off with it at once, of course, but Philibert told us what was in it, he'd got the whole story from Jeanette.

We all knew it was good news. Crespin thought it was a wonderful coup, Stefan was laughing in admiration, even Bernadette nodded approvingly and said Anne was a clever lady. Then we looked back at the house where André had gone and went quiet.

I went in after him. He wasn't banging up and down or anything, just sitting on the edge of the bed with the letter in his hands like he was still reading it. I watched him for a minute, then said 'André?'

He looked up. 'You've heard then?'

'It's brilliant, isn't it?' I said quickly. 'They'll really trust her now.'

'That's right,' he said, and looked at the letter again. 'And she's not really going to marry him, it's only pretend. We'll have her out long before it comes to that.'

'Of course.'

He nodded. 'It won't matter, them being betrothed. They won't be alone together, he won't get a chance to . . . do anything. He won't touch her.'

'No,' I said. 'That's not what he's after anyway, he's only doing this to –'

'I know why he's doing it,' he said. 'I know why he's bloody doing it.'

I couldn't think of a word to say.

He didn't seem to expect it. He stood up, stowed the letter carefully in his coat, and said 'Promise me one thing, won't you? When it comes to it, nobody kills him but me.'

Twenty-Three

Jacques de Roland

We stayed at the Porchiers' to wait it out. We kept a guard on the track in case anyone came looking, but no one ever did. Bouchard probably thought the lackeys had just run off with his money, and I suppose the authorities assumed André was out of the country and gone.

We lived together in the barn, and that was good actually, it was like being back at the Hermitage. Stefan took turns on guard, Charlot came to help when his shoulder was better, and best of all I'd got Bernadette by my side. Grimauld couldn't do much, one of his legs had healed wonky so he couldn't stand long, but he made André laugh and helped him through the waiting, and that was worth a lot.

He was really chafing, the boy, he got worse all through spring. Anne's letters said the betrothal didn't make any difference and she hardly saw Bouchard at all, but he hated even the thought of it. If it had been anything else he'd have just stormed back into Paris and grabbed her, but the treaty was his only hope of justice and he'd simply got to get it.

Everything was concentrated on the signing of that treaty. We knew d'Estrada would be there, so André had us working on our fence for hours every day, always with two swords or a *main-gauche* to teach ourselves how to face a left-handed attack. We knew it might be in enemy territory, so André got Gaspard to give us half a dozen volunteers from his family's estate and asked Stefan to train them to the musket. I watched him in the woods one day drilling a nervous bunch of gardeners, and it felt like 1636 all over again.

The Comte paid for it all. I'm not sure how much he believed in what we were doing, he might have just been trying to make up for the *amende honorable*, but he gave the Comtesse cash every week and I used to sneak in to visit her hidden in the Porchiers' vegetable cart. She always knew what was for supper from the way I smelt when I walked in, but she didn't care as long as I brought her news. I kept saying 'Maybe we'll hear tomorrow.'

Those bloody tomorrows, I smelt each of them in turn in that vegetable cart. The sprouts and beetroot went first, then the radishes and salad leaves, then May brought the peas and beans. The situation in Flanders was hotting up, but the King was ignoring it to throw everything at Roussillon and everyone wondered why. Richelieu might have pressed him, but he was lying ill at Narbonne and out of things entirely. All we'd got were Gramont and Harcourt wandering round Champagne doing nothing while Spain was mopping up Lens then going on to lay siege to La Bassée. We kept saying 'Why aren't we stopping them, why aren't we bringing them to battle?' and then of course we finally did.

The news hit Paris on the 28th of May and everything went silent with shock. Honnecourt was a massacre. We'd got a victorious Spanish army less than five miles from Le Câtelet and we heard people muttering about the year of Corbie everywhere we went. Even the Porchiers were asking if the Spaniards were coming, and all André could say was 'They won't till they're invited.' He didn't point out that they were obviously expecting it any day.

We all felt completely hopeless. Charlot even wondered if the treaty had already been signed and we'd missed it. André didn't say anything, but I don't think he slept much that night. When I crept out for my turn on duty he was still sitting with his arms hugged round his knees and staring blindly into the dark.

It was a cold dawn. I was smacking my arms against myself to warm up when I heard fast hooves turning down the track and there was Gaspard riding right up to my lookout tree. I slithered down in panic because I knew what that meant. Anne had put the signal out, she'd dropped a message, she was in danger, we'd got to get her out right now.

But Gaspard was smiling. He looked kindly down at me grovelling at his horse's feet and said 'My friend, we have a letter.'

Anne du Pré

Extract from a letter to André de Roland, dated 29 May 1642

My very dearest,

We have it at last. This latest victory is all the Spaniards have been waiting for, and we are to join Don Miguel at his lodging near Honnecourt from the 7th of June. I do not know where exactly, we are to be given directions at the village of Éspehy, but I can pass them to you then, my darling, because <u>I go with them</u>. Don Miguel has asked for me himself and my detestable fiancé is delighted. He thinks to show me off to his friends, and little suspects it will be the last time I ever have to endure his company.

Now it is so nearly over I can admit how wearisome I have found it. I have always told him our marriage cannot be thought of until he has what he calls his proper title, but he is becoming increasingly less tolerant of this answer. But now it does not matter, I can even agree to a date if he wishes, for I will not be here to honour it. Instead I shall be with you . . .

Jacques de Roland

André went thrashing up and down the barn smacking his sword against his leg and saying 'This is it, Jacques, this is bloody it.' I agreed. The treaty was going to be signed, we'd soon know where, all we'd got to do was break in and get it out.

But Anne was a worry. We needed her to lead us right to the house, but no one liked the idea of her being alone with the enemy and maybe getting stranded if it came to a battle. Philibert couldn't help, they'd never let Jeanette bring a follower on something this private, we'd got to find someone else.

'It needs to be a woman,' said Bernadette. She was sat cross-legged in the straw sewing up a rip in my shirt with hundreds of neat little stitches. 'Someone who can be in her very bedchamber.'

She sucked at a bead of blood on her finger and considered. 'I think it had better be me.'

André stared at the top of her head. 'Bouchard might recognize you. Florian himself . . .'

She tied the thread in a knot and bit off the end with her teeth. 'Not if I were her personal maid and stayed in her room. If I were there she would have a companion who can climb out of a window or shoot a musket at need. If I were there she would be quite safe.'

'But you wouldn't,' I said. 'I'm not having it.'

She gave me that complicated woman's smile that means you can't trust a word they're saying. 'Naturally you are not, since it is the one way to guarantee Mademoiselle's safety and the treaty for the Chevalier. Naturally you will put your love for me first.'

If there was a right answer to that I couldn't see it, but André just laughed. 'Oh sweetheart, of course we want Anne safe, but you must know we won't put you in danger.'

'Perhaps I do,' she said. 'Perhaps I know what you have done to avoid that already. Do you think it is only men who honour their obligations?'

We said 'No' very quickly.

'Good,' she said. 'Then it is agreed I will go.'

I've never known how to argue with women. But she was right this time, so we sent her off with Philibert and by evening she was Anne's new *femme de chambre*, hired to accompany her on the journey.

It did seem safe. We'd be just outside the whole time, no Spaniards were going to go pouncing on them with us around. We didn't worry about them inside either, not considering who their host was going to be. We knew the women were safe with d'Estrada.

Carlos Corvacho

My Capitán would never countenance disrespect to a lady, Señor, least of all this one. He'd always had what I'd call a soft spot for your Mlle Anne, right back to the days at the château when she was sat mousy-quiet with her embroidery and never missing the littlest thing.

But in a manner of speaking that's what put us on to her, my gentleman thinking highly of her as he did. He sends her an invitation to join her father and brother at the house party, but bless me, what comes back but a letter from Bouchard saying he'll bring her himself as she's now his betrothed wife. My gentleman quite forgets himself and lets out a little oath, which was most unlike him, most.

'What the devil?' he says to me. 'A girl like that consenting to marry this Bouchard?'

I brought him his coffee. We'd an Arab servant used to make it for us, Señor, it was my Capitán's latest fancy. I said 'It'll be his rank, Señor, he's a better match than she'd anywise hope to aim for.'

'Rank!' says my Capitán. 'Anne du Pré sell her country for a title? Her family must be forcing her into it.'

Now I won't say I'd my gentleman's knowledge of women, but I'd seen this one controlling her weak-minded brother more times than I can rightly speak to. I said 'As you say, Señor, but I'd think she's some purpose of her own or she wouldn't be doing it at all.'

My gentleman stops with the cup halfway to his lips. 'You're right,' he says, and puts it back down. 'She's up to something, she must be.'

He springs to his feet and prowls about the floor. It was a good, big house we'd the use of, Señor, and not a speck of damage from the battle, saving maybe a wee bit of looting inside. We were only borrowing it as a base, you'll understand, my Capitán being left to keep watch round Honnecourt in case the French tried to creep back.

'De Roland,' says my gentleman. 'She loved him, didn't she?'

I told him what I'd heard of the *amende honorable* and let him make his own judgement. My gentleman wouldn't hear a word about it before, but he listened now and rubbed his hand up and down his cheek.

'And there's another puzzle. A man like de Roland could never endure such a thing, and yet Bouchard's still alive. What's he waiting for, Carlos? The chance to clear his name? And if Mlle du Pré is helping him . . .'

I saw the way his mind was going, and can't say I liked it. 'Maybe we should rethink a little, Señor, and suggest she visits another time.'

'Uninvite a lady?' That was my gentleman, chivalrous to a fault and maybe a little over. 'On the contrary, we'll give her complete freedom the whole time of her stay.'

'And we watch her?' I said.

He smiled. 'We watch her. Every single thing she does I want reported at once to me.'

Jacques de Roland

We couldn't follow the du Prés, I mean you can't follow someone over a hundred miles and have them not notice. We went ahead of them instead.

Éspehy's a tiny place, no bigger than Dax, but at least there was only one inn where the du Prés could be staying. We couldn't stay there ourselves, of course, we didn't want to end up eating breakfast with Bouchard, but it was June, the barns were cleared for the harvest, and Charlot found two at a seigneurial farm called Malassise we could use as a base. There was bugger all in them, Philibert had to go and buy straw to lie on, but I didn't think we'd be getting much sleep anyway. We were like a little army ourselves now, and less than a mile away was the enemy.

There were a lot of them too. We'd met remnants of our retreating troops as we journeyed north and nothing they told us about Honnecourt was encouraging. Gaspard was half Spanish so he trotted over the border to see for himself, but he came back very quickly saying the whole place was teeming with troops. There were Germans and Spanish in proper billets, Italians wandering round living off the country, and Walloons just about everywhere. The only soldiers he didn't see were French, or at least not live ones.

I still thought we'd got a chance. There were fourteen of us now, and mostly experienced soldiers. The musketeers were only gardeners and stablehands, but Gaspard had them equipped with buff jackets and bandoliers, and they sloped arms for Stefan like their lives depended on it. Grimauld said 'Dear oh dear, oh dear' every time he looked at them, but I knew what amateurs could do when it came to it. I'd been one myself.

All we needed now was information, so André and I went into the village to wait for the du Prés. We were supposed to meet Bernadette that evening in the inn's stables, but we arrived far too early, it was still daylight and no sign of guests at all. We'd got the right place, though, we heard carriages coming while we were still in the courtyard and had to nip into the horrible privy to hide.

The first carriage was battered and dingy but the people who got out were richly dressed gentlemen, the kind who'd never slum it at a village inn unless they'd got some kind of purpose. The next removed any doubt at all. The man who got out stood a moment gazing at the buildings, and the thick rope-like scar on his neck identified him at once as d'Arsy.

That's when it felt real. We'd set out two years ago from a border village just like this one, we'd been in Paris and all over since then, but everything led back here to this little strip of land where Spain met France. D'Arsy was part of that other life, Paris and the salons and politics, but here was where we were really going to fight it out.

'Here they come,' whispered André.

The du Prés made rotten conspirators, they'd got their arms emblazoned over both carriages. I watched the servants getting out and felt my heart squeeze at the sight of a little maid in a thick cloak scurrying indoors with Jeanette, but then the main carriage doors opened and the first man out was Bouchard.

We should have guessed he'd be travelling with them, but it was still a shock to see him so close to Anne. He handed her down himself, and I saw his fingers actually caressing her elbow when he did it. Beside me André let out his breath in a soft little hiss, and I daren't even look at his face.

It was still light when the courtyard finally cleared, so we went out for fresh air and felt we bloody needed it. It was comforting just walking through the village and reminding ourselves this was still France we were in, people coming home after working the fields, a blacksmith mending a ploughshare, a bunch of women gossiping round the well. They were Champenoise, of course, but the patois is very close to Picardie's, we sat down to join them and it felt like home.

Then a man rode by. He was just an ordinary traveller in a heavy cloak and hat, but I knew his face and quickly lowered my own. It was Carlos Corvacho, d'Estrada's servant, riding openly into a village in Champagne. When I lifted my head again the women were still talking but I wasn't looking at them any more, I was seeing another well on top of this one, a well with no bucket and a rusty chain in a hamlet called Petit-Grouche long ago.

Anne du Pré

Extract from her diary, dated 6 June 1642

Carlos himself delivered our instructions. No one seemed anything but happy to welcome him, while Père Ignace chatted to him in Spanish as if he had missed the language.

Florian alone seemed uncomfortable at Carlos's appearence, as if overcome by the memories it reawakened. Carlos said 'Ah, but we're all good friends now, aren't we, Monsieur?' and patted him on the shoulder, but I saw Florian resented the familiarity. He had forgotten that they used to treat him as a feeble-minded child, and I hope the recollection will *do him good*.

With me Carlos was even more effusive, and stressed the warmth of Don Miguel's welcome with such significance that my abominable fiancé said 'Not *too* warm, I hope,' and laid a proprietorial hand on my arm. He always sits so close.

But dusk was falling and Carlos wasted no more time. He gave us directions to a frontier road behind a farm called Malassise, said an escort would meet us at six in the morning exactly, and gave us a safe-conduct from Don Miguel. I handed it to Bouchard myself that I might have the opportunity to examine it, but it is covered in so many seals I have no hope of trying to copy one for André. I saw indeed the name of the 'Château d'Escaut', but since I have no idea where it is I'm not sure it is much help.

André must still have the information. Bernadette will tell him at the rendezvous tonight, and perhaps, oh perhaps, he will work out a way to use it.

Jacques de Roland

We crossed the border just before dawn. The sky was paling and the fields beyond Malassise were edged with a faint yellow shimmer, while behind us in the gloom the St Nicolas clock struck five.

There wasn't even a wall at the border. The farm track just stretched between Malassise fields, crossed a road in front of the first Artois farm, then went on through more fields like nothing had changed. Even the crops were the same, we rode between wheat and barley the whole way. It felt really exposed, the land was open on all sides and anyone could have seen us, but André said 'No one's watching, Jacques. We're the ones who've been beaten, no one's expecting *us* to invade.'

We followed the track into the wood just before Ossu and settled down to wait. It was still dark among the trees, and I couldn't make out much more than shapes. I hoped it would stay that way, I wasn't convinced any of us looked right, but Gaspard said it didn't much matter with all these different troops about. 'My dear, such a mess,' he said, stifling a yawn. 'No one knows *anyone*. I assure you, I was more than once mistaken for a Walloon.' It was easy for him to be calm about it, we'd dressed him in our best stuff and even ripped out the lining of Crespin's cloak to make him a red sash and ribbons. We were counting on him today.

André was all right, of course, he was completely relaxed now we were smack in enemy territory and real danger. He set the positions, sent Philibert up a tree to give us early warning, then hunkered down among the musketeers, asked for a volunteer to help carry the branch, and tried not to recoil when six voices all said 'Me, Sieur,' at once. He picked the biggest, a rather dim-looking gardener with the most enormous hands I'd ever seen, handed him over to Charlot, and told the rest that if he'd had a dozen more like them we'd have liberated Dax in half the time.

The Ossu clock struck the half. Grey light was starting to filter through the trees, and above us the first birds began to twitter.

Crespin cleared his throat. 'I say, they're cutting it a bit fine, aren't they? What do we do if the du Prés come before we finish?'

André glanced quickly at the musketeers, then put his arm round Crespin's shoulder and began to walk him away.

'They won't,' he said. 'We've seen to it. Now let's look at the rear, I need you and Philibert there in case anyone tries to run back that way.'

The musketeers turned their heads to look after him, their eyes gleaming in a single movement. One pair flashed like enormous white discs, and when the man turned back I saw he was wearing eyeglasses.

A cock crowed in the distance. The birds in our own wood were quiet again, there was only the rustling of leaves, the occasional snort from the horses, and the murmur of Stefan's voice as he talked to our musketeers. They'd never fought before, and their voices were sort of hushed and trembly. 'M. Ravel,' a young one was saying, 'M. Ravel, I don't understand. I can't load the musket while this bayonet is in it, I don't see how to fire.' 'You're not going to bloody fire it, are you?' said Stefan patiently. 'I told you, no noise. You're going to stab them like we practised.' There was a little pause, then 'M. Ravel, how can we stab a man on horseback?'

Grimauld muttered 'Oh dear, oh dear,' but Stefan only sighed. 'You can't, soldier, that's why we're making them dismount. Leave it to the officers, they'll see to all that.'

I was an officer, me and André with Gaspard. I didn't like the idea of them all depending on us.

'How many will there be, M. Ravel?' came another voice, hoarse and with a faintly German accent. I thought it was the one with eyeglasses. 'Do we know how many?'

It might be forty, it might be four, we'd no bloody idea at all. The musketeers weren't the only ones craning forward to hear Stefan's answer.

'One at a time, soldier,' he said. 'Same as it always is. The man in front of you, then the man behind him. That's all you ever need to know.'

Anne du Pré

Extract from her diary, dated 7 June 1642

The clock struck half after five as we gathered in the courtyard. I'd hoped Bouchard would be late as usual, but today he was there even before us and determined to waste no time.

Why André wished us delayed I did not know, but Bernadette had been definite that he did. She said he'd remained behind in the courtyard when she left it, and I wondered if he had perhaps done something to hinder our departure, but everything seemed quite as usual. The carriages were all functioning, the gates opened without incident, and we travelled through the village without anything untoward at all.

The Malassise Farm was less than a mile away and we were there in what seemed only minutes. Bouchard leaned across to pat my knee and said 'Don't worry, everything will be all right,' and I had to smile and thank him without saying that was exactly what I feared. I pressed myself further back in my seat, but was at once thrown almost out of it as the coach juddered and slewed to one side. Our driver shouted, and the vehicle jerked to a halt.

Bouchard thrust his head out of the window. 'Go on, fellow, why have you stopped?'

I heard Vincent explaining that the road was blocked, then felt the jolt of the boards as he jumped down from his place.

Bouchard swore, wrenched the door open and leapt out. I moved to the opening to see what was happening.

The other carriages had stopped behind us and their drivers were hurrying to join the conference. The reason was plain, for at the entrance to the farm track was a wagon loaded with branches of wood, and a great many seemed to have spilled across the road, blocking our path completely. I wondered how long it had taken André's men to do it.

One of the drivers was calling the servants out of their carriage to help shift the debris, and I sat back in my seat, confident that all was going as André had planned. Then Bouchard's voice rose above the others, and with horror I heard him insisting we continue regardless.

'Go round, fellow,' he said. 'We don't stop for a few logs, go round over the fields.'

D'Arsy's driver was a brave man, I heard him protesting about the damage to the wheat. 'It's June, Monseigneur, a month off the harvest, we'll do no end of damage.'

Bouchard almost spat at him. 'And I should care? Let them eat rye instead.'

They will eat rye anyway, the wheat is for the flour to pay their taxes, but it would never occur to André that a man would not know that or not care even if he did. The other drivers were already walking back to their own vehicles and I knew all was lost.

I jumped down. Bouchard said roughly 'Get back in, we're going on,' but I curtsied and said 'Forgive me, Monseigneur, but surely we can wait a few moments?'

He shook his head. 'Corvacho said six o'clock.'

'For the escort,' I said quickly. 'But you cannot believe they would not wait? The Duc de Montmorency visits their country and they will not wait?'

He stopped and looked at me. After a moment he said 'They're Spaniards, they may not even know who I am.'

I forced myself to touch his hand. I said gently 'They will know.'

'I wonder,' he said. His other hand came towards me, and his finger traced the line of my jaw. 'By God, I wonder. But it is still my duty to show a gentleman honours his appointments. We will go on.'

I returned to the carriage in wretched silence, having shamed myself to buy André perhaps one minute, no more.

The carriage jerked forward. We turned sideways, and the reluctance of the horses was evident in the slowness of our progress, but Vincent urged them on to the wheat and I heard the crackle of breaking stalks beneath our wheels. The floor dipped as we encountered the first rut, there was a bumping sensation through the seat, but we cleared it and lurched on.

The light darkened through our window as d'Arsy's carriage pulled level, then seemed to black out completely as something smashed hard against the door, rocking us violently sideways.

I grabbed the strap in panic as I slid down the seat to crush against Florian, and for a moment the whole carriage wobbled precariously before Vincent brought it safely to a stop.

I subsided into my seat, but voices outside sounded high-pitched in alarm, people were running, and someone yelling for help. Florian fumbled with his door, but Bouchard threw ours wide open and dropped furiously down to the field. I slid quickly to the opening to look.

D'Arsy's carriage had lost a wheel, and must have struck our own vehicle as it tipped. The servants were assisting the shaken occupants from the wreck, while the driver complained bitterly that it was not his fault, the field was too bumpy, it had been madness even to try. Vincent clearly agreed, for he made no attempt to resume his seat, but only took the reins of our lead horses and began to walk them purposefully back to the road.

Jeanette hastened to make sure I was unhurt, but behind her I saw Bernadette watching the chaos with evident satisfaction. For a moment our eyes met with understanding, and we exchanged a smile.

Albert Grimauld

Philibert calls them at about a dozen, then slithers down his tree in a shower of leaves.

'Only twelve?' says André. 'Hardly worth bothering.' He's cool as cotton, the laddie, gives no more than one little pat on his sword, then he's straight in position, standing plumb in the track to face the enemy.

Jacques and Lelièvre stroll up beside him. Ravel takes two of his so-called musketeers back towards the fields, Charlot and the big one go for their branch, the Gascon legs it to the rear with de Chouy, and the rest of us try to look like we're shrubbery. I'm propped against a tree myself, my left foot still can't carry no real weight, but I've a musket with a plug in it and I know right where it's going.

There's quiet when we all stops moving, and we hear the clip-clopping of the Spaniards approaching. Lelièvre clears his throat. 'Hem,' he's going, 'hem,' and I know his trouble, the man's got no spit.

Through the trees they come, officer in front, but not one of they senior ones, no big sash or plume, just a few bitty ribbons and that's his lot. Lelièvre looks far the better man as he steps forward with his hand up, saying 'Whoa there, whoa.' It's in Spanish all this, if you get me, but don't go asking me to give it you that way. I knows the gist and that's enough.

The officer reins to a hard stop, and I hear them others all banging into each other behind. He starts with 'What . . .?' but Lelièvre cuts in right away.

'Du Pré escort?' says he, with authority enough to flog a regiment. 'I need to borrow your men. The track's blocked, the carriages can't get through.'

That's the cue, and up come Charlot and his bulky musketeer, carrying a huge branch between them like they've lugged it off the road.

The officer hesitates, but Lelièvre speaks him proper sharp. 'They're Don Miguel's guests, man,' says he. 'Every consideration, those are *my* orders.'

The men know that tone, oh my word they do, they're all legs in the air as they slide off their horses and rush up to help. Not a one with a weapon ready, no armour bar a little back-and-chest, they haven't the chance of a lark in lime.

Or so I think. They're going too eager-fast, see, the officer's still in his saddle and the last ones ain't past me when the first reach the edge of the wood and see there's no blockage. 'What?' calls one. 'Where . . .?' then we all hear the gurgle as the sword goes in. That'll be Ravel.

'Now!' shouts André, and it's time to put the lambs to slaughter. My two musketeers step forward cautious and that's no ruddy good. I yell 'In you come, boys!' and stamp down my good foot, lunging sweet into the nearest man's guts. That does it, they're all but trampling me in their haste to give it a go. There's a couple turning and belting back towards Ossu, but de Chouy will have them, him and young Philibert, they're too busy running even to draw sword. Lelièvre's got one and Jacques another, and as for that Charlot, he's swinging that branch like no more than a twig, knocking them down like he's threshing wheat.

But the officer's the one to watch, he's up out of reach, struggling to turn his beast to gallop the bleeding hell out of it. André's got the bridle and lashing up with his sword, but the man's full-armoured and the horse twisting round at every wrench of its reins. The officer slashes down like 'get out of it', and André can't pull him off, not with reins in one hand and sword in the other, he's yelling for Jacques to help. But as his head's turned the officer's hand whips down, he's going for his ruddy pistol, and if he fires it we're fucked.

Jacques de Roland

I struck wildly up at him, but my blade slid down his armour and only scratched the horse The gun was already clear of the holster, the man's thumb on the dog, I flailed again uselessly, but something screamed past my head, the blue flash of metal as André swung. I heard the crunch and the howl, then blood sprayed out at me, I saw the dreadful stump of the wrist, then the hand still holding the pistol as it thumped to the ground.

André hauled the man down and ended it with the blade in his throat. I stumbled back with the horror of warm blood on my face, but when I reached to wipe my sleeve over it André grabbed my wrist.

'No,' he said urgently. 'Not your clothes. You need to look right, remember?'

I'd forgotten the plan, I'd forgotten everything except the killing and the muck on my face, but André's hand was cool on my wrist and his eyes steady on mine, and I felt my breathing start to ease. Everything was still around us. The fight was over, there were only bodies on the ground and Stefan strolling back from the field whistling.

Anne du Pré

By the time the wheel was replaced and the logs moved we were afraid our escort would have abandoned us to travel through hostile

360

country alone. It was almost a relief when we crossed the frontier and saw Spanish horsemen awaiting us in front of a small wood, though the sight of those hated helmets was still enough to make me shiver.

The officer dismounted to approach our window and Bouchard gave him Don Miguel's safe-conduct. He studied it, placed it inside his coat, and said 'That's quite in order, Monsieur, it will be our pleasure to escort you.'

'I am Monseigneur,' said Bouchard, drawing back haughtily. 'My name is Montmorency.'

The officer was profuse in his apologies, but I had much to do not to laugh aloud, for as Bouchard sat back I saw this officer's face for myself and recognized him as Gaspard.

I couldn't understand how this could be, and was filled with a wonderful relief at being so unexpectedly among friends. As we again moved forward I leaned close to the window to see who else was there, and thought I could determine in one of the cuirassiers the great form of André's man Charlot. My eye was quickly drawn to the young officer at his side, and though his face was shadowed by the helmet it would have taken more than that to disguise him from me. He saw me looking and smiled.

That André himself should be here both terrified and exalted me, for he is known by sight to almost everyone of our party. I turned away in consternation, but Bouchard was sitting back as a prince among lesser men and would never compromise his dignity by paying heed to common soldiers. I saw then it was really quite safe, for the carriage was lower than the riders, it was only the more distant horsemen whose faces we could see, and André was quick to move right alongside our door.

It was extraordinary to have him so close. After a while he dangled his hand low down his side, so I rested my arm on the window ledge and raised my hand above the opening. A second later our fingers touched. At once I was struck with my folly and snatched my hand away before the driver of the following coach should see, but above me I heard André laugh.

I could almost have laughed myself at his audacity. He had found a way of accompanying us to our destination and was actually leading us there himself. I had no idea how he knew the way but we were travelling confidently through the little hamlet of Ossu and I knew we were safe in his hands.

Jacques de Roland

We hadn't a bloody clue. Our troops had told us stuff about the fields and abbey by Honnecourt, but no one had mentioned a Château d'Escaut.

So we asked. We met a Spanish patrol in Ossu, and André just rode ahead, showed them the letter, and asked for directions. Our presence may have made the carriages look official, but theirs did the same to us. We were an escort with a proper safe-conduct signed by Don Miguel himself, the patrol sergeant not only gave directions, he even asked if he could help.

André actually said yes. He had them bully a farmhouse into getting refreshment for our passengers, which gave us the perfect excuse to hang about and wait for Stefan and Philibert. They'd stayed behind to hide the bodies and drive the riderless horses over the border into Malassise, but they must have been quick about it, they caught up with us in minutes.

They'd got something useful too. Stefan had rifled the baggage and found a letter in the officer's pouch which André said were his orders. The dead man was an alférez called de Geres who'd been detached from a company on its way to the Rhineland, and his orders were to deliver the guests to d'Estrada then report to him for duty. That was good in a way, it meant we could go right to the château without anyone realizing we weren't the same people who'd set out, but the bad bit was we'd be expected to stay.

André wasn't bothered. He told Gaspard to say he'd got despatches to deliver first, but if it didn't work we'd just fight them and run. 'They'll still only think we're deserters,' he said. 'No one would imagine a bunch of Frenchmen actually choosing to visit the headquarters of the enemy. Who'd be mad enough to do that?'

His confidence was catching. We were in a horrid situation really, dressed up sweaty in dead men's armour with enemies all round us, but I watched the boy springing cheerfully back on Héros like he couldn't wait to be off, and realized actually he was right. What we were doing was amazing, we ought to feel bloody elated. As we set off again even our musketeers were grinning.

We reached the château in less than half an hour, and that looked encouraging too. It was a good half mile away from Honnecourt in walled grounds and as private as we could possibly want. I thought how easily we'd broken into the château in Verdâme and the barracks in Dax, and knew this would be no different.

The guards at the lodge were obviously expecting us, they took one look at the safe-conduct and opened the gates right away. A cabo was already waiting to take us to join the company, but Gaspard told his story, said he'd report in officially tomorrow, and the cabo just looked weary and accepted it. Armies are the same everywhere. When officers start countermanding other officers' orders there's nothing you can do except try not to get stuck in the middle.

André made us play it out till the end, so we stepped back and saluted the carriages as they filed through the gate. I watched them winding away from us down the drive, then lifted my eyes to what they were riding into and my heart seemed suddenly to stop.

It wasn't like the château at Verdâme, and it wasn't like the barracks at Dax, it was like both of them together and much, much worse. The building was massive and stone-built, and even from this distance I could see all the soldiers wandering about like it was home. The grounds were swarming with them, and I guessed they'd got a full company of three hundred men, some billeted inside, others at the lodge, more in the outhouses and even some in bloody tents on the grass.

'We can do it,' said André. 'We've done it before, we can do this too.'

We couldn't. Last time we'd had an army to help us and a detailed knowledge of the inside, but now we were just fourteen and knew no more about the building than what we could see.

'Forget it,' said Stefan bluntly. 'Let the women sit it out and come home, there's nothing we can do here. We couldn't even get in.'

André looked at the château, at the grounds, at the tents and the lodge, then he turned round to study the rest of us. I felt his eyes on me in an oddly detached way like I wasn't me at all, then he looked in turn at Stefan, at Grimauld, at Charlot and Philibert, and last of all at the musketeer with glasses. Then he smiled.

'Yes we can,' he said. 'We're going in right now.'

Twenty-Four

Stefan Ravel

If he'd given us more time to think about it I'd have told him to fuck off. But the lodge guards were already hovering to close the gates, so I said 'All right' like a good little soldier and dropped myself in it right up to the balls.

We weren't all going in, Abbé, just those with the best chance. Lelièvre couldn't, he'd never have bluffed through his report to d'Estrada, and de Chouy couldn't, he was too refined to pass for a foreign mercenary. We needed men on the outside anyway, people free to move without three hundred dons watching every step.

André briefed Lelièvre at speed. 'Tell them you don't need all your men, you're going to leave half here. Say I'm your abanderado and I'll look after them, but they're due a rest day after hard campaigning and have to be rostered off till you get back. That's crucial, Gaspard, it's no use if they start giving us duties. Can you do it?'

Aristocratic sang froid has its moments. Lelièvre said 'Relax, Dédé, I shall be both persuasive and eloquent. I shall also give him two pistoles, which may help more than either.'

André grinned. 'Make it five.' He turned to the rest of us, said 'Don't worry, we'll say you're Walloons or Germans,' then started confidently after Lelièvre towards the lodge.

I watched them deciding our fate with the guards, and wasn't even sure what to hope for. Oh, I'm all for audacity, and André had enough for a regiment, but I'd rather have had a day to work it out than approximately one minute. The others didn't look too confident either, especially those without the gift of tongues. It was all very well to pretend we were foreigners, but we'd still come from a don regiment, we'd be expected to understand a bloody order.

'We'll be all right,' said Jacques feebly. 'I understand Spanish, so does Charlot, just watch us and do the same.'

'Ah,' said Grimauld, and spat unattractively. 'But what if they wants us to do something different?' He shouldered his piece, caught sight of our lone musketeer attempting to do the same, muttered 'Dear, oh dear,' and went wearily over to help him.

It did seem a bit much to rope in the one German from my musketeers. I said 'Go with the others, Henne, we're all right with six.'

He looked at me reproachfully through his eyeglasses. 'But the Chevalier has chosen me, M. Ravel. Out of all our number he has chosen *me*.' Poor sod. He hadn't much brain and no sense of humour, I doubt he'd been picked first for anything in his whole little life.

Well, it was too late now. André and Lelièvre came back with a mounted cabo in tow, Lelièvre and the lucky ones galloped off with suspicious haste, and we were left in the hands of the Spanish army. They weren't very enthusiastic, I'm bound to say, the cabo just muttered something in don speak and started morosely down the drive, but I can't say that bothered me. What mattered was that he was leading us right into the château itself.

We followed him through a stone archway to a grassed courtyard with a fountain, and in through a side door to the ground floor where the military and livestock were housed. Not us, of course, nothing so useful, the cabo told André all the inside billets were taken and we'd have to go under canvas in the grounds, but at least our horses would be comfortable.

We handed ours to the gloomy horse-master, loaded ourselves with baggage, and followed our cabo across the courtyard to the main administration area. It was like a lot of these big châteaux, with no passageway, just a lot of rooms leading each to the next. We went through a nest of pen-pushers, a police office with defaulters' cells, a barber's room with a spiral staircase rising out of the back, then finally into a sub-office of the fiscal militaire where we were presented with a quill and a dirty piece of paper and invited to sign our names. I watched André writing his, and suppressed a smile when I saw he was calling himself 'de Castilla'.

Next was the anteroom to the furiel mayor's office, and off it the stores. A yellow-faced don handed us out a six-man tent and talked a lot of gibberish which apparently meant it was coming out of our pay, but he wouldn't give André his own till the kid forked out gold.

That's the one good thing about Spanish domination, there isn't anywhere in Europe that doesn't accept the pistole. It was just as well, as it happened, since the tent was all we were getting, and everything else we'd have to buy from the sutlers in the grounds.

And there we were, Abbé, soldiers in the army of glorious Spain herself. André led us back outside, reported to an alférez, which is the dons' idea of a lieutenant, was told to bugger off and not bother him, then cheerfully chose our pitches as close as possible to the château and got us to erect our tents. He was sharing one with Philibert, whom he'd had the sense to introduce as his servant, but the rest of us had a single tent between five, of which one was bloody Charlot who needed half a field just for his legs. We were supposed to be what they called *las camerados,* a bunch of men who sleep and mess together and bond for the greater good of the tercio, but all I could think was if the rest of *las camerados* were as ill-assorted as we were then Spain had better surrender right now.

It's a strange thing, the illusion of security offered by a few feet of flimsy canvas, and it was remarkably tempting to stay hidden right behind it. But our only safety was in a good solid plan, so I braved the open lawn to find the man who'd talked us into this madness.

There he stood, legs apart and arms folded, watching critically as Philibert and Jacques struggled to erect his personal tent. He looked every inch the kind of arrogant young bastard you find in officers' ranks anywhere.

I muttered 'You ought to take the plate off, no one wears it off duty.'

He never varied his imperious expression. 'I can't, my shirt's bloody under it. Give them a hand with the tent, will you, then I can get changed.'

He couldn't muck in himself while the occupants of the next tent were watching, but I still suspected he was enjoying it. When I next looked round he gave me an encouraging grin and told me to put my back into it.

I wandered back up to him when we'd finished, saluted respectfully and said 'This isn't a fucking game.'

'You think I don't know that?' he said, and for a moment something fierce flashed in his eyes. He turned to look at the château, and I saw it then, Abbé, what was boiling underneath. His freedom, the future of his country, the woman he loved and the chance to destroy the man who'd humiliated him, all those things were to be had if he could just get through those walls, and it's possible in his place I'd have felt a little strongly myself.

I said 'I don't suppose you've got a plan, have you?'

He turned and looked vaguely at me, so I said it again.

'I'll think of something,' he said dismissively. 'I've got to, haven't I?'

I looked at Philibert standing anxiously at the entrance to the tent, then at Jacques trying hard not to look towards the watching soldiers. I thought of the others in our own tent, Henne's trusting gaze, and the underlying smells of blood and sweat and fear.

I said 'Yes, little general. I think you have.'

Carlos Corvacho

Oh no, Señor, I'd never deny it was a very bold thing to do. To join our own army right under our noses, well, you can only laugh, can't you? Not but what it wasn't rather foolhardy when you think about it, but there, it's all down to luck in the end, isn't it?

But we knew there was something up all right, there was no fooling my Capitán. It was your young lady gave it away, as ill at ease as she was, and all but shuddering whenever her fiancé looked at her. My gentleman says 'We're right about this, Carlos, she's here for her own reasons and we need to find out double quick what they are.'

He never let it show, though, not my Capitán, he greets her warm as an old friend. 'Satisfy me on one thing, Mademoiselle,' says he, holding both her hands. 'De Roland could never have raided your château without help from the inside, and I've always had my suspicions that help came from you. Am I right?'

She lowers her lashes demurely. 'We all helped,' she says. 'But it was André de Roland who deserves the credit and no one else.'

There was no shuddering when she said that name, Señor, she blushes pink as a rose, and very fetching it is too. My gentleman smiles.

'Perhaps,' says he. 'But I know who was my most worthy adversary, and am so very glad we are now of the same side.'

Now there's nothing in that a lady could take offence at, but her blush deepens dark red and she hides her face fast. Over her head my Capitán's eyes meet mine, and there's triumph in them, Señor, his old hunting look when he knows he's got a scent. She's no more on our side than Richelieu his own self, and she still loves de Roland to boot. If that isn't trouble in a nest full of conspirators such as we'd got here, well, I ask you, Señor, what is?

I never let her out of sight after that, or not in a manner of speaking. I watched her to her room and saw she had no one in with her but her maid, and she never stirred hand nor foot outside of it all morning. Her companion wandered around a little, that I did see, the one called 'Jeanette', is that right, Senor? She walked up and down the gallery taking notice of everything, but there was nothing untoward in it, I'm sure. She was a very friendly lady, Mlle Jeanette, stopped to talk to me more than once, and I'm guessing she hadn't much in the way of presentable male company at home.

Then at noon your Mademoiselle's safe under my own eyes again as they all come into my Capitán's rooms for the signing of the treaty. Our job was easy enough, to witness the arrangements they'd made among their own selves and sign to say Spain would respect them, but it's a nasty business to my mind, nothing a gentleman would want to put his name to. Your Mlle Anne's father, he's the worst. 'Where's my name?' says he. 'Two hundred thousand livres I've given, and there's no mention of du Pré in this whole document!' 'Oh, there is, Papa,' says Bouchard, his voice sweet and sour like a Moorish delicacy gone off. 'Here, where it says "family dependants of the Duc de Montmorency". When I become your son-in-law I believe that will be you.' Your poor Mlle Anne closes her eyes in shame, and I can't say I wonder at it. My Capitán's of the same mind himself, which makes it all the more pity we have to break her as we do.

Oh yes, Señor, we're all but sure of it now. When my gentleman takes the paper to the éscritoire the company's eyes are burning on it at every move. They all watch the lid closed, the lock turn, even the key dropping into my Capitán's doublet, all but your Mlle Anne, who sits with her head resolutely turned away as if she's not the slightest interest in the matter. And no more she might have, Señor, if I hadn't been watching close enough to see her following the whole business in the glass.

That's what she's after, that document. Not that she's a chance of getting it with guards on the door every minute, but it casts what you might call a serious light on our situation. She won't be alone in it, not a slip of a girl like that, and for all we know there's a force outside planning an assault on the château itself. My gentleman says no, there's not a French army big enough in the region, but he still has the guards on the gate doubled for what he says is 'just in case', and takes a little extra precaution to protect his own room.

He doesn't like not knowing, Señor, and that's the truth. I put a couple of men on to watching Mlle du Pré's door with orders to follow whoever comes out, but it's my gentleman prowling up and down like an animal that's caged. 'We have to force her hand,' he says to me. 'She'll lie low and wait till our guard's down, we have to make her act now.'

I said 'We can wait, can't we, Señor? They're only staying a few days, she'll have to make her move soon.'

'And what if we can't counter it?' says he. 'What if she's only gathering intelligence for a raid after she's gone?' He picks up her empty Madeira glass and runs his finger silky-soft round the rim, for all the world like reading her thoughts from her touch. 'No, it has to be on our terms and at a time of our choosing.'

I knew that look on him, I'd seen it often enough when he was playing chess, but this was a woman, and no more predicting them than a cat. I said 'A girl like this, who knows what can push her into something rash?'

Round the rim his finger goes, and then it stops. 'A girl like this,' he says, and puts the glass down in the exact same spot he took it from. 'Well, I think we know what she's afraid of, don't you?'

Jacques de Roland

We sort of clung to the tents to begin with, but by noon Grimauld was sitting with our neighbours telling funny stories about chasing fellow Walloons at the Battle of Honnecourt. He'd got it from our own troops, of course, but you'd never have known it, he was saying 'No, you've got it all wrong, see,' and had them laughing at every word. Henne was with them too, nodding and not saying much, but Grimauld rolled his eyes and said 'German,' and people laughed kindly and patted him on the back.

It was harder for me and Charlot because we weren't sure how things worked in the ranks, but we sat and polished muskets like I did in the Occupied Army and it felt comfortable and familiar. Philibert was even more at home. I saw him haggling furiously with the sutlers over the price of a cooking pot, his voice getting shriller and his gestures getting wilder till they just threw up their hands and gave in. Stefan was just Stefan of course, like he'd probably been in every regiment he'd ever belonged to. He lounged by our tent smoking his horrible pipe and telling everyone to fuck off.

Even the language wasn't a problem. Most armies have got mercenaries, they've been in occupied towns and fought alongside foreign allies, there's hardly a soldier doesn't speak a bit of at least three languages. There was even a bunch of Italians from the Strozzi a few tents down, and they weren't having any difficulty getting by. Everyone was friendly and chatty, it started to feel like this was our own army and we were perfectly safe.

But we weren't, of course, we'd got a job to do and not much time to do it. We'd be found out as soon as Gaspard didn't come back, and André maybe even sooner. He was an officer, d'Estrada was bound to want to meet him, the alférez said he'd probably have been invited for dinner already if the château hadn't been busy with guests. As soon as we heard the treaty was signed we'd do the raid and get out.

We started by making a way to communicate with Gaspard. There hadn't been time to arrange anything clever, he was just going to come back at midnight and slink round the outside for a letter, but André'd promised to hang something over the wall to show him where to look. I wasn't sure about that, I mean the wall was twelve feet high and people were sort of bound to notice us shinning up it, but at the rear of the château we found an orchard of apple trees that seemed perfect. Soldiers were camped round that side too, but they couldn't pitch tents where the trees were so close and we were able to get right to the back without anyone looking. André tied his handkerchief to the tip of a branch growing over the wall, then scribbled a note asking Gaspard to be here at six tomorrow, wrapped it round a stone and simply chucked it over.

We gathered dead branches to look like we'd been collecting firewood, then set off to walk round the château itself. That was more depressing, because it actually looked easy to break into. There was a door on every side, and only two pikemen guarding each of them. All the rooms on the upper storeys had open balconies like extra bits of floor stuck out into the air, and it would have been the simplest thing in the world to get a grapnel hook on the railings and nip up a rope. There were twenty different ways into that house, but the second you turned round you realized there were none at all.

The soldiers. They were camped on every side with nothing to do but lounge round their cooking fires and watch other people. They looked up even when we just walked by, we couldn't have put a hand on the walls without fifty of them giving an alarm. They'd be maybe less suspicious on our own side of the building where they knew us by sight, but they were so bloody friendly they'd have probably come after us to see what we were doing.

André said 'All right, we'll do it from the inside. The spiral stairs off the barber's room, they've got to lead up to the living quarters somehow.'

'The block'll be locked after dark,' said Stefan. 'There's money in there, stores, supplies, they're not going to leave that lying around for the taking.'

Grimauld snorted. 'Locks,' he said. 'You leave it to me, laddie, I'll do you your locks.'

We all looked at him. He seemed to realize what he'd said, went red and stared at his feet. 'Locks,' he said. 'Just saying, that's all.'

He wanted wire to work with, so we unravelled the decoration on the grip of Charlot's rapier and he spent all afternoon making it into little hooks and loops and thick bits twisted together he said were 'hammers'. None of us asked how he knew, not even Stefan. André did say 'Jacques, do you think it's possible Grimauld . . .' and I said 'Of course not, it's just a soldier's skill, that's all,' and he said 'Yes, of course,' and went away.

Next he needed to examine the lock, so at dusk we strolled round to the courtyard we'd gone to when we first arrived. It was dark in the administration block, so we stood casually in front of the door and started talking loudly about nothing. Henne began telling this long joke in German which no one understood, then I heard Grimauld cursing behind him.

'Locks?' he said. 'There ain't no ruddy lock. What's keeping this shut is buggering bolts on the inside, that's what.'

We'd have to smash it, and everyone would hear. I looked in alarm at André, but he shook his head. 'There'll be another staircase on the other side, it's probably symmetrical. Let's look.'

We went back to the stables and through the indoor billets. Officers raised irritated eyebrows, married soldiers stood quickly in front of their women, but we walked calmly through them all, and the boy was right, there was another spiral staircase exactly opposite where the barber's would have been. It was wooden and very creaky, but we set off up it like we'd a reason to be here, and there was a pikeman round the second bend, saying 'I'm sorry, Señor, no entry past this point.'

'Ah,' said André, leaning against the wall and smiling lazily at him. 'Sorry, soldier, my mistake. Château living quarters, is it?'

'That's right,' said the man, showing willing to an officer. 'I'm very sorry, Señor, but . . .'

'No, you're quite right,' said André. 'My fault, I got lost, that's all.'

The soldier beamed at us in anxious relief. There was sweat on his balding head and I remember hoping it wouldn't be him on duty tomorrow night, it wouldn't be him we'd have to kill.

Because this was our way in, there wasn't any doubt. I wasn't sure about the getting out bit, I mean we'd have the women with us and maybe hordes of guards in pursuit, but André said 'We don't need to go back through the billets, we'll go down the other stairs and open the bolts from the inside.'

We all felt more confident now we'd got a plan. We went back to our tents and lit a fire like everyone else, then Philibert made casserole out of our beef ration, given to us free by the Spanish army. André had to eat by himself, but it was only for this one night and tomorrow we'd be on our way home with the treaty.

'Provided they've signed it,' said Stefan, chucking down his empty dish. 'Provided the women find out where it is and how the fuck we're going to get to it.'

That sobered us. We could pass in a crowd of Spanish soldiers, but we were planning to burgle a grand château full of guests and servants who'd scream at the first sight of us.

'It'll be all right,' said André. He was standing in the entrance to his tent, his figure a black blur above the firelight. 'We've got three brave women in there, they'll manage it between them.'

I thought of Bernadette, how she'd saved herself from being abducted, what she'd done under fire at La Marfée. Of Jeanette, who'd risked execution in the old days just to get our messages to Anne. Of Anne, who'd fought two Spanish officers all by herself to save her sister, and gone back among them now to save André and France.

'That's right,' said André. 'The women will find a way.'

Bernadette Fournier

Indeed, Monsieur, we had done very well. Anne had found out exactly where the treaty was kept, while Jeanette had walked over the entire gallery and made the most beautiful map.

But yes, I remember, this is how it worked. Ours was the east wing of the château, with a number of grand apartments set about the main staircase down to the great salons of the first floor. A railed gallery ran all about the stairwell so a person might walk round and see into the anteroom of each apartment, and although Don Miguel's was closed with an oak door we still knew what lay behind it. Anne had seen the treaty signed there, and told us the inner door was flanked by two soldiers with crossed pike.

Anne wrote all this in a letter for the Chevalier and we hoped he would see a solution. He had arranged to meet me at half after ten this evening and we hoped he would achieve that too, though how he would penetrate the grounds we could not imagine. He had told me to look for a rose garden, and if there was none for an orchard, and if there were neither I was to walk as close as I could to the stables and he would find me.

But I was just placing the letter in my bosom when we heard raised voices in our anteroom. We heard Jeanette saying that her mistress was indisposed, but M. du Pré was arguing with her, and the third voice was Bouchard's.

She was quick, our Mlle Anne. She pushed me at once to the connecting door of her brother's room, saying 'If he is here he cannot be there, you can pass through unseen,' and of course she was right. I walked out and through M. du Pré's antechamber, round the gallery to the back stairs, then out into the dark to look for a rose garden as arranged.

There was none, as doubtless Monsieur already knows, but there was an orchard to the rear and I made my way towards it past the ranks of soldiers' tents. Yes, there were men still about and all inclined to be gallant with a woman walking alone after dark, but I did not think they would dare touch a guest of Don Miguel's. My fear was more for André, for he too must somehow pass through all these enemy soldiers and his danger was greater than mine.

Yet still I believed he would have managed it, and remember a sense of disappointment when at last I lost myself in the apple trees and saw no figure of a man waiting. Then a twig cracked behind, I turned to see a young Spanish officer entering the orchard after me, and a voice I knew said 'It's all right, Bernadette, it's only me.'

I said 'You startled me, Chevalier.'

'I'm sorry,' he said, taking my hands. 'But I couldn't let you go by those soldiers alone, I've been walking behind you all the way.'

He did still care, Monsieur, the coming of Mlle Anne had not changed that. I was woman enough to find pleasure in it, and when he asked if I had run any other danger I told him truthfully how near I had come to being caught by Bouchard.

In this I was a fool, for he caught fright at once. 'In Anne's room?' he said. 'Dear God, what was he doing in there?' He turned wildly to the château as if he would storm it alone, and I hastened to assure him that there could be no danger, since both M. du Pré and Jeanette were present.

He subsided and looked indeed a little shamefaced. 'I'm sorry,' he said again. 'But I couldn't bear it if harm came to either of you, you must see that.'

I did and do, Monsieur, I understand a man's pride. So I made no more of our risks, but gave him the letter and map, and explained it all myself since it was too dark to read.

He seemed elated to hear the treaty was signed, and surprisingly untroubled to learn it was in a locked desk. That it was in Don Miguel's own room gave him more difficulty, for while this was placed next to our own apartment there was no connecting door and the only access was through the anteroom with the guards.

'Only two,' he said thoughtfully, tapping the letter against his teeth.

'No, Chevalier,' I said at once. 'There are many public rooms down the staircase, and below them the soldiers' billets. The pikemen would only have to shout to bring fifty men to their aid.'

I thought his eyes gleamed in the gloom. 'We could do it quietly.'

'And invisibly?' I said. 'Even to reach the inner door would take perhaps three strides, and that alone would be enough for the pikemen to give the alarm.'

He was silent, and after a moment his head turned back towards the château as if drawn there by a string. Above us the trees rustled softly.

'Then we'll do it from the balcony,' he said. 'The soldiers won't see us after dark.'

He was right, Monsieur. The château was lit by great sconces on the walls, but the very brightness of the lower levels served only to darken the thick shadows above the protruding balconies.

I said 'At night Don Miguel will be in his rooms. He is there now.'

'Then we'll do it when he's dining,' said André. 'Do you know when that will be?'

I could say only that the gentlemen had remained downstairs until after ten tonight, but who knew when it might be tomorrow.

He nodded. 'It's dark by nine, we'll come up straightaway. We'll get you and Jeanette out immediately, and if Anne's at the dinner I'll wait to bring her down myself. Does that sound all right?'

Naturally it did, Monsieur, I could not have known anything else. So I said 'Yes,' and committed us, and the memory of it troubles me even now.

O God, God, help me, I cannot think what to do. I can hardly think at all.

Perhaps I should have guessed. I was so anxious to hurry Bernadette away I did not stop to wonder why Florian wished to do this unprecedented thing and bring Bouchard into my room. Only when they entered did I feel the impropriety, for it did not seem right to have Bouchard so near my bed, gazing about the room with unashamed interest.

'You have been writing, Mademoiselle,' he said, observing the ink-stained quill that lay on the paper and the fine scattering of sand over the inlay of the desk.

'Only my diary,' I said.

'Ah, the famous diary,' he said, and sat heavily on a silk-embroidered chair. 'I shall enjoy reading that when we are married.'

'Of course, Monseigneur,' I said. 'When we are married.'

Florian cleared his throat. 'That's actually what we want to talk about, Anne. Monseigneur has asked for a little chat with you, and I want you to know he's doing it with my blessing.'

My alarm was growing. 'Blessing?'

'And our father's, of course,' he said. 'I know you'll be sensible about it and not make a fuss, so I'll just wait outside and let Monseigneur speak to you himself.'

I said 'Florian, it's not seemly,' but he waved his hand, said 'I'm just outside, for heaven's sake,' and quickly went out. I know Florian. I know he is only angry when secretly he is ashamed, and the thought terrified me. There is so little he is ashamed of now.

'Don't look so worried,' said Bouchard, leaning back comfortably in his chair. 'It's just about the wedding. I think I'd like it a little sooner.'

I sat down to face him. 'It cannot be thought of until you have your title. We have had this conversation before.'

'You want to rise from your knees as Mme la Duchesse, do you?' he said. 'Then so you shall. I am Duc here, so it is here we will be married.'

I said 'But Don Miguel –'

'Don Miguel suggested it,' he said. 'He thinks it would set the perfect seal on our agreement. Your father is delighted, since without the alliance the paper we have signed today awards him precisely nothing. Your brother is delighted because he's my friend, I'm delighted because I've waited rather longer than I'm used to for something I want, and you too will be delighted because it's what you said you wanted. It's to be tomorrow evening, and Don Miguel has arranged a feast to follow.'

I will not write what I felt, to write it is almost to make it real. I said we could not marry in this furtive fashion, I wanted a proper wedding in Paris with all my family present. He said I had no family to speak of, and those who mattered were here. I said it was not enough to call myself Mme la Duchesse here, I needed my title recognized by all, and he said 'The coup is to be any day, if we linger a fortnight we can return to Paris in triumph.' I said my trousseaux was not prepared, and he said 'You do not care a spit for such things, Anne du Pré, and that is one of the reasons I have set my heart on you.'

His effrontery took my breath away, and with it the last of my self-control. I said 'You have *not* set your heart on me. You do not love me, you do not even like me, you only marry me to hurt André de Roland.'

I remember the quiet. The singing and laughter of the soldiers drifted over the balcony, and to me at that moment they sounded as innocent as children.

Bouchard stood abruptly and closed the doors. 'De Roland?' he said. 'I've had him on his knees begging pardon. I don't think we need trouble ourselves about him, do you?'

He lies. He is frightened of André, I know it, his valet tells Bernadette he has always a servant with him for bodyguard and sometimes screams in his sleep.

I said 'Then why?'

'Ah, there's a question,' he said. He still did not turn, but remained at the balcony, staring at the dark glass. 'So many answers. Perhaps you were a challenge, Mademoiselle, and I enjoyed forcing you into the pretence. But there are other things.'

He turned to look at me and I could not bear his eyes. I looked at the desk, the ink-splatters and sand, I thought of André and my letter and said 'What other things?'

'Your ruthlessness,' he said. 'You were all for de Roland as long as he could get you the tabouret, but the minute he couldn't you dropped him.'

'I defended him at the *amende honorable.*'

'True,' he said. 'And even that in a way I admired. You think I care for society's opinion? Do you know what they say of *me*?'

I do, but he told me anyway. Bastard, he said, filth, mongrel, jumped-up nobody. The words poured in my ears and despite myself my heart ached.

'I could have other women,' he said. 'If they knew I'd be Duc I could have half Paris. I wouldn't have them now if they begged, not even for the pleasure of teaching them better at the point of the only kind of sword they understand.'

I was shocked. Not that he should say it, but that he should think it right to say it to *me*. He knew it, I think, for he smiled and walked towards me.

'Not you,' he said. 'You're different, Anne.'

He stopped close in front of me, and I screwed my nails tight into my palms. 'You really do believe in me, don't you?' he said, his finger tracing a snail's trail across my cheek. 'You argued with such passion that the escort would wait this morning, and of course you were right. Even I didn't believe as strongly as that.'

I had never thought I could do such damage. I compelled myself to look into his face and say 'But Monseigneur, I do not love you.'

His eyes widened, and then he laughed. 'Why should you? This is an alliance, not an affair.' He took my hands in his and stepped back to look at me. 'You've suffered from it too, haven't you? You've seen the scorn in people's eyes, you know what they say of your father and his tradesman's lineage. You want to throw it back at them, don't you? To watch them squirm as you take precedence? We'll do it together, you and I. It starts tomorrow.'

I said weakly 'Not tomorrow, give me time to prepare. Perhaps Monday?'

'Tomorrow,' he said, and his mouth set in a sulky line. 'Don

Miguel suggested it, and I'm not losing face in front of that Spaniard. I'll fetch you at half after eight.'

I could say only 'Please,' and clutch his hands in supplication.

He smiled. 'It's only natural for you to be frightened, I shouldn't respect you otherwise.'

He released my hands and leaned towards me. I could do nothing but watch his face coming closer, his mouth opening, and then my head was jolted forward and he was kissing me, his clammy lips squashing mine. I could not breathe. His palm was sliding round my face, pulling the skin taut, his lips working on mine and forcing them apart, and then he thrust his tongue inside me, *his tongue inside my mouth,* my throat gagging with the need to spit and expel him, but he held my head firm and did what he liked inside while my knees shook beneath me and my mind screamed.

The pressure eased and his head lifted, I pressed my hands on the desk to support myself upright and faced him with a mouthful of his saliva my body was too disgusted to swallow. He smoothed down his hair, stepped away and gave me almost a kindly smile.

'It'll be all right,' he said. 'I won't hurt you more than I can help.'

Twenty-Five

Jacques de Roland

I woke to the sound of a bell clanging, and found the soldiers being called to Mass. All around us men were crawling blearily out of their tents and drifting across the lawns to sit in a huge circle round a wooden table and a couple of robed priests.

We'd got to join them. Everyone was but the lodge guards, it would have looked suspicious if we'd slunk in the opposite direction. Only Henne refused, but then he was a heretic, he started spouting stuff about the Whore of Babylon with his glasses getting all steamed up, so Stefan said 'We'll give her your love then,' and chucked him back in the tent before anyone noticed.

It was quite safe for the rest of us, I mean it was something we were used to. We huddled together in an anonymous lump at the back, and I was feeling quite comfortable with it all till I saw a figure striding across from the château and recognized d'Estrada.

I'd forgotten how dangerous he was. I'd seen him armoured and on horseback at La Marfée, but this was the d'Estrada I remembered from Dax, a handsome young Spaniard with that relaxed assurance that said he wasn't scared of anything. His walk was a bit like André's, that same light swing in the hip to bring his sword ready to his hand, but he hadn't the boy's restlessness, he seemed like a man with all the time in the world. He was just strolling along, inclining his head courteously to listen to a junior officer by his side, but it didn't matter how polite he was, he made you feel inferior just by being there. André watched him with a kind of yearning intensity, and I knew without looking his hand was on his sword.

'Head down,' said Stefan roughly. 'You think he won't spot you in a crowd?' He was watching d'Estrada himself, but there wasn't any yearning in it, just the narrow-eyed stare of a man who's seen a snake and wants it killed quick.

I don't want to say much about the service. It ought to have felt good, all of us together listening to the same language, but it was odd praying next to people I might have to kill the same night, it somehow didn't seem very holy. We didn't chat to people when it was over, we just waited till d'Estrada was out of sight then started to make our way back to our tents.

'Mlle Jeanette,' said Philibert suddenly. 'Look, Messieurs, it is my Mlle Jeanette.'

There were about a hundred soldiers between us and the terrace, but I glimpsed the light flutter of a dress moving beyond all the dark bodies, and a moment later she came into full view. Jeanette taking the air, and beside her Bernadette.

'She is a fine woman,' said Philibert complacently. 'If it were not for Agnès . . .'

We watched them a moment, Sunday and ladies in the sunshine, then André said 'They're here for a reason, something must have happened. We'd better go to the orchard.'

I wasn't convinced, I thought they might just want a bit of air, but we wandered to the apple orchard just in case. The sun hadn't got round there yet, it was chilly under the trees, but it was a chance to see Bernadette and I didn't mind waiting for that.

So we did, we waited more than an hour. We waited till the sun had crept round and glowed yellow on the apple trees, but the women never came.

Bernadette Fournier

It was a nightmare, Monsieur, the thing you dream as a child. André was so close I even saw him in the crowd, but we could not reach or talk to him, we could do nothing at all.

And oh, we needed him so desperately. At nine he was to come tonight, nine, when Anne was to be married half an hour before. We had been at a loss how to find him, for we could scarcely search the tents of so many soldiers, but then this Mass had come as a chance from God Himself, for the soldiers were every one of them out in the open. We walked round the terrace a full twice to make sure André would see, but as I turned for the orchard Jeanette's hand clamped on my wrist and she whispered 'We are being followed.'

She was sure, Monsieur. She even pointed him out to me by a movement of her eyes, a soldier who had been on the gallery when we left and was now on the lawns staring most busily at nothing. Jeanette said 'He walked all round the terrace with us, Bernadette. Not once, but both times. Now, I ask you, how much of an accident is that?'

'Then we will separate,' said I. 'Sit on the bench while I walk round again, and when he follows me you must go for the orchard.'

I strolled on alone, but had hardly turned the corner when footsteps pattered behind me and there again was Jeanette. She took my arm in a show of friendly companionship and led me back to the bench, a great cold stone thing with arms like the heads of roaring lions.

'There are two,' she said under her breath. 'That was another went after you. I've seen him twice already on the gallery this morning, don't you tell me that's coincidence.'

Two we could not beat, there was nothing we could do that would not lead them right to the Chevalier. We sat and pretended to talk and laugh in the fresh air, while our minds hunted furiously for answers.

I said 'They cannot know, we have given them no reason to watch us.'

'But they do,' she said, picking at scabs of lichen on the grey stone. 'Not us, I think, but our door. I've caught that Carlos hanging about across the stairwell more than once. The empty room opposite, they're using it as a spyhole.'

I said 'Then they would have followed me last night, and I will swear no one did. André himself came behind me all the way across the gardens.'

Jeanette thought a moment, then brushed the lichen off her fingers. 'Ah, but you didn't come out of our room, now did you? It was M. du Pré's, and we must thank God for it.'

My head swam with the thought of what would have happened had the visitors not forced us to change our plan. I said 'Then I shall go that way again. M. du Pré will leave his room for dinner . . .' and there I stopped, Monsieur, for I remembered dinner would be too late.

'We won't find the Chevalier again anyway,' said Jeanette. 'Mass was our only chance.'

It was, and it was lost. We could do nothing but return wretchedly to poor Anne.

She was very quiet when we told her, very quiet and very calm. She said 'Then I have given myself away somehow and the danger is acute. Are you sure they watch up here?'

We had seen it for ourselves on our return. Only one man had followed us up the back stairs, but we glimpsed the other slipping into their anteroom as we reached the gallery, and knew he must have run up the other stairwell to watch which room we should enter. They were not stupid, these men, and were taking their job very seriously indeed.

'I'm sorry, Mademoiselle,' said Jeanette, her bright face crumpled in misery. 'I don't see how we can tell the Chevalier what's to happen, I really don't.'

'It doesn't matter,' said Anne, and again I was struck by the calm in her voice. 'What matters is that they watch the door, and when André comes tonight he will be caught.'

We were silent a long while. It was an enormous apartment we were in, yet we sat huddled close together as if crushed in a net we could none of us see. I thought of a great many things in that silence, Monsieur, of why I was here, and what the Chevalier had put himself through to save me from torture and death.

I rose and went to my own little bed in the alcove. Underneath it was my box, and I had only to remove my linen from the top to find what I needed. André had said they were for the very last resort, but I knew that was now come.

Anne and Jeanette sat still in silence as I returned. I said 'I will deal with these watchers, Mademoiselle. I shall ensure they see nothing at all,' and on the table in front of them I placed a knife.

I saw in the widening of their eyes that they understood, yet neither exclaimed in horror. We were three very desperate women.

Jeanette stood with determination. 'You don't do it alone. Tell me what to do, and I'll help you.'

'But not now,' said Anne. 'If the alarm is raised now . . .'

Oh, but she was right, Monsieur. A dead guard could lead only to us, and we should all be imprisoned long before the Chevalier could come.

Anne stood and smoothed her sleeves purposefully over her wrists. 'Do it after I have gone down. Don Miguel and Carlos will be engaged with us, so will my father and brother and Bouchard, this whole floor will be empty but for you and the valets. André should be here very soon after.'

Jeanette stared. 'But it will be too late, the wedding will be happening.'

'Yes,' said Anne. 'I'll have to go through with it, it's the only way.'

Even I was shocked. I said 'There is no question of it. We shall do it right now, then we will all three go out to find the Chevalier. We will not be able to return, it is true, but he will get us out somehow, you can be sure of it.'

'I am,' she said. 'And then he'll lose all chance of the treaty and of clearing his name. Anything is better than that.'

Ah God, but she had fortitude. It was Jeanette who seemed the more distressed of the two, and indeed her eyes grew wet with tears.

'But you can't,' she said piteously. 'That man, you can't.'

'And I won't,' said Anne, turning away and hugging her arms across her chest. 'The service, yes, then I'll come up to get changed, and please God André will be waiting for me. We can have the marriage annulled afterwards, it's only words.'

Jeanette shook her head wretchedly. 'It's a lie before God Himself.'

Anne turned back to us, and I saw a brightness in her face as if what Jeanette had said had cheered her. 'André did it,' she said. 'André did it, and so can I.'

Jacques de Roland

By six o'clock I was in the orchard talking to Crespin and Gaspard over the wall. I hadn't got much to tell them, André could only ask them to be in position by dark and listen for a pistol shot, but they'd simply got to be ready when it came.

'We will be, Jacquot,' said Crespin, nodding his head in desperate seriousness. 'We've got five jolly keen musketeers and surprise on our side, tell André we won't let him down.'

I bloody hoped not. The lodge guards seemed to have been increased since we arrived, and the musketeers were our only hope of getting out.

The rest was down to us. We'd sharpened our swords and fed the horses, we'd packed up our gear and taken it bit by bit to the stables so as not to attract attention, there was nothing left to do but wait. I remember just sitting on the grass and watching the soldiers milling about like a play with no plot. Two came staggering by with an enormous basket of flowers and I wondered what it was for. 'The château,' said one. 'Festive dinner or something.' I guessed they were celebrating their bloody treaty.

Bernadette Fournier

They came for her at half after eight.

She was determined not to resist, for the rooms would then be surrounded by people and André would stand no chance at all. She said we must not even tell him what was happening, since he would arrive too late to prevent it and nothing must stop him securing the treaty. Love is not a soft thing, Monsieur. It is a grand lady standing obediently as a little girl as we dressed her, but her hands clenched into small tight fists by her sides.

It was not to be much of a wedding, but there were still enough of the trappings to make it feel the travesty it was. They had found for her a dress of gold and silver, and Don Miguel had even sent to Honnecourt for imitation orange blossoms. Wax flowers are pitiful things, Monsieur, and as I dropped the garland over her newly curled head there was only the faintest scent of singed hair.

I was not to attend the ceremony, and was able to stay in the alcove with my head well down when her family arrived with Bouchard. It might have been harder for Jeanette to excuse herself, but

Anne had insisted the service be very small and her father had not cared enough to argue. He had no interest in anything but the piece of paper, and when Anne knelt for his blessing his face showed nothing but satisfaction. The brother at least had the decency to look unwell, and I noticed he counted his rings with almost feverish urgency.

We watched them to the door and saw it close behind them. We listened to their footsteps descending the stairs until all was silent and Anne was gone. Then Jeanette and I looked at each other, and I gave her the second knife.

'It is sharp,' I said. 'The Chevalier saw to it himself. It will slice a man's throat if you strike hard and do not hesitate.'

'Don't fear me,' said Jeanette. "They have taken my Mlle Anne, and someone is going to pay.'

She concealed the knife in her sleeve, but I placed mine in my bosom for I needed a hand spare for the wine. Then we crept to the door and peeped out.

There was no sign of our quarry in the anteroom across the stairwell, nor did we expect it, for they concealed themselves hard to one side of the opening. The stairs themselves yawned in front of us, and I saw now their steps were scattered with petals for the passage of the bride.

'Slippery,' said Jeanette. 'My poor lamb, walking over that lot, it's a wonder she didn't break her neck.'

I steadied her with my eyes. She took a deep breath, nodded, and awaited my lead.

I pulled our door full open, crossed the antechamber, looked from left to right along the gallery and forced myself to give a girlish giggle. Jeanette came stiffly after me and attempted a laugh herself. It was not good, Monsieur, but it was surely sufficient to disarm suspicion from across the way. Together we almost scampered across the gallery, our bodies compelled into terrible gaiety while we thought only of killing, and then we were at the opening of the opposite antechamber and I peered coyly round the wall.

There were two, as we suspected. One was the first man who had followed us that morning, and the other was a stranger with a beard scarce grown. I swayed coquettishly into the doorway and said

'You've been watching us, haven't you, Messieurs? We have seen you, Jeanette and I, and could not help wondering why.'

The older one covered his confusion with an ease that surprised me. 'Two such pretty ladies, what else would a man do?'

His French was excellent, and I guessed he was also employed to listen at doors. I stepped full into the room and waggled the wine bottle.

'Well now is your chance,' I said. 'The grand folk are all gone, there is no one but ourselves, what say you we have a celebration of our own?'

He hesitated, but I was close enough for my purpose and my hand already reaching into my bosom. His eyes followed it, what man's would not, but they had time only to widen in shock as the knife came clear, for I struck in the same movement, stabbing only the smallest amount before sweeping wide into the slice. His neck opened upwards like a lid, and oh, the blood that came, hot and wet, it stung my eyes and blinded me.

I heard a gurgling, but it was not my man, he seemed only to make a sighing exhale that belched more blood, it was Jeanette's, for she had stabbed not sliced and the knife still protruded from her man's throat. His hands groped for the hilt, she released it and backed away in terror, but I blinked my eyes clean, put my hand over his and pushed hard. His eyes bulged but the gurgling ceased abruptly, his knees buckled, and I took his weight myself to lower him to the floor. My own man was already sliding down the wall, his body wiping a clean whiteness in the spray of red he left behind.

I went to each and completed the cut to make sure of them, then stood to face Jeanette. She stared at me with as much horror as if I had been the enemy myself, and her mouth worked in soundless speech. I grasped her wrists and said 'Help me move them,' but she only stared at the red smears left by my fingers on her skin.

I opened the inner door to drag the first body through myself, but it took all my strength to slide him as much as a foot. Then the weight lessened as Jeanette took the other arm, and between us we manoeuvred him through and returned for the other. We worked in silence, and she did not meet my eyes.

We closed the door, but still the carnage was evident to anyone who happened to pass by. There was no help for it, Monsieur, I pulled my dress over my head and stood in my undergarments while I used it to wipe the wall clean. Jeanette watched in silence as I resumed the dress, and I could not read her expression.

I dared not delay further, for fear of missing André's arrival. We crossed the gallery noisily, so that if Don Miguel's guards had heard us pass they would also hear us return, then slipped into Anne's apartment, lit a candle from the fire against the growing darkness, and regarded each other in silence.

'Bernadette,' whispered Jeanette at last. 'Your face. Your dress . . .'

I looked at the wine bottle, wiped it roughly, and opened it.

'You will need this then,' said I, 'for I think you have yet to see your own.'

Anne du Pré

I moved in a dream and nothing about me was real. We came at last into an antechamber with an iron crucifix on the wall, and shame stirred inside me, for never before had I been afraid at the sight of the cross. A servant pulled open the heavy door beside it, and as I stepped into the chapel I heard it close behind me with a soft thump.

Oh dear God, it was far grander than our own chapel at home, and dressed almost as a small church. There was a little altar with a kneeling step, a dozen carved oak chairs, and a side table almost concealed beneath a bowl of trembling white flowers. I looked about me and saw only faces of the enemy. Don Miguel advanced on me with a deep bow, Carlos smiled ingratiatingly by his side, the only guest was d'Arsy, the priest at the altar was Père Ignace, and the man by whose side I stood was Bouchard. The dream fell away from me, and I was as panicked as a small child that finds itself lost in a crowd of strangers.

I whispered 'I must go back. There is something in my room. I must go back.'

A woman would have asked what this precious thing might be,

but the men naturally assumed it was some mysterious female object too delicate to name. Don Miguel turned smoothly away and began to speak to the priest.

My father lowered his brows in annoyance. 'Not now, Mademoiselle, we can't keep people waiting.'

'I'll go,' said Florian. 'Your maid will know where to find it, won't she?'

The thought of what Florian might see upstairs frightened me back to sense. 'No, no, it's not so urgent. I can fetch it after the ceremony when I change my dress.'

'Change your dress?' said Bouchard. 'Not tonight you won't.'

I could not believe him. 'But Monseigneur, I can surely return to my room . . .'

He laughed, a great masculine sound that bounced round the stifling walls. 'Now, Mademoiselle, did you really think we wouldn't try to honour the traditions? After the feast we'll be escorted to my own chamber where doubtless d'Arsy will arrange some appalling riot, and then we'll be alone, you and I. The only dress you'll need is this.' He flicked the wax flowers of my garland with his large fingers. 'You know it would be unlucky for anyone to remove this but me.'

The chapel seemed to shimmer and shift before my eyes, for a terrible moment the ground swayed, but then a steady arm supported me and a voice said 'Mademoiselle is unwell.' I looked up into the eyes of our enemy, the Don Miguel d'Estrada. They were brown and soft and filled with compassion, and I said 'Help me,' and meant it.

He sat me in one of the oak chairs, and I heard him say 'Just one little moment, Messieurs.' He was their host and they had to heed him, they stood back and murmured among themselves.

He lowered his voice and spoke only to me. 'If you do not wish this marriage I may be able to stop it. I would not have harm come to a woman beneath my roof.'

There was agitation in his face, contrition in his eyes, and I had never before heard him say 'woman' instead of 'lady'. I had all but opened my mouth to speak when I remembered the watchers upstairs and who must have set them there. He knew I was his enemy. Perhaps he knew everything and sought only to trap me into an admission that would endanger us all.

He said 'We don't have to talk here. I can have you escorted upstairs to my own room where we will be undisturbed.'

Where we would now find André. If I resisted or feigned illness the same thing would happen, they would take me upstairs and find André. I had no choice left. I must not only go through the service but also what came afterwards. André would wait for me in my room and I would never come there, I would never see him again. After tonight he would no longer want it.

Perhaps the very horror of it helped me. My feelings seemed to die like an echo until there was nothing left but listlessness and a desire to drift until it was over.

I said 'No, I'm all right now. Let us resume.'

Jacques de Roland

We didn't even have to kill the grumpy horse-master. He was shutting up the stables as we arrived, and simply trudged off into the billets for the night. He'd never know how lucky he really was.

There was no one else in the courtyard. We nipped into the stables, saddled up the horses and loaded the pistols in the holsters, and that was everything ready for a speedy departure. I looked back at Tonnerre as I went out and wondered how I'd feel when I next saw him. That was stupid really, I mean I might never come back here at all, but I didn't actually believe that. You somehow never do.

Going in was even simpler than last time. We walked straight through the billets, and the married men actually nodded because they'd seen us before, we were familiar and harmless. The officers looked up and looked down again, then we were round the bend with the door to the kitchens in front of us and to our right were the spiral stairs.

No one spoke. We clustered in a group in case anyone walked by, then Stefan sat on the steps and removed his shoes. He stuck his knife in his teeth, grinned at us over the top of it, then started up the wooden stairs in his stockinged feet.

We were ready to start talking and laughing to cover the sound of a struggle, but everything was quiet. I hoped the guard hadn't just wandered off somewhere to come back at the most inconvenient moment, but then came a soft creak of the boards and Stefan was back with us, his knife bloody in his hand.

'Easy enough,' he said, sticking it in his belt. 'Poor bugger was asleep.' He didn't meet our eyes when he said it, and I'm not surprised. I tried not to look when we went past, but I had to climb over the guard's legs and so of course I saw. It was the balding man who'd been here yesterday, the one who'd given us that anxious smile.

But I couldn't think about that now, we were in new territory past this point and all we had to guide us was Jeanette's map. We climbed past the doorway to the first floor, stopped at the second and listened. I thought I heard the faint thump of a closing door, but otherwise everything was quiet. After a moment we crept forward and looked through.

We were completely exposed. It wasn't like downstairs, with each room leading into the next, there was a bloody great stairwell in the middle and a railed gallery all round. At the top of the staircase was a landing with an ornate wooden bench set into the wall, but the rest of the gallery was just bare boards leading past the open doors of a dozen anterooms. The only bit I liked the look of was the arched opening exactly opposite our own, which we hoped led to the stairs in the administration wing and the way out.

Stefan studied the map. 'This is the south staircase, so Anne's room is on the right. That's d'Estrada's next along with the guards in it, the one with the closed door.'

André turned to Charlot. 'You'll be all right, they won't even see you going past.'

'It won't matter if they do, Chevalier,' said Charlot, removing his soldier's coat to reveal the smart grey doublet underneath. 'I will do nothing to rouse their suspicions.'

André nodded. 'We'll deal with it if it happens. All that matters is you get that bottom door open and hold the stairs for our escape.'

Charlot straightened. 'Of course, Chevalier.'

'There could be another guard,' said Stefan. 'You'll have to deal with him alone.'

Charlot hardly even turned his head. 'I think I can manage,

M. Ravel.' He flipped up the skirt of his doublet to show us the beautiful *main-gauche* in his belt. 'It is just possible I have been managing these things before you were even born.'

He smoothed his hair over his shoulders, then set off round the gallery with the soft tread of the experienced servant. His head never turned as he passed the open anterooms, he was a valet about his business. He reached the opposite opening, disappeared through the arch and was gone.

'Now us,' said André. 'Quiet as you can, but they won't hear us with the door shut.'

We crept cautiously along the gallery. Grimauld's good foot was going down with a hard thump on every step, but no one heard or bothered if they did. All the anterooms were empty, the place was deserted. We passed the stairwell, then I bumped into André as he stopped.

'Strange,' he whispered. 'Look.'

There were flowers all over the stairs, pink and white petals scattered down the steps. They'd formed clumps where people had walked over them, but it was still very pretty.

'A wedding,' said Henne. 'In my village it is always done so for the passage of the bride.'

Something odd was happening to André's face, it seemed to be getting older, the skin almost sagging as his eyes widened.

'For the groom it is different,' said Henne. 'For him we place briars and he has to . . .'

André took two strides and was into Anne's anteroom with me hard behind him. There was no one there, nothing but an odd little streak that glimmered faintly in the darkness, and when my shoe lifted off it I heard a faint sticky tear.

André stared with terrified comprehension, then spun away and shoved open the inner door. We shot after him.

Bernadette, her hands and face streaked with blood and her dress slathered in it. Jeanette, wine slopping from a goblet in her hand as she jumped back in alarm, but that wasn't wine on her cheek or spattered on her bodice, she reeked of the slaughterhouse as much as Bernadette. André let out a cry, and behind us Stefan had the sense to close the door.

Bernadette was babbling 'It's all right, Chevalier, we had to kill some guards, that is all. The way is clear, see, the balcony door is open.'

Grimauld was already hobbling purposefully towards it, Philibert after him, but André didn't even turn. 'Anne,' he said. He took Bernadette by the shoulders and almost shook her. 'Where's Anne?'

Jeanette's face was white under the bloody streaks. 'She's at dinner, Sieur, that's all. You're to get the treaty, she'll be here directly.'

I grabbed André's elbow and pulled him away from Bernadette. He looked at me dazedly and said 'Sorry. I'm sorry, but . . .' and looked helplessly back at her. To my amazement she dropped her eyes.

'Jeanette says what she has been told to,' she said. 'Mlle Anne is downstairs in the chapel being married to M. Bouchard as we speak.'

André's face almost lit up with terror and his eyes weren't seeing anything, not me, not Bernadette, he thrust us both back and groped for the door.

'The treaty, laddie,' said Grimauld from the balcony window. 'Come on, the treaty.'

'Fuck the treaty,' said André and wrenched the door open. I grabbed his arm, I said 'It's too late, they'll kill you,' and then something crashed smack into my cheekbone, my head went bang against the wall, and when I got my eyes open again the boy was gone.

Stefan Ravel

He hit his own brother, bolted through the door, and pelted for the stairs before anyone else drew breath. No more skulking, no more disguises, he didn't give a fuck who heard him and was drawing his sword as he ran.

Yes, I went after him. It wasn't the easiest of journeys, those petals slipped and slithered under my feet the whole way, but André practically flew over them and landed on the floor below with a soft thump.

He swivelled this way and that, sword up and no one to kill, then saw the trail of flowers and chased it round the stairwell to the rooms behind. I skidded after him, yanking out my own sword as we went.

Jacques de Roland

I was only dazed for a minute or two, and then I knew exactly what was happening. I jerked myself upright and my mind was cold and clear.

I said 'Grimauld, you know the plan, can you do it alone?'

'Course we can,' he said. 'Me and the boy here.' Philibert nodded with determination.

I turned to Henne. 'Get the women out, both of them, do it now.'

'Yes, M'sieur,' he said, happy to be given an order he could follow. 'To M. Charlot I will take them.' He seized Jeanette's arm as if she were a horse and reached for Bernadette.

I turned for the door. Bernadette was grabbing at me, saying 'Jacques, no,' but I couldn't stop, I was out and bolting down those stairs in a second. I knew it was too late to save Anne, but I couldn't lose my brother, not again. This time I'd got to bring him back or die.

Twenty-Six

Anne du Pré

The step was hard beneath my knees, but the service still seemed very short. Bouchard was asked for his consent and gave it. I was asked for mine and gave it. My voice faltered as if my own throat sought to stifle it, but before God I lied and said I would be his wife. His, that terrible word 'his', like his horse, his house, the food on his plate, *his.*

Père Ignace smiled archly and raised his hand to begin the *ego conjungo,* but the door banged open and the priest's hand was arrested in air. I turned, we all turned, and it was André, dressed as he had been when he broke into my rooms all those years ago, a young Spanish officer with drawn sword.

He did not break step in the doorway but was already through and running, commotion all about him as chairs were pushed back in alarm. Don Miguel was leaping to his feet and Bouchard pulling at my arm, but then André's voice spoke close to me and said 'Please, Messieurs, I am really hoping someone will move.' His blade was outstretched past my face and the tip was at Bouchard's throat.

'At the altar?' said Don Miguel. 'An unarmed man at the altar of God?'

André's blade wavered and steadied. Behind him I heard another man rush in, but it was Stefan, he pushed the door shut behind him and again our world stifled into silence.

'Come on, Mademoiselle,' said André. His hand appeared in front of me and I grasped it. 'I'll take you home.'

'You can't,' said Bouchard. 'She's my wife now. Before God.'

André said 'Not before any God I know,' and tightened his hand round mine.

I said 'He has not pronounced . . . the priest has not . . .'

Bouchard shouted over me at Père Ignace. 'Say it, man, say it now!'

The priest said *'Ego . . .'* but then stopped in horror as André's blade pressed into the soft flesh of Bouchard's throat.

'Say it by all means,' he said evenly. 'Make her a wife and I'll make her a widow.'

The priest swallowed and was silent.

'All right,' said André, his eyes still steady on Bouchard. 'Now take back your consent, sweetheart, and it will never matter again what he says.'

My voice came freely now, for my whole heart was behind it. I said 'I do not consent to this marriage, it is forced upon me, and before God I belong only to André de Roland.'

I heard the shock rippling round the chapel but cared nothing for it, for in that one instant André turned his head and at last his eyes met mine.

Stefan Ravel

He looked at her. Jesus Christ, he *looked* at her. He'd done it, the stupid, lucky bastard, he'd caught them all out and got control, then he took his eyes off the target to look at a woman. Bouchard flung back in an instant dragging Anne away with him, and d'Estrada snatched out his sword.

André whipped round but d'Estrada was already coming at him and I had to wade in myself to keep the others back. I batted down the blade of the one with the scarred neck, but Corvacho was drawn too and I had to waste a second slashing him out of my way. I swivelled back to André, but now the brother was in front of me, and heaven help him, he'd a sword in his hand. I smashed it aside and yelled at him to back off, and then he knew me, he recognized the man who'd carried him out of the Château Petit Arx and saved his miserable life. His face burned scarlet with what I'd like to think was shame, his sword drooped and he stood back. Beside him the Baron stood with his mouth open in an 'o' of bewildered outrage, but his fashionable sword was safe in its scabbard.

D'Estrada was the only real danger, but André didn't seem up to it, he was shocked and off balance, and even glanced over at Anne out of reach. The Don was straight in, of course, and André only saved himself by snatching at the blade with his left hand. I guess it wasn't edged near the hilt, but the shock still woke him, he jumped back smartly and got his own sword up in at least some semblance of a guard. D'Estrada began to weave towards him, making elegant little balletic feints, and I realized the bastard was forcing a duel.

We had no choice. It was Anne was the problem, Anne with Bouchard on the other side of the room. We could cut our way to the door together, but we'd have to leave the woman if we did. We could go for Anne instead, but then d'Estrada would reach the door. We needed that door shut, Abbé, it was one of those big heavy ones designed to protect the pious from the noises of the worldly, but get it open and the sound of clashing swords was going to bring the world right in among us. André had to beat d'Estrada to give us any chance at all.

I couldn't help him either. Corvacho was down and clutching his hip, but the scarred man was at me again and his swordsmanship was rather out of my league. I snatched up a chair in my left hand and walloped him sprawling to the floor, then grabbed the moment's respite to turn again to André.

Too late. Bouchard had his sword out and was heading straight for André's back. Anne screamed, I yelled 'Behind!' but André's sword was tangled with d'Estrada's, he hadn't even turned when Bouchard lunged.

Carlos Corvacho

And missed, Señor, missed by a foot, because your young lady seized his sword arm and dragged it to one side. A brave little girl, your Mlle Anne, but she paid for it this time. Bouchard wrenched his arm free and struck at her, his sword on a woman and a guest of ours too. She didn't skip back fast enough, and the blade slashed down her arm, tearing the sleeve to the flesh beneath. I saw blood gleaming on her white skin.

That's too much for de Roland. He's screaming with rage and trying to beat my gentleman back so he can turn and get to her. Oh, he was wild, Señor, no control at all, my Capitán could have pinned him easy, but he was torn in his own mind because of what Bouchard had done and his honour wouldn't let him take advantage.

Bouchard was another kind of creature. He was swearing and cursing, a terrible thing in a house of God, and what's more he was still swiping after the woman. Her brother was pleading with him no, no, and Bouchard hissing at him to stand back, but du Pré's stiffened himself up with something and when his sister screams 'Help me, Florian!' he's like a man waking out of a dream. His face clears almost sensible, and he's in with his blade to parry Bouchard back. A feeble kind of blow it was, Señor, but it drives Bouchard mad to be resisted. He beats the lad's blade away and plunges him right through the middle and out the other side.

For a second everything stops, even de Roland and my gentleman, all shocked by what's done. Mlle Anne's down on her knees saying 'Florian, Florian,' and the Baron stumbling up to them, all the dignity fallen off him like a cloak.

Bouchard stares round, teeth bared as he sees the condemnation in every face. He yells out something, telling us all to go to the bad place I think, then thrusts past my gentleman and heads for the door. Your Chevalier throws himself after him, but the priest steps in front, and de Roland can't touch him for fear of his soul. He's crying out with fury and trying to dodge past, but as Bouchard reaches the door it opens itself and another man charges in with upraised sword. It's Jacques Gilbert, Señor, and I think Bouchard's a dead man, but M. Gilbert wavers, he really does, he ducks out of the killing blow and just stabs in the side to bring the man down.

Ravel at our end bellows 'Shut the door!' but it's been open long enough for the noise to reach our honour guard round the corner, and in they shoot, both of them straight for the man fighting their officer, straight for your Chevalier.

Jacques de Roland

I slammed the door and turned to charge after them, but there wasn't an opening anywhere. André wasn't fencing, he was just

399

fighting wild, nothing but blade and fury. He'd got his *main-gauche* and was whirling both blades, slashing all round him, driving them back, no one could get within four feet. He was screaming at me too, and after a second the words made sense, he was yelling 'Get her out, get her out, *get her out!*'

Anne. I saw her now, the candles lit up her hair as she huddled against the far wall by someone on the ground. Stefan was nearer, but he'd got d'Arsy coming off the floor at him, he just yelled 'Get that bloody woman out,' and swung back to his own fight.

He was right, so was André, Anne was a liability. I vaulted over a row of chairs to get to her and saw the man she was bending over was Florian. Her father was sat on a chair above them, his head in his hands, but he lifted it as I reached them and looked at me with eyes that didn't focus. He said hoarsely 'They killed my son. What good is a title without a son?'

I couldn't look at him. I took Anne's arm, but there was blood under my fingers, she was wounded. She looked up at me, red eyes in a white face, and whispered 'Florian saved me, he really did, I hope he knows that now.'

He didn't know anything. His eyes were blank and his jaw sagging open.

'Come on,' I said gently, pulling her to her feet. 'André wants you out.'

He was still bloody shouting it, but he never dropped his guard, not once. One of the guards was reeling back with an arm flung over his eyes, the other scrabbling backwards into the chairs to escape the sweeping blades, but d'Estrada was standing back patiently, watching André tire himself out, watching and waiting for his chance. I hesitated, but Stefan was bawling 'Go on!' and our only hope was speed. I lifted Anne off her feet, stuck her arms round my neck to keep my sword arm free, then waded straight through the chairs to the door. I pulled it open, steered us through, and pushed it soft shut.

There was suddenly silence. The sound didn't reach out here, there was nothing but a distant tinkle of voices and laughter. There was no shouting, no footsteps, no one was coming, and I realized the alarm hadn't been given at all. This floor was salons and dining rooms, probably the only soldiers around had been the two now in the chapel.

I headed for the back stairs and Charlot, my confidence rising with every step. André could hold for a couple more minutes, the guests would stay in their dining room waiting for the wedding feast, Philibert and Grimauld would be getting the treaty, we could do this and get out without raising any alarm at all.

Albert Grimauld

'Piece of piss,' André'd said to me, or something similar. 'All we've got to do is jump from Anne's balcony to d'Estrada's and get in through the windows.'

Oh dear, oh dear. The gap didn't look much from the ground, but up here's a different thing, see, there's maybe six feet of air between us and the next balcony, and nothing below it but sky.

'I'm not afraid,' says Philibert, fear dripping off him you could smell in Senlis. 'I'll go first.'

I watched him clambering over our rail and teetering on our little ledge. His hands uncurl on the railing, he's leaning forward over thin air, he's reaching and leaping, and *slap* his feet are landing on the other ledge. I lets out my breath as he climbs over, nonchalant-proud as a man who's had his first maid.

'Come on,' he says, wiping his hands down his breeches. 'It's easy.'

Oh, my word. I gets over the rail right enough, but I need a good foot to kick off with and a good one to land on, and that's one more than I've got. I reckon it's the kick matters most, so I warn the kid to be ready to catch and springs off that ledge like a fucking gazelle.

And lands like a crippled soldier. The jolt's shooting up the bone like another shiv in that bastard boot. The twisted bone can't take the pressure, something goes *snap* and my knee cracks against the rails as I whack up the second foot and stamp down hard. Now that's pain, that's worse nor it was when I couldn't take it and spilled the lies that sent the laddie to the Place de Grève. But I took it now. No choice, see, there's not one of the others can do what I can do,

401

they're fucked to Frankfurt without me. Philibert knows, he clamps his hands on my wrists and hauls me up like precious china till I can get my good leg over and on solid stone. The other's over easy then, but it's broken and useless, the foot dangling like something doesn't belong to me at all.

But we're here and over and a job to do, so I leans on the good leg and has a look at the window. There's no curtain over it and candles lit inside, nice and cosy for our don officer to come home to. No one there. But the door's opposite us with two pikemen leaning on the other side, so I lowers the window handle soft and slow and eases it open with never a sound, then in we tiptoe like a pair of mincey mice.

It's a pretty room, I'll say. Tapestries everywhere, even on the floor where people could trample them, and not them muddy brown colours neither, all reds and blues and yellows, bright as sun on a field of poppies. But they're nice and handy for us right then, they keep our footfalls to no more than little sighs as we creep up on the desk. That's pretty too, rounded lid painted with flowers and inlaid with mother-of-pearl leaves, but best of all there's a clear big lock with a brass ring round it, simple as sweet. I lifts the candle off the top, gets the wires out my coat, then behind me I hear a soft, firm click.

I look round at Philibert. Behind me someone laughs and says something in Spanish.

Slowly, slowly, our heads turn towards the sound, but there's no one, only an arch I'd guess leads to a bedchamber. I blink at Philibert, and he starts to creep silently towards it. I pay him no nevermind and go back to the lock.

'Two,' whispers Philibert behind me. 'They're playing chess.'

Now that's tricksy, that is, that's the kind of man we're up against here. Locked desk, guards on the door, and he's only stuck another couple in his own bedroom. But he still don't know soldiers. He's imagined them straining to listen for the first sign of trouble, but they're thinking 'We'll hear when the door opens,' so there they are sat on his bed playing chess.

I go on fiddling. The projection's talking to me now, loop round her neck to pull her back, but she won't come past the sliding tongue, so it's in with a little hammer to press it back, and through she comes sailing easy and the little click as the spring yields. Philibert reaches with trembling hands for the lid, and it opens.

You want to see inside a man's head, just look in his desk. Little drawers, little packets, everything labelled up neat, the man wasn't human. I think I've only to look for a label saying 'Treacherous treaties – France' and I'm home.

'Here,' whispers Philibert. 'Here.'

His plump young finger points to the papers right at the front. No label, none needed, I read that opening line and know what we've found. 'The Sieur de Fontrailles has been sent as an envoy from Monsieur le Duc d'Orléans to the King of Spain with letters from His Highness for His Majesty . . .' That's treason, that's what that is, treason in any language, and this is plain French. I grin round at Philibert, and he grins back. I reach for the papers, find the top one's sticking, and give it a little pull to bring it clear. There's half a blink as I realize the corner's caught under a stack of tiny drawers, another half when I try to stop my hand pulling, then *crash*, down they tumble, rattling and rolling like rocks in a bucket.

I drop the papers and go for my sword. Two troopers come leaping out the other room, swords up and businesslike as if they've never heard of chess, then one shouts, there's a scuffling at the door and in burst the two pikemen. Four against a boy and a cripple, we was done like pigs on a ruddy spit.

'Drop the weapons,' says a pikeman in the worst accent you ever heard. 'You're French, aren't you? Drop the weapons.'

I lower my sword, but Philibert's already seen hisself a hero and ain't having it took away that easy. 'Run, Grimauld,' he says to me, me a bleeding one-leg who's struggling to so much as stand, 'run and I'll hold them.' He flourishes his blade and runs at them like a hero bloody born, and oh Christ in a crucible he's buying me time.

Stefan Ravel

André couldn't last much longer. He'd downed both guards, and the one slashed across the eyes looked good as dead, but he was still back where he'd started with d'Estrada to beat. D'Estrada was fresh, but André'd been imitating a windmill for the last five minutes and looked just about exhausted. His face glowed with sweat, one sleeve was slashed and flapping, and I could hear his breathing from the back wall.

We'd still got to beat that bastard aristocrat if we were going to get out. Bouchard was nursing his injuries behind the altar, Corvacho was calmly bandaging his wound and watching the swordplay, the Baron didn't count, young Florian was dead, there was only the one with the scarred neck to watch, and even he'd taken another bash from my trusty chair and sat himself down out of reach. That only left d'Estrada.

He was standing back, assessing André the way a man looks at a joint he's about to carve, then in he came again with those smooth liquid movements like butter melting in a pan. Sword out straight, André's out to meet it, the blades tickled and separated, but d'Estrada had his underneath, a back-handed flip up, out and round, and André wide open for the lunge. The Don was hard in with it, but André spun on his heel, left arm slashing back in the turn, and the *main-gauche* slammed d'Estrada's blade safely aside.

They faced each other again, and I thought d'Estrada looked a touch less complacent. He glanced reproachfully at André's *main-gauche*, then at his own empty right hand.

'Fight fair, Chevalier?'

Jesus *Christ*. We were fighting for our lives here, we were outnumbered three hundred to seven, and the bastard was talking like this was a gentleman's game.

For an unbelievable moment André hesitated, but the dagger was his best defence against that left-handed freak, and he knew it. 'I regret, Señor . . .'

D'Estrada gave a graceful shrug that suggested he'd only been trying it on. He called 'M. d'Arsy!'

My friend of the mangled neck jerked himself to attention, then fumbled awkwardly at his belt, produced a short blade like André's own, and chucked it to d'Estrada.

It was a chance and a good one, I'd have had the bastard while his arm was up to catch, but André stood back like a fool and let them do it. Then there was d'Estrada facing him again, dangerous with one blade, lethal with two. The games were over, and it was time for the kill.

Carlos Corvacho

I'd my doubts about your Chevalier after that blasphemy at the altar, but I won't deny he did the right thing about the dagger. He'd his own sense of honour, in a French sort of way.

So did M. d'Arsy, which surprised me in a traitor of his kidney. When he sat back down I said 'Don't you worry, Señor, my gentleman will settle him,' and he turned me a grey face and said 'That's what I'm afraid of. De Roland's the only man alive who can give me back my honour.'

Well, I didn't rate his chances and that's the truth. My gentleman was as much at home with rapier and dagger as he was with just the sword, I knew how it would end. They were moving faster now, as men do with two blades, there's no 'off' beats, if you understand me. There's maybe less craft in it, my Capitán always said the single blade was the purer form, but he'd the strength and speed for the business, he was weaving that dagger in and out to draw the Chevalier's eyes while he's in and up with the sword. Twice, three times he nearly had him that way, and the last his tip's that close it gashes a clear red streak across the forehead.

I says to M. d'Arsy 'He'll have him next time.'

The tanner gives me a filthy look and, if you'll forgive the expression, Señor, he tells me to shut my gob.

Stefan Ravel

André looked fit to drop, but there was something else in his sword-play now, a glimmer of the old joy I remembered when he was a kid. He shook his head and almost smiled when d'Estrada cut him, and when the thrust came again he dropped on one knee to duck it and stabbed sharp into the bastard's thigh. Corvacho yelped, but d'Estrada didn't, there was never a sound out of him. He merely stepped back with his guard up, tested his weight on the wounded leg, and gave André a tight-lipped smile.

'Very good,' he said. 'You have improved since your last lesson.'

André bowed. 'Or perhaps you are a little slower.'

D'Estrada's eyes narrowed, but his only answer was to level his sword and slide back into the attack.

And Christ, it was fast. Two quick crosses, then he dodged André's rapier and closed distance in less time than it took to blink. He slammed his hilt at the jaw, André's sword flailing uselessly wide, and jerked up his short blade to stab. André got his *main-gauche* to it, but the blade still scratched him, another line down his throat, and d'Estrada stabbing again low. Corvacho was on his feet with excitement, but André wasn't done yet, he used his own sword hand to punch d'Estrada in the face and jump back from the dagger, streaking up his rapier to keep the man at bay. One breath, no more, and d'Estrada was in again, attacking the sword this time, clashing and clashing at it, the dagger glittering in the candlelight as it poised to find the opening.

The door banged but they neither of them turned, they were close again, wrestling rather than fencing, and now I heard d'Estrada, *now* I heard the bastard, his breathing as ragged as André's as they struggled and swayed together before the kid managed to stumble back out of reach and slash out again with his sword.

Jacques was in the doorway, and I knew from his face we'd got trouble.

'The alarm's given,' he said. 'Not us, but a guard's run downstairs yelling.'

Time to be out. André and d'Estrada were still fighting, and I noticed a new gash on the Spaniard's arm, but neither was near admitting defeat. I checked my scarred-neck friend was still safely seated, then turned and belted for the door.

Jacques was staring in shock at his brother and the Spaniard. 'We can't leave André.'

I'd no intention of leaving André. They were apart again, d'Estrada starting that weaving motion before another attack, so I just struck out with another chair and knocked the legs from under him. I didn't waste a second on André's cry of chivalrous outrage, I just yelled 'Now, soldier!' and held the door open.

He hesitated, but only a second. He saw d'Arsy up and heading for us and the terror on Jacques' face, he heard my order and came. He babbled 'I'm sorry,' at d'Estrada as he passed, but he fucking came, and as soon as he was out the door I grabbed his arm and pulled.

We made it through to the grand stairwell, and I heard it then, the swelling roar of voices downstairs as the guards were dragged out of billets and thrust towards the stairs.

'Grimauld,' said Jacques wretchedly. 'My fault, I asked them . . .'

There wasn't time for apologies. 'Back stairs,' I said. 'Now.'

'And leave the others?' said André. He didn't want an answer, Abbé, he was already wrenching away for the central staircase.

I yelled 'There's no time!' but he was gone and Jacques already following. I said a few choice words and went after them.

Jacques de Roland

We stormed up those stairs and swerved round for d'Estrada's room. Familiar sounds were coming from it, swords and yells and furniture going over, like part of the same fight I'd been in for years and was never going to see the end of, but as we panted towards the room the noises stopped, and that was even worse.

The anteroom was empty, the inner door open, and men moving in front of me, but as we ran in I saw the fight was over. Grimauld was down with blood over his face and a man menacing him with a pike, while two swordsmen were turning from a crumpled figure I knew at once was Philibert. They thought we were reinforcements and actually lowered their weapons, we charged and finished them in three seconds.

I dropped by Philibert, but his chest was slashed open and he was dead. Dozens of cuts on his face and arms proved he'd put up an incredible fight before they killed him, and I wanted to cry like a dog because I hadn't even seen it. At least Grimauld was alive, Stefan flung him over his shoulder and we hurtled back to the gallery, but soldiers were already pounding up the stairs and some almost at the top.

André jumped to the stairwell and swiped out with his sword to drive the first man back. 'Take Grimauld,' he said to Stefan. 'Get him out, I'll hold here.'

Stefan swore at him, but the boy was already fighting again, sweeping the sword in a great arc before him while he jabbed with the *main-gauche* at anyone who got close. He was ragged and bleeding, his face and throat were cut, his shirt hanging off one arm, but he was the same bloody stupid André who never ever gave up. Something pumped up inside me like water in the Samaritaine.

'Go on, Ravel,' I said, and took my place beside André. 'Go on, we'll hold.'

A soldier pressed forward and I took him myself, just a simple slash and he fell. I actually wanted to laugh, because of course it was easy. They were below us on narrow steps but we were on solid ground and striking down, we could take the whole bloody lot. André darted a thrust at another, and it didn't just get him, the two behind got knocked off their feet when the man fell against them. I saw Stefan disappearing through the archway and it made me oddly exultant. Grimauld was out, Anne was out, Bernadette and Jeanette were already out, I could mourn for Philibert but we'd bloody well saved the rest.

'Fence your front,' said André, stabbing across me at a soldier sidling up my flank. 'Fence your bloody front and we'll be all right.'

We wouldn't be really, my brain was clear enough for that. We could buy time for the others, but there wasn't a hope for ourselves. We couldn't do this for ever, and the second we left the stairwell they'd have us from behind. It didn't matter. I thought of Philibert and his heroic stories and hoped he'd approve of me now. We were holding the stairs, me and André, we were going to fight to the death and go out together in the grandest way there was.

Anne du Pré

It was cold in the stables after the stuffiness of the chapel, and I remember shivering while Jeanette dressed my arm with a strip from her own chemise. I could not even cry for Florian as I wished, for all my emotions seemed in a state of suspension, waiting to learn for certain which way I should let them flow.

Footsteps were approaching, only one man's, but heavy as if he carried a great burden. Our German escort shooed us like chickens into the shadows and stood by the door with levelled bayonet, but the figure who appeared in the doorway was Stefan, and in his arms he carried Grimauld.

'Heavier than he looks,' he said, lowering the poor man carelessly to the straw. 'Get them mounted and out, Henne, there'll be all hell let loose in a moment.'

Henne saluted him briskly but in the same moment came the clang of a great bell from the château's tower, rung repeatedly and vigorously as if to rouse the soldiers in the encampments outside.

Stefan grimaced. 'Better make that now.' He grabbed the bridle of Jacques' horse and thrust it into Henne's hand, then turned and ran back across the courtyard. Even the slap of his footsteps was drowned in the clamour of the great bell.

Jacques de Roland

I heard it but was too weary to care. My arm was aching, and I wasn't even achieving much. The soldiers weren't pressing forward any more, just jabbing in enough to keep us jumping, waiting for the moment they could grab and drag us down.

'Not much longer,' said André, and I thought he was right, one more swipe would finish me. 'They'll think of the backstairs in a minute and come at us from the billets.'

I hadn't even thought of that. 'If they try the other wing they'll get Charlot.'

'They won't get Charlot,' he said, spiking one of the bolder ones in the arm. 'You'll see.'

I tried not to think of Charlot, big and safe and solid on the backstairs. I lashed out at a big bearded man taking a determined step forward, I actually screamed at him to leave us alone, but someone was shouting below them now, an officer gathering them for the rush. I heard more yelling from the gallery and nearly threw down my sword in frustration as I realized they'd got us from both sides.

A great tearing rip behind me forced me to look round. Charlot was there, single-handedly wrenching the wooden bench out of the plaster that fixed it to the wall.

'Jacques,' said André urgently, and I turned back to fence the rising press, hope shooting down into my hand so I forgot the pain in my arm and everything except what was happening behind. It was Stefan who was yelling, and he was saying 'On three, got it? On three.' It didn't make sense, then I heard him yell 'One!' and it did. 'Two!' and I slashed at that bearded man as he turned to shout a warning, then 'Three!' and jumped back on to the gallery, as Charlot and Stefan hefted the bench between them and simply hurled it down the stairs.

I wish I'd seen more of it, but I was running for the archway and couldn't risk more than a glance. The soldiers were tumbling back on each other and the bench rolling over them, I heard cries of fear and pain and thought 'Good, you bastards, you should have left us alone.' Then we were clattering down the backstairs, down and into the barber's room, through the police office which had a dead guard sprawled by the empty defaulters' cells, through the clerks' room and the open door into cool fresh air and night in the courtyard, and there was Tonnerre waiting for me like I'd dreamed, Tonnerre with Bernadette safe on his back.

But that bloody bell was still banging and soldiers already running into the courtyard to see what was up. As I leapt on to Tonnerre I heard a shot zing past me and saw men firing down from the windows. The soldiers in the courtyard took cover in the confusion, it was our chance and we grabbed it. Charlot was taking off already with Jeanette, Stefan was screaming 'Go, go!' while ahead of me André urged Héros to the gallop, with Anne clinging on behind him. She was straddling the beast like a man and so was Bernadette, I didn't need to worry about her, I could just get my head down and bloody charge.

And I did, we all did, André was even shouting it as he pounded through the panicked infantry and on to the drive. He wasn't firing the signal, there'd been enough shots from the windows to alert fifty Gaspards and I just hoped like hell he was ready. We were out of range of the château, no one was mounted to come after us, we were home and free except for that bloody gate. I fixed my eyes on the lodge in the distance and prayed.

A crack of yellow light ahead of us, and I still wasn't sure, it might be us being shot at, but then another and another, and men fleeing the gate in panic. It was open, standing wide open and the horsemen on the other side were Gaspard and Crespin. Spanish soldiers came pouring out of the hut opposite the lodge, but Crespin waved his hat and more shots broke out, one, two, three in quick succession, then a fourth at their retreating backs. Stefan had done a good job of training our musketeers.

We were nearly there. A shot barked from the lodge and Henne jerked in the saddle, his horse rearing in panic, but Charlot swerved to get a hand to the bridle and drag the beast after his own, Henne still hunched on its back. Another long barrel poked out as we drew level, but something roared right behind me and it disappeared. A pistol clattered on the road beside me, Bernadette slipped her other arm round me, and I understood. The musketeers fired again, the lodge went silent and we galloped clean past it, through the gate and on to the road with woods ahead of us, woods and beyond them open country, I dug in my heels and rode on.

We went through Ossu like a forest fire. We were too many to stop, too fast to shoot at, and no one could even be sure who we were. We passed a few soldiers on half-hearted picket duty, but all I remember was the blur of white faces below us as we charged by. We galloped straight through the village and out of it, then we were back at the turning to farmland, and suddenly there were night-blue fields of waving crops on both sides.

There was no one coming after us. We picked our way more steadily down the track, and I became aware of little noises about me, the creaking of saddles, the high trill of nightbirds and the soft brushing of wind over the fields. As we cleared the trees of the little wood I looked up and saw the moon. Its pale light outlined the tips of the corn stalks and shimmered whitely on a flat surface in the distance, making it glisten like a river in summer. It was the little road that divided the fields, and as Tonnerre finally crossed it I knew the ground under his hooves was France.

No, Abbé, I didn't think it very likely the dons would cross the border after us, but if they did I wanted them to see nothing but empty roads and the whole of France in front of them.

So we stopped for the night at Malassise. The barn wasn't the most comfortable of billets, but we'd left our heavy baggage there and it didn't take much to make it like home. I tended to the wounded first, but there weren't very many, I'm glad to say. My own hide was intact, and there wasn't a mark on Lelièvre's men, not one between them. He'd got the gate open by presenting his papers and saying he'd come back as ordered, then my musketeers simply lurked in the shadows and took pot-shots to stop them shutting it. Nice work if you can get it.

The one I was worried about was Henne. It had looked like a chest-hit to me, but when I got the coat off him I found the wily bugger was wearing his Spanish cuirass underneath. Oh, he took a lot of ribbing, but the fact is the plate had all but stopped the bullet and it was hard to argue with that. He said confidentially 'I like to be safe, Messieurs,' and carefully stowed the dented armour in his bundle to show his admiring friends back home.

Grimauld was another matter. He'd a pike-wound to the thigh which I cleaned and dressed, but a quick look at his other leg showed a nasty break above the ankle. The bone had already been twisted and crushed, I thought this might be a chance to get a decent surgeon to set the thing right, but there wasn't much I could do for him now but strap it comfortably and give him brandy for the pain. He liked that part of it all right, he clung on to my flask and sucked at it like his mother's breast.

The rest were easy, and young Bernadette helped with the dressings. Anne's was a pity, she was going to have a scar on that lovely white arm, which was one more little item Bouchard was going to have to pay for in the end, but she said listlessly it didn't matter, she always kept it covered anyway because of the scar on her wrist. I told her she was obviously hanging around with the wrong men, and earned a nasty little kick from André for my pains.

He was a mess himself, of course, but none of it was going to be fatal. The cut to his neck was bad, I gave it a couple of stitches and hoped for the best, but the rest weren't going to spill anything important. The one on the forehead might scar, but I told him a man wasn't a man without d'Estrada's mark on his face somewhere.

He looked darkly at me. 'You shouldn't have tripped him, it was cheating.'

I mopped the blood off his chest. 'You weren't going to beat him otherwise, you know that as well as I do.'

He thought about it. 'Well, he wasn't going to beat me either, so we'll just have to settle it next time.'

There's always a next time for people like André. I patched up the rest of him and kept my mouth firmly shut.

But we hadn't done badly this time, and the only man lost was Philibert. Jeanette was weeping for him, and Jacques not much better, but the one really moping was Anne. For the little Gascon, for her worthless brother, for the wounds on the rest of us, and all on the usual womanly grounds of it being her fault. She'd been strong enough all this time, but now it was over she sat huddled in André's cloak like a feeble little girl.

Lelièvre eyed her thoughtfully and opened another bottle of wine. 'We should celebrate, my friends,' he said. 'Yes, we mourn our losses, but we have snatched the bride from under the nose of the pig Bouchard, we have taken on a whole nest of Spaniards and won.'

Anne shook her head. 'It's not what we set out to do. You've all been so brave and done so much, but because of me it's been for nothing. If André had gone after the treaty and not had to rescue me . . .'

André wrapped his arm round her shoulders. 'Is that really what you wish I'd done?'

She looked up at him, and suddenly couldn't say a word.

'Well then,' he said, giving her a little squeeze. 'Don't ever say it was for nothing.'

Grimauld cleared his revolting throat. There was definitely more colour in his face, and I was willing to bet my flask was that much lighter too. 'That's right, laddie,' he said importantly. 'Young Philibert weren't a hero for nothing. He kept them soldiers busy enough to buy me time.'

'Time for what?' I said, firmly removing my flask from his clutching fingers.

He pulled a sheaf of papers out of his coat and chucked them on the floor. 'That,' he said, nodding at them. 'Them papers there.'

Jacques de Roland

The sheet on top had the flamboyant signature of Fontrailles, and below it one I could hardly believe I was seeing. 'Philip', it said, just 'Philip'. The King of bloody Spain.

André touched it with his fingertips to be sure it was real. 'But this . . . Grimauld, this is . . .'

I turned over a page, then another to be sure. Next came a couple of newer sheets in a different script that clearly weren't part of the treaty itself, but as I pushed them aside a name flashed out at me, one I knew better than anyone because it was my own. De Roland.

It was a formal agreement drawn up in Bouchard's name. His signature came first on a huge list with d'Estrada's as witness, but above the names came a long paragraph describing services they'd all rendered, and one was to give evidence against André, Chevalier de Roland. It didn't say 'lie our bloody heads off' but it might as well have done, you don't get paid for speaking the truth. I realized the value of what I was holding, and when I remembered how nearly we hadn't gone back for Grimauld my head went dizzy.

André was poring over the long treaty, reading bits out and exclaiming. Cinq-Mars was named in a contre-lettre, so was Bouillon, and the King's own brother Gaston d'Orléans. He scrunched his hands in his hair and stared at it in amazement.

'It's everything the Cardinal could possibly want.' He looked up at us, eyes shining in the candlelight. 'You know what you've done, all of you? You've saved France.'

I took a deep breath and held out the other agreement. 'This one clears you, André. This is your pardon.'

He turned very slowly, the brightness gradually fading from his face. I said 'Here, have a look,' and shoved it into his hand.

He looked at me with wide, dark eyes, then lowered his head to read. It seemed to take him a long time. At last he looked up and into the darkness at nothing. 'You're right,' he said. 'This should do it. Richelieu will . . . We'll get this one to Richelieu too.'

He stood up abruptly, and took a single step towards Grimauld. He said 'You did it, you old bastard,' and laid his hand lightly on his shoulder.

'Payday, Chevalier?' said Grimauld happily.

'Payday,' he said, and turned away. 'I'll see to the horses, they'll need feeding and watering, someone's got a long ride to the Cardinal at Noyons.'

He went out, leaving an odd kind of hole in the barn and a silence no one liked to break. Then Stefan stretched out a long leg and prodded me with his boot. 'What are you waiting for, stable boy?'

I got up and went after André.

He was in the smaller barn getting nosebags on the horses, but there was a clumsy impatience in the way he was working, and when Crespin's mare tossed her head he tugged roughly on the bridle to bring her back.

'Careful,' I said, and fondled her ears.

He turned for another bag. 'Did you read that paper, Jacques?'

'Yes,' I said. 'It couldn't be better.'

'Better.' He was overfilling the bag, the poor horse was going to have oats up its nose. 'Did you see whose name it was in?'

I took the bag off him and removed a fistful of fodder. 'It wasn't personal, just politics.'

He made a furious noise and snatched another bag. 'Politics! It wasn't Fontrailles made them all lie, it was Bouchard. All this, the *amende honorable*, Anne, it was that bloody blond bastard and all because I fucking beat him.' The oats were spilling between his fingers.

I dropped my own bag and gripped his wrists. 'It's all right, André. It's over.'

His arms stayed rigid. 'I've got to get him, Jacques. I've just got to. I've got to . . .'

His breathing was suddenly harsh and jagged, his shoulders

straining, his wrists tightened under my fingers as his hands clenched. The next breath came as a gasp, then there was voice in it and I knew.

I dropped his wrists and grappled him into my arms. I was ready for resistance but there wasn't any, he clutched me like to stop himself falling, one arm smack round my shoulders, the other crushing hard against my back. I squeezed him back till I could hardly breathe with it, and for a moment we simply clung to each other in the dark. His breathing slowed, caught, then slowed again, and gradually I felt him relax. Everything was quiet around us except for the stolid munching of horses. I rested my forehead against his, but we neither of us spoke a word, because there wasn't a single thing left in the world to say.

Twenty-Seven

Stefan Ravel

It was a start. We'd got thousands of pissed-off Spaniards just across the border, but admit it, Abbé, it was a fucking good start.

We didn't waste it either. De Chouy caught up with Richelieu on the 11th, and I'm told the man practically got off his deathbed and danced. Personally I didn't care if he performed a fucking ballet as long as it was out of our hands. Oh yes, Bouchard was our affair, André would have killed the Cardinal himself if he'd tried to lay hands on him, but the rest were for Richelieu and he was welcome to them.

And by Christ he had them. He got word to the King on the 12th, and next day they arrested Cinq-Mars himself. It was all very discreet, nothing to alarm anyone while Richelieu scooped up the rest. Fontrailles was on to it, he slipped out of Narbonne the night before it blew, but Bouillon was so unsuspicious they got him mid-shag in a barn at Casale. Orléans was cannier, but even he couldn't wriggle his way out of his name on that treaty. The King was beginning to think that executing a Bourbon might not be such a bad idea after all, and poor old Gaston was forced to do the usual and drop everyone in it but himself.

De Chouy hung about Lyons while the trial was going on, but I can't say we had much interest in it. Bouchard was still in Flanders and unlikely to be tempted out for a while, so we packed Anne off to the Comtesse for the sake of propriety and went back to our cosy little hidey-hole at the Porchiers to wait it all out.

The Spaniards did the same. All that panic over Honnecourt, and they never put a foot over the border the whole summer. Oh yes, we knew why, de Melo had been so confident of his invitation he'd scattered his troops all over the Rhineland, he'd have struggled to muster two tercios by the time he knew no one was asking him anywhere.

It wouldn't stop him another time, we knew that too, but I imagined it would take a little while before he found another ally to help him get rid of Richelieu. And yes, dear Abbé, there's your proof that even Stefan Ravel doesn't think of everything.

He didn't know everything either. There were some surprising things came out at the trial, such as the attempt to assassinate Richelieu that rumour said the King himself had approved. Oh, fuck knows, I can only tell you the whole thing stank. Bouillon kept his head in return for ceding the Sedan, Orléans got away with publicly rapped knuckles, and Fontrailles was permitted to exile himself at his family estate. The only people executed were a young innocent called de Thou and poor Cinq-Mars himself.

Me, I didn't give a toss, I was only waiting for them to do something important like clearing André's name. He needed that pardon, Abbé, he needed the freedom to go after the bastards who really needed their heads detaching, but naturally Richelieu wanted to deal with his own little vendettas first, and it wasn't till mid-October that the Comte brought news.

It was a grey day, I remember, the rain hadn't let up all morning and André and Jacques were fencing in the barn. It was quite spectacular when they did it indoors, Abbé, a man needed to tuck himself well out of the way while they flung themselves about, leaping and charging and bouncing off the walls. Oh, I still used to watch them, other opportunities for entertainment being somewhat limited in a field of sprouts. Grimauld did too, he'd lounge in the straw making unhelpful suggestions, furtively scratching under his leg cast when he thought I wasn't looking. Bernadette always watched. She'd sit with her knees drawn under her chin and her arms tight round them, saying 'Go on, Jacques, go on, you can beat him,' in a voice she probably thought was under her breath.

Charlot had the watch that day, poor bugger, he was sodden with rain when he squelched through the door to announce the Comte. That wasn't too funny at his age, so I nobly volunteered to take over while he dried himself off, but I'd hardly taken a step to the door when the Comte raised an imperious hand and said 'That won't be necessary.'

He made a strange figure in that barn. He was heavily shrouded in his fur-lined cloak, a masked and huddled creature facing two flushed and sweaty young men in their shirtsleeves, but there wasn't much doubt where the power lay. He held out a paper almost invisible under important red seals, and said 'You won't need a guard now, Chevalier. You're a free man.'

André didn't exactly cheer, I don't remember him speaking at all, but there was something about the way he wiped his face with his sleeve and laid his sword carefully down in the straw that I thought said rather a lot. He took the paper, broke the seals, and read it aloud.

He was pardoned. Not cleared, I noticed, the King didn't seem desperately well disposed towards the people who'd made him execute his own favourite, but it was at least a pardon. André got his property back and was graciously permitted to go wherever he wished in His Majesty's realm.

'It's not much,' said Jacques depressingly. 'It doesn't even admit he's innocent.'

The Comte turned the blue beak in his direction. 'They need to be discreet, surely you understand that?'

Jacques looked mulish. 'People might go on thinking things.'

The Comte's defensiveness gave its own answer. 'What if they do? Everyone who matters will know the truth. Bouchard's been banished, so has d'Arsy, everyone who signed that document.'

André looked up from the paper. 'Even the Baron? Anne's father?'

'No exceptions,' said the Comte. 'But in consideration of Anne's loyalty she's to be allowed to keep the confiscated property herself. You'll be marrying a rich woman, André.'

André gave him the predictable glare. 'You think I care about that?'

'No,' said the Comte, and smiled. 'Why don't you come back with me now and see her?'

André picked up his shabby coat and shoved the letter into a pocket. 'I'm not going to Paris, Uncle. Not even to see Anne.'

The Comte made a huffing noise. 'Now that's just childish.'

'Perhaps,' said André, pulling down his shirtsleeves. 'But I said I wouldn't, and until they can find a way of undoing the *amende honorable* I'm not going to. Anne knows that, we've decided to marry in Dax.' He began to put on his coat.

Jacques reached for his own. Bernadette stood to brush the straw from her skirts, and even Grimauld made feeble heroic movements to at least sit upright. I picked up my hat.

The Comte looked round in confusion, then back at André. 'Where are you going now, for heaven's sake? I've brought the carriage to take you back.' He turned to Charlot for support, but the big valet was sticking his own soggy hat back on his head, and only gave him a deferential bow.

André buttoned his coat. 'I'm a free man now, Monseigneur? I can go wherever I like?'

The Comte looked at him, and I'll swear he was starting another smile. 'Yes, Chevalier.'

'Good,' said André, reaching for his hat. 'Then I'm going to find Bouchard.'

Jacques de Roland

We based ourselves in Dax. It was right on the Artois border, the perfect place to start looking, and more than anything else it was home.

For the first time we could stay openly together without doing stupid stuff like hiding in vegetable carts. Crespin hung about Paris for news of Bouchard, but the rest of us lived at the manor, even bloody Stefan who had a perfectly good house of his own. Bernadette stayed with Mother for the look of things but actually I think she liked it, it was sort of like having a home of her own. You remember my mother, she hated making decisions about anything, but Bernadette used to just take the pan out of her hand and say 'No, today we are going to make an omelette because Jacques likes them.' Mother used to look at her in awe.

Anne couldn't stay at the manor, of course, she was Dame of Verdâme and lived in her own château, but André still visited every day. They were very proper about it, they always had chaperones and things, but we hoped it wouldn't be for long. They were planning a spring wedding, which we thought gave us lots of time to deal with Bouchard.

But finding him was harder than we'd expected. When the boy was on the run I felt he'd be caught any minute, I didn't see how they could miss him, but now it was our turn to be the hunters it seemed the most impossible task there'd ever been. The Comtesse wrote to friends in England and Rome, but they said Bouchard wasn't in any of the obvious places that exiles head for. Crespin heard nothing at court, and Stefan got nowhere with old soldiers in Amiens and Abbeville. Charlot managed to track down some of his old servants, but all they knew was that they hadn't been paid. André, Gaspard and I went over the border to get friendly with Walloons in Sus-St-Léger, but no one had heard anything about a fair-haired Frenchman with odd eyes. We even carried Grimauld to Lucheux to talk to some mysterious people he said sometimes 'knew things', but nothing came of that except him getting pissed. No one knew anything at all.

I was starting to wish I'd killed Bouchard in the chapel when I'd had the chance, but André said 'I have to kill him myself, Jacques, I'm dishonoured for ever if I don't.' I did understand, I mean it's shameful to let anyone insult you without fighting them, but what Bouchard had done was far worse. He'd destroyed André's reputation and humiliated him in public, he'd even taken a sword to the woman he loved. If André didn't kill him he couldn't hold his head up anywhere, not even in Dax. We kept on bloody looking.

We'd got one last chance, and that was Anne's father. The Comtesse's friends said he was in Rome, so Anne kept writing and sending him money in the hope of a reply. I wouldn't have bothered myself, I mean he'd signed that paper, he was as bad in his way as Bouchard, but she said he'd never understood that what he was doing was wrong. I remembered the du Pré carriages rolling into the courtyard at Éspehy with their crest blazing openly on the panels, and thought she might even be right.

In November he finally replied. I guess he was pretty snotty, Anne said he still couldn't see why he was being blamed for a simple political arrangement, but he did tell her that Bouchard was in Flanders with d'Estrada. That sounded odd to us, I mean the coup had failed, there was no reason for him to be still hanging round the army, but the Baron seemed sure, he'd heard it from fellow exiles.

Flanders is still a big place, and not even Gaspard could wander over all of it asking for d'Estrada. We needed proper military information, so André simply wrote to Richelieu and asked. I thought we'd a good chance, actually, I mean Richelieu owed us something, he'd have been dead or banished by now if it wasn't for us. Crespin took the letter himself, and we waved him off feeling full of hope.

I remember the day he came back. It was the first week in December and Grimauld was trying to walk round the terrace for the first time. His leg had healed much straighter since being reset but it didn't stop him leaning heavily on André and swearing horribly at every step. I was sat on one of the stone benches, feeling the cold seeping through my breeches and thinking 'One more round then I'm going indoors.'

Sound carries further in a frost, and I heard hooves on the drive long before we saw Crespin. He spotted us on the terrace, reined to a skidding stop and dismounted on the gravel. Then he took off his hat.

'What's happened?' said André, dumping Grimauld on the bench. 'Crespin, what is it?'

He said simply 'The Cardinal.'

It wasn't till I heard the tolling of the bell of St Sebastian's that I understood. For a second I just thought 'That's a bugger, now we can't find Bouchard,' then I remember the blankness as the real shock hit. No one was bigger than Richelieu, he couldn't just die. But there was and he had, and Spain had found another ally after all.

Carlos Corvacho

Now, that was more like it, Señor. The old devil was gone, if you'll excuse the expression, and France had lost her own head. 'No more dealing with traitors, Carlos,' says my Capitán joyfully. 'We can go back to good clean war.'

He'd had enough of politics. You'd never credit it, but there were people blaming that treaty business on my Capitán his own self, as if he'd ever wanted to be involved in their dirty dealings in the first place. One of our guests bringing the French in, another committing murder, well I ask you, it's not what a gentleman expects. We were all for throwing Bouchard out on a dung heap where he belonged, but the Conde-Duque said he'd something else in mind and made us keep him and M. d'Arsy round our necks all winter.

Not that it looked like mattering now we were going back to war. The Conde-Duque wanted the pressure off Catalonia and the French kept out of the Franche-Comté, so a campaign in northern France seemed just the thing to distract them. The reports were coming in very tasty too. Your new First Minister, this Cardinal Mazarin, he'd left all the northern forts under strength, and given the command to a mere boy. The Duc d'Enghien, Señor, barely twenty-one, and little more experience than Arras and Perpignan.

De Melo made his plans. We'd enter through the Ardennes, but we wouldn't repeat the failures of the past, Señor, we were going to take a fortress to make a base in France herself. Now that's a tricky business and de Melo knew it, he didn't want another Corbie we could only hold till the winter. 'We'll give them a governor France will accept,' he says. 'We'll give them a son of Montmorency.'

My poor gentleman, he's stuck again, lumbered with Bouchard and his hangers-on to nursemaid through the whole campaign. All I can hope is we take the fort quick and get rid of him before my Capitán loses control and duels the man his own self.

At least de Melo's already chosen the place, a fort close to the border with a garrison under a thousand. Nicely fortified, I'm bound to say, star-shaped before your Vauban ever came near it, but de Melo says we'll take it in a week, install Bouchard and move on. My Capitán hears those last words and says 'Yes' with as much enthusiasm as I've ever heard. That's the only advantage I see in it myself, Señor, a rustic bit of nowhere I wouldn't spend an evening in for choice.

'Never heard of it,' says Bouchard, examining his glass for finger-marks. 'Now Amiens, perhaps, or Doullens . . .'

'Precisely, Monseigneur,' says my Capitán. 'We would never endanger your person by placing you somewhere even this Mazarin would feel compelled to relieve.'

Bouchard swills his Jerez in his mouth before swallowing it. 'Well, perhaps. We have friends in Champagne, of course, and can count on a high degree of support.'

'And can encourage more,' says my Capitán. 'We thought of printing handbills for the populace.' He hands the brute the papers, and I see him wiping his hands when he's done it.

Bouchard studies them complacently, as well he might, them all being heroic captions over pictures of his own self. 'Not bad,' he says, 'but I think I can do better. Perhaps I'd better speak to your artist.'

'You have something special in mind?' says my Capitán, ringing the bell in haste to be rid of him.

The animal smiles. 'Oh yes,' he says, throwing me his empty glass to catch, yes, Señor, throwing it as if closer contact would give him plague. 'I've thought of something that might be rather fun.'

Anne du Pré

Extract from her diary, dated 16 April 1643

It may be wicked, but I would like to see Bouchard *burn in hell*.

Today was always going to be hard. The Comte and Comtesse have arrived to stay until the wedding, and today they took us to the notary in Lucheux to sign the papers. We had Jacques with us to make it a family occasion, but André was still dreading it. He has avoided the towns for months, and I knew he was afraid people would sneer.

Even the carriage was an ordeal. He had not been in one since that terrible journey out of Paris, and I knew from the way he looked at it that the associations still linger. He sat beside me as tense as if he were about to enter a fight, and when the door was shut on us I felt his arm quiver against my own. Beneath my cloak I let my fingers find his and we held hands all the way.

The Comte sat opposite, his eyes flicking between us behind the mask. At last he said 'Come on, Chevalier. It doesn't matter if people look, does it?'

André gazed out of the window. 'It depends how.'

The Comte smiled faintly. 'No, it doesn't. You'll get used to it.'

André's fingers felt stiff in mine. 'I've no intention of getting used to it.'

The Comte settled back into his blanket. 'Then you're a fool. Just ignore it, André. It's the only way, you'll see.'

André's mouth tightened. He leaned back in his seat with half-closed eyes and did not speak another word.

Jacques de Roland

We had to walk through the crowds to get to the notary's. André's shoulders were all hunched and defensive, and when a woman bawled next to him he shied like a nervous horse, but no one took the slightest notice and gradually he got less bristly and more like himself.

The signing seemed to help too, he and Anne were looking soppily at each other all the way back. The Comtesse took us to wait inside St Léger's while Charlot fetched the carriage, but André and Anne lingered to look at market stalls as if the other two hundred people weren't there at all.

There's not much to see in St Léger's except statues and paintings of him with his head off, so after a while I wandered out myself. Someone was selling trussed-up chickens by the porch, all squawking and flapping and scattering little brown feathers, but beyond them I saw a bunch of people clustered round a handbill on the wall. The murmur of their voices drifted over the clucking chickens, and then someone said the name 'de Roland'.

I remember moving very slowly towards them. People parted for me politely, but the ones in front kept their noses to the handbill and went on talking like I wasn't there. A woman said 'I don't know, I've heard he was innocent,' a man with a high voice said 'All the more shameful. No gentleman should take such a thing lying down,' then a porter said 'Didn't, though, did he? Took it on his knees like an Abbeville whore.'

The paper was in front of me. Broad black letters spelt out *'Dieu aide le premier Chrétien baron!'* which was the old war-cry of the Montmorencies, but I was being hit in the face by the picture. Bouchard was standing with his hair swirling round him and an upraised sword in his hand, but kneeling in the dirt at his feet was André. The picture blurred and bulged in front of me, the Place de Grève, André in his shirt, the faces of the crowd, I watched my own hand reaching out and grasping at it, making a fist to rip the whole thing off the wall.

'Hey,' said a man behind me. 'I haven't seen that yet.'

I turned away with the bill. A woman protested 'Put that back!' but others were muttering and shushing, I heard the name 'Vallon' and looked up to see the Comte in front of me, my grandmother on his arm.

He said 'What is it, boy?'

I hesitated, but he just clicked his tongue and held out his hand for the paper. They bent their heads over it together, then the Comte muttered 'Dear Christ.'

I said bitterly 'You still think he should get used to it?'

He looked up so suddenly I had to step back. His eyes burned at me from behind the mask.

'Never mind that,' said the Comtesse, her voice clipped with urgency. 'Where's the Chevalier? What will he do if he sees it?'

I knew exactly what he'd do, and so did she. He'd fight, he'd have to, I'd got to find him and stop him. I looked frantically round the parvis but people were milling about in front of me, faces blurring, backs in my way, flashes of market stalls, and in the distance angry voices. It wasn't a crowd, it was a mob, and somewhere in the middle of it was the boy.

Anne du Pré

We were only looking at the flowers. André insisted on buying me a basket of pink and blue anemones, and when I pointed out he had flowers as good at Ancre he said only 'These are here and so are you.'

A voice behind said 'Lilies would be more appropriate,' and someone laughed.

André did not hear, he never does when his back is turned, but like a *fool* I allowed my face to betray me and then of course he looked round.

Three elegant young men lounged against the stall consulting a handbill. They returned André's look of enquiry with knowing smiles, and one even sniggered.

André's face changed. 'You wish to address me?'

'Not I,' said the one who had laughed. His moustache was a thin black line that curved upwards as he smiled. 'We admire the façade, that is all.'

André said 'You permit?' and extended his hand for the paper. It was his left hand, and I did not have to look to know where the other would be. His happiness was all gone and in its place was the hardness I remembered from the Parvis Notre-Dame.

'Of course,' said the youngest-looking of the men, handing it over with a smile. 'There are plenty to be had about the town.'

André looked at the bill, and for a moment the parvis seemed to recede into a blur of gaudy colour so that I saw only him, standing alone in utter stillness, his hands clenched tight on the paper, his cheek a sudden painful crimson which faded only slowly to white. Then he looked up.

The faces of the others shifted suddenly into sharp relief as they moved. The first straightened so fast he dislodged a basket of narcissus from the stall, the second stepped abruptly backwards, and the third clapped his hand to his sword.

'Where did you get this?' said André, and I did not know his voice.

It was the one with the thin moustache who answered. 'An inn somewhere. An inn. There's no crime.'

The voice of the man with the sword was louder than the others. 'Or if there is, it's not ours.'

André swung round on him. 'Do you say it is mine?' The paper dropped to the ground as his left hand slid to his scabbard.

I could see none of our friends in the crowd, no one to intervene and save him. I moved to his side and said 'André,' but he did not even turn. He saw nothing but the man and the sword and the chance to fight his own shame. He said again fiercely 'Do you say it is mine?'

'Perhaps,' said another voice. A plainly dressed gentleman stepped from the crowd, holding a copy of what looked like the same bill. 'This is Picardie, this monstrosity shames us all. Do you know it is to be seen by our neighbours in Champagne?'

André flushed. 'And you would blame me for that?'

'It's you, isn't it?' said a woman at the lace stall. 'That's you on your knees to a Montmorency?'

André swung round again but he could not fight a woman, least of all when what she said was truth. 'It was the King's order . . .'

'King's order!' said the man with the little moustache, finding courage among so many allies. 'A gentleman would die before doing such a thing.'

They were baiting him, he was turning round and round like a bear at a fair and meeting with nothing but derision. Again I moved towards him, but people were pressing up behind me, something banged into the back of my knee, I stumbled and half fell, my basket of flowers flying out of my hands to scatter on the stones.

People said 'Shame!' and a gentleman assisted me to rise, but André had already seen it and was half mad with fury. He whirled back on his accusers and now his sword was out and in his hand.

'Is this your honour?' he said. 'In God's name –'

'Honour?' said the loud-voiced man. 'This Montmorency's still alive, isn't he? One can only wonder –'

'How long for?' said a deep voice behind me.

Relief snatched away my breath as I saw it was the Comte himself, standing tall and straight as if he had never huddled into a blanket in his life.

He said 'Because the creature hides himself, do you question the courage of my nephew?' and his black-gloved hand rested openly on his sword.

Jacques de Roland

I'd heard of him, Hugo, Comte de Vallon, one of the deadliest swordsmen in Paris, and now here he was, like an old legend coming to life. He spoke in my father's voice, he stood and even looked like him, and my chest swelled with pride.

André felt it too, it flashed on his face as he spun round, but there was something else underneath it, an uncertainty like fear. He said in a low voice 'Monseigneur, I beg –'

'No, Chevalier,' said the Comte, pitching his voice to the crowd. 'These men have insulted my family, this is my quarrel now.'

That got them, that bloody got them, everyone knows what's meant by 'quarrel'. The crowd backed off at once, and I didn't blame them. Even if one of them had the guts to fight André, whoever seconded would have to take my uncle, and there wouldn't be two swordsmen like that here, there wouldn't be two like them anywhere.

But the loud-voiced man seemed determined not to lose face. He leaned against the stall, pushed back his hat, and said 'I seek no quarrel. I merely asked a question to which I have yet to receive an answer.'

There bloody wasn't one and he must have known it. Of course we knew Bouchard had got to be killed, it wasn't André's fault he wasn't dead already, but there aren't any excuses for a gentleman. It was stupid and unfair, the frustration on André's face was suddenly boiling inside my own head, I'd got to relieve it or burst.

I stepped forward and stood at my uncle's side. I couldn't remember the proper stance, but found my body sort of doing it for me, my feet square like a fencing lesson, my hip already tilted and the hilt of my sword brushing my hand like an invitation.

I said 'What right have you to question the Chevalier de Roland?'

I was nobody really, but the crowd still murmured and more of them sloped away. André looked at me, his eyes went bang on mine, and suddenly I wasn't nobody, I knew exactly who I was and all I wanted was the chance to prove it. I looked back to the man causing the trouble and something inside me was saying 'Draw, you bastard, draw.'

He licked his lips. 'None, Monsieur. My concern was for the family's reputation, for which I naturally have great respect.'

'And you doubt is in safe hands?' said the Comte, unmoving. Behind us I heard the Comtesse muttering 'Good, Hugo, *good*.'

'Not I,' said the man quickly. 'I wish the Chevalier godspeed in his quest and assure him he has all Picardie behind him.'

'Behind him,' said the Comte, his mouth twisting in amusement. 'Quite so.'

The crowd rippled with laughter. The man coloured with irritation, but he was practically on his own now, his friends were already retreating. He said stiffly 'Then we are in agreement,' made the quickest bow I've ever seen, and turned to follow the others.

I felt oddly flat for a moment. I'd loved the feeling of the three of us standing together, I'd wanted it to go on, but they were all bloody going and it was over. Then I looked round at André sheathing his sword and knew we'd done what we needed to, there was no trace of that awful lonely desperation I'd seen when we first arrived. He squeezed both our hands, said 'For God's sake, Uncle, what if they'd called you on it?' and went past us to Anne.

I was puzzled. I said 'We'd have fought, wouldn't we?'

My uncle grimaced. 'I'd have tried.' He saw my blank expression, sighed, took my hand and guided it to his upper arm. 'Here, feel that.'

He had a coat on and something beneath it like a padded gambeson, my fingers were sinking through for ages before I felt anything hard. His arm was like a stick.

'That's right,' he said. 'I'd have been sliced veal if it had come to it.'

He patted my arm and swung away to the Comtesse, saying 'Now then, Mother, the show's over, where's the damned carriage?' He walked with such confidence, the beautiful rapier jingling cheerfully at his hip, but I felt only an awful sadness as I began to understand.

I looked for André to share it with, but he was standing by Anne and I saw with alarm he was poring over that vile handbill. I shot up to him and said 'Give it here, André. Let's burn it and forget it.'

'Forget it?' said André. His head came up, but there wasn't the fury I'd expected, he looked almost excited. 'Jacques, have you read this? Do you see what it means?'

I said 'It means Bouchard's a bastard and we already knew that.'

'But to plant posters about it in Picardie?' he said. 'Don't you see? No more hiding in Flanders, Jacques, the bastard's *coming out*.'

So he was, Abbé, but unfortunately not alone. The poster claimed France's exiled heroes were returning to bring peace and prosperity to the world, which was all very fine and uplifting until you realized 'heroes' meant 'traitors' and 'the world' meant 'Spain'.

Oh come on, think about it. Even exiles like Guise hadn't the muscle for a comeback like this, and Bouchard hadn't enough to get in the gate of Amiens. Someone was backing them, and it wasn't hard to guess who. André'd always said Spain would never give up, and for once in his life he was right.

Yes, yes, we checked it. The countryside was slathered in these papers, so we talked to every innkeeper displaying one. They said the man who brought them was foreign, some even said half-Spanish, but two went further and gave us a name. Corvacho, Abbé. Carlos Corvacho, the little friend and bedmaker of Don Miguel d'Estrada. That irritatingly persistent bastard was at it again.

It was imminent too. There were other things moving in Champagne that spring, and one was the young Duc d'Enghien. In our little hunting trips for Bouchard the one thing we heard loud and clear was that he'd got the army of Picardie strung out along the Champagne border between Albert and Saint Quentin. We weren't the only ones expecting invasion.

That put a different colour on it. I'd as soon be wringing Bouchard's fat neck as not, but if he was in the middle of an invading Spanish army I could see a rather more worthwhile target right there. There was only one obvious way we could get near either of them, so the Comte trotted off to Brichanteau at the Picardie to ask if he'd a place for André de Roland among his Gentleman Volunteers, along with a few assorted followers such as my good self.

I admit I was looking forward to it. Oh, it was all very comfortable lounging around at Ancre, and almost worth it to see the look on Jacques' face when I stuck my feet on the furniture, but I'm a soldier, Abbé, there was a campaign to be fought and that's what I do best. Grimauld felt the same. Jacques and Charlot fussed about organizing horses and a wagon, Lelièvre sat down to polish his pearl-handled pistols, while André sharpened his sword and whistled.

Then the Comte came back. I'd love to have heard how tactfully they'd put it, but the gist seemed to be that the Picardie needed to be careful of its reputation, and there were a few 'uncertainties' about André's recent history. Oh, fuck knows, maybe because he'd never been publicly cleared, maybe because he still hadn't avenged Bouchard's insults, who knows how the nobility think? I only know that if I'd ever doubted Bouchard was worth it, André's pinched face as his uncle said the Picardie wouldn't have him was enough to put steel in a Carmelite.

We waited till the Comte and Comtesse had retired then slipped over to the château for a council of war. It was quite a little problem we had now, winkling Bouchard out of the ranks of the Spanish army without the slightest help from our own, but we were every one of us up for it. We sat round a table eating oranges in an atmosphere of pure venom. 'He is a coward, this Bouchard,' said Bernadette, spitting out pips. 'He will not be with the army, Chevalier, you will find him hiding at the back.'

Anne shook her head. 'Not if anyone can see. He has too much pride, that's all he thinks about. That's why he set out to destroy André in the first place.'

'Pride,' said André. He looked up from his plate with a light in his face I found ominously familiar. 'You're right, that's his weak point. So let's hit it.'

André de Roland

Cartel issued to Henri Bouchard, dated 4 May 1643

To HENRI BOUCHARD, who falsely takes to himself the name of MONTMORENCY, and is currently believed HIDING in FLANDERS

Monsieur,

You have defamed my honour and I will meet you to discuss the matter anywhere in Europe you choose to name. You have SEVEN DAYS to respond to the Chevalier de Roland at Dax-en-roi in

Picardie, and fail at peril of being exposed to all France as a LIAR and COWARD.

No man of HONOUR would refuse such an invitation. No man of honour will conceal or harbour a man who does so. Prove your honour by responding, and give me the opportunity TO PROVE MINE.

A. de Roland, Chevalier, Sieur of Dax

Stefan Ravel

It seemed a lot of balls to me. I wasn't even sure it was legal, but André said Bouchard was the non-person now, and no one would mind if he killed him. I rather thought Bouchard might, but knew better than to say so.

De Chouy had hundreds of the things printed off in Paris, and we dutifully trailed round Picardie and Champagne sticking them up everywhere there'd been one of those bills. André and I even rode across the border to Ossu, found an alehouse packed with Spanish soldiers, wrapped the cartel round a stone and smashed it through the window. Childish, possibly, and we had a hell of a race back to Éspehy, but it was the best way of ensuring d'Estrada heard about it, which naturally meant Bouchard would too.

It still didn't fetch him. André watched for couriers like a condemned man waiting for reprieve, but the seven days stretched to ten, then eleven, and no word came at all. I thought we were wasting our time.

And there I was wrong, Abbé, as perhaps I should have guessed. Me more than anyone, as it happened, since I was the only one who'd heard that conversation in the chapel of the Château d'Escaut. I was the only one who could have guessed that if the cartel didn't fetch Bouchard there was a fucking good chance it was going to fetch someone else.

Bernadette Fournier

We were to dine in the manor that night. We did not normally do so while the Comte and Comtesse were staying, but the wedding was only a week away, tomorrow would come grand relatives from Paris, and the Chevalier insisted on spending this night with his friends.

I had only a short walk from the home of Mme Gilbert. It was growing dark as I crossed the lawns but the sound of an approaching horseman did not trouble me, for M. de Chouy was expected from Paris. I waited by the drive to greet him as he arrived.

The figure moved fast down the avenue and I felt a moment's unease. M. de Chouy had tinkling bells on his harness and often sang as he rode, but this man came silently and with purpose. I thought it might be one of the grand relatives arriving a day early and stepped back respectfully, but the rider shouted after me 'You! You there, girl! Wait!'

It was not polite, but such an address is common among gentlemen, so I turned and waited as he reined up on the drive beside me. He bent from his saddle and said 'I need a message taken to de Roland, you can do that, can't you?'

He was little more than a dark shape in the gloom, but I knew the voice now and for a moment could not find my own.

'Are you dumb?' he said, and fumbled inside his coat. 'Here, a silver écu, you know what that is, don't you? I need a message taken to de Roland, I'm too busy to go myself.'

'Or too afraid?' said I. 'You are a fugitive here, M. d'Arsy.'

Oh, but it was good to see his fear. For months I had curtsied and taken the insults of these fine gentlemen, and now it was I who stood erect with a whole estate of important friends behind me while he cringed in his very saddle and said only 'Good God. Bernadette.'

'Good God indeed,' said I. 'You had better leave, Monsieur, before I decide to tell my friends that here is a man who ducked me in a horse trough, and who sat and watched as the Chevalier de Roland paid an *amende honorable* he knew was undeserved.'

He was silent a moment, and I heard only the tired snorting of his mount. At last he said 'All right, be a bitch if you like, but you've a brain about you somewhere, you must have had to fool us so long. Tell de Roland Bouchard is in France with the army of de Melo, they've already crossed into Champagne. He'll be looked after safe somewhere, they're to make him governor of the fort they're taking. De Roland ought to be able to pick him off if he wants.'

He was turning to ride away, but my mind was still in confusion. I seized his bridle and said 'Do you expect me to believe you wish to help the Chevalier?'

'I don't expect anything,' he said. 'What does a woman like you know about honour? But there's the message, take it or not, I've done my best.'

The reins were ripped out of my hand as he turned. I saw the chance disappearing and cried after him 'Where, Monsieur? You have not told me where!'

He checked the horse to look back over his shoulder. 'Some godforsaken town in the Ardennes no one else wants. They call it Rocroi.'

He turned again and galloped away, his horse's hooves pounding faster and fainter into the distance. I stood now with a head as clear as the moonlight and at last the news the Chevalier had sought for so long. This is where it would happen, this is where he would regain his honour.

A place called Rocroi.

Twenty-Eight

Jacques de Roland

We set out at dawn.

Anne herself came to see us off. She knew André might not be back for the wedding, but she helped tighten his horse's girth herself and said only 'I'll be here when you get back. Whenever you get back. You know that, don't you?' He took her behind Héros to kiss her, but none of us blamed him. I felt like bloody kissing her myself.

Even the Comte was there, saying 'Is there anything else I can do? Are you sure?' I understood that better now and felt shit for never seeing it before. I looked at him standing with his chin up like André when he was hurting inside, then slid down off Tonnerre.

I said 'Uncle, will you lend me your sword? André's got our father's, I'd like to carry yours for you, if you'll let me.'

He didn't speak for a moment, then reached down and fumbled with his sword.

I said 'Let me.'

I helped him with the frogs and for a second his gloved fingers touched mine, the leather cold for a second before it was warm with the man beneath. Then he passed me the scabbard and said 'Look after it, will you? It's a good blade.'

I said 'I know,' and he understood. When I got back in the saddle he didn't look small any more, he looked the way he had at Lucheux, tall as my father and standing by my side.

But we'd plenty of men by our side today. Charlot had the Comtesse's permission, but I think he'd have come even if he hadn't. Crespin was there, he'd only got in about three hours ago but looked brighter than anyone and was humming under his breath. Gaspard was there, his hat so low over his face I'm bloody sure he was asleep under it. Stefan was there, smoking his stinking pipe and scowling but at least he was bloody there. Grimauld was there, perched up on Duchesse like he thought she was going to bolt with him, but with the same obstinate look I'd seen when he picked up that axe in the Luxembourg.

We were seven, that's all. But if you've got the right seven that's as good as an army and when we set off into the mist I knew that's just what we were.

Stefan Ravel

Well, if you want to look at it like an amateur. The truth is we were seven innocents riding into a battle zone without the slightest idea what was waiting for us at the other end.

There were clues if we'd looked for them. We headed for Albert where the Picardie had been last time we looked, but it seemed d'Enghien had started the whole lot for Vervins to relieve a rumoured siege at Rocroi. I still wasn't worried. The dons would be out in the open, we ought to be able to pass round the lines and find the man we were after unguarded while his comrades were fighting a battle.

We followed in the army's wake. It was very different from La Marfée, but then it always is when the battle's ahead of you with all the hope in the world. There were no straggling wounded, no crying women and abandoned baggage, only a lot of flattened crops and pissed-off civilians who'd been eaten out of their last winter stores. The only thing the same were the rumours. A one-armed veteran at Moislains said he'd heard the Spanish were thirty thousand strong, and a lot of people were listening.

We spent the night at Éspehy, but there was no mistaking the smell of fear the next day. Sunday and the church bells ringing, the righteous flooding in to pray for deliverance and the rest quietly packing their bags. We passed handcarts rattling along with household possessions piled on top, a mattress, a kettle, a brass dinner bell, and the men pushing them with that old, old look that said

'Why don't you kill each other someplace else and leave us the fuck alone?' Civilians. They wouldn't have had the food in their bellies let alone their sodding dinner bells if it weren't for the army and people like us.

We camped outside Vervins, then ploughed on towards Maubert-Fontaine. There was a lot of traffic round Aubenton and Rumigny, and when we saw heavily guarded wagons in the fields it wasn't hard to guess why. D'Enghien had left the baggage train behind and was pushing on through the woods. We were getting close.

If you're ever looking for a pleasant ride through Champagne, Abbé, you can forget the Forêt de Pothées. Ditches, bogs, up-and-down fucking chasms, it was a nightmare with flies. We were still in the middle of it by late afternoon when we got our first hint of what we were really riding into. A low, distant rumble, and birds flapping out of the trees in alarm. Another, like a thunderstorm getting closer, and that warhorse of Jacques' lifted its head and neighed.

'Guns,' said André.

'Guns,' said Grimauld, and spat. 'That's artillery, laddie, heavy ordnance. That'll be the dons.'

We told ourselves it was only what we'd expected, and went on. We rode maybe another hour and dusk starting to fall, then the sounds ahead of us changed. We were hearing more cannon, but the salvos seemed lighter than before.

'They'll be ours, won't they?' said André, batting the branches out of his face as he rode. 'Our army's got there, they'll turn it round.'

'Not with that kind of firepower they won't,' said Grimauld, who was clearly first cousin to the comforters of Job. 'Hear it? That's not a patch on the first.'

A deep answering boom made the point with depressing emphasis. There are a few things one likes at the start of a battle, and being outgunned isn't one of them.

'That won't stop them,' said André, sweeping aside generations of military experience as if they were more branches. 'That's the army of Picardie ahead of us, you'll see what they can do.'

That was just it, Abbé. I was rather afraid we would.

I'll stop you right there if I may, Señor, and we'll have a few things straight. I know what the French say about Rocroi, but if it's truth you're after let's keep it fair. It wasn't just the Picardie we were up against, we'd half the army of Champagne as well, and us with four thousand of our own men stuck up in Chateau-Regnault with Beck. Now I'm not saying we didn't have a wee bit of an advantage with the artillery, but that's good generalship, Señor, that's planning a campaign in the proper style.

We made gruel of the French lines that night. Two and a half hours we were banging away and my Capitán guesses there's a thousand down at the least. We should have followed it up with steel in my opinion, my Capitán said we should have attacked them while they were still coming down the defile, but de Melo didn't want them driven off, he wanted another Honnecourt. He saw more value in destroying a French army than seizing a little fortress in the middle of nowhere, and with morale what it was going to be in a day or two's time I won't say he wasn't right. Oh, yes, Señor, we knew what had happened in Saint-Germain-en-Laye. We knew before most of the French did, your Duc d'Enghien having decided to keep that touchy little titbit to himself.

So we do nothing till they're all formed up and the guns fall quiet. Some French cavalry try a charge down the far end, but someone orders it back, we shift our infantry along a wee bit, and there we all are, standing with nothing but a strip of valley between us and never a move on either side. The light gets dimmer, the French stand down for the night, and us, we do the selfsame thing. The fires are lit, then the men settle down to eat and sleep right in the lines as if there's no such thing as a French army no more than a few feet away.

We're on the left wing, Señor, back with the Flanders cavalry where we belong. Not that we hadn't still got Bouchard to look after, him and his exiled friends, so we have them set comfortably inside a screen of gabions as if they're precious as cannon. It's no more than a gesture really, seeing as they're cavalry-trained and happy to take their chance alongside us in the morning, but to lose them in a battle's one thing, to have them picked off under our noses while we sleep is quite another. My Capitán doesn't trust the French troops one bit, especially when they're quiet.

'Not too many of them though, are there?' says Bouchard. 'We shouldn't have much difficulty seeing them off.'

'I'm not so sure,' says d'Arsy. 'L'Hôpital knows what he's doing, and we've already had a taste of Gassion. Is General Beck joining us, or do we go it alone?'

It's a fair question, Señor, and our own men asking it already. My Capitán reassures them that de Melo's already sent a message and Beck is expected to join us in the morning, then has me give them wine to keep them quiet and goes back to prowling about the lines his own self.

He's uneasy, Señor, and not the only one that night. De Melo's wandering up and down encouraging the men and leaving them jumpier than he found them. The young Duque of Albuquerque in charge of our own wing, even he's twitching, saying our deployment's more like a parade than a battle order. There's no denying the ground's tricky either, that's an enemy fort at our backs and no lines of circumvallation dug, de Melo being confident we can take the fort without. There was plenty not to like, Señor, and no call for the French moaning we had the advantage from the start.

My Capitán leaves off at last and joins me at the fire for a bite of supper. I'd kept some cold fowl back for him special and it did me good to see him eat it.

I said 'That's right, Señor, you relax now, you've done everything you can.'

He stopped mid-bite. 'Never say that, Carlos. What you mean is I've done everything I can think of.'

It was the selfsame thing in my opinion, but I gave him his wine and said never a word.

Neither did he. He sat sipping his wine, looking round at the men and the horses and the little campfires, seeing it all safe and secure in his head. We were nicely sheltered where we were, Señor, a little wood in front of us like a screen so we couldn't even see the waiting French in front. It was quiet all about us, the rustle and murmur of men sleeping, some of the horses maybe snorting a little, and the wind blowing soft through the trees.

My Capitán turns towards the sounds and his eyes glisten black in the firelight. Then he lets out a little sigh and stands up. 'You think I've thought of everything?'

'Yes, Señor,' I say. 'You always do.'

'Not always,' he says. 'But perhaps I have now.'

Stefan Ravel

What you have to understand is that we weren't looking for a battle. Bouchard was important, so we naturally expected to find him tucked safely behind the Spanish lines a long way from the fighting. It didn't occur to us he might simply have got stuck in it.

We didn't fancy that ourselves, Abbé, so we left the army's tracks and slithered down into the marshes to find a way round the whole lot. It didn't help much. We had to follow the Ruisseau right to its source before we could cross it, and when we emerged from the last straggling trees above Sévigny-la-Forêt and saw what was in front of us I was tempted to turn straight round and go back.

We were looking at a battlefield. It was night, of course, but the two lines were clearly marked by the dots of little fires spread out over the plain. The town of Rocroi was ahead all right, a neat mass of grey stone bastioned walls, but there was something in front of it I didn't care for at all. We'd passed most of the French lines by going through the marshes, but before us was the biggest single enemy force I'd ever seen.

'Spain,' said André, his tone quite expressionless. 'They're back.'

I'm afraid they were. Oh, there'd been Spanish troops at La Mar-fée, but they were mixed in with Imperials and a bunch of Sedanaise, they'd just been 'the enemy', nothing more. Here was the real enemy, right here. The firelight flickered on the planted standards, blue, red, fucking pink, any colour you can think of, but across them all that jagged slash of the Burgundy cross of Spain. We'd been fighting them in the dark for three years now, but here they were, finally out in the open, doing exactly what André said they'd do all along. They were back and invading France.

I whispered 'If you want Bouchard in that lot, little general, you're on your own.'

He dragged his head round as if he'd forgotten I existed. 'What does one man matter in the face of all this?'

I was tempted to agree. When you come to the lines of a great battle, Abbé, you're on the edge of the world.

'Let's at least look,' said Jacques, a man with the imagination of a coal bucket. 'There's a wood ahead, we can spy out the land, see if there's a way behind the lines.'

'I suppose,' said André, but his eyes never left the campfires. He was a soldier, that boy, he should have been with his own kind, not skulking in the night like an assassin. But that was something else Bouchard was responsible for, and I for one wasn't inclined to forgive it.

I said 'We've come this far, let's see if we can get the bastard. On foot, mind, and only three, we don't want anyone getting the wind up and blowing our heads off.'

That was quite a possibility, as it happened, since when two armies sleep this close they tend to be a little careful in the matter of sentries. Charlot led the rest back into cover, then André, Jacques and I proceeded at an undignified crawl past the French right wing. Cavalry, Abbé, I could hear the horses. D'Enghien had gone for a standard formation, with infantry in the middle and wings of cavalry to either side.

It wasn't long before the night thickened, there were dry leaves under my hands, and I knew we were safe in the thicket. It looked dense and dark in the middle, so we kept to the edge and inched our way cautiously up towards the dons. I was hearing more rustling than I had in the open, and a murmur of voices suggested the Spanish lines were closer than we'd thought, so we only went halfway before sticking our heads out for a look.

And there were the dons, illuminated by their campfires like a panorama in flame. I couldn't see more than the left wing immediately in front of us, but that was cavalry too, the same formation as d'Enghien's. There were more tents on this side, dark shapes of baggage wagons and distant siege cannon, but otherwise it might have been the French lines we were looking at all over again. There was just one thing out of place, an enclosure of gabions where you'd expect to find cannon, but with nothing inside but a tent and four men round a little fire. They were chatting in a desultory kind of way, then one lifted his head and laughed.

'André,' whispered Jacques next to me. 'André.'

Oh, he'd seen him, his face had already changed. It was sharper, hungrier, burning eyes beneath dark brows. If Bouchard had been powder he'd have gone up like a battery.

I drew my pistol, but André's hand clamped down on mine. 'I'll kill you if you do.'

Well, it's always nice to know where one stands. I said 'You want us to go and kidnap him so you can fight a fucking duel?'

He looked away. 'I don't want to murder him.'

I did, I'd have done it and taken Mass on the same day. 'Then what?'

He didn't know, poor kid, he'd the will but nothing like the conscience. 'I could go down alone. If d'Estrada's there he'll . . .'

His voice was rising. I got a hand up to warn him, but something was already rustling behind us in the thicket and then a sleepy voice said '¿Qué pasa?'

We weren't alone. I turned my head warily, and dear Christ, the wood was full of them. We'd crept in round the edges, but the centre was one great pile of sleeping soldiers, curled up on the ground like so many twisted roots. Some even sat upright against tree trunks, and in the distance ahead of us were a couple standing sentry.

André's eyes showed white in the dark. 'No es nada,' he said, then something my don-speak isn't up to repeating but that sounded like an attempt at humour. Under other circumstances I'd have found the contrast between his face and voice rather comical, but not right then, Abbé. Not just then.

There was a grunt where the voice had come from, some muttering nearby, then quiet returned. It wasn't total, of course, and I'll admit I did a little cursing of myself for not realizing the rustling wasn't all made by ourselves and the voices weren't all coming from the lines. Now my eyes had adjusted I estimated we'd got several hundred of them around us, making the wood look double the trees.

André whispered 'It's an ambush. We have to warn d'Enghien.'

I was rather more worried about ourselves just then, but either way the priority was to get the fuck out. That didn't look too easy either, since we could hardly crawl back to the French lines right under the noses of several hundred puzzled dons. We'd have to go round the outside in full view of the Spanish lines.

We were on the edge of the wood anyway, so we just slid gradually round the trees till we were facing the field, then dropped to our bellies and crawled. I expected a shout, maybe a shot, but nothing came. I suppose we were in the dark with a thick background of trees behind us, and anything beyond the sentries' own fires was probably just black.

But we weren't the only ones taking advantage of the dark, and we'd only been moving a minute when André stopped so suddenly I nearly crushed my face on his boot. Something was moving down near the Spanish lines, a low black hump steadily working its way across the field. Someone was doing as we had, and crawling furtively towards the little wood.

I murmured 'He's in for a shock when he gets there.'

The figure crawled on. It lifted its head a moment, a pale blur in the dark, then bent again for another determined haul forward.

'We have to warn him,' whispered André.

I sighed. 'He's a deserter. Fuck him.'

'We can't,' said Jacques. 'He'll start an alarm, and we'll be caught in the open.'

That at least was rational. André was already slithering back to intercept the stranger, so I contented myself with crouching against the trees to block the way in. I also drew my knife.

The figure made it safely into the shadows of the trees, then jolted to a sudden stop as André raised his head. André whispered quickly '*Tranquilo, Señor, soy un amigo . . .*'

The man sprang forward, pinning André to the ground and crushing in to throttle him. We leapt out and on him, Jacques forced his wrists apart while I jammed my blade under his throat and hissed at him to stay still. André started to slide groggily out from under-neath, but suddenly froze to a stop and stared stupidly up at the stranger's face. I got it myself then in the sensation under my fingers on his neck. There was a thick, ridged line in raised bumps, one hell of a scar if you saw it in the light, and I knew quite suddenly I'd done just that.

'D'Arsy,' whispered André.

'De Roland,' said the man. 'What . . .?'

'All right,' I said, and eased off the blade. 'But can we save the explanations for somewhere a little less public?'

We were maybe safe enough. I guess from a distance we looked so close to the trees the dons imagined any movement was from their own musketeers, but it wasn't a theory I wanted to test. I urged them all back on their bellies and led the crawl at my best pace until we could round the wood and get out of sight of the enemy.

We stopped in a wretched clump of rye that had somehow sur-vived the winter harvest, and I got out my flask. We were out of range of the wood, out of sight of the Spaniards, and at least out of whispering earshot of the French. Ahead of us I could see the safety of the forest where the others waited with the horses.

I had a slug of brandy and passed the flask to André. 'What now, little general? Crawl in to warn d'Enghien? We can deliver a traitor to prove our good will.'

D'Arsy gave me a look, but he couldn't hold it, Abbé, he knew what he fucking was. He stared at the ground instead.

André studied him, and I'd guess he'd rather mixed feelings. He took a gulp of brandy, winced as it hit his bruised throat, and said 'I got your message.'

D'Arsy grunted.

'You're trying to leave the Spaniards?'

'Obviously.'

'To get away from the battle?'

D'Arsy's head shot up. 'You dare imply –'

'I don't imply anything,' said André wearily. 'You lied at my trial, you sat there at the *amende honorable,* what the hell do I know?'

D'Arsy looked at the ground again. 'I've got information. De

Melo's written to Beck, they'll be reinforced by morning. If d'Enghien's still here he'll be massacred.'

Even Jacques sat up at that. André was more cautious. He reached for the flask again and said 'Why are you doing this?'

D'Arsy didn't answer for a moment, then lifted his head as if it was heavy and looked André directly in the eye. He only lasted a second then it was back to the boots, but something happened in that second or I'm a Walloon.

He muttered 'Maybe I'd like to go back where I belong.'

André was silent, then bowed his own head. I heard him say to the ground 'So would I.'

I watched him, feeling his indecision. Distant voices came from the French lines, the clanking of water cans, the occasional burst of raucous laughter. Someone was scraping a violin nearby, and I knew we'd got Hungarians in there somewhere, making those dismally soulful noises that remind them of home.

André's shape blurred in the darkness in front of me, his feet scuffled on the ground, then he was up and on his feet, standing in clear view of the French sentries and waving a handkerchief to draw their eyes.

'Attention, the guard!' he called. 'Permission to approach the line.'

There was more consternation than attention, judging by the babble of voices, and it took a good few seconds before he got the official *Qui va là?*

'Volunteers to join,' he said. 'We have a message for M. le Duc d'Enghien.'

It was our cue, Abbé. I lifted myself out of the mud feeling about as dignified as a worm-cast, and the others followed. From the forest ahead I saw Charlot leading the others out into the open.

Our troops didn't seem too impressed. A voice called grudgingly 'Advance and be recognized.'

André strode forward. No creeping, no crawling, he fucking strode till he stood in the light of their fires, head up, legs apart, arrogance enough to smack you in the face at fifty paces.

'I am André de Roland,' he said. 'I am André, Chevalier de Roland, and I am coming in right now.'

He didn't wait for permission, he'd spent enough years waiting as it was, he walked straight into the lines and we followed him. Excitement was building in me the way it does at gunfire, everything feeling urgent and important. I think the sentries felt it too, they gabbled to a sergeant who bowed and led us hastily towards the rear. A smart aide-de-camp escorted us for the last bit, and I realized we were being taken to the Duc d'Enghien himself.

The aide seemed to be leading us right back into the forest, but at the foot of one of the trees sprawled the figure of a young man wrapped in a black velvet cloak, his elegantly booted legs stretched carelessly out over the field. His head rested comfortably against the tree trunk and he was fast asleep.

The aide knelt beside him and coughed. 'Monseigneur.'

The man's eyes snapped open, and I had to suppress the urge to step back. They were dark and sharp as a bird's, and even his nose was fine and pointed like a beak. For a second he was motionless, his face tense with listening, but the night was still quiet and I sensed him relax. He lifted his head, dragged a hand through his tangled brown curls, and said 'Oh damn you, Brunel, it's nothing like dawn.'

The aide murmured that the Chevalier de Roland had a message. The Duc sat up. 'De Roland? I didn't know you were with us. What's up?'

André told him about the musketeers in the wood. D'Enghien stood while he was doing it, slung off his cloak and roughly brushed down his breeches, but he was listening all right, he wanted estimated numbers and when he'd got them he sent at once for Gassion.

'Excellent,' he said. 'But what were you doing in the woods anyway? Trying some heroics of your own?'

André hesitated. 'No, Monseigneur.'

D'Enghien looked at him. 'Ah,' he said. 'Bouchard, I expect. I heard he was with them. Well, don't trouble yourself about it. You shall have him in the morning as a present.'

André recovered himself. 'The morning, Monseigneur, I'm afraid there's a problem.' He introduced d'Arsy to explain about Beck.

D'Enghien's smile never faded. He let d'Arsy finish, then waved a hand to his aide. 'Better rouse them all, Brunel, the fun's about to start.' Then he turned back to André. 'Anything else? A detailed plan of the Spanish lines, perhaps?'

'I regret not, Monseigneur,' said André. 'But we'd like to stay and fight if we may.'

'May?' said d'Enghien. 'Tonight I'd take a convent of nuns, but you're offering me the man who held the Dax Gate and opened the way to Arras.'

I think I loved him for that. He spoke like the *amende honorable* wasn't important any more, we were on a battlefield and all that mattered was how a man fought. That's obvious really, but it was only him who made me see it: Louis II de Bourbon, the Duc d'Enghien, the man we know now as the Great Condé.

Stefan Ravel

Oh yes, Abbé, hallelujah and all that balls, but all I saw was a kid who'd been given an army before he'd properly learned to shave.

He'd guts, though, I'll give him that. There was none of that Châtillon havering about d'Enghien, he told his officers to stuff waiting for dawn, we'd start the battle right away.

'Let Beck come,' he said cheerfully. 'It won't be till morning, and by then I'll have beaten them.'

He was a cocky bastard, but it was the right decision. I doubt anyone but himself had really been sleeping anyway, it's something most of us find hard to do in what might be the last hours of life.

No one was sleeping now. The men were already rousing themselves as we were escorted back through the camp, and everywhere around us were the old familiar signs of preparation. Artillerymen were selecting their first balls, cavalry tightening their girths and climbing wearily into the saddle, musketeers were blowing patiently on their slow-matches, while pikemen looked superior and yawned. It's the same everywhere, Abbé. Movement from the Spanish lines suggested they were already responding, and I'd guess you could have walked the two lines and not seen a straw's difference between them.

Not that we were part of any of the proper units, oh dear no, the army doesn't care for that kind of irregularity. We were handed over with great ceremony to the Baron de Sirot and told we were being dumped with the reserves. André was visibly disappointed but the Baron laughed and said 'Look at what's against us, Chevalier. I think we've a better chance of action than any other men on the field.' I thought he was probably right.

We were all mounted except for d'Arsy, so they found him a horse and stuck us with the cavalry. I wasn't sure that was such a good idea for Grimauld, the man was an affront to horsemanship, but when I suggested he go with the infantry he mumbled something about 'staying together' and I didn't press. He was right, Abbé, a soldier fights better when he feels part of the men around him. Even d'Arsy became less morose once he was in the saddle like the rest of us, and seemed at least able to look people in the eye. We didn't know a soul in those cavalry lines, we looked decidedly underdressed next to the sleek black armour of the gendarmes, but in a way we'd become a little unit of our own.

The one I'd expect to feel strangest was André, since he'd never stood in the line of battle before, but I watched him going through the drill, checking his pistols, adjusting his sword, soothing the horse, I watched it all and smiled.

'It'll be all right, André,' said de Chouy anxiously. 'I was awfully nervous myself before La Marfée, but if we all stick together then it's quite all right.'

André thanked him gravely.

Sirot was pacing his horse up and down our lines. He had a watch in his hands, a wonderful thing like a miniature clock on a chain, and was tilting it to the moonlight to read what it said. 'Remember, Messieurs, wait for the orders. Our rallying cry today is "d'Enghien".'

'D'Enghien,' repeated Jacques, as if it were something he needed to memorize. 'D'Enghien.'

Artillery boomed. I heard small-arms fire underneath it, and guessed the musketeers in the wood were being treated to a nice little ambush of their own. But even the guns were drowned in the shout that followed, a great roar from our right echoed again way down to our left, then the ground vibrated with the pounding of hooves. Our cavalry were going in. Sirot looked up, snapped shut his watch and tucked it inside a pouch on his saddle.

No, he didn't tell me what it said, Abbé, but everyone knows now. It was four o'clock in the morning of the 19th of May 1643, and the Battle of Rocroi had begun.

Twenty-Nine

Carlos Corvacho

Straight at us. They charged straight at us screaming 'D'Enghien!' and the Duc his own self at their head. There was no mistaking him, Señor. He wore a great broad hat fluttering with white plumes, wore it like a flag to show the men he was there.

Well, we knew he was there, and that's a fact. And not only him, there's Gassion's lot crashing into our flank and others charging through the wood, scattering our hiding musketeers like chaff. Now that's got to be treachery, Señor, and we all know whose. That d'Arsy disappeared in the night without so much as his baggage.

Not that we're bothering about that just now with the French hurtling into us. Some of our squadrons are driven right on to our second line, and there's a few for falling back altogether. But not my Capitán, he's shouting like a madman and wheeling us round to come back at the French cavalry while they're scattered. Alburquerque's doing the same and the second line steadying nicely, so round we go with never a pause, it's round we go and at them.

Now you know me, Señor, I've never pretended to be a great warrior in the saddle. I was a servant and infantry-trained, my job is to stay by my Capitán's side and protect his back. But that's fighting work today, we're in the thick of the enemy cavalry, and my arm aching with cutting them out of the way. We're downhill at first as we drive them back into the valley, but that's not enough for my Capitán, he charges right on up the hill after them. And so do we, every one of us, Bouchard and his friends with the rest, all our spirits lifted by the best thing a soldier can ever see, the enemy cavalry scattering and fleeing before us.

It's no ruse, Señor, no feint, they're fleeing for their lives and leaving their infantry exposed behind them, two whole battalions looking at us in horror like a baby when the nurse takes the blanket away. They thought they'd a nice scavenger's job in front of them piling in after the cavalry, but they took one look at us, broke and ran. I won't say there weren't a few musketeers still banging away, but we charged straight at them and routed the lot.

Albuquerque was straight after them, but my Capitán sees his chance and wheels off to the infantry centre now they're unsupported by cavalry. There's maybe two other squadrons following and that's all we need, the infantry's panicked and almost parting to let us in. My Capitán's striking down hard all round him, the enemy dropping back either side, then in the empty space we see cannon, the gunners falling and dying with the rest. I won't pretend it was the main battery, it was Issembourg's cavalry took that, but it was five pieces and we took them, Señor, took them with three squadrons. The French hadn't another cannon in the field.

Jacques de Roland

André was desperate. Héros must have felt it, he kept jerking forward, and the boy had to tug him hard back. He didn't want to, he was biting his lip with frustration, but we were under orders like everyone else and couldn't move till we were told.

It was unbearable. As men advanced ahead of us we were allowed to inch forward on to the heights and get our first proper view of the plain. I'd never seen much at La Marfée, it was all confusion and nothing beyond the man next to you, but here it was laid out like a dinner on a table and we saw it all. We saw La Ferté's cavalry charge on the left wing, and we saw them break. We saw d'Enghien and Gassion charge on the right wing, fight through to the Spanish lines, then there too we saw them break. We saw the infantry beaten and falling back, the battery taken, both wings in disorder and the centre breached. We saw something I'd seen before and prayed never to see again, French soldiers routed and running, and I knew it was only a matter of time before we were running too.

'Not this time, Jacques,' said André. I might have believed him if I hadn't seen the tears on his cheeks. 'Never again, I told you. This time we're going to make the bastards run.'

I'd sworn never to doubt him again, and I tried, I really did, but he was a boy in his first battle and it was hard. I looked ahead to Sirot, willing him to give us something to fight other than fear, but he was standing half upright in the saddle, his eyes fixed on the right wing of our cavalry as if that alone held the answer. I looked there myself, and then I saw.

One man. In that whole sea of wavering cavalry, one man without a helmet but wearing a hat with white plumes that floated above the carnage like a swan. The men with him saw it too, they were rallying to his cry, turning back and fighting, crowding towards him, a great press of them turning like a tide and roaring back.

'D'Enghien,' a voice said, and I think it was me. But others were saying it too, it was rippling down our lines, even the Swiss and Hungarians were murmuring it. D'Enghien. It grew as it went, André stood in his stirrups and shouted 'D'Enghien!' and others followed him, the night went white with the flash of their swords.

More voices yelled beyond ours, and horsemen were galloping in our direction, yellow and red, yellow and orange, the Alsace cavalry broken through our lines and coming right at us. There must have been a signal but I didn't see it, I only remember Sirot saying calmly 'Messieurs, we are invited to join.'

Then André was streaking by so fast he nearly ripped my foot out of the stirrup, my own heels were digging in, Tonnerre was leaping forward, and beside me the others were doing the same, Stefan, Charlot, Crespin, Gaspard, d'Arsy, even Grimauld was saying 'Fucking hell' and lurching after us. The reserves were in, we were part of it, and charging all together into battle at last.

Stefan Ravel

It was hardly a charge, Abbé, we just turned and rode smack into them. Beasts were colliding head on, armour crashing against armour, swords clashing with steel-breaking ferocity. There was a moment's total scrimmage when I could hardly get my elbow out to wield my sword, then Lelièvre fired a pistol into the chaos, de Chouy another, the living wall of men and horses gave back a little, and we had room to swing.

And swing we did. Jacques was almost scything his way forward, Charlot's arm rising and falling like a woodman with an axe, and André was cleaving through their ranks like wire through rotten cheese. We halted them, we thrust into them, and by God they were giving back, faster and faster, some in such haste they were backing their horses rather than take time to turn. Oh, there was no magic in it, Abbé, the poor sods had fought through our whole left flank to get to us, they were weary and battle-sore and their pistols were empty, while we were steaming with an hour's pent-up frustration and threw the lot at them like burning pitch. I doubt more than a handful got past us and the infantry had them, our musketeers were primed and ready and only too keen for something to shoot at.

'They're running,' said André, almost sobbing with passion as he slashed his last opponent from his horse. 'Look at them, Jacques, they're bloody running.'

More than running, they were trampling each other in their haste to fall back. Their infantry were legging it too, some belting after their cavalry, some dropping their weapons and simply scattering for the woods. We were driving them clear off the field.

Officers urged us forward, but the only trouble they'd have had was calling us back. We leapt after the Alsatians, gathering up remnants of our broken left flank as we came. La Ferté had been taken, L'Hôpital was wounded, the poor sods were dazed and leaderless, and there was André waving his sword like a banner, yelling 'Come on, look, they're running!' He was hope on a fucking horse and they followed him all the way to the front of the lines.

There were more enemy there, different colours, different units, but we weren't fussy, we tore into them anyway. Half didn't even have their swords up or their muskets loaded, they'd never expected a reserve as big as ours. Some had even stopped to loot the bodies, ripping the clothes off dead and dying men in their hurry to find any valuables before their fellows did. We had them, Abbé. A few may have cried for quarter, but we hacked them down and trampled them like the carrion crows they were. Even André didn't hesitate.

Fallen gabions were rolling about the field, we had to dodge to stop them tangling our horses' hooves, but André swerved towards them and I saw what he was after. Wicker fencing marked our first battery emplacement, but in front of it stood a screen of cavalry carrying the yellow and black of the army of Flanders, and more of the bastards were moving inside.

The guns, Abbé. They'd taken the bloody guns.

Carlos Corvacho

It was a disgrace, Señor, our flank-guard dropping their guns and looting, my Capitán could never have predicted that. They'll have been Croats, in my opinion, it's not what you look for in an army of Spain.

But the damage was done and hordes of enemy cavalry thundering at us with nothing but our own horsemen out front to meet their charge. We're in the little enclosure ourselves, Señor, with earth-filled gabions all about us and screens of wicker fence to either side, but it's only a lashed-up field emplacement, nothing to rely on as a defence. We've men further back to secure the magazine, but otherwise there's no more than twenty of us inside and only a handful of infantry.

'We must retreat, Señor,' shouts our alférez. 'We must fall back, or be cut off.'

'And leave the guns?' says my Capitán. 'Get them spiked, Salbador, if we can't hold them we must disable them.'

The alférez calls our infantry to the guns, but there's a horse already leaping right over the screen, gabions and wicker fence flying to either side, and the man on its back is de Roland. No helmet, no armour, André de Roland as we remember him from the Dax Gate, and his sword smashing down as he lands. Left, right, and two of our men down before we've so much as blinked.

My Capitán's straight at him, but de Roland blocks the blow without looking and forges on past. It's the helmet, that's what it is, he can't have recognized my Capitán, but what he does see is infantry round the cannon and one's already found a hammer.

'The guns!' he calls behind him. 'To me, quick, they're spiking the guns!'

He cuts down at the man with the hammer, but our infantry leap at him, one seizes his bridle and two more reach up to drag him down. He kicks one clean in the face and whirls his blade round on the other, but he's sliding out the saddle for all that, and our pike leaping forward to impale him on the ground. He'd have died right there but for more horsemen pouring through the gap after him, a great wedge of them rallying to the Chevalier like his own private army and routing our infantry as they come. There's one huge great brute, really scarcely natural, he spits one of our pikemen so hard he lifts the man clean off his feet.

'The guns!' cries my Capitán. 'Protect the infantry, they must spike the guns!'

We turn to fight off the newcomers. I'm finding quite a pleasure in it too, seeing as the first man I'm up against is that traitor d'Arsy. There he is fighting bold-faced with the enemy, riding past me like dirt because I'm nothing more than a servant. Well, I have him, Señor, I get both hands to my sword and chop right across his middle as he passes. Off he rolls, sprawling on his back over one of the cannon, dead as he deserves.

Even Bouchard joins in. He's striking about him like a lion at jackals, driving the enemy back and away from the cannon so our men can do their duty. And they're trying their best, Señor, working right in between the guns to keep out of reach. It's the gun carriages, if you understand me, yards of wood sticking out the back and tangling up in the horses' legs, making it tricky for a rider to get deep enough in for the strike.

But your Chevalier's up to that little problem, and next thing he's leaping on one of the cannon his own self, right on the barrel, and hacking down at the men beside it. It's a wonder he doesn't slip, it is really, but my Capitán always said fencing taught a man balance better than ballet. Still, there's one little thing escaped his notice, and no doubt you see it as well as I did. He's stuck up higher than any other man on the field and a more promising target you never saw.

Bouchard takes his time. He draws his pistol and wipes it on his sleeve, watching your Chevalier all the while. Then he levels the barrel across his elbow, narrows his eyes, and fires.

The boy jerked to the impact and the sword dropped out of his hand. He stamped down hard but slipped and thumped sideways against Charlot's horse. Charlot stooped to clamp him to its flank, but André was still swaying, his hand crossing to grasp his arm below the shoulder, and between his fingers was oozing thick, red blood.

Some bastard Spaniard got in front of me, I belted him away backhanded and saw Charlot helping André to the ground. Another soldier in my way, I struck at him, but he ducked and shot past, and I was dimly aware of a Spanish voice calling a retreat. Horsemen were crossing in front of me, I saw Corvacho, even d'Estrada galloping at the rear, but they were going and irrelevant, I just wanted them out of the way so I could get to the boy.

I urged Tonnerre through the bodies and fallen horses, but the first thing I saw was Gaspard, propped up against a cannon wheel with a horribly white face, hands clenched tight round his thigh. He said 'It's an awful bore, Jacquot, these were my best breeches,' but the words were hissing through his teeth and I knew it was bad. Crespin was already dismounting to help him, so I just reached down to pat his shoulder, said 'I never liked them anyway,' then hurried past to André.

He was leaning against the cannon while Charlot furiously wrapped strips of his own shirt round the wounded arm, but the white was turning red as it touched, and he had to wrap faster and faster to make it stop. André's face was pale and glistening with sweat, but he looked up and smiled and I almost sagged in the saddle with relief. 'Are you all right?'

He gave a tentative waggle of his fingers. 'It's not broken, look.'

Voices were shouting outside our enclosure, Sirot rallying the reserves.

'Come on,' said Stefan, reining up beside me. 'We're being ordered –' He stopped at the sight of André. 'Oh, for fuck's sake, what have you done to yourself?'

'Nothing,' said André at once. He pulled his bandaged arm away from Charlot and reached his other hand to Héros's bridle. 'Don't wait for us, we're coming.'

'Not me,' said Grimauld. He was unhorsed, of course, he probably fell off in the first charge, but he was rolling up his sleeves and eyeing the two unspiked cannon with something like relish. 'These ladies have still got a bang or two in them and I'm the man to make them.'

Someone was shouting 'To me, the reserves! You in the enclosure, to me!'

'Go, Crespin,' said Gaspard, pushing him away to finish his own dressing. 'I shall stay and assist the noble Grimauld. Go and be a hero for me and Raoulet.'

Horsemen were charging off all round us, we were going to be the only ones left behind. Crespin leapt back on his mare, and I turned to see Charlot helping André back on Héros and Grimauld passing him up his sword. But something was wrong, the boy couldn't seem to lift it, his face sort of spasmed with pain. He turned his head quickly, thrust his bandaged arm through the loop of the reins and took the sword in his left.

His sword arm. It was his sword arm that was wounded, he must have had a musket ball straight through it. André in a battle and he couldn't lift his sword.

Stefan Ravel

No, I didn't see it, Abbé, not till we passed d'Arsy splayed over a gun carriage. He was dead all right, and with him his chance to win back his honour, but André said sadly 'I think he's already done it,' and reached down to close the staring eyes. His left hand, Abbé, and the right hardly holding him steady on the horse. I knew then all right, but it was already too late. We galloped after Sirot, and I could only hope the kid stayed in his saddle till there was time to sort him out.

There wasn't time for anything. By the time we caught up with the others they were already squaring up to face a charge from the enemy reserves. They looked fewer than us, but this time they were the fresh ones and we were the knackered wrecks.

'Get to the rear, André,' said Jacques, furiously loading his pistol. 'They'll never break through that far.'

André didn't budge, so I just nudged closer to his right side and saw Jacques doing the same on his left. Charlot went one better and planted his great bulk right in front. We had him corralled, and as long as we weren't ordered to advance I thought he'd be all right.

Pistol fire cracked into the front of our ranks, and the few of us who'd managed to load fired back. Seconds later and they were into us, more horses thrusting in our faces, more yelling, more swords waving about everywhere and mine right along with them. But there wasn't the force in it I'd expected, they seemed as tired as we were. One young cavalier rode whooping right up to me, but when I slammed his blade aside with a snarl he skipped nimbly back and tried somewhere else. A minute later they fell back.

I couldn't really blame them. We'd routed the Alsatians, and d'Enghien and Gassion had seen off Albuquerque's lot, these miserable reserves were about the only Spanish cavalry left on the field. They regrouped and came on again, but I can't say I was worried. De Chouy said 'I say, they're not awfully good, are they?' and André began to ease casually out of his little pen. I stuck out my arm and said 'Don't fucking push it.'

They were building up speed, but we were loaded this time and picked off dozens before they were halfway over the ground. Then someone yelled, horses thrust forward behind me, and we'd been given the bloody order to advance.

No choice, Abbé, we'd be trampled by our own cavalry if we waited, so we lurched forward with the rest. André was still up, the horse knew him and didn't need much steering, but then we slammed into the enemy and I lost sight of him in the mêlée. Horses' heads and men's torsos, arms thrashing up and down with heavy sabres, it was all I could do to keep the blades out of my own space.

We still ground forward, but the enemy started to veer away, and the ones who'd got through the first ranks were struggling to turn and ride back. Horses neighed and stamped as riders tugged at their bridles, our formation scattered like straw, and one confused gendarme blazed his pistol right over my shoulder. André reeled in front of me half off his saddle, and one of the retreating cavalry crashed into him broadside on. I heard him cry out as I shoved up to him, then his weight smacked into my shoulder as he toppled back. I grappled an arm to pin him to my side while he kicked out to get his leg back over the horse.

Riders were still crashing past all round, but Charlot got his mount across us like a wall, and Jacques shot up André's other side to pull him straight in his saddle. De Chouy was turning to cover our rear when a fleeing rider stumbled into us from the other flank. My sword hand was on the reins, I could only spin sideways and didn't really see it, just the man's panicked face and the grey streak of a sabre, but I heard the chop and de Chouy's cry and glimpsed him falling away as I turned.

The soldier was past us, three more blundering after him and streaking away across the plain. André cried out again and I saw it myself, de Chouy sprawled on the ground, his back bright scarlet from the slash down his spine. Oh Christ yes, he was dead, his head was caved in from the blow of a hoof, and there was little left of it but pink pulp. Crespin de Chouy, Abbé, blond hair, innocent eyes, the man who used to sing for sheer enjoyment as he rode. I looked at the mess of blood and bone and brain on the green field and thought 'Yes, that's about what it comes to, that's the size of it right there.'

Jacques de Roland

It was really only the horses that carried us along after that. I know we went sweeping after the fleeing reserves and drove them off the field, but I don't remember my mind being there, everything felt numb and pointless. When we headed back to the valley I heard our guns firing again and knew that was good, but it felt like we were right back at the beginning and the battle only starting. André lifted his head and said 'Grimauld,' but then the greyness came back over him and his head went down. He was exhausted and in pain, he couldn't go on much longer.

But when we got back to the field everything had changed. The Spanish cavalry had all gone, and the infantry had trouble of their own. D'Enghien had brought his cavalry right round the field to attack them from the other side, they'd got us coming at them from where their own reserves ought to have been, and now in front they'd got artillery. The Italians were actually leaving. It was all civilized and in good order, but right in front of us were thousands of men calmly marching away, the great Italian tercios withdrawing discreetly from the field. I saw the Strozzi among them, remembered those jolly Italians in the grounds of the Château d'Escaut, and was stupidly glad they were out of it.

Sirot was getting excited. 'One more push, Messieurs! These last little remnants, one more push!'

It looked a bit more than that to me, but at least we'd got infantry support. Our centre had been mangled by the Spanish cavalry, but we'd extricated some, d'Enghien had done the rest, and I saw four whole regiments drawing themselves up alongside. The Persan, the Piémont, and the Marine, then our own, the Picardie, the regiment I'd never fought with but felt part of since I was little. Red and white, the colours sparkling in the morning sun like my childish dreams of joining the army and one day being a soldier for real.

'The sun,' said André. 'What time is it, do you think?'

I'd forgotten about Beck. It had to be close on nine, he could have been here ages ago. Sirot obviously knew it, he was rallying the infantry to break those last remaining tercios before it was too late, but then a man in a gold cloak reined to a halt in front of him and everything sort of stopped.

'De la Vallière,' said someone behind me. 'What's up, I wonder?'

Sirot was actually yelling. 'I refuse to believe it. The Duc would *never* order withdrawal when victory is so close, he would *never* ask such a thing.'

La Vallière shouted back. 'You do what you like, but d'Espenan's battalions are to withdraw. The field is lost, don't you understand?'

It was enough for the infantry. They'd been fighting for five solid hours and were only too glad of the chance to stop. Pike and muskets were lowered, the soldiership trickled out of them like sawdust, they turned and began to shamble away.

'No,' said André in a small voice. '*No.*'

'No!' yelled Sirot, cantering after the retreating men. 'No, you cannot! There is only this one force to beat and the field is ours.'

They weren't listening. Sirot rode alongside them, crying that he'd complain to d'Enghien, he'd complain to the bloody King, their names would be mud all over France. They listened politely and a few started murmuring, but some round the sides were already drifting away. All these people killed, Gaspard wounded, André crippled, Crespin dead in the mud, everything we'd all done and they were bloody throwing it away.

André pushed out of the ranks before I could stop him. He streaked along the regiments, yelling for them to turn and listen. 'Wait, wait, we're not beaten! We can still win!'

He stopped Héros right in front of them, sat upright like a proper officer and spoke in his grandest, most carrying voice. 'Listen to the Baron. Do you want your regiments broken, dishonoured, famous for letting Spain into France? Or do you want to be the men who gave her her biggest defeat in a hundred years?'

Stefan muttered 'Oh, for fuck's sake.'

The infantry seemed to feel the same. 'Defeat?' shouted a grey-haired pikeman. 'We're already defeated!'

'Only if you choose,' said André. 'Stay and fight!'

They were turning away. One grimy-faced musketeer even shouted 'You fight if you want to, we've had enough.'

André suddenly lost his temper. He stood in the stirrups and bloody well yelled. 'So have I, I've had enough of all of it. I've had enough of Spain trampling over our homes and villages whenever they want to.' He'd forgotten his officer's voice, and what was coming out was as rough as the first day we came to Paris. 'It's our chance, our one single bloody chance to turn things round and drive the bastards back, and if you don't care then bloody well fuck off and leave it to the people who do.'

Sirot was listening. His eyebrows went up at André's language, but he must have seen the men didn't mind, there were more of them turning to him all the time.

André began to turn on Héros, appealing wider and wider. 'Picardie, you know me, I'm de Roland. You remember '36? You want that again? And again and again till somebody bloody does something and turns them round for good?'

His voice was breaking, but it didn't matter, he'd got them. He

462

was one of theirs, and someone to be proud of. He'd got a bloody great bandage on his arm and was visibly struggling to control his horse, but his left hand was up and in it the sword.

'I was at Corbie,' yelled a musketeer. 'I'm with you, de Roland.'

He didn't say 'Chevalier' or 'Sieur', just 'de Roland', but it was enough, and others started yelling too. 'La Capelle', I heard, 'Le Câtelet', and others saying 'The Saillie, the man who held the Gate.' The Picardie began to surge back towards us.

There was movement in the other ranks, then a sergeant stood in front of us, musket sloped like he was on parade.

'La Marfée,' he said in a great bellow that boomed round the plain. 'Come on, Piémont, remember La Marfée? The man who saved the women at the baggage train? Piémont for de Roland!'

He did it, that sergeant, he turned the bloody lot. They were all crowding forward and shouting, and someone was waving that great black-and-white flag back and forth, grand and beautiful against the blue sky. I remembered when I'd last seen it in the hands of the enemy on the field at La Marfée, and then I couldn't help it, I was suddenly crying, great hard gulps that hurt my throat.

'Fuck the Piémont,' another man was shouting. 'Don't forget the Persan, we were there too. My wife was in that train.'

I saw them through a blur of tears, all coming to André, the boy I'd thought was a fool. Even the Marine were coming, they didn't know him from before, but the army's its own family and André was one of theirs. 'De Roland!' they were shouting together. 'To de Roland!' I heard another voice close to me, muttering under its breath 'Fuck, fuck, oh fucking bloody fuck,' and there was Stefan with his face flushed red and his bristly cheeks glistening with the brightness of tears.

Stefan Ravel

Oh, come on, Abbé, do I look the kind of man to weep at a speech? I've heard a hundred and they're all the same. It's always 'Never mind being safe and comfortable, let's get ourselves killed instead.'

Oh yes, it did the trick all right, they were mustered and ready just as d'Enghien came galloping up with the rest of the army to join us. Sirot was straight in to defend his refusal of an order, but we all heard d'Enghien denying ever having given it. Oh, I believed him, that man wouldn't have known defeat if it bit him on the balls. I never did understand what went on there, Abbé, and if you ever find out I'd like to know.

It didn't matter anyway, we were poised for the finish. When you start a battle an army's in different sections: left wing, right wing, centre, reserves, but when you end it the divisions disappear. We weren't the reserves any more, Abbé, we were part of the army of France, and against us was the army of Spain. The Italians had gone, the Germans, most of the Walloon and Alsatian cavalry, we were left with just the native tercios to beat.

Forgive me if I laugh.

Carlos Corvacho

Oh no, Señor, you don't catch a man like my Capitán leaving the field till he's ordered, and maybe not even then. Albuquerque had gone to rendezvous with Beck, but there was no call for us to follow him, was there? We were free men now, with even the Frenchmen disappeared and no one knowing or caring where. It was every man for himself those last hours, and seeking sanctuary with any unit that could stand.

And it looks like we can. We've the remnants of five tercios and old Fontaine gets them sorted into a kind of square. We've still some cannon and odds and ends of cavalry, we're expecting Beck any moment, my Capitán thinks we can hold. But well, the French get their artillery going again, we've nothing to protect our flanks, and gradually we're whittled away from the sides. The tercio of Velandia's gone, Castellvi, and Villalba, and still no sign of Beck. My Capitán says 'He could have been here at dawn, Carlos, the man's four hours late.'

Four hours was too late, and that's all there is to it. The men cluster round the squares of the two last tercios, some to the Garciez and some like ourselves to the Albuquerque. It was home to us, if you understand me, they were part of the Army of Flanders.

Then they come. Charge after charge and we held them all. They had infantry, we had muskets to bring them down. They sent cavalry, and we'd pike and cannon to drive them back. They were losing more men than we were, and that's the truth. Well, no, I won't deny we'd a few casualties round the outside and Fontaine already dead on his litter, and it's true the ammunition was running a little low, but we were holding, Señor, you don't want to get the wrong idea about that. We were holding.

'Of course we are,' says my Capitán. It's hot work in that square and he's shed his coat and cuirass long ago, but now he drags down his collar to open his shirt, and I've never seen him do that before, never. He's smiling at me too, and there's something soft in it, almost kind. 'Of course we are, Carlos,' he says. 'We're Spain.'

He was right, Señor. You can keep the French and their little private armies, the tercios made soldiering a profession a man could be proud to put his name to. We were the best and most experienced in Europe, everything the world meant when it talked about the might and glory of the Spanish army. That's what we were back then, Señor.

We were Spain.

Jacques Gilbert

They just wouldn't surrender. Maybe they were waiting for Beck, but four thousand men couldn't make a difference now. Nothing would happen now but us losing men trying to break those tercios and the Spaniards all dying to gain nothing at all.

The field went quiet and our artillery stopped. Then a trumpet sounded, a drum rolled, and a small group of horsemen moved out from our front, d'Enghien with his right hand up for parley. The Spaniards sent out men to meet him.

The silence deepened until I could even hear the distant murmur of voices as d'Enghien talked to the men of the first tercio. Next to me André's face was frighteningly pale and his bandage sodden with blood.

Voices rose in excitement and I looked out again to the field. A big

Spaniard with a grey beard was writing something on the skin of a drum, and behind him I saw the tercio sort of sagging at the sides of its square as if everyone in it had relaxed at once.

'Thank God,' said André. 'Oh, thank God.'

The tercio was breaking up. It didn't look much like a surrender to me, they were still keeping their weapons and didn't seem to be prisoners, but they were bloody going and nobody really cared how.

D'Enghien was talking to the second tercio, and all around me people were starting to shift and ease themselves in their saddles. It sounds stupid, but your arse really aches after bouncing around for that long, I felt mine had actually changed shape.

'Shit,' said Stefan.

D'Enghien was already riding back, and the men of the second tercio returning to their square. Pike were levelled again, and in the middle of the square someone upraised a green-and-pink flag and waved it flamboyantly above them all. The tercio of Albuquerque was going to fight on alone.

All I remember is numbness. Orders were shouted, and we were shuffled along till every man in the French army was positioned round that single, small defiant square. No one spoke now, no one laughed, we all knew what we were going to do and what it really was.

'Fuck them,' said Stefan. His voice was rough with defiance, and I wasn't the only one turned to look. 'They came to do what they always do, to invade an innocent French town doing nothing but minding its own business. The only difference is this time we caught them at it. They won't even surrender decently to save lives on both sides.'

'It's still brave,' said André, looking wonderingly at him. 'You're a soldier, you can see that, it's still brave.'

'So's a rat,' said Stefan. 'Catch one in the corn bin and you'll see.' He drew his pistol, and sat back in his saddle to wait for the order.

It came, and we charged. There wasn't much gusto in it, but we rode through their musket fire and got clean to the front line before we were called back. We got a few with our pistols, but we never set steel to them and I didn't feel cheated. We rode back and reloaded. Our musketeers were returning fire, and so was our artillery, someone had even moved the field guns to the front so we could pound the square head-on. My fingers were shaking as I closed the pan.

It couldn't go on, it was pointless and stupid, I could hardly believe it when it was our turn to charge again. But even as we lined up I heard a chorus of voices, and then I saw it, someone waving something from the middle of the square, a shirt, anything, but it was white for parley and I almost vomited with relief.

We stood down. D'Enghien started forward with his officers, and I heard it again, that babble of voices in excited relief.

A shot, then another, and d'Enghien clamped a hand to his head as the wind of a ball nearly swept off his hat. They were shooting at him, the bastards were shooting at our own general under cover of a truce, I was almost howling with rage and so was everyone else. No one waited for the order this time, we wouldn't have taken it from anyone, we screamed 'D'Enghien!' and bloody charged.

Carlos Corvacho

It was a mistake, Señor, my word of honour on it. A mistake. The army of Flanders doesn't surrender, and if someone in the middle chose to ask for parley, then you can't blame us for it, now can you? All we knew was young d'Enghien riding out again as it might be another charge, so we fired at him, naturally we did, it's what you do in a battle. But the French thought it was treachery, and it made them fair boil with rage.

I'd never seen it myself what happened then, there's few have and lived, but when a young abanderado wets his lips and says 'The *furio francese*,' I know just what he means and what we're in for. They were madmen, Señor, madmen. They cared nothing for our bullets, they swept the pike aside like straws, they charged right through the middle of us, slashing down men like sheep. It's all up then, our sargento mayor's crying out the surrender his own self, and his aide ripping the shirt clean off his chest to wave as a flag of truce.

But these are animals we're reasoning with, not men. They're stabbing and hacking and seeing nothing but their own bloodlust. My Capitán sees one of our little drummers go down, and now he's screaming his own self and striking out with his sword at anything that comes near. But this is butcher's work, no room for finesse, and next thing there's a sabre whistling between us and he's down, my Capitán, the Don Miguel d'Estrada, he's down on his hands and knees like a little boy in the earth and a great red gash cut off half his ear and gone blazing across the skin of his chest. I'm yelling 'Señor, Señor,' but he thrusts me away and says 'Run, Carlos, you've done your duty, now run.'

I don't. There's his voice in my head saying 'We're Spain' and I don't. I stand upright as a man should, and then I see him, Señor, the Duc d'Enghien, tall on his horse in front of the tercio and saying to his men 'Back, back, they're surrendering, in the name of God go back!' He says it in the name of the Almighty himself, and I know this is a gentleman with an honour worthy of Spain. That was the Duc d'Enghien, Señor. That was Condé.

I bend to my gentleman and say 'It's all right, Señor, we're surrendering, come with me to the Duc d'Enghien.' But he says no, he says to me no and hits out like a child in a tantrum, he says 'I've told you to go, now bloody go and do it.' My gentleman, Señor, blaspheming and swearing like a trooper. I look round and see some of our men have made it safe to the Duc, clutching at his bridle, his horse's legs, anywhere to be free of the steel and the maddened enemy, but there's Frenchmen too far gone to heed him and they're scything down as if we're weeds on their land, mowing us down like grass.

A voice calls 'D'Estrada!' A young voice, and I know it even before I see him, the Chevalier's fought to the front and is doing just like the Duc, rallying our own poor soldiers to his side. He reaches down his hand and calls again 'D'Estrada!'

My Capitán shies back, and grasps his sword firmly. He says 'I don't ask favours.'

The French infantry have almost reached us, Señor, broadswords flailing round like soldiers of Herod his own self. De Roland leans further over, hand stretching out with fingers spread. 'No favour,' he says. 'For God's sake, man, I owe you.'

My Capitán lifts his head. De Roland does owe him and he knows it, that business with the tanner tripping him, there's a debt of honour to be paid. I hear the sargento mayor calling hoarsely 'Lay down your arms, do nothing to inflame them!' and then, then my Capitán lowers his sword.

I help him to his feet, then he reaches out to de Roland, left hand to left hand, and I push him towards the Chevalier's horse to bring him out of the path of the infantry. My Capitán stands himself calm and upright as befits a gentleman of Spain in defeat, but his hand's firm in de Roland's, and we're both of us safe by his side.

Jacques de Roland

There weren't many left to surrender. When the last survivors left the square there was only a great pile of bodies in the middle and one old man lying dead on a litter. D'Enghien knelt by the body and said 'If I couldn't be me today, I think I'd choose to be him.'

I was just glad to be me and alive, and the boy still in one piece. By the time he'd left d'Estrada he was swaying in the saddle from loss of blood, and Stefan said we'd got to get him seen to quick.

Charlot carried him on his own horse while we looked for a quiet place to patch him up. When everywhere's strange you go for the thing that's familiar, so we headed towards that wood where we'd found the musketeers. It was still chaotic even there, with d'Enghien's scouts galloping about and Gassion's cavalry checking round for those enemy we'd driven from the field. Most had probably gone to find Beck, but there were still odd pockets hiding round the woods, I heard gunshots cracking all over the plain. Then another banged just behind us, a man cried out and it was Charlot. I turned in horror to see him toppling off his horse with André still held to his chest, and both thudding heavily to the ground.

Everything was blurry in panic as I yanked at Tonnerre's reins to bring him round. I thought it was just a stray shot, I wasn't even looking, just trying to get to Charlot and the boy. I vaguely heard hooves coming from the wood, then Stefan yelled 'Bastard!' and I turned.

Three riders galloping at us, and the one holstering a pistol was Bouchard. I never even thought about not killing him, I just charged, wrestling out my sword as I came, but he swerved away, another man came at me with sword already drawn, and I hardly even saw him before it hit. Steel sliced down my shoulder as I hurled myself sideways, he slashed after me and I was sliding down Tonnerre's flank, the ground hitting me in one great smashing jolt. I had time to think 'It's all right, I haven't hit my head,' and then that went bang too, like my brain was being shaken inside my skull.

It took me a second, because it does. Swords were clashing as I got my head up, and I saw Stefan and another man, both unhorsed but going at it anyway. I saw André on the ground, pale and bloody, left hand making desperate sweeps of the ground for his sword. Then boots landed with a thump in front of me as my own man dismounted and I saw the sword that was going to kill me come scything down. I closed my eyes.

A clang of blades and a rush of air before my face, I thought stupidly 'André!' and opened my eyes. The boy was still yards away, it was Charlot on his feet, wielding his sword two-handed to beat away the man's thrust. His back was torn and bloody where the pistol ball had hit, but he was somehow up and fighting to save me.

It only took seconds. Charlot's arm still had strength in it, he powered forward in the lunge and took the bastard clean through the chest, but the man's sabre was already swinging and struck into Charlot's side even as he went down. It wasn't a deep blow, but Charlot was done already, his eyes went blank, his knees crumpled, and he folded gently to the earth.

I struggled over to him but his hand was limp and his face already empty. I think he died standing, I think he was dead before he fell. I whispered 'Charlot,' but there was nothing there, only the distant clash of steel that was Stefan and the other man still fighting. Then I remembered the third man and forgot the pain in my shoulder and the ache in my heart, I turned so bloody fast I nearly wrenched my neck.

André. He'd found his sword and managed to claw himself up on his knees, but I was looking at him through the arch of a man's legs. A glinting sword was dangling down into the picture, and even as I watched, it flicked forward and touched the boy gently under the chin.

'Anywhere in Europe, Chevalier?' said Bouchard. 'How about right here?'

Stefan Ravel

Of course I saw it, he made fucking sure I saw it, the bastard wanted an audience. Jacques was down and helpless, I had my hands full with another of them, but Bouchard was spinning the whole thing out like a play. When I next got myself facing the right way he was prodding André's chest with his rapier, bringing up little dots of red blood.

More fool him. André was dragging himself up, elbow cradled in one hand but the sword dangling from his fingers and a glare in his eyes that told me he meant business. If I'd been Bouchard I'd have stuck him and run, but that wasn't what he was after at all. There was a cartel out against him, he needed to duel André de Roland and win, and this was the only chance he'd ever have to do it.

André straightened. Bouchard gave a last little tickle with his rapier and André bashed it aside like a kid with a stick, then stepped back, shoved his hair off his face, and took guard. Bouchard smiled and took position opposite. He was really going to do it, Abbé. He was going to fight a one-armed man.

Even my own opponent looked dubious, though it didn't stop him banging away at me. I'd no time for him, Abbé, there was a murder to be stopped, I slammed away his blade and gave him a good hard kick in the shin to discourage him. It seemed to be effective, or perhaps he was just starting to realize what he was involved in. He backed out of reach, looked over again at Bouchard, then turned and loped off for the woods.

I swivelled back to André. He was fighting now, or at least his sword was hitting Bouchard's, but there wasn't the force in it I was used to, and none of his usual fluidity. He was having to fence with his left hand while his right hung limp and useless by his side.

I belted towards them. Bouchard's head jerked towards the movement, then he spun round and saw Jacques climbing to his feet. He looked for his friends, saw one dead on the grass and no sign at all of the other, and glared at us in frustrated fury. He took a step back towards his horse and yelled 'Keep back! He challenged me, you can't interfere!'

Balls. I kept right on coming and so did Jacques, but then André swung round himself and shouted 'Stop!'

Jacques stopped. I didn't, Abbé, I never even broke stride. Bouchard took another step towards his horse, but André yelled 'Wait!' then turned back round to me. 'Get back, Stefan, you've got to. He's right, I challenged him.'

I said 'Fuck off, André, you can't fight him now.'

André's bandages were blood-sodden, his face was the colour of whey, his legs weren't even steady, but he wasn't going to wait another day. He said 'Yes, I bloody can.'

Jacques de Roland

We couldn't stop him, we'd no right. We had to stand and let it happen.

I could hardly even watch. I sort of kept my eyes half open, ready to shut them any second. I heard it though, the clashing and grunting, and twice André crying out. It was the jolting of his arm that was doing it, he couldn't balance properly, it was swinging every time he struck. Another stifled cry, and now André was nursing his wounded arm into his body, and Bouchard only pausing to choose his target before he lunged.

André slammed up his left hand to parry, Bouchard twisted to reprise, but somehow his blade sliced only air, he stumbled off balance and had to jump back. A second later it happened again, but this time André got in a quick riposte and Bouchard didn't seem to expect it, he only just got his sword round in time to block. I opened my eyes fully, watched the next clumsy exchange, and finally understood. Bouchard was thrown by the left-handedness. He was struggling with it just as André had against d'Estrada.

And André was getting better. All that practice with his left hand, all that stuff he'd done to face d'Estrada, he was using every bit of it now. His left wasn't as good as his right, but it was bloody good enough and his confidence was rising all the time. His rhythm was coming back, and a second later I saw him fling out his right arm for balance as naturally as he'd ever done with his left.

I stared. It was hurting him, it had to be, I saw him grimace every time, but he was making that arm do what it had to and fuck what it cost him. Bouchard deliberately knocked it with his forearm as he curved round for a stab at the face, we all heard André's gasp of pain, but it didn't stop him swivelling into the riposte, he never even broke tempo.

And that was Bouchard's second mistake. He'd come into this fight for the sheer cruel joy of it, but André was fighting for his life and his honour, he was going to kill Bouchard if he had to die himself to do it and nothing in the world was going to stop him. I looked again at Bouchard's face and all I saw in it now was fear.

But Stefan was right, and even a cornered rat will fight with all it's got. Bouchard stepped out of reach, bent down swiftly and came up with Charlot's sword. He'd realized what André had, that the best way against a left-hander is to give yourself a guard on that side. He was going to fight two-handed.

'You can fight the gentleman's way, can't you, Chevalier?' he said. 'Or didn't they teach you that in the stable boy's home?'

The bloody, bloody bastard. I looked desperately at the boy, but he only looked angry and wary. He was still going to kill the man, he was set on it, his brain was just furiously trying to work out how.

I think maybe I was as mad as he was. I reversed my sword in my hand, said 'Catch!' and threw it to him.

He caught it. His arm might be torn up, but no one had a stronger hand or wrist than André, he caught it and hardly winced.

I said 'It's our uncle's, André. You've got them both now.'

Something happened in his face, his eyes blazed with something that wasn't just hate and revenge, something only I understood. Then he bent his right elbow, extended his left arm in the proper two-sword guard, smiled at Bouchard and said 'What are you waiting for?'

It was impossible what I was looking at, and Bouchard knew it too. I can't imagine the pain André was in, but he used that wounded right arm to block and guard like it was steel itself. He did all the skilled stuff with the left, he was feinting and dropping, binding and sliding under Bouchard's blade, he pricked him in the arm, the thigh and the hip, but he used his right to keep the blades away from his own guard and the bastard never touched him.

I actually sat down. André had his father's sword and his uncle's, the one I'd used myself, it was like we were every one of us there in the fight with him, us and the one man who'd fenced us and loved us all four. I looked down at Charlot and thought he'd have been proud of his Chevalier now.

'Making yourself useful, I see,' said Stefan, sitting beside me.

It was nearly over. The neat four-rapier formation had long since broken up, Bouchard was backing away, doing little more than slash down with each hand alternately like he'd never had a fencing lesson in his life. André was more ragged now, his face grey-white, his bandage smearing red wherever it touched, he was panting and gasping, he was all but bloody sobbing, but his footwork was perfect and his hands never wavered, he was driving the bastard back for the kill.

Hooves were crossing the plain behind us, but I didn't turn, there'd been movement round us the whole time and no one had approached us. But these were slowing, I felt a presence at my back, then someone said 'Good God!' and I whirled round fast because it was d'Enghien.

He'd got Brunel with him and an officer I recognized as Gassion, but none of them were looking at me. André was fighting, André with two swords and the kind of passion you go to hell for. He was upping the tempo, in and out and sharp back, he feinted at Bouchard's face, dropped for the chest and got him, right hand slashing clean across to sweep away the parry and nearly slicing Bouchard's face in the process. The man was jerking his head back, feet stumbling, doing nothing but parry wildly with both blades as if they were great wide broadswords and could save him like armour.

They couldn't. He tried one last thing, a great strong thrust on the high inside line with all his weight behind it, but André'd expected it. He dropped my sword, smacked his right hand on the grass for balance, thrust back his leg and threw the force of his whole body in one almighty lunge at the groin. The *passata sotto*, and I've never seen it more savage. Bouchard screamed high as a woman, dropped both swords and dashed his hands to his mutilated torso, knees crumpling as he collapsed and writhed on the hard ground.

André stood again and wiped his face. There was no expression on it at all.

'Bravo, Chevalier,' said the Duc.

André whipped round, then lowered his sword and relaxed. Bouchard went on screaming, but he was sobbing too, a horrible, embarrassing noise that made me want to look away.

'Finish it,' said d'Enghien. 'The creature's an affront to humanity.'

Bouchard was openly weeping, on his knees and weeping, rocking to and fro as his hands clutched his groin. He looked up at André with tears on his face, and said 'Please. No. It's not fair. Please.' When André raised his sword he almost wailed, and I felt my own cheeks burn with shame.

André turned away. 'Might he have a surgeon, Monseigneur?'

D'Enghien leaned forward. 'You wish him to live to face trial?'

André said 'I wish him to live.'

Stefan muttered under his breath 'Mistake, kid. Big mistake,' but d'Enghien gave a pleased laugh.

'Magnanimity. You're right, it's one of the pillars of honour.' He turned to Brunel, said 'See to it,' then leaned back in his saddle to look at André. The boy was battered and bloody but d'Enghien didn't seem to mind. He was scruffy himself, come to that, his velvet torn and his face bloodied, he looked like a dirty little boy playing at war.

He bowed. 'You've done well today, Chevalier. His Majesty will be delighted.'

André bowed back. He nearly fell over but he bowed back. 'I doubt His Majesty will be delighted at any achievement of mine.'

'Ah,' said d'Enghien. 'Perhaps you should know that King Louis XIII died five days ago at Saint-Germain. I don't think His Majesty King Louis XIV will care for past prejudices of that kind, do you?'

The King was dead. There'd been a Louis XIII since before I was born, but all I felt just then was hope that maybe the old politics would die with him and André would get a fresh start.

D'Enghien began to turn his horse. 'Do you join us for the campaign, Chevalier?'

André managed a better bow this time. 'I regret, Monseigneur, that I am to be married in four days.'

'Regret?' said d'Enghien. He laughed so loudly his horse sort of shied. 'Then we have more in common than you think. But come to us afterwards when your wound's healed.'

André hesitated. 'If I'm welcome in your army . . .'

'Don't be a damn fool,' said d'Enghien. 'You're welcome anywhere I say. Who's going to say no to the victor of Rocroi?' He gave a huge grin and cantered away with Gassion.

I didn't blame him for being triumphant. He was right, he'd be really powerful after this, and now the King was dead we'd got a chance of real justice at last. Then I watched Brunel's minions carrying off Bouchard as a bleeding, sobbing wreck, and thought in some ways we'd already had it.

We'd won something else too, and there was evidence of it all over the field. Trumpets were sounding in Rocroi, soldiers gathering up Spanish flags as trophies, and little bursts of music were coming from all over, drums and singing, and from the Écossais that horrible wailing of pipes. We'd done the impossible. We'd fought a huge battle and smashed the Spanish tercios to pieces, we'd done what the boy always said we'd do and were driving them right out of France.

I turned to him in wonder, but he was knelt down by Charlot, gently massaging his injured arm as he gazed about the field. Stefan said 'Not bad for Trooper Thibault,' and André said 'Fuck off, sergeant,' and they laughed together at a joke I didn't understand. I looked at his face and didn't see anything like exultation in it, just a kind of quietness that hadn't been there for a long, long time.

I looked again at the field, and now I noticed other things among the noise and jubilation. Chaplains were praying over the fallen, surgeons' assistants going around with litters, boys clanking along with buckets to give the men water. I remember one musketeer pouring his mug all down his face and the white runnels it made on his smoke-blackened cheeks. I remember a pikeman hauling a friend's arm across his shoulders, saying 'You're all right, chum, I'll get you to the surgeons, you'll be all right.' I remember civilians coming out of the town, women and children who'd have fallen to the Spaniards if we hadn't driven them off, and the children were running round making banging noises like guns, and nobody cursed them, even the wounded ones looked at them and smiled. I remember seeing two figures staggering towards us over the grass, and one was Grimauld with a face so black he might have been a Moor, and the other was Gaspard with bandages right up his leg, but both of them smiling with the same kind of quiet in their faces I'd seen in André's.

Then I understood. After all the fog and lies of politics we'd come here to the smoke of cannon and the open green field where ordinary people fought and died to make the lies come true. We'd come to the shattering violence of the battlefield at Rocroi, and what we'd finally found there was peace.

Thirty

Bernadette Fournier

We dressed her ourselves for her wedding, she would have no one but me and Jeanette. Her dress was not Spanish gold and silver now, Monsieur, it was creamy white and cascading like a waterfall with lace from Reims. I myself placed the orange blossoms round her neck, fresh that morning from the Ancre hothouse, and their scent warmed the air like a promise. She touched them with tentative fingers and said 'Do I look silly, Bernadette?' and I looked at her and said 'No.'

So we rode with her into Dax, and as the carriage approached the square we saw André ahead of us by the church steps, pacing anxiously as if convinced she would change her mind and refuse to come. I laughed and said 'How silly he is, he must hear the carriage,' but Anne looked at me wonderingly and said 'But he is deaf in one ear, Bernadette, did you not know?' And then I felt foolish, for indeed I had not.

But that is how it is, Monsieur, there is always more to a person than any one other can ever know. Even I had my own little piece of André de Roland, for I had shared his lowest times like no one else, and nothing would ever take that away.

It did not trouble me, for as I descended the carriage there was Jacques waiting for me with a look on his face that was brighter even than Anne's. I stood on the church steps with the sun on my face and my hand in his arm and would not have changed places with a queen. I watched Anne walk the last steps over the scattered blossoms, I watched the look on André's face when he turned and saw her, and I did not grudge them one scrap of their happiness, for I knew I had something precious of my own.

Anne de Roland

Extract from her diary, dated 23 May 1643

I had thought to write this last night, but had scarcely trimmed the quill before there came a rustle of bedclothes behind and I saw André watching me.

He said 'Anne, please tell me you're not writing your diary.'

I said 'I thought you were asleep.'

'I was,' he said, and looked at me through half-closed eyes. 'I was dreaming I'd married the most beautiful woman in the world, but when I reached for her I found nothing but pillow.'

I said 'I couldn't sleep, I was too happy and wanted to write it down.'

He smiled like a king and stretched himself out over the bed as if he would conquer it all. 'That's all right then, you can read it to me if you like.'

Something squeezed like a fist inside me for love of him, and I could not resist. I looked at the blank page and said aloud 'Only to my diary can I write this, for I would not wish my husband to realize my disappointment on my wedding night . . .'

There was only a flurry of bedclothes to warn me, and I had hardly time to lay down the pen before his arm was about me and I was thrown flat on my back on the bed I had so recently vacated.

I said feebly 'André, your arm.'

'Never you mind my arm,' he said, and indeed his hands were already busy removing my nightdress. 'This is a question of duty. I cannot have my wife disappointed.'

He knew I was not, he could not fail to know, but it was so much pleasure to have him prove it I could not bear to say anything that would make him stop.

But in the morning he was quieter. I lay with my head on his shoulder while he kissed the back of my neck, but then his lips lifted from my skin and I felt his breath there instead, warm at first, then leaving little cool patches in its wake.

I said 'André?'

He quickly kissed behind my ear. 'Yes, sweetheart?'

I said 'What's wrong?'

He stilled. Then his hand pressed down into the softness of the mattress and he twisted round to face me.

'Nothing.'

I put my hands either side of his face and looked at him.

He lowered his eyes. 'I don't want you disappointed in anything, Anne. You should be in Paris, being fêted, attending court. You shouldn't be hiding in a little village in Picardie, because your husband is afraid to go out.'

I said 'You're not afraid. You'll be going back to the army, won't you? And I'm sure the Duc will make things all right everywhere else.'

'I think he will,' he said, and began absent-mindedly to play with my breasts. 'But I still won't go to Paris, my darling, because I don't think I can face it.'

I have never heard him admit such weakness, and was astonished how fierce it made me feel.

I said 'Then we shan't go. Why need we? We're perfectly happy here.'

'Are you?' he said. 'Perfectly?'

I stroked his chest, then let my hand stray down to follow the fine little hairs that pointed like an arrow to the thicker growth below. 'Well, perhaps if . . .'

Afterwards we clung together in the warmth of our own sweat, and for a little while there was no other world beyond the curtains of our bed. I was careful not to allow the talk to return to Paris, and he did not ask again.

Jacques de Roland

He'd got no choice. He'd only been married a week when we got a letter from d'Enghien saying he'd been writing to people and the King wanted to meet him. He wrote 'You're to be publicly cleared in any event, but it will look rather ungracious if you don't at least visit.' Even I knew 'rather ungracious' was another way of saying

480

'bloody rude', which is not a good thing to be to a new King. The Comte knew it too, he ignored all André's excuses and made an appointment to present him right away.

We'd got time to do a few things first. Crespin's body had been returned to his family, but we'd brought Charlot's back to Dax to lay in the family vault itself. He was the only one in there who wasn't actually a Roland, but André said he might as well have been, and the Comte and Comtesse both agreed. We even had a plaque put up for him in St Sebastian's alongside Philibert's to say he'd given his life for the Sieur of Dax. I said that wasn't true any more, I hadn't been Seigneur since André officially got his property back, but the boy just smiled and said 'You'll see.'

I did. We went to the notary's to make André's new will, and my uncle changed his at the same time. He didn't need me as a spare any more, but he included me anyway, he made me a proper official second son so when André became Comte I'd still get Dax for my own. I saw it on the paper myself, then I went to tell Mother and she cried. Bernadette didn't, she drew herself up and said 'Now you are truly nobility and will not want to know me,' so I showed her I did, then we sat in the back meadow and I put a chain of daisies round her hair like a crown.

My uncle and grandmother set off for Paris first, and they took Gaspard with them to convalesce with his family. We got a litter to take him to the carriage, but he said 'It's a coach, Jacquot, not a hearse, I shall enter it in the style of a gentleman,' and walked to it all by himself. I felt very solemn watching him being driven away, waving an immaculate hand from the window. He was the very last of the Puppies.

Stefan and Grimauld weren't coming to Paris, they were too bloody comfortable where they were, but they were both joining us for d'Enghien's campaign afterwards. That puzzled me with Grimauld, I mean André had given him a pension, he didn't need the money, but I think the truth is he just liked making things go bang. André said he'd get him a position with the engineers and he went round grinning with all four teeth. I didn't understand why Stefan was coming either, he'd always banged on about wanting to be independent in the army, but he said 'Maybe I like having an officer I can tell to fuck off,' and stared me right out.

André was very quiet the last day. Anne told me he'd been having nightmares, and we both knew what about. He was doing it again, that stuff he did straight after the *amende honorable*, that twitching with his shoulders when he felt people looking. He went out alone in the afternoon, and when it got near dusk I set out to find him.

He was doing what I'd guessed he'd do, fencing all by himself on the back meadow where we'd trained together all those years ago. I stood and watched till he noticed me and lowered his sword.

I said 'You shouldn't be doing that, you're meant to be resting your arm.'

His face darkened at once. 'It's always "should", isn't it? Doesn't it ever matter what I want to do?'

I waited. After a moment he looked down and flicked his sword irritably through the grass. 'All right. I know I've got to go to Paris, you don't have to tell me.'

I said 'You're being publicly cleared now, no one will say anything.'

'Say!' he said, and slashed the sword the other way. 'They can say what they like, I just don't want them looking.'

I saw it again in my head, André barefoot in his shirt and that mob of people staring. I said 'I know. I was there, I know.'

'You don't,' he said, and began prodding the grass with the point of his sword. 'You weren't there for the journey.'

I'd always tried not to think about that. Anne told me the state he'd been in just going in the carriage to Lucheux, and I'd sort of guessed the rest.

'They threw things,' he said casually. 'Mud and – things. The carriage shook with it. People pressed up to the windows to look at me, some even thrust their heads inside. One spat.'

To be spat at and not allowed to retaliate. André de Roland. I squeezed my eyes shut, but it was no good, I'd started to picture it.

'Then the gate,' he said. 'The Porte Saint-Martin. The carriage is theirs, so you have to leave it at the gate and let the guards push you out. Or kick you, if they want. They can, you know, you don't exist any more, they can do anything they like.'

You, he said. But it wasn't me, was it, I'd been the one floating around thinking myself big and heroic while they were doing all this to my younger brother. I said 'André . . .'

'Oh, I'll go,' he said. 'It'll be all right at the court, the King will be there, and if anyone stares I'll bloody challenge them. But it's the streets, Jacques, do you see? The ordinary people. How the hell can I challenge a crowd?'

I thought of an answer. 'They won't see you. We'll take the carriage for Anne and Bernadette, you can just go in it too. No one will know you're there.'

'I suppose,' he said unhappily, spiking the grass again. 'But you know what the real trouble is, don't you?'

I didn't.

He sighed, stood upright and sheathed his sword. 'It's that I don't blame them. They supported me at first, but then I told those lies and let them all down, everyone who'd ever believed in me or my family or anything we ever did.'

I said 'You had to, you were ordered. You did it for all of us.'

'Perhaps,' he said. 'But who's going to understand that, Jacques? Even more now they know I'm innocent. Who the hell is going to understand?'

I remembered that man at Lucheux saying 'All the more shameful,' and couldn't think of an answer. He knew it, he just put his arm through mine and we walked home in silence.

We left early next morning. The women travelled in the carriage, but the boy didn't want to be confined yet so we went in front on horseback. I remember how it felt riding out of the Dax Gate and seeing the beech forest on the horizon, just like that day in 1640 when we'd set out together hopeful and excited to our new life in Paris. That was June too, but then it had been sunny, the fields green and the sky blue, but today was overcast and heavy, the sky a dull grey.

It was much slower travelling with the carriage, but we still reached the Faubourg Saint-Martin on the fourth night. The gate was shut, but we weren't expected till morning so we spent the night at the farm instead. I thought it would do the boy good to remember there were ordinary people who loved him, but he couldn't relax even with the Porchiers. Paris was just too near.

We went out in the dark to look at it together, and it did look pretty horrid, the walls tall and forbidding like an evil castle in a poem. It still stunk too, but when I offered him the vinaigrette he waved it away and said 'I have to get used to it, don't I?'

A voice behind us said 'Yes, it smells, Chevalier, and always has. But it is the smell of people, that is all, and you will have little trouble with them, I think.'

I turned to see Bernadette in a thick travel cloak, smiling at us like we were children who didn't see.

André said 'I'm afraid there's more to it than that.'

'Is there so?' she said. 'The last time I stood here I made a promise for us all, and tomorrow is the day it will come true.'

André said softly 'What did you promise?'

She wrapped the cloak tighter round her and glared at the city as if it were a monster waiting to be defeated. 'I said you were coming back. And so you are, Chevalier, you have beaten everything it had to throw at you, and tomorrow you will enter it with your head held high. Do not tell me you are now to let me down.'

Silence, the three of us in the dark, the night air brushing gently through the leaves, and behind us from the farmhouse Mme Porchier yelling at someone about warming pans.

'No,' said André. 'I won't let you down.'

I heard the rustle of her curtsey as she left us, but all I could see just then was the boy. He stood up straighter as he said 'Sod the carriage, Jacques. We'll ride in together, you and I, and if anyone wants to look let them bloody look.'

I said 'If you're sure . . .'

He actually laughed. 'I'd better be. I've just been called out by a woman, and God help me if I lose.'

The morning was still cloudy, but the air felt tingly and fresh. André had made an effort to look the part, he was dressed in black and silver and had even given himself a shave. His face was still pale and the skin under his eyes dark from lack of sleep, but he had the fighting look on him and I felt my own rise to meet it. Anne suggested we might like to go through a different gate this time, but

André squeezed her hand and said 'No, Madame, we shall go through the Porte Saint-Martin and damn it every inch of the way.' Bernadette watched him and suppressed a smile.

Wagons were rumbling over the bridge as we approached, just like the day we came to the Porte Saint-Denis and the porter jerked his thumb to signal us in. That didn't happen this morning. We were with a smart carriage bearing the Roland arms, the porter took one look and bawled at a fish cart to let us cross first. We rode sedately over the bridge, totally ignored the bowing guards, and swept through the thick walls into Paris.

For a second the noise was just how I remembered it, an insane tumult of wheels and horses and bells and voices that hit us like a second wall, but this seemed less random, it had more of a purpose, and it took me a full second to realize it was us. Carts were trundling aside to clear our passage, horses protesting with indignant neighing as they were reined back, but people were swarming into the gaps and their yelling began to clarify into words. 'De Roland!' people shouted and the boy flinched beside me, but others cried just 'André!' and some called 'Chevalier, Chevalier,' as if they only wanted him to notice them.

André's alarm faded into confusion. 'But they can't have . . . How did they . . . ?'

'The Comtesse,' I said. 'She must have told people. And our friends.'

I could see one right in front of me, Gaspard lounging in a sedan chair by the side of the road and waving beautifully. He'd a bunch of other people round him, and a glint of eyeglasses drew my eyes to a beaming Henne.

'That's it,' said André. 'She's asked people to do this, she's got the servants to . . .'

A window opened above us, and out fell a shower of petals, lilies and roses, white and pink fluttering down like snow. A red-faced woman shook her basket empty and gave us a smile that was broader than Henne's.

I said 'No one's been told to do this, André. They're here to welcome you home.'

The strain dissolved from the boy's face as we began to recognize faces. There were servants from inns we knew, a cavalry officer I recognized as Danthan, a sergeant I'd seen at Rocroi, a Cardinal's Guard I remembered from the duel by Notre-Dame, a fat woman with a loud voice from the baggage train at La Marfée. There were strangers too, old men and women, beggars and soldiers, women and children, some in grand clothing, others in rags, but all cheering and waving and saying 'Chevalier,' over and over again, 'Chevalier.'

They were lining the road, leaning out of the windows, the buildings alive with movement and ringing with human voices. They were as much part of the city as the bells I was hearing, clanging wildly and gloriously, near and far. Saint-Martin, Saint-Sepulchre, Saint-Denis, even Saint-Sulpice were all ringing together, and my eyes followed the sound to the great towers and spires of the skyline of Paris. I'd seen it so many times, I'd been awed by it, frightened by it, I'd even hated and despised it, but never till that moment had I seen that it was beautiful.

The crowd quietened as André leaned down to a little boy tugging at his stirrup. I guessed what was being asked, because André sat back looking oddly self-conscious, then reached down and drew his sword. The shouting died to an expectant murmur as I heard the soft ring of the blade sliding out of the scabbard. André looked at me, his face alight with sudden wickedness, and hefted the sword in his hand.

I said 'You'd better not bloody drop it.'

'I won't,' he said.

He wouldn't, I knew it as if I'd already seen it falling back into his hand. I remembered describing it to Praslin and the way his eyes had followed my hand into the air, I remembered the crowd outside Chagny willing him to do it again and their disappointment when he didn't. I said 'Throw it, André,' and urged Tonnerre back to give the crowd a better view.

His eyes met mine and he nodded, just once and just for me. Then he drew back his arm once, twice, then thrust it hard upwards as he threw.

We all gazed after it, up, up, up into the clean air above the city where the smell and the smoke never reached, where everything was fresh and corruption never came. A little gleam of sunlight pierced the greyness overhead, fringing the Paris spires with gold, and sparkling on a sword that shone with the brightness of silver as it spun in the summer sky.

Historical Note

History has never recognized André de Roland. In the surviving records of his time only these documents of the Abbé Fleuriot mention his name or those of his close friends and most intimate enemies. The events through which they lived, however, are extremely well documented, and these may require some explanation for the lay reader.

The years 1640–3 were a convulsion in the history of France. Still heavily embroiled in the Thirty Years War against the forces of Spain and the Holy Roman Empire, she faced two near-successful coups from within, followed by the deaths in rapid succession of the two men who had done most to define her role on the international stage: Cardinal Richelieu and King Louis XIII. Within days of this last blow she endured yet another Spanish invasion, and stunned the world by turning it into her greatest victory at the decisive Battle of Rocroi.

The importance of this last has been much debated in recent years, with the historian Juan Luis Sanchez Martin leading the way in debunking the 'myth' of Rocroi as a great turning point in European history. His arguments have considerable validity, and the testimony of Carlos Corvacho supports his assertion that the primary purpose of the Spanish invasion was to deflect French troops from the assault in Catalonia and avert a threatened invasion of the Franche-Comté, in which light it can be seen only as a resounding success. It is difficult, however, to dismiss as entirely meaningless the victory of an untried twenty-one-year-old commander against the most seasoned fighting troops in the world, or to overestimate its effect on French morale.

The account of the battle in these pages matches closely those of other primary sources, including the eyewitness testimony of Albuquerque and Sirot themselves, but also throws light on some of the darker corners. The role of d'Arsy, for instance, may explain why the mysterious figure who told d'Enghien both of the planned ambush in the woods and also of the imminence of Beck's arrival has never been identified as de Roland. This man is described in various sources as a deserter, a Spaniard named Francisco Bernáldez (Ragel in *El sombrero de Rocroi*), and most significantly as 'a French gentleman fighting on the Spanish side but overcome with remorse' (Gerrer/Petit/Sanchez-Martin in *Rocroy 1643*). It is unsurprising that none of the sources name d'Arsy, whose identity would naturally be withheld out of consideration to his family.

Perhaps most enlightening, however, is Corvacho's assertion that the tercio of Albuquerque made no official surrender, and that the men inside the square must have acted independently. This would explain the disagreement of witnesses and historians on the event, some insisting that the tercio never capitulated at all, others aggrieved at the apparent treachery of the Spaniards in firing on the Duc d'Enghien when he came to accept a capitulation believed to have been given in good faith. If Corvacho is right then both sides acted honourably, and that is what I choose to believe. Few would deny the heroism of the tercio of Albuquerque (now known as *La Fidèle*) or the magnanimity of d'Enghien in his attempts to stop the final butchery. On the field that day was shown the very finest qualities of both nations, and if Rocroi is now remembered for nothing else, then let it be for this.

The Battle of La Marfée is viewed very differently. Disastrous to both sides, such few eyewitness accounts that remain are riddled with contradictions in the furious struggle to evade blame. In none have I found any mention of the Aubéry or the role it supposedly played on this day, but since the name is not to be found in regimental lists it seems likely its memory has been thoroughly expunged from history. The lists do, however, clarify one memory of Jacques'. The Scottish regiment who behaved with such courage under fire was the Douglas, previously the Hepburn, and better known to us today as the Royal Scots.

Other facts we know are confirmed by the narrative of Jacques. The preliminary movements of the armies are as he states here, as was the completeness of the rout, and the heroism of Fabert. The Duc de Bouillon's cavalry did indeed take the baggage train and war chest, and the Duc himself ordered his men to stop the carnage. The Marquis de Praslin did save the advance guard at the Pont-de-Douzy, and apparently died in just such circumstances as Jacques describes, for Tallemant des Réaux relates the rumour that he received 'a hundred blows after death' for breaking his word to the Comte. The nature of this promise is unknown, but Jacques' suspicions of a previously treacherous attachment are consistent with Puységur's own account, which relates the offer of quarter as recorded here and adds coyly that Praslin refused it 'for reasons I will not mention'. It is Puységur also who gives us the detail of the deserting cavalry saying 'That's for your 50 écus!' repeated here by Jacques, but it is Grimauld who offers an explanation when he speaks of a recruitment bounty that had not been paid.

Possibly most revealing is the light shed by both Jacques and Ravel on the death of the Comte de Soissons, which explains many of the contradictions in other sources. Châtillon's claim that he was killed in the battle might be explained by Fabert's slaying the Sedanaise officer on a white horse, while Jacques' presence among the cavalry of the Orléans may explain Roussillon's belief he was killed by a 'gendarme of Monsieur'. Bouillon's assertion that he accidentally killed himself by lifting his visor with his pistol accords with Jacques' description, while Montrésor's suggestion that he was murdered by an agent of Richelieu might have risen from the presence of André himself. Personally I am inclined to believe that while Ravel did indeed fire at Soissons, the bullet that killed him came from his own pistol. Bouillon claims the paper of the cartridge was actually embedded in the Comte's forehead, which would not have been possible from the distance Ravel fired.

On the conspiracies themselves the Abbé's accounts have less to offer, for there is clearly a great deal our characters never knew. In the Soissons conspiracy, for instance, only Corvacho mentions the important role of Gondi, later Cardinal de Retz, with whom André is to have more dealings in the future, while in the Cinq-Mars affair only Ravel mentions de Thou. André's companions were clearly only involved with the smallest fry of the intrigues, and I have found no mention of Bouchard or his companions in any other history.

The accounts here are still in accord with what is generally known, particularly concerning the role of Fontrailles and his disguise as a Capuchin monk. It seems likely Richelieu made more use of this information than even Anne was aware, for Fontrailles' own 'Relation' tells us he was followed part of the way back from Madrid with the signed Spanish treaty in his possession. Since Fontrailles was already on this journey at the time of André's trial it is easy to understand why the fear of the conspirators was so acute.

Possibly the most startling revelation in the Abbé's manuscripts is the explanation of how Richelieu finally came to lay hands on this treaty. The official story was that it had been retrieved from a shipwreck, but this gained little credence even at the time, and several authorities have even suspected the hand of the Queen herself. That she knew about it is almost certain, and Anne's account of Bouchard's 'carte blanche' gives vital support to the claim made in the memoirs of the Comte de Brienne that he had obtained from the Queen blank sheets of paper with her signature for the purposes of the conspirators.

The nature of the relationship between the King and Cinq-Mars himself must remain a mystery. The Abbé's manuscripts certainly echo the rumours and anecdotes current at the time, but provide no new evidence. That Cinq-Mars enjoyed sufficient influence to cause the King to shout at Richelieu is also already known, and we can thus put a date on Jacques' visit to Fontainebleau of 2 February 1642, since that is when the famous row occurred, after which Gassion specifically observed Richelieu's pallor.

The various places mentioned also generally correspond with documents of the time, with the major exception of the Gardens of the Luxembourg. In 1640 this would have still been in the original layout devised by Jacques Boyceau de la Barauderie for Marie de Medici, but I have been unable to discover any record of a maze in his design. It is, of course, possible that it was simply never replanted after the fire, and certainly John Evelyn's account of a visit to the Gardens in 1643 makes no mention of a maze at all.

The Hôtel de Roland is never pinpointed beyond its frontage on the Rue de Roi de Sicile, but Jacques' reference to roses on the wall suggests it backed on to an alley running from the Rue des Rosières itself, although no such alley appears on the period maps. Other locations mentioned in Paris are true to what we know of the time, although the modern reader may be disconcerted by the fact that so many names have since changed. The Place Royale, for instance, is now the Place des Vosges, while the Place de Grève is simply the Place du Hôtel de Ville.

Another name that puzzled me was the border village of 'Éspehy', but the 1588 *Routes et Chemins de la Somme* gives this as an old name for modern Épehy. There was a Malassise Farm there even in the 1640s, though it is better known to us today as the site of a major battle in the last days of the First World War. All the other towns and villages mentioned are easy to locate, and sufficient of the original fortifications survive at Saint-Jean Aux Bois to give us a picture of how it appeared even in 1641.

The only location of which I have found no trace at all is the little hamlet mentioned by Jacques as having been destroyed by the Spaniards. The village of Grouches-Luchuel exists indeed on the road between Lucheux and Milly, but there is neither record nor memory of a Petit-Grouche itself. That in itself, perhaps, is the most telling indication of the reality of the world in which André de Roland lived.

Edward Morton, March 2011

He just wanted a decent book to read ...

Not too much to ask, is it? It was in 1935 when Allen Lane, Managing Director of Bodley Head Publishers, stood on a platform at Exeter railway station looking for something good to read on his journey back to London. His choice was limited to popular magazines and poor-quality paperbacks – the same choice faced every day by the vast majority of readers, few of whom could afford hardbacks. Lane's disappointment and subsequent anger at the range of books generally available led him to found a company – and change the world.

'We believed in the existence in this country of a vast reading public for intelligent books at a low price, and staked everything on it'
Sir Allen Lane, 1902–1970, founder of Penguin Books

The quality paperback had arrived – and not just in bookshops. Lane was adamant that his Penguins should appear in chain stores and tobacconists, and should cost no more than a packet of cigarettes.

Reading habits (and cigarette prices) have changed since 1935, but Penguin still believes in publishing the best books for everybody to enjoy. We still believe that good design costs no more than bad design, and we still believe that quality books published passionately and responsibly make the world a better place.

So wherever you see the little bird – whether it's on a piece of prize-winning literary fiction or a celebrity autobiography, political tour de force or historical masterpiece, a serial-killer thriller, reference book, world classic or a piece of pure escapism – you can bet that it represents the very best that the genre has to offer.

Whatever you like to read – trust Penguin.